How to
Kiss a
Cowboy

JOANNE
KENNEDY

sourcebooks
casablanca

Copyright © 2015 by Joanne Kennedy
Cover and internal design © 2015 by Sourcebooks, Inc.
Cover art by Craig White

Sourcebooks and the colophon are registered trademarks of Sourcebooks, Inc.

Published by Sourcebooks Casablanca, an imprint of Sourcebooks, Inc.
P.O. Box 4410, Naperville, Illinois 60567-4410
(630) 961-3900
Fax: (630) 961-2168
www.sourcebooks.com

Printed and bound in Canada
MBP 10 9 8 7 6 5 4 3 2 1

To Mum, who taught me to love reading and let me read her racy romance novels when I was too young to understand the racy parts. You showed me that anything worth doing is worth doing well, and you loved me no matter how much I screwed up.
This one's for you!

Chapter 1

SUZE CARLYLE EDGED THROUGH THE SHADOWS AT THE far end of the Rodeo Days beer tent, praying she could make it back to her trailer before anyone noticed her. A hubbub at the bar made her pause, and when she saw the cause, she couldn't help but smile.

Brady Caine had arrived, strolling into the tent with a loose-hipped swagger that said "cowboy" as clearly as the worn spots on the seat of his jeans. Tall and tan, with rugged good looks and an easy smile, he barely had time to rest one hip on a bar stool before he was surrounded by a flock of pretty cowgirls who fluttered around him like hummingbirds squabbling over sugar.

He had a woman under each arm and another in his lap before Suze had time to blink—a blond, a brunette, and a redhead. Did he do that on purpose, or what?

Suze knew who the women were. Miss Wyoming, Miss Montana, and Miss Arizona. All three were perfectly coiffed, with curls spilling out from under their fashionably tilted hats. They wore jeans so tight it probably hurt to move, but their practiced smiles never wavered.

Neither did Brady's, though his smile was as real as the rest of his cowboy credentials. Most guys worried about something—a tough bull, a bad score, or getting nacho sauce on their shirt—but not Brady. Whether he was chatting up women, riding a rank bronc, or eating sloppy fair food, he was equally at ease.

Watching him, Suze wished she could somehow absorb the magic that made him fit so securely into the world he'd chosen. Unless she was in the saddle, she always felt at least a little bit awkward and out of place.

She wondered which woman he'd choose, but to her surprise, he was easing his way out of the three-way clutch. For a second, she caught a rare glimpse of panic in his eyes. The redhead had entwined herself around him so thoroughly he looked like a motherless calf tangled up in a barbed-wire fence.

Suze looked down at her boot tips and smiled. She couldn't help it. Sometimes she felt like she had a mean little devil inside her, because watching Brady Caine reject those rodeo queens made her feel *good*.

But it wasn't sheer meanness that made her feel that way. She and Brady had been friends when they were younger, and she hated to see him snagged by the wrong kind of woman.

She gave herself a mental slap. She didn't know what the right kind of woman was. Not for a man like that. She just wanted him to be happy, healthy, and...hers.

A little alarm went off in her head. *Danger. Stupid thought alert. Danger. Danger.*

She continued to skirt the dance floor, staying in the shadows until she slammed into Miss Arizona, who was heading for the ladies' room in a huff. Excusing herself, Suze had almost made it to the exit when she was startled by a voice in her ear.

"What are you smiling about?"

Brady Caine. She was so shocked to see him, she told him the truth.

"Those women," she said. "They thought they'd caught you."

"Nope." He smiled, his brown eyes warm and sweet as hot fudge. "They didn't catch me. You did."

"I—what?"

"You caught me. I watched you ride today." He shook his head. "Man, oh man. Never saw a woman ride like that. You're not scared of anything, are you?"

She told her heart to stop beating faster. She told her face not to flush. She told herself not to admit she was scared of *him*, and of the way he made her feel.

She told all the other parts of her body not to react too, but it was useless. Brady Caine made her shimmer inside. She didn't know how to respond to the compliment, so she dug down deep inside herself and found a little sass left over from the day's victory lap.

"I don't know how I caught you, 'cause I wasn't fishing." She struggled to keep a tremor out of her voice and pasted on a confident smile. "Why don't you go unbreak the heart of one of those poor rodeo queens? I'm going home."

"I'll walk you there."

How could she say no? He was just being nice. *Nice*, dammit.

She knew Brady's attention didn't mean a darned thing. He thought he was being nice by talking to the girl in the baggy jeans and scuffed boots, the social misfit who didn't know how to dress or flirt or sparkle like the other girls.

So he'd go and make her feel special, like he always

did, and when she was back at her trailer alone, she'd have to deal with all the foolish hopes and stupid dreams he'd left behind. Meanwhile, he'd move on and be nice to some other girl.

It had taken years to learn that lesson, but she'd learned it well. She had no hopes and no dreams where Brady Caine was concerned—although there were a few fantasies left over from high school.

When he'd looked at the rodeo queens, he'd seemed mostly interested in their shirt buttons. But he kept glancing at Suze's face, and she was sure he could see what she was thinking.

She chased those fantasies out of her head and undid an extra button, hoping to distract him, but he kept scanning her face. Reading her. Analyzing. It felt—*what was the word? Invasive*. Something like that.

"Stop it," she said without thinking.

"Stop what?"

She waved her hand vaguely. "That."

"What? Walking?"

They'd stepped outside the tent now, into the soft, blue night. It had rained earlier, a quick summer storm that was all flash and rumble with barely a sprinkle of rain. Strings of twinkle lights dangled from the edges of the tent, and the distant lights of the midway were reflected in a few scattered puddles, giving the asphalt a supernatural sheen. Suze could hear the carnival barkers hawking their games in faraway voices, luring fairgoers with the promise of giant teddy bears and Elmo knockoffs.

Brady took her hand and stopped so abruptly she couldn't help spinning around to face him.

"I've stopped walking." His voice was low, and he pulled her a little closer. Not too close. No more than if they'd been dancing the two-step. But it was closer than they should be. She could feel those hopes and dreams billowing from her subconscious like ghosts rising from the grave.

"That's not what I meant." She stared down at her toes.

His tone gentled. "Then what did you want me to stop?"

Suze shook her head, further undoing her long blond braid. As usual, it had loosened from the day's riding, but not enough to hide her face.

"Stop looking at me."

She wished she'd worn a hat, so she could tug the brim down and hide her eyes. Nerves were making her stomach burn, but there was another kind of heat in her belly—a warm, rich stew of sensation set on a slow simmer.

He tugged her closer. "I like looking at you."

He was teasing her. It should make her mad, but there was something so gentle about it that it felt good. Was teasing the same as flirting? Because this felt like flirting.

Surely Brady Caine wasn't hitting on *her*.

"Go back to your rodeo queens," she said. "They're into this kind of stuff."

"What kind of stuff?"

She waved a dismissive hand. "Boy-girl stuff."

"And you're not?"

"No. I'm not…" *What was the word? Dammit, he'd shorted out her brain.* "I'm not available."

"Got a boyfriend?"

She shook her head and felt her braid flop from side to side. "Don't take this wrong, but my relationship with my horse is about the only one that matters right now. I need to focus, and you're distracting me."

"Distracting you from what?"

"From being the best." The answer came quickly to her lips. "I need to get back to my trailer so I can watch videos of my races today. To see how I can improve."

They stood at the edge of a puddle, and the glistening swirls at the edge framed their reflections in light. It was like seeing their auras—Brady's golden, her own a dim blue.

"Don't you ever think about anything but winning?"

"It beats thinking about losing."

He laughed softly and touched her face. Just a touch, at the temple, but it felt invasive again. Invasive? No, *intimate*. That was the word. It drew her in, somehow, making the world around them fade away.

"When did you ever lose anything?" he asked.

"I win races. But other stuff…" She dropped his hands and shoved hers in her pockets, staring down at the puddle. "I lost my mom to cancer, my dad to—I don't know. I think I lost him to my mother's ghost, or something. And if I don't keep winning, I'll lose the ranch. Dad mortgaged it again when Mom…you know. The medical bills."

She regretted the words as soon as she'd spoken them. You didn't go talking about serious stuff when a guy flirted with you. You were supposed to keep things light. Flirt back, if you liked the guy. But she had no idea how to do that, so she'd blown it.

It was just as well. Brady would leave now. The hopes and dreams would haunt her for a while, but eventually they'd slip back into their graves and life would go on as usual.

"I'm sorry." He said it simply, as if he really meant it.

Poor guy. She really shouldn't have dumped all that on him. Sucking in a deep breath, she tilted her chin up and gave him a smile straight from the winner's circle. "There's nothing to be sorry about. It's made me stronger. I might have lost a lot in life, but on horseback, I'm unbeatable."

"You are." Brady grinned and chucked her under the chin. "You are unbeatable."

She was glad she'd had the nerve to brag a little. Basking in the light of his smile, she actually felt like the winner she was. Prize saddles, gold buckles, and blue ribbons couldn't compare to the ultimate prize: the smile of Brady Caine.

Chapter 2

BRADY WATCHED THE LIGHT FROM THE FESTIVE BULBS that lined the eaves of the beer tent dance across Suze's face as she talked. She wasn't the prettiest girl in rodeo, but something about her had always drawn him.

Maybe it was the way she rode, fast and reckless, always balanced on the knife-edge of disaster. Maybe it was her independence, her loner mentality. Most women needed a man around, and the single ones traveled in packs. But Suze seemed perfectly happy on her own.

Well, not happy. She never seemed happy, and no wonder. She'd lost her mother, and her father—well, he was a strange one. He'd lived through his wife's accomplishments, supporting her while she rocketed to rodeo stardom, but now that she was gone, he seemed to have lost interest in her talented daughter, and in life itself.

"You drive yourself so hard," he said. "You don't always have to *be* the best. Isn't it enough just to try? To *do* your best?"

She shook her head. "Maybe if you're in kindergarten. Then everybody gets a trophy, right? But in the real world, another world championship would get me more endorsements. And I need endorsements. That's where the real money is."

He walked beside her in silence for a while, wondering what was wrong with him tonight. Normally he'd have bailed on this conversation as soon as it started. He wasn't big on the serious stuff, but here they were, talking about riding and living, winning and losing.

Brady's goals were simple: buckles, broncs, babes, and beer. By that measure, he was definitely a champion. It had never been hard for him to stick to the back of a bronc, and once he won the buckles, the beer was free and the babes came easy. The cowboy life, footloose and careless, suited him down to the bone.

Well, almost. Sometimes it bothered him that nobody took him seriously. His brothers claimed everything was a game to him, even sex. They said he took love about as seriously as a game of pickup basketball, and maybe they were right.

That's why he needed to stay away from Suze. She took everything seriously, and he knew she liked him. It would be easy enough to seduce her, and he'd always wondered if she made love like she rode—all out, with her heart leading the way.

But she'd expect more of him than he had to offer. He made it a rule to stay away from girls who didn't know how to play the game. He wasn't out to hurt anybody.

The two of them strolled through the rodeo grounds in silence, heading for the area where the contestants kept their trailers. The crowds were mostly gone, and the place looked melancholy in the moonlight. The brightly lit stands that sold funnel cakes, fried Twinkies, and turkey legs were shuttered and dark, and the empty parking lot beyond was scattered with discarded day sheets and cigarette butts.

Suze was staring down at her feet as she walked, lost in thought. She seemed to have forgotten he was there.

He wasn't used to that. Women generally paid him close attention.

"How do you do it?" he asked.

"Do what?"

"Focus the way you do? Everyone says I'd ride better if I'd apply myself. I apply my butt to the saddle, but apparently that's not what they mean."

She flashed him a smile, and her step took on a little bounce as she counted off points on her fingers.

"You have to live and breathe your sport, every minute of every day. You need to watch videos, of yourself and of the winning riders. You analyze what you do right and what you do wrong. You ask questions. You make sure everything you do is dedicated to succeeding. You eat right, you sleep right—everything goes toward the goal."

She finished the speech with a little hop step, as if she was so excited, she could hardly contain herself. Now he was the one watching his boot tips as they walked.

"Doesn't sound like much fun."

She spun around and walked backwards in front of him. He'd evidently hit on her favorite subject. Talking about rodeo lit her up. She looked different. Animated.

"It's not *about* fun."

"So it's all about winning?"

"No." She turned and walked beside him again, the animation gone, her tone flat. "It's all about making a living."

"Shoot," Brady said. "That would take all the fun out of it."

He knew he'd been lucky when old Bill Decker plucked him and two other boys from a group home for foster kids and gave them a home on his ranch, teaching them to rope and ride. Now that Bill was gone, they all lived on the ranch, except for Brady's oldest brother, who ran a spread up north of Wynott. They shared expenses, so they didn't have much to worry about.

He and Suze slowed their steps as they crossed the parking lot and left the noise of the beer tent behind them. They were alone, and it was getting dark. Brady stopped and took her hand, and their eyes met.

"You must get tired, trying so hard all the time," he said. "Don't you ever want something more? Something better?"

She looked at him for a long time, the yearning in her face so strong it made him want to smooth her hair, to comfort her somehow. To kiss her.

"Don't I." She said it in a whisper so soft and sad it made his heart ache. "Don't I ever."

Suze was surprised to feel the sting of rising tears in response to Brady's question. She loved her life. Granted, she had problems and pressures, but everybody did.

She didn't want anything more than what she had—two national barrel-racing championships and a successful season building toward a three-peat. She had a great horse, the skill to ride him right, and a stable to keep him in. What else did a girl need?

Brady Caine.

No. He was the last thing she needed. He was a distraction.

"I don't *need* anything else. I love what I do." She said

it fiercely, so he'd know she meant it. "I love racing like nothing else. When Speedo's prancing in the alleyway and we're waiting for the start, I can hardly hold him back. All that power under the saddle, you know? I can feel the tension in him, how much he wants to run. And then I nudge his flanks, and *bang*." She clapped her hands, pointing one up toward the sky as if she was tracing the course of a rocket. "It's like being shot from a gun."

"But you must have to think about strategy and technique, right? Once you hit the barrels, you have to think through your turns."

"Not really." She felt like she was bragging, but hey, he'd asked. "It's muscle memory at this point."

"I guess it would be. How many times have you ridden that pattern?"

"Too many to count."

No wonder Brady got any woman he wanted. Forget the dimples and the soulful brown eyes, the hard, sinewy cowboy muscles, and the wild bronc-riding courage. He listened—really *listened*—to what she had to say.

"What are you thinking about when you're out there?" he asked.

"I'm not really sure." To her relief, her thoughts about Brady shut down once she was focused on racing again. "Once we cross the line, Speedo and I are like water running, smooth and fast." She spread her hand and made it tilt and turn. "The path between the barrels is a riverbed, and we're just flowing."

He smiled. "Sometimes I get a bronc like that. The crowd sees a fight, but if you ride 'em right, it's more like a dance." He laughed. "The bronc definitely leads, though. It's up to me to just counter his moves, move with him. Most times it ends up being sloppy and messed up, even when I make it to the buzzer, but once in a while, it's like you said. Water flowing."

She glanced at him, surprised he understood so well. Brady never seemed to take anything seriously, and she had to admit he was right—a lot of his rides were a little on the sloppy side. He had courage to burn, but his technique could use some improvement.

"Your mom raced too, right?"

"Sure did." Suze was surprised he had to ask. Not only had her mother had been a National Finals champion, she'd also been one of the most beautiful and charismatic cowgirls in rodeo. Everybody knew who Ellen Carlyle was. "She won Frontier Days twice," Suze continued. "And Pendleton, and the Calgary Stampede. Plus she was a national champion."

"Impressive. You were a champion too. And you won Fort Worth twice, and Amarillo. And how many times did you win Prescott?"

She smiled. "Three times. But I never won Frontier Days."

He was looking at her curiously, and she realized she might have revealed too much.

"You know exactly which rodeos she won that you didn't? That seems like a weird way to think about things."

"Yeah, well, tell my dad that."

"He does that? Compares you to her?"

"Yeah." She sighed. "She was a tough act to follow."

She tossed her hair like it didn't matter. The effect was somewhat spoiled by the fact that her braid lashed out and smacked him on the cheek like a bullwhip.

He laughed, and she would have gladly given money to hold on to that picture forever. The way he tossed his head back, the way his eyes lit up and his dimples flickered to life—there was something wild about him. Something joyous.

Dang it, she had it bad. Brady just seemed so—*real*. The guy might be a player, but at least he didn't pretend to be anything else. He probably couldn't. He was honest to the core, even if that core was pretty badly flawed in some ways.

Deep down, Brady was a good guy.

That loud, annoying alarm bell was blaring in her mind again.

Stupid thought alert. Warning. Warning.

Good guys didn't make it with a different woman every night, and walk away the next morning with a wave and a smile. Good guys didn't break hearts from Fort Worth to Pendleton. Good guys weren't players, honest or not. Brady might think he was just having fun, but a lot of the women he bedded were hurt by his casual rejection.

They'd left the parking lot behind and were traipsing through a miniature model of a frontier town where various vendors hawked their wares during the rodeo. The little shacks representing saloons and general stores had closed up hours ago, and the wooden boardwalk sounded hollow under their boots. The silence and shadows surrounding them made her feel like they were walking through a ghost town.

"I always wondered why barrel racing wasn't more popular," Brady mused. "It's exciting, it's easy to understand, and honestly, it's amazing how pretty all you girls are. There's nothing sexier than a woman on horseback, you know, with her hair flying and all. And for some weird reason, it's like all the top contenders in your sport happen to be gorgeous."

She felt her face warming with embarrassment. She knew she was no great beauty—nothing like her mother or the other girls on the circuit. She never seemed to fit in with them, partly because she didn't care about clothes or makeup. Unless they were talking about racing, she was always left out.

Brady cast her a sidelong glance. "You don't know it, do you?"

She must have missed something. "Know what?"

"You're just as pretty as they are. Prettier," he said. "You look just like your mom."

Suze hated it when people said that. She knew it wasn't true, because she had the world's greatest expert on Ellen Carlyle right at home—her father. He was always ready to point out how Suze came up short in comparison to her mother.

"My nose is bigger," she said. "And my mouth is… never mind."

She flushed. Why was she talking to Brady about this stuff? Or any man, for that matter? He flashed her a puzzled look and, to her relief, let the subject drop.

They'd finally come to the Cowboy Corral, where contestants parked their rigs during the rodeo. Living quarters ranged from deluxe fifth wheels hauled by huge diesel pickups, to battered ranch trucks with a few cowboy bedrolls laid out in back. Suze had a Dodge Ram Super Cab and a Featherlite trailer that combined deluxe living quarters with a tack room, plus stalls for two horses. It was a gift from a sponsor, and sported a larger-than-life photo of her and Speedo circling a barrel, with dirt flying up from Speedo's hooves.

As usual, she'd pulled out the frame that supported a little awning to create a front porch, but instead of unrolling the canvas, she'd strung chili pepper lights along the edge. They were glowing red, welcoming her home.

Most of her temporary neighbors were back from the rodeo. Light spilled from trailer doorways, and cowboys sat on tailgates drinking beer, re-riding the day's broncs and re-roping the calves that got away. The faint hum of conversation blended with the usual insect chorus to create a backdrop of sound that was as familiar as her own backyard.

Stepping onto the lowest of the metal steps that led to her front door, she turned to say good-bye to Brady and thank him for walking her home. But her words stuck in her throat when those brown eyes met hers. The step had brought her face to his level, and he was close enough to kiss.

He rested one hand on the siding. The screen door at her back opened outward, and the frame of the awning blocked any other escape route. She was trapped.

Not that she wanted to go anywhere. Those brown eyes did something to her. She felt *seen*, just as she'd felt heard when they talked. If Brady focused as hard on his sport as he was focused on her right now, he'd ride every bronc to a standstill.

"You're every bit as beautiful as your mother. Only stronger. Like an Amazon." He touched her temple again, but this time he let his fingers trail down the side of her face. "Your nose makes your face look stronger. And your mouth…" He traced a fingertip along the seam of her mouth, and she resisted the urge to flick her tongue out and taste. "Trust me, there's nothing wrong with your mouth. Your lips…"

The chili pepper lights warmed his skin and made his eyes shine. It took her a minute to realize he was going to kiss her. She leaned toward him, mesmerized and so ready, so *very* ready for that kiss.

Then she fell off the step.

She fell into him, and awkward as it was, it was romantic too, because he caught her and she slid slowly down his body to the ground. The hard planes of his body answered her curves, and she caught his scent— leather, sage, and the familiar combination of dust and sweat that spelled *cowboy*.

And then he kissed her, and it was the only thing she'd ever felt that was better than riding a fast horse.

Chapter 3

SUZE KNEW THIS KISS DIDN'T MEAN ANYTHING TO Brady. He'd dallied with most of the other barrel racers, and there was no reason she should be special to him, no matter what sweet nothings he whispered. But after a while, the warnings in her head faded away, because he knew exactly, *precisely* how she wanted to be kissed.

His lips slid over hers slowly at first, softly, in a sort of experimental way. Her knees turned to jelly, but then a plume of warmth rose inside her and she felt suddenly strong. Lacing her arms around his neck, she kissed him back and the night noises that surrounded them faded away.

She'd wanted this kiss since the day she'd first seen Brady swaggering down the halls of Grigsby High. He and his foster brothers were from the group home in Wynott. It was the home where the bad kids lived—or so said the school gossips. Brady Caine, Ridge Cooper, and Shane Lockhart walked like men, not boys, and they could send a girl stumbling through a haze of hormones just by glancing her way.

The girls whispered that they were so bad, their parents couldn't handle them. So bad, they'd been sent to the foster home. So bad that when the place shut down, all the other kids got adopted and those three stayed.

The other girls' eyes glittered when they talked about the brothers, and they tossed secret, flirtatious glances at them from under their lashes. They seemed to think being bad was a *good* thing. Suze didn't get it any more than she understood why her own eyes always sought out Brady in the hallway, or why she felt a strange flutter inside whenever he caught her looking.

Tonight, Suze got it. Apparently, bad boys knew how to kiss a girl senseless, and Brady was no exception. She'd dated a few times, but she'd never been kissed like this. Brady seemed to be tasting her, testing her, drinking in her secrets and her needs.

Then the kiss changed—the angle and the intent. It was as if the *conscious* part of kissing was over, and the two of them were lost inside a fog of sensation. His breath came hard, and she could feel his heart pounding under his shirt, because, oddly enough, she actually had put a hand on his chest to push him away at first. Not because she didn't want him to kiss her, but because Brady was famous for teasing the girls and she was afraid it was a joke.

This was no joke. Something about laughing, good-natured Brady had changed. His tongue tangled deliciously with hers, stroking, probing, exploring as if he needed to know every part of her.

Suze knew a Sunday night affair with Brady wouldn't last through Monday's sunrise. But just this once, she let herself go. She felt like what they were doing was meant to be, as inevitable as the flowing of a river or the whisper of the wind in the trees.

She knew she was feeling too much. Men like Brady didn't want women to fall in love with them. Sex was a game to them, and if you took the game too seriously, nobody would ever pick you for a partner again.

She broke the kiss, turned away, and walked smack into the side of her trailer.

"You okay?" Brady took her by the arm and looked her up and down.

Oh, those eyes. Hot fudge. Warm and sweet.

"I'm fine," she said. "Just clumsy." She laughed, and it came out a little too high. She sounded kind of crazy.

Brady smiled, putting the killer dimples on display. "We're all clumsy sometimes. I fall off horses a lot."

She laughed. "You do, don't you?"

He sobered. "Sometimes I'm clumsy about kissing too," he said. "I hope you didn't mind."

"No," she said. "No, I didn't mind. It was fine."

He looked so deeply hurt she almost rushed to reassure him before she realized he was joking. "Fine?" he said. "Just *fine*?"

"More than fine." She gave him her best smile, but she could feel it trembling at the edges. How could she tell him how much she'd liked it without sounding like a seventh grader? She needed to be honest somehow, without giving too much away.

"It made my night." She finally found the right, light tone. "Thank you."

She opened the door, flicked on the light, and turned to face him. Miraculously, she didn't slam her face into the door or fall off the step.

"Good night, Brady."

"Aren't you inviting me in?"

Another land mine. How was she supposed to politely refuse what he was offering? Because he wasn't angling for an invitation to tea.

She'd just say no.

"No," she said.

"Oh." He looked so disappointed, she kind of felt sorry for him. He'd ditched the three rodeo queens to follow her, after all.

He strolled over to the folding camp chairs she'd put beneath the chili pepper lights and sat down. Slouching until his long, lean body was practically horizontal, he crossed his ankles and folded his arms behind his head, making himself very comfortable in her space.

Her *private* space. She liked to sit alone outside her trailer in the evenings and listen to the conversations all around her. When it got late and the talk died down, she'd turn off the tiny lights and gaze up at the stars, feeling just as small as those faraway twinkles, lost in the vastness of the universe.

"Come on," he said, patting the other chair.

"What?"

"Dang, girl, is it that bad?"

"What?"

"My reputation. Is it so bad you're afraid to sit out here and talk to me?"

To her surprise, she realized she wanted that. Just to talk.

It would be foolish to sleep with him, but there was nothing wrong with talking for a while. She could use a friend, and who better than Brady? He seemed to understand her.

"You want a beer?" she asked.

"Sure."

She reached into the little refrigerator, which was only a foot or so from the doorway, and grabbed an ancient six-pack of Bud. She'd had it for months, and it had been in and out of the fridge. Probably tasted like panther pee by now, but what the heck.

She stepped out of the trailer, letting the door slam behind her, and sat down in the second chair. She'd always wondered why she bothered to set up two when she almost always sat out there alone.

Now she knew.

Pulling two beers out of the plastic six-pack carrier, she handed one to Brady and popped the other one open for herself. She didn't drink, but this seemed like a good time to start. She took a healthy gulp and nearly coughed it out.

Yup. Panther pee.

They sat silently, awkwardly, until Suze knew the time had come and gone for some sort of exchange. But she didn't know what to say, and he seemed oddly content to sit there, staring out into the darkness. She'd parked at the edge of the Cowboy Corral, beside a line of scrub that bordered the dirt parking lot. The lot was empty now, and the darkness seemed to go on forever.

Finally, he spoke.

"Is your mother the reason you barrel race?" he asked. "To honor her memory?"

"No. Not really. I mean, sure, it helps me remember her." She stretched out her legs, crossing them at the ankles, and looked out at the sky. Sipping her beer, she felt dreamy for a moment, as if she could float up there and catch the stars. "But mostly, I do it so I can ride really, really fast on a good horse."

He smiled. "Escaping?"

"Probably. I never thought of it that way."

"So are you running *to* something or running away?"

She didn't even have to think. "Running away."

Brady gave her a sharp, appraising look, and she wished she *had* thought before she'd admitted that. It didn't sound like much, but it defined her life—and that was kind of pitiful.

Time to change the subject.

"So how about you? Why do you do what you do?" she asked.

"Well, that's the thing," he said. "My brothers say I do it for buckles and babes, and that bothers me."

Suze grinned. "I don't see why. If they want to judge you by that standard, you're a howling success."

He laughed again. She so loved to watch him laugh. Maybe they'd be friends after this—if she could keep that trailer door closed. She didn't want to be another one of the women Brady left behind. She wanted to be his friend. The challenge was to resist the sexual magnetism that emanated from him like the reflected aura that had shimmered around him in that puddle on the asphalt.

"Everybody thinks I'm superficial," he said.

She almost laughed. Of *course* he was superficial. That's what everyone loved about Brady. It might not feel good to be called shallow, but in a way, it was another word for *honest*. Brady never lied about his motives or pretended to be anything other than what he was. And that was refreshing.

But right now he was being serious, and nobody wants to be laughed at. Staring up at the sky, she thought about how that would feel—to have everyone think your only purpose in life was to have a good time. She supposed life could feel a little empty that way.

"There's a lot more to you than buckles and babes," she said. "Otherwise, you wouldn't be here, with me."

He grinned. "Some people would say different."

She whisked away the comment with a wave of her hand. "I'm no babe. You left them back at the bar."

"You're right," he said. "You're not a babe. You're something more."

She felt his eyes on her and tried not to blush. The things he was saying—this was better than any fantasy she'd ever had. And she'd had many fantasies, all of them starring the man beside her.

The man who was looking for something from her. Not sex, but meaning. She needed to quit mooning about him and *talk* to him.

"Just think about it," she said. "What's the real reason you do it? The deep down reason?"

"Same reason you do, I think. The way you talked about riding before, about that moment when you start the race? That's the kind of thing I do it for." He looked up into the star-spattered sky. It was smudged with a few streaky clouds, but they didn't obscure the bright speck of light that drew a quick arc across the sky and disappeared.

Brady turned to Suze, a question in his eyes, and she smiled. They shared the rare experience without a word. She liked that.

Maybe Brady wasn't as superficial as they said.

His voice went low and soft. "I collect moments like that. Rare moments." He reached over and took her hand, and she was so dazzled—star dazzled, Brady-dazzled—that she let him.

Moments. Rare moments. She wondered if he knew he'd just created one for her.

But he was still talking rodeo.

"When I get settled just right in the saddle, and I brace my feet and give the nod—I guess that's my equivalent of your moment, when Speedo starts his run." He was warming to the topic now, edging forward in his chair and gesturing as he talked. "It's the possibilities. A thousand things could flow from that moment, and you don't have a clue what's going to happen. You could win; you could lose. The bronc could make one of those high, straight-legged jumps where you leave the saddle for a second and float above him, weightless." He raised his hand, palm down, in the air. "I love that feeling. Or he could sunfish and crash down on you, like that danged Tornado did to my brother." The hand flipped over, palm to the sky, and crash-landed in his lap.

"How is your brother?"

"Better," Brady said. "He won't rodeo again, though. Dang bull rolled over on his hand, and he has no grip at all. But he's married now, and happy."

"That's good." She shuddered. "He's lucky he's alive. That was a terrible wreck."

He nodded. "Every time I board a bronc, I feel how little separates life and death."

Suze grabbed another beer from the six-pack. Popping the top, she took a long drink. "I try not to think about that when I watch you."

"Why not?" He grinned. "Half the crowd's hoping I'll wreck."

He seemed to have forgotten about the falling star they'd shared, which was all right with Suze. She'd hold that moment for a long time—the way he'd turned and smiled, the way he'd taken her hand. It would become a treasure, like a shiny toy kept hidden away so she could play with it whenever she felt down.

"How can you know they're hoping you'll get hurt and not be—I don't know, angry or resentful?" she asked.

He shrugged. "That's just how it is. So when I get bucked off, I try to dismount slick. I want to land on my feet and tip my hat, like it's nothing to me. I don't want to give them that wreck."

"It always seems like it really is nothing to you." Suze flushed. "I mean, I know you want to win as much as anybody, but you're so good-natured when you don't score. I don't know how you do that. I think it's why you're so popular."

He shrugged. "Rodeo's the best thing that ever happened to me. It's my world, the best one I ever knew. If that crowd wants me to get stomped, frankly, I don't mind giving them a show once in a while. Long as I can stand up and climb back in the saddle the next time my name's called, I'm good."

One part of her was listening to his words; the other part was reading the current that flowed beneath them. Brady had survived an ugly childhood in the foster care system, and an uglier one before that, with abusive parents. He didn't talk about it, but she knew his real life had begun when Bill Decker pulled him out of the system and onto the ranch.

She looked up at the trees and stars, and thought how lucky she'd been to be born into this life. Her father might be hard to please, and she sure wished her mother had lived. But she had horses and blue jeans and a country world so wide, she'd never run out of dirt roads and rodeos.

"Rodeo saved you, didn't it?" she asked Brady.

He was quiet for a long time, looking up at the sky as if he'd find the answer written in the delicate tracery of the stars. It felt to Suze like the world held its breath, waiting to see if he'd let her in.

At some point, he'd moved his chair closer, and he still held her hand. Now he took it in both of his and smiled.

"You're right. Rodeo, and Bill Decker." He kissed the back of her hand and dropped it. She wondered if he was dismissing her or if the kiss meant something. With some effort, she resisted the temptation to obsess over interpreting it and paid attention to his words. "I'll never forget when Bill took us to our first rodeo. For me, it was like stories I'd heard about the circus—so big and full of life and lights and pretty girls. I never wanted anything else after that. Nothing else in the world."

"Nothing?" She fluttered her lashes and felt her heart lift like a rowboat rising on the crest of a wave. She was flirting. She'd figured it out.

And it worked.

"I guess there is one other thing I want," Brady said. "One other thing."

She pulled another beer from the six-pack and lifted it in a toast. Brady didn't need to know she was celebrating her first successful effort at flirting.

"Are you thinking we might have a moment?" she asked.

He took his hat off and smiled. "I think we're having one now."

Suze felt her heart ramp up to a fast trot, and her breath came quick and shallow. Brady was right. They were having a moment, and it was moments that mattered—life's little diamonds, scattered through even the most commonplace life. Those rare gems were what everyone lived for, when it came down to it. And right now, she had a chance to have more than a moment with Brady.

Rising from her chair, she opened the trailer door. She wanted to turn and flash Brady a saucy look, but instead she tripped and banged her shin on the step.

"You okay?" he asked.

"Fine," she said. "I'm fine. Um, you want to come in?"

This wasn't quite the way it happened in her fantasies. But it was happening for real.

Chapter 4

BRADY WAS SURPRISED SUZE CARLYLE WOULD EVEN talk to him. Normally, she wouldn't let him close enough for conversation. The moment he entered a room, she'd toss that tawny gold braid and leave. He'd always figured either she hated him or she was in love with him.

Tonight he'd found out she didn't hate him. And that meant he shouldn't flirt with her. Shouldn't even be having this conversation.

Suze was serious about everything she did, and he didn't do serious.

She didn't look serious right now, though. She was smiling like she did this all the time.

He'd always thought she disapproved of him. She'd see him with some buckle bunny, and she'd lift her chin and toss her hair, and he'd feel like dirt. Or she'd run into him with his friends, drinking and fooling around, and look at him like he was an idiot.

So the open door of the trailer and the woman standing in its square of golden light were too tempting to resist. He stepped up and kissed her, harder than he meant to. She grabbed for the door frame, but it was too late. The two of them fell, laughing and kissing, onto the kitchen floor.

They crawled inside in a tangle of limbs and laughter. She'd start to stand, and he'd pull her down for another kiss, and then she'd scramble a few feet toward the back of the trailer and he'd pull her back to him.

He heard footsteps passing by on the gravel lot and wondered how much anybody could see by the dim red glow of the chili pepper lights. He tried to kick the door shut, but his boot hit her shin instead. She yelped and laughed, kicking him back, but then she escaped his grip and shut the door. The two of them sat on the floor, panting for breath and grinning at each other.

He glanced around, realizing he'd never seen the inside of a two-time champion's trailer before. Sponsors fought for the privilege of providing trailers for rodeo royalty like Suze, and Montana Saddlery was proud to emblazon their name across the side.

The trailer might be just the thing to light a fire under his lazy ass, because it was as knock-you-down gorgeous as its owner. It was fitted out like the inside of a ship, everything either gleaming teak or spotless white, all with brass fittings. The space was small, of course; it had to be hauled all over the country, and it needed to carry two horses as well as Suze herself. There was even a small tack room at the back, and a space for hay and grain.

Her bed was all the way at the front, a platform that could be propped up to double as a sofa. It was covered with a bright Native American blanket and heaped with pillows in various solids that matched the stripes on the blanket—blue and burnt orange and brown.

What was it about girls and pillows? There was barely room enough for two people there.

Suze took care of that in no time, sweeping the pillows aside and letting half of them fall to the floor. One particularly shaggy one turned into a hairy little dog who jumped up and treated Brady to a ridiculous display of doggie machismo, barking and growling from behind a curtain of gold and gray hair that covered his eyes.

"Hush, Dooley." Suze turned to Brady. "Don't mind him. He's all bark."

"More like he's all hair. What kind of dog is he?"

"He's a Dooley dog." She laughed. "There's only one."

He reached out to pet the dog, and it turned into a wriggling, tail-wagging bundle of glee. "You don't seem like the type who'd have a hairy little yapper dog," he said.

"Yeah, well." She flushed. "He needed a home." She lifted him off the bed. "Shoo, Dooley."

The dog scampered away and Suze plopped down in the middle of the pillows, bouncing on the bed, and looked up at Brady, seeming suddenly shy.

When she'd opened the door to her trailer, he'd been sure she'd made up her mind to let him into her bed. But maybe he'd assumed too much. She looked up at him with a smile that was a little tentative, as if she was wondering what she'd started.

He sat down beside her. "Remember how you said I was good-natured even when I get a no score?"

She nodded, biting her lip.

"Well, you're right. That's one of the things that drives my brothers crazy." He kept his tone conversational, and he could feel her starting to relax. "I'm just not very goal oriented. Sometimes a moment is enough." The light in his eyes softened as he took her hand. "I don't have to score. And I don't even like to hear this called that."

Her smile quirked up on one side. "This?"

He looked her straight in the eye. "You know what *this* is."

"I sure do." She kicked off one boot, then the other. They hit the floor with two solid thumps, and she shot him a sultry look from under her lashes. "I'm a big girl, Brady. I can handle it."

He sure as heck hoped that was true.

And for the first time ever, he found himself wondering if *he* could handle it.

Brady had been bucked off in the first go-round that day, so he'd had time to go home and clean up before hitting the beer tent. Suze, on the other hand, had won the barrel racing, which was the final event of the day. She was still dressed in her riding clothes, which didn't look all that different from her everyday clothes—a long-sleeved Western shirt, Wrangler jeans, and boots. It was the same thing Brady was wearing, but his clothes were clean. She probably smelled like a stable—or worse.

"I need to take a shower," she said.

Brady rolled over, pulling her close, and breathed deep.

"Are you going to use all kinds of fancy soaps and shampoos, and squirt yourself with flowery perfume when you're done?"

Suze huffed out a laugh. She should have known she wasn't good enough for Brady. Might as well let him know that now.

"I don't own any fancy soaps," she said. "And I use Mane 'n Tail shampoo.

Brady laughed. "Is that the same shampoo Speedo uses?"

Suze nodded. She wasn't really ashamed of using horse shampoo. Brady might not know it, but lots of the girls used it. It seemed to strengthen hair and make it shiny better than anything else on the market.

"Seems like it's working," he murmured.

She realized then that he'd undone the rawhide tie at the bottom of her braid and was working his fingers through the plaits, undoing it from the bottom up. It felt good, his fingers stroking through her hair, and she didn't want him to stop. But she needed to tell him...

"I don't have any perfume either."

"Praise the Lord." He buried his head in the crook of her neck and shoulder, and inhaled her scent, which was probably nothing pretty at this point. It might look like a girl just sat up there in the saddle and the horse did all the work, but riding barrels was a workout.

"Dang, girl." He kissed the side of her neck. "You don't have anything to apologize for. You smell fantastic."

He probably said that to all the girls, but, heck, she'd take it.

Whatever he wanted to give her, she'd take it.

He tugged her collar aside so he could nuzzle her throat. One button slipped open somehow, then the next, and then she was lying there in low-slung jeans and a plain white sports bra. The outfit was hardly the stuff of randy male fantasies, but at least she didn't have to be ashamed of her body. The workout she got from riding might not make her smell pretty, but it kept her in shape. And the stretchy bra tamed her curves a little bit, which was a good thing.

Brady sat up on his knees and looked down at her. She'd ended up sprawled on the pillows in what probably looked like a wanton, come-hither pose. Come to think of it, she was feeling pretty wanton and sexy. And it was obvious that Brady liked it.

"You should dress like that more often."

"Like this?"

Only a man would say that. She had way too much up top to parade around in her next-to-nothings. There were girls who did, but they were attention hounds, and wore things far more lacy and sparkly than her plain white bra.

"Just like that." He reached out and ran his finger gently down the edge of one strap, then across the front, taking his fingertip on a hilly journey across the top of one breast, down into her cleavage, and across the other.

Just one touch of his finger made her breath catch. What would it be like if—if this went further?

"If you dressed like this all the time, I could look at you and think about doing this," he said, tugging one strap down her shoulder. "And this." He loosened the other strap. "And this." He stroked his hands down her sides. The nerves just under her skin rippled with the sensation, making her gasp. "You like that," he murmured, bending down to kiss her.

She couldn't help herself. She *did* like it. She liked it a lot.

She tried to stay cool, to control her breathing, but she loved kissing, and kissing Brady was sheer heaven. He smelled so good and tasted better, like toothpaste and mint and very, very faintly of beer.

Come to think of it, she probably tasted like a

brewery. She'd had how many beers? Two? Three? She couldn't remember, but she suspected that however many she'd had, they were responsible for her newfound courage—the courage that let her stroke her tongue across his upper lip and dart it into his mouth, the courage that let her pull him down on top of her so she could writhe under his body and press her hips to his, making her needs perfectly clear.

God, he felt good.

She could feel the tension of the day unwinding as she gave herself over to pure feeling—something she rarely did. Her mind was always running, always worrying, always obsessing about something. The only other time her mind cleared was when she was racing.

Like water flowing.

That was how this felt. It shouldn't. She didn't really know Brady that well. She hadn't spent much time with him—except in fantasies. If fantasies counted, she'd spent a lot of time with him.

She needed to be careful. Brady was a man, not a fantasy. A...*man.*

The proof of that fact was pressing into her at this very moment, making her body heat and soften, opening to take him in, to make him a part of her memories forever. Because whatever happened, she'd never forget this night.

Chapter 5

BRADY LOOKED DOWN AT SUZE AND TRIED TO FORGET that he was breaking every rule he'd ever set for himself when it came to women.

Never sleep with a woman who takes things too seriously was number one.

Never sleep with a woman who has a yapper dog was number two, but Suze might be exempt from that one, since she wasn't your typical yapper-dog woman.

The third rule was *Never talk to a woman about anything personal.* He normally kept his conversations light. He'd talk about rodeo, about music, and about drinking, but never about a girl's home life or his own goals and dreams. But he'd let Suze spill her heart to him, and he'd told her more than he'd intended about himself.

The fourth rule was one he hadn't expected to break tonight.

Never sleep with a woman who makes you feel too much.

Something about Suze's combination of strength and vulnerability spoke to him, deep down inside in parts of his heart he usually kept walled off. As a foster kid, he'd learned that caring about people only made it hurt more when they left you, so he was careful to keep his relationships superficial.

Suze had always seemed so standoffish that he'd never dreamed she'd get under his skin like this. Being with her felt like stepping into a kiddie pool and discovering it was six feet deep. He was way out of his depth, and he couldn't figure out how he'd gotten there.

And they'd only just started.

He glanced toward the door. He could make a run for it.

But then he looked down at the woman lying beneath him and decided he'd regret running for the rest of his life.

"Something wrong?" she asked.

"Nope." He smiled, hoping she couldn't read the fear in his eyes. It was fading anyway. She looked so sweet, lying there—a word he never thought he'd apply to Suze Carlyle.

That long blond hair, freed from her trademark braid, lay uncoiled on the pillow. Her body was uncoiling too. He could feel her relaxing, softening, letting him in.

But there was still one hill to climb. Actually, it was looking more like a mountain. She'd relaxed enough to let out a little whimper a while back, but then that V between her eyebrows had returned and he knew she was taking this way too seriously.

"Suze," he said.

She opened her eyes and blinked up at him.

"Stop thinking."

"I'm not." She squirmed against him. "In fact, I was just thinking that—oh."

"Yup," he said, grinning. "Exactly."

Green. Her eyes were green and had a strange crystalline clarity to them. They reminded him of a stream flowing through a forest, the cool, clear water reflecting the spring green of the leaves.

She shrugged, prettily embarrassed. "I guess you won't believe me if I told you I was thinking about how I wasn't thinking?"

"Guess not." He rose to his knees. "Turn over."

"What?"

"Turn over. Don't worry. I'm not going to spank you."

She grinned. "Darn it. A girl can hope."

Wow. He'd expected Suze to be shy, or maybe cold—not feisty and funny and warm.

Once she turned over, he let her wait a bit, partly so he could enjoy the sight of her and partly so she'd wonder what was coming. For him, that was half the pleasure of making love with a new partner—wondering what was coming next.

Or *who* was coming next. It would be her. He'd make sure of that.

Now *he* was thinking too much. He put his hands on her shoulders and kneaded the tight muscles there, pressing hard with his thumbs until she moaned aloud.

"Oh, Brady," she said. "I didn't realize how tense I was." She moaned again. "Don't stop. *Please* don't stop."

"Man, you're easy," he said, moving down to press his thumbs along her spine. "You're already calling my name, and I'm still fully clothed."

"I was going to talk to you about that." The joke tapered off into a moan.

Brady had had his share of massages, from physical therapists and from women who wanted to impress him with their skills. He did his best to remember everything that felt good, and he used that knowledge to knead her neck and rub hard under her shoulder blades.

"Loosen your belt," he said.

She was so lost in the massage, she didn't seem to think at all as she hiked up her very fine butt and struggled with the clasp to her belt. Tugging her jeans down until they were dangerously low, she relaxed again. He had a little trouble getting started again, since he hadn't expected the combination of tight athleticism and hourglass-shaped sexiness her body revealed. She always wore those baggy pants and shirts. He wondered why.

He kneaded her lower back, making her moan even more.

"Dang, I didn't know I was so sore," she said. "I should do this more often."

"A lot of times you can get a massage at the Justin tent," he said. Justin was a boot company who'd put their brand on the map by sponsoring sports medicine stations at every major rodeo. They patched up the cowboys who wrecked and offered advice for those with chronic injuries. Since a lot of cowboys rode hurt, the tent stayed busy through every rodeo.

"I guess I should try that."

She sighed, giving herself over to the massage. Brady gradually gentled his touch. He was a little worried she'd fallen asleep, but hell, if she had, he'd lie down beside her and count himself lucky he didn't have to break *all* his rules.

Maybe he should pretend he was just here to give her a massage. He glanced at the door again, then back at Suze, who had suddenly turned over. Her eyes were wide-awake, and he was now straddling her hips.

There was no turning back. His pardner down under

was ready for action, and though Brady himself might be a coward, his pardner never let a good woman down.

"Um," he said.

She smiled. "Were you going to say something?"

"I was. But danged if I can remember what it was, now that I looked in your eyes."

She turned her head.

"That won't work," he said. "Now I'm looking at the way your lips turn up at the corners and the sweep of your jaw." He reached down and stroked her jawline with one finger. "You have a strong face," he said.

"Is that a compliment?"

"From me it is. I like strong women."

"Is that what you were going to say?"

"Nope." He kissed the corner of her mouth. "Whatever that was, it's lost and gone forever."

Suze closed her eyes and gave herself over to sensation as Brady kissed his way down her jaw, then trailed his lips and tongue down her neck, down her throat. He reached her cleavage and tugged at her sports bra, but it wouldn't budge.

She tugged at it, trying to help, but the danged thing was designed to hold tight, no matter what kind of pressure it was subjected to. It was more like armor than lingerie. She let out a mew of frustration—a very embarrassing mew—and sat up, hauling the thing up over her breasts and off.

Oh Lord. What had she done? He was staring at her as if something was wrong. And no wonder. She'd stripped like she was in gym class or something. There was nothing sexy about what she'd done. Nothing sexy at all.

And her breasts, always too big, were bouncing all over the place. She started to cover herself, but he shook his head no.

"Perfect," he said, his voice low. "You're so perfect." He reached out and cradled her breasts in his hands, running his thumbs slowly over her nipples until they peaked and ached. She squeezed her eyes shut, overwhelmed by the feeling, and resisted the urge to cover herself again. Losing herself in sensation, she threw her head back, inviting him to touch and fondle and stroke and kiss.

He did all that and more. Sensation swirled from his touch, and she tugged at his shirt until the snaps came undone and she could run her hands over his chest. There wasn't an extra ounce of fat on the man; he was all muscle as far as she could see. How someone who spent all his time carousing could stay so fit was a mystery she'd never solve.

He flipped her over. She wasn't sure how; one minute she was on her back, the next she was on all fours, with him behind her. She could feel how hard he was, pressed against the tight seat of her jeans, and she rocked against him while he cupped her heavy breasts in his hands and pushed back.

She suddenly realized she hated blue jeans. Sure, they were great for riding and comfortable for most everything else, but they were practically impossible to remove with any kind of grace. After that scene with the bra, she wanted to entice, to tease.

She wished she were wearing yoga pants. And she wished Brady wasn't wearing any pants at all.

Well, her mother had always said that if you had a wish, it was up to you to make it come true. Suze kind of doubted this was the kind of situation she'd been referring to, but it was still good advice.

She reached behind her and tugged at his belt.

"Take these off," she said.

"Is that an order?" His tone was easy and humorous—a total contrast to hers, which was desperate and out of control.

"Yes, it was," she said. "Are you going to follow it?"

"Not unless you take yours off too."

"Bet I can beat you."

She squirmed and wriggled in a desperate effort to peel her Wranglers past her hips. She didn't wear pants as tight as the other girls, but dang it, they fit well enough. It was a struggle and well, this was embarrassing. She ended up feeling like a turtle on its back, trapped, waving its legs in the air.

Brady, who'd shed his own jeans with relative grace, helped her out, but with maddening slowness, taking the time to pull off her belt and set it aside, then easing her jeans down while she tried to hide the fact that she had to hang on to her panties or they'd be gone too.

Finally, the two of them lay face-to-face, a little worn out from all the struggling and heaving and squirming but happy as a cowboy and a cowgirl could be.

She ought to do this more often. One-night stands were actually kind of fun. She felt better than she had in days. Months. Years.

There were other good-looking cowboys out there who probably wouldn't mind a roll in the hay with the women's barrel racing champion. She'd had some offers, but she didn't know how to make love to some-one she didn't even like.

And that was the problem. She was no virgin, but this was the first time she'd taken off her clothes for a man she wasn't in a relationship with. It was also the first time she hadn't been nervous or even reluctant. Because the kind of guys she could stand having around all the time weren't like Brady at all. They were thoughtful, sensitive guys, guys who watched her race and brought her flowers. Guys from other worlds.

In the past year, she'd dated a financial advisor and a real estate agent. Both were the kind of guys her father said she should be dating—men with responsible jobs that didn't involve risking their lives on the backs of broncs every day. She wished she had a dollar for every time her father had warned her about cowboys, about their drinking and carousing, their lying and their cheat-ing and their evil hound-dog ways.

But eventually, she'd had to admit that she just didn't have the kind of feelings for those nice, ordinary men that made for a successful relationship. They made good friends but lousy lovers. So she'd broken up with them and gone back to fantasizing about Brady Caine.

Who was here now, in her trailer, making love to her.

Well, having sex, anyway. Her father was right about the hound-dog ways. The wandering, town-to-town life of the rodeo cowboy made it easy for a man to leave women behind, and a lot of the cowboys—including Brady—took full advantage.

Brady nuzzled her right where her neck and shoulder met. "You're thinking again."

He was right, but something like goose bumps or

tickles or happy-dancing nerve endings spread from the spot where he was kissing her, taking over first her body and then her brain.

So this was the solution. One-night stands, all the time, with cowboys. Look how good Brady made her feel. All she had to do was dress up a little and visit the beer tents and barrooms in the small towns where rodeo held sway, and she could have a cowboy every night.

But it wouldn't be Brady. And Brady was the only one she wanted.

And he'd never settle down with someone like her. When he got ready to start a family, he'd find someone as attractive, clever, and good-natured as himself.

So this was it. Not just a one-night stand, but a limited engagement, once-in-a-lifetime event. She'd better make it count—for both of them.

She wanted to be the best he'd ever had. She wanted him to remember her. She wanted him to wish, once in a while, that he'd hung on to her.

"You're thinking again," he said between kisses.

"Trust me," she said. "I'm thinking good thoughts."

"Like what?"

She whispered in his ear, making sure her lips and tongue did a lot of the talking, and was pleased to see his eyes widen with surprise.

He pushed her down onto the bed.

"Tell me something," he said, stroking her hair and smiling as if he'd just won the lottery. "Why haven't we done this before?"

Chapter 6

BRADY COULDN'T BELIEVE HIS LUCK.

He was in Suze Carlyle's trailer, on Suze Carlyle's bed, making love to Suze Carlyle. It was truly a rodeo miracle. He'd always thought Suze was far too high above him in the rodeo hierarchy of champions, strivers, and deadbeats to give him so much as a glance.

In fact, she probably considered him one of the deadbeats. Most people did. His rides *did* look sloppy—he'd seen the agreement in her eyes when he'd said so. But he knew what he was doing, and he won more often than people realized. His sloppy rides gave the audience exactly what they wanted: the impression that he was going to get bucked off and stomped at any moment. That's why he was popular enough to get endorsement deals for everything from trucks to Tony Lamas.

The other miracle was that Suze seemed to be experienced. He'd been a little worried she'd turn out to be a virgin. As far as he knew, she'd only dated a couple of guys, and they were losers—some accountant and a real estate huckster who wasn't man enough to shine her boots.

But judging from what she'd just told him, she knew exactly how to please a man.

"Now *you're* thinking." She laughed, lying beneath him with her gorgeous body laid out like a feast.

The massage had worked. That laugh hadn't come

from the tightly wound Suze he'd picked up at the beer tent. It had come from a woman who was comfortable in her own skin—maybe more comfortable in her skin than in her clothes, come to think of it.

"Why do you cover yourself up?"

"What?" He could see why she was confused. She sure wasn't covered up now.

"Normally," he said. "With those baggy jeans and big shirts."

"I don't know." She looked away. "My breasts are too big, and my butt—you know."

"Not yet I don't. But I will." He touched her lips—just touched that full lower lip—then stroked her chin, her throat, her chest, working his way down through the valley of her cleavage to her tanned, flat stomach. She rippled at his touch, catching her breath.

That was all the encouragement he needed. All the encouragement he could *take*. He bent to kiss her, and the tender touching was all over—for the moment, anyway. They pressed their bodies together and kissed *hard*—deep, wet, hotly sexual kisses that left him nearly exhausted.

If this was what kissing Suze was like, what would it be like when they got to the main event?

It's going to be fantastic.

But Brady was determined to take his time getting there. He was going to enjoy those breasts—the one place where her long, lean body offered a little something extra. He wanted to feast on them, make the nipples stand up till they ached, and then taste them, touch them, drive her wild. He couldn't get enough of the feeling of her flesh filling his hands. He wanted to squeeze and stroke and fondle, and she didn't seem to mind letting him.

That's why it took him by surprise when she reached down and cupped her palm over his erection. The warmth of her hand, the pressure, but most of all the fact that it was Suze touching him there, nearly made him come right then, like some high school kid, but he hung on and let out his feelings in a groan of pleasure.

Was that what she wanted? Was she in a hurry for this to be over?

He groaned again at the thought, and that seemed to drive her wild. Grabbing his shoulders, she pulled him down on top of her again, pushing her hips against his pelvis, demanding what she wanted without saying a word.

She was in a hurry, all right. But not for it to be over.

They were just getting started.

Suze was not a passive woman. She wasn't willing to lie there while Brady did all the work, much as she enjoyed his efforts. No, she wanted to touch him the way he was touching her. She wanted to drive him wild.

He was experienced, obviously. The accountant and the salesman hadn't exactly taught her the *Kama Sutra*; their lovemaking had reflected all the excitement of their occupations.

A cowboy would expect something more. Brady was an adrenaline junkie. They all were, herself included. You couldn't deal with the hazards of rodeo unless you fed on danger like horses fed on hay.

So how could she match the thrills he experienced every day on broncs and bulls—not to mention the buckle bunnies?

She met his eyes, and her thoughts skidded to a stop. She could look at him, that's what she could do. She could make love to Brady, the Brady she knew, and not some version of him out of a Wild West storybook.

She didn't take her eyes from his as she pushed him gently to one side. He figured out what she wanted and rolled over, letting her straddle his hips so his erection rose, hard and proud, from the spot where their bodies met. But she didn't touch it—not before she'd bent over and kissed him, long and thoroughly, and then licked her way down his body.

She could feel a fluttering excitement between her legs as her body yearned for release. It was going to have to wait a while longer.

She stroked Brady's abs, watching his muscles ripple and clench under her touch. He started to sit up then, but she pushed him back with one hand while she wrapped the other around his cock.

It was bigger than she'd expected—bigger and harder and altogether more tempting than anything she'd seen before. She moved her hand gently up, then down. Then she squeezed, and Brady closed his eyes and threw his head back, his hands reaching out for her, then knotting into fists at his side.

She had him right where she wanted him. He opened his eyes and gave her that smile. "You're enjoying this, aren't you?"

"Aren't you?"

"Oh, yeah."

She shimmied backward on the bed, until she lay between his legs.

"You're not going to—you don't have to…"

He cut off his words with a moan as she ran her tongue up his shaft. She hoped to hell she knew how to do this. She'd never done it before, and she'd die if he knew that. All she knew was that it gave men pleasure, as much pleasure as the real thing, so why not do it for Brady?

Evidently her lack of experience didn't matter. She hadn't thought he could get harder, or bigger, but that's the effect her warm mouth had on him. He let her lick and taste and suck for a while before he clutched her shoulders with both hands.

"What's wrong? Did I…"

She was about to ask him if she'd done it wrong, but it was a good thing she didn't get the words out, because he was gazing at her with such an expression of wonder it almost made her laugh. Apparently, she'd done something right.

Very right.

"Dang, girl, where'd you learn to do that? I didn't expect—I mean, I'm glad, but I thought…"

"You thought this was going to be plain vanilla, didn't you?" She gave the head one final swirling lick, making his ab muscles tense. "Well, surprise. You got chocolate."

"I got strawberry," he said. "Strawberry swirl." He drew out the last word like he was tasting it—or like he was passing out from pure pleasure. But he revived soon enough, when she added a little hand action. "Oh," he groaned. "There's a cherry on top."

"We haven't gotten to the cherry yet," she said.

"I know." He grinned, and before she could do more than squeak with surprise, he hauled her up and flipped her over. Now it was his turn to kneel at the foot of the bed and her turn to widen her eyes with surprise as he slipped off her panties and parted her legs with both hands.

Both hands. That meant he was going to touch her with…ooooh.

But first, he just looked. How could he make her squirm so much without even touching her? The fluttering was so strong now she thought it must be visible, and she could barely breathe as Brady looked his fill, as if he was memorizing all her secret places.

By the time he touched her, she'd closed her eyes, so she floated away on a warm river of pleasure as he licked and stroked and licked again. Her body felt more alive than ever before. A shimmering of lust and need gave way to the hum of pure pleasure, and then the lust and need came back stronger than ever. Panic and pleasure followed each other, one after the other, so fast that she couldn't tell one from the other.

She felt her body tensing like a taut string as she tried to hang on to sanity just a little bit longer, but the force of her orgasm was too much. Squeezing her eyes shut, she felt that string pull tighter, tighter, tighter—and then it broke and she was spiraling up, up, up, and up, her mind spinning as sensation overwhelmed her. She'd never felt more free, and yet she'd never felt more frightened. She was seriously afraid she wouldn't be able to come back to the real world.

She felt herself break into a million glittering pieces,

and then she was falling. Limp, sated, spent, she landed safe in Brady's arms.

Brady gazed in wonder at the woman beside him. He'd been right—she made love with the same wild, reckless spirit she brought to her sport. She might think it was watching videos and asking questions that made her the extraordinary woman she was, but she was wrong. He had no doubt that the secret to her success was the way she gave all of herself to everything she did. She held nothing back, and he'd never seen anything so beautiful as her body responding to his touch. Her cries and moans made his own desire burn even hotter.

But before he could take what he wanted—what he *needed* now—he had to help her down from the heights. She lay in his arms limp with exhaustion, her lashes fluttering as she gradually returned to reality. She looked up at him, blinking, and he gave himself a mental high five when he realized she didn't know where she was.

"You okay, darlin'?" He pulled her head down on his shoulder and stroked her hair.

She shook her head as if to clear it, and her brow furrowed. "I think so." She looked up at him, then quickly looked away, but not before he saw a hot blush steal over her features. "Sorry," she muttered.

"Sorry?" He gave her a little shake. "What have you got to be sorry for?" Tugging her close, he stroked her hair again. She seemed to like that, so he did it again and kissed the top of her head. "That was the most beautiful thing I ever saw," he said.

He actually *meant* that. He was starting to get nervous.

"I kind of, um, get carried away," she said, looking at the walls, the ceiling—everywhere but at Brady. "It's embarrassing."

He shook his head, wishing he could get hold of that accountant and the goddamn salesman she'd been seeing. "Honey, you've got nothing to be embarrassed about. Not in my world."

"That's right," she said. "You're a cowboy." She gave him a hot look from under her lashes, then sat up and slung a leg over his body, straddling him again. "I guess it's okay to get carried away."

He was more than ready to go, but she'd put him in an awkward position. He had a condom in his wallet, but his wallet was in his jeans pocket and his jeans were somewhere beyond the foot of the bed.

"Honey, I just need to do one thing," he said. "We cowboys believe in safety first."

"Of course," she said. "You need your packet."

He laughed. "Exactly."

The term *packet* had become part of the cowboy lexicon a few years ago, when some do-gooders had decided those wild rodeo cowboys and cowgirls needed reining in. Notices were posted in the restrooms at every rodeo, advising safe sex and offering free packets at the medical tent. *Packets* were, of course, condoms—which apparently couldn't be mentioned by name.

He'd never seen packets offered at rock concerts or motocross races. Only rodeos. Apparently, cowboys had quite a reputation to live up to.

He was happy to do his part.

Bending to retrieve his jeans, he slipped his wallet

out of his pocket and the condom out of the wallet. He had himself gloved up and ready before he even turned around.

Now it was his turn to blush as he met Suze's very frank, very interested gaze and realized he'd bent over without even thinking about the view from the bed.

"Nice." She ducked her head and smiled shyly. "Very nice. Now how about if you show me how to ride?"

He laughed. "I don't think I can show you anything," he said. "Except maybe a good time."

"That's enough for me." She turned serious all of a sudden. "Really, Brady. Just so you know? That really is all I'm here for."

"What's all you're here for?"

"A good time." She gave him a sunny smile. "Don't have to worry that I'll expect anything more. I know the score, Brady. I know this is just for fun."

Huh. So breaking the rules wasn't a problem. He'd been sure Suze would want to be treated better than that. She wasn't some one-night-stand buckle bunny, after all. She didn't seem like the kind of woman who would give herself away to just anybody.

That had made him feel special, but now? Not so much.

He turned away, pretending to adjust the condom so she wouldn't see the expression on his face. For some reason, it really stung that she didn't take him seriously. She took *everything* seriously.

Everything except him.

Chapter 7

SUZE THOUGHT SHE'D HIT JUST THE RIGHT TONE TO keep Brady from thinking she was one of those women who would follow him around and make doe eyes at him, but for a minute she thought she'd offended him. There was something fake in his smile, and his eyes held shadows she'd never noticed before.

Maybe she wasn't supposed to talk about how casual their casual sex was.

But when he joined her on the bed and looked down at her, she decided everything was okay.

The rest of the night was everything she'd dreamed of, with Brady taking her up to the heavens twice more before they were done.

Everything felt right. Everything but the knowledge that crept into her mind whenever she let herself think. *This is just for tonight. Just for now.*

But she didn't mind—or at least, that's what she told herself. She'd remember this night forever—treasure it and run it through her mind like a home movie whenever she felt blue. It would be her own private porn stash.

The thought made her giggle.

"What's so funny?" he asked.

What if she told him?

"Nothing," she said.

When it was over, the two of them lay side by side, glistening with sweat, smiling at the ceiling like a couple of fools. Which was probably what they were, but she wasn't about to admit it.

Suze woke the next morning with a smile on her face. Last night might not have meant anything to Brady, but it had been a rare gift for her. Once, just once, she'd wanted to have a man she really desired. A man who made her feel hot and loose and sexy.

Brady must have known what it had meant to her, because he was kind as could be. He'd made love almost as if he cared.

Not made love. Had sex. She needed to remember that was all they'd done.

Still, he'd made her feel almost beautiful. No wonder women loved him.

She wondered where Dooley had gone. Normally he was curled by her side, but he must have gotten up early. She hoped he hadn't pooped on the floor. Up until now, pooping outside was the one thing the dog did right.

She turned over, ready to step out of bed, and got the shock of her life.

There he was. Brady Caine, sleeping like some kind of Wild West angel, with her hairy little yapper dog clasped in his arms.

She'd never noticed what long lashes Brady had. And she'd never seen his face relaxed like this. The tough guy was gone, and she could almost see what he must have looked like as a child. Her heart, which she'd hardened in anticipation of waking alone, softened at the sight. She was kidding herself if she said she wasn't crazy about him. She had been for a long time.

But a lot of other girls felt the same way, and it wasn't like Suze could compete in that arena. Horses she could handle, but love? Not a chance. Winning took practice, and she had no idea what the hell she was doing when it came to relationships—or anything that pertained to humans, for that matter.

Brady stirred in his sleep and turned over, clutching Dooley tighter. She'd better enjoy the view while she could, because the dog would leap up at any moment, yapping out his morning demands for walkies, breakfast, playtime, *now*!

But Dooley only lifted his head and looked at her—or at least, she thought he was looking at her; you never could tell with all that hair—then settled down with a deep, satisfied sigh. Apparently he liked sleeping with Brady almost as much as she did.

She shuffled off to the bathroom to brush her teeth. It was bad enough she'd had beer breath last night. She didn't want to blow it in his face in the morning.

Besides, brushing her teeth and throwing cold water on her face gave her time to think about things. Why was Brady still here? She'd assumed he'd leave right after—after *that*—and been surprised when he'd held her, stroked her hair. She thought she'd dreamed that she drifted off in his arms, but apparently not.

She stared at herself in the mirror. She didn't look like the kind of woman Brady liked, but he'd been more than sexy last night; he'd been tender and kind. And he'd stayed.

He was experienced enough to know that a man didn't stay the night unless he wanted to see a woman again. Breakfast was pretty awkward when you had to look across the table at a woman you planned to leave behind like a used towel.

So maybe he wasn't going to leave her behind.

Suddenly, the morning seemed a little brighter, and the night before took on new meaning. She hadn't dared to hope that Brady saw her as anything more than a little bit of fun. But here he was.

And here she was, mooning over the possibilities when she should be making breakfast.

French toast, she decided, with eggs on the side. Over light, scrambled—she'd make whatever he wanted once he woke up.

She fished out her best coffee, the stuff she saved to savor after special victories. The scent of it brewing should wake him up. Then she set out the eggs, milk, and two kinds of cereal, plus bowls and everything else she'd need to make a great breakfast.

Humming, she set the table with her best lace place mats and put out butter, maple syrup, and salt and pepper.

Brady was still sleeping. That meant she had a little time to pretty up. Humming a happy tune, she headed back to the bathroom for a quick shower.

—⁓—

The first thing Brady felt that morning was a kink in his neck. Then he remembered how he'd gotten it, and smiled.

Suze Carlyle's body was the best-kept secret in Wyoming. Under her frumpy clothes and tacky old hat, she was as pretty as any rodeo queen—prettier, because you could see her strength in the set of her jaw and the steel in her eyes, and sense the grit that made her a champion. She wasn't any ordinary beauty. She was truly a strong woman in every way.

He opened his eyes and stared up at the ceiling.

Where the heck was he? Once in a while he tied one on and woke up in a strange place, but that hadn't happened for a while.

He felt something soft under his hand. Soft and silky. Like Suze.

Oh, shoot.

He'd spent the night.

He felt her hair again, and she woke up and licked his hand.

Wait. What? That was weird.

He opened his eyes just in time to see Dooley's furry face coming at him, tongue first.

"Hey, buddy. Wait a minute. No." He pushed the dog away and sat up, rubbing his eyes. Shoot. He was still in Suze's bed—and in deep, deep trouble.

Fortunately, he could hear the shower running, so he'd be able to make a quick and quiet exit.

He hadn't meant to spend the night. He liked Suze, and he respected her. He wouldn't mind sleeping with her again, but he didn't want a relationship. For one thing, the woman was wound a little tight. For another, she seemed to have a lot of problems. It wasn't her fault that her mother died or that her dad was so peculiar. But he wasn't exactly panting to join the family. He knew his own limitations. Those complications were too much for him.

Speaking of panting, here came Dooley again. This time, he had one of Brady's socks in his mouth.

"Hey, thanks, little buddy." Brady reached for the sock.

Dooley dodged away, making a playful little growling sound.

"Hey. Give that back." Brady lunged for the sock, and Dooley dashed off to the kitchen. Brady followed, hot on his furry heels.

The dog ran under the table and growled, shaking the sock as if it were a rat that needed killing.

But Brady wasn't watching the dog. He was taking in the sight of the kitchen.

A dozen eggs sat on the counter beside a fry pan. There was a loaf of bread, a jug of milk, and two boxes of sugary cereal, including Frosted Flakes—his favorite.

The table was set with lace place mats. *Lace.*

This was serious. She'd put out butter and maple syrup too, so they weren't just having a quick, simple breakfast. He could deal with eating a quick bowl of cereal while standing at the counter. But a whole cooked breakfast, served on lace place mats? No way. That was way too domesticated for him.

He headed back to the bedroom and hustled into his clothes. Dooley could have the damn sock. He shoved his bare foot into his boot, wincing at the rough feel of the leather against his skin.

His cell phone buzzed in his jeans pocket. He had an alert.

Meeting, Lariat Western Wear. Today, 9:00 a.m.

Today? No, the meeting was tomorrow. Lariat was his biggest and most important sponsor. He wouldn't forget when the meeting was. Would he?

He looked at the screen again. *Today.*

Shit. He glanced at the top of the screen for the time. 8:55.

Double shit.

He was going to be late.

Well, at least that gave him a good reason to rush out the door.

Chapter 8

SUZE COMBED OUT HER DAMP HAIR AND SCOWLED AT herself in the mirror. Even after a hot shower, her eyes showed every possible sign of a short night's sleep. They were red and rheumy, with big pouches underneath. Her skin looked sallow and dull, and every freckle and blemish showed in the harsh white light.

She certainly didn't look anything like the kind of girls she'd seen Brady with. They probably rose from the bed with perfect, dewy skin and temptingly tousled hair, all ready for another round.

Why couldn't she look more like her mother? Ellen Carlyle had certainly never looked like this in the morning. Her father had said once that his late wife rose in the morning fresh as a summer day.

She could hear her father's voice in her head. *You should try harder to look like your mother. She was a beautiful woman*. Once he'd scowled and said she looked more like him. How could that be her fault?

Besides, it wasn't true. He was short and slight, with dark hair that had receded rapidly since her mother had died, leaving a little tufted island in the middle of a sea of pink baldness. He was nearsighted and squinted from behind thick glasses, and he wasn't the least bit athletic.

She shut out the thought of him. Thank goodness she could do that now. He used to go with her to every rodeo, critiquing her riding, comparing her to her mother until she wanted to scream. She'd actually gone out to the barn and done a private happy dance when he'd told her he wouldn't be traveling with her anymore. She felt guilty, since it was his arthritis that kept him home, but she was also relieved. Rodeo was hers now, a sanctuary from his constant carping and the cloud of grief that hung over his head.

It had been twelve years since her mother died— *twelve years*, and yet her father still seemed to be grieving. All the pictures of Ellen that hung around the house probably didn't help, and he talked about her constantly. He even watched *Bonanza* reruns on television because Ben Cartwright, the patriarch of the Ponderosa clan, was a widower too. Three times over.

Ben Cartwright dealt with it. Why couldn't her father?

Suze grieved for her mother too. She'd been ten when Ellen Carlye had died, so she had some memories to treasure—although her mom had spent so much time on the road that Suze thought of her almost like that falling star she'd seen with Brady: a bright presence that arced across her life, then disappeared.

But instead of shutting down, like her father had, she'd built herself a mental treasure box of memories to carry with her, so she wouldn't miss her mother so much. Every time her father told her something about her mom, she added it to the treasure box and felt a little bit richer. Her father was right about one thing: Ellen Carlyle had been an amazing woman. Suze just wished she could live up to the legacy of being her daughter.

She wasn't doing it right now, that was for sure. Looking at her sallow reflection, she couldn't believe Brady had stayed over.

She fished out the emergency makeup kit she kept under the counter for TV interviews and that kind of thing. She almost never wore makeup. She didn't have time to fuss with that kind of thing, and besides, her father disapproved.

Makeup? Why do you want to spend money on that garbage? Your mother never needed more than a touch of lipstick.

She really needed to stop letting her father intrude on her thoughts. Because he was wrong about her. She was just as pretty as her mother. Brady had said so. At the time, she'd thought he was just trying to get her into bed, but now she realized he'd really meant it. After all, he'd stayed.

Still, she needed a little work this morning.

She was inches from the mirror, applying concealer under her eyes, when Brady appeared behind her. He was leaning on the door frame with one hand gripping the top, looking all handsome and Brady-ish.

It wasn't fair. Why didn't men have to wear makeup to look good? It seemed like the less they fussed, the better they looked. He had more than a day's growth of beard, and he looked raffish and hot. She remembered that beard scraping her skin and blushed, which probably turned her skin blotchy and made her look even more hideous.

Brady was fully dressed, which was disappointing. She'd love to have seen him all rumpled and shirtless, but he'd even put his boots on.

"Hey," she said. "Good morning."

"Good morning." He shifted nervously from one foot to the other. He obviously wasn't used to waking up with a woman. He was probably the type who left in the dead of night.

But those days were over. It was hard to believe it, but she'd actually tamed the great Brady Caine. No doubt she'd earn the irrational but intense enmity of thousands of hopeful buckle bunnies—an army of pubescent teens in tight pants who'd come after her with shotguns and pitchforks. The thought made her giggle.

"What's funny?" he asked.

"Nothing." She spun around and gave him a quick smooch on the lips. "Give me a minute here and I'll be out to make breakfast."

She wanted him to protest, to grab her and haul her off to the bedroom for a repeat of last night. But having breakfast together would be just as intimate, in a way.

"Do you like French toast?" she asked.

"Um, no thanks." He shifted uneasily. "You didn't have to go to all that trouble."

"I don't mind, Brady. I like to cook."

"No, I mean I, ah, have to go. I'm really sorry."

She stared at him, her mind frozen by a cold whoosh of hurt and humiliation. He had to go?

Of course he did. He hadn't stayed over on purpose. He'd overslept. By about four or five hours.

She hadn't *tamed* Brady Caine. She'd just worn him out.

She laughed. It sounded high and unnatural, but it was the best she could do. "You think I went to 'all that trouble' for you?" She forced out another laugh. "Haven't you ever heard of the Breakfast of Champions? If you don't eat right, it's no wonder your career's not taking off. I eat a huge breakfast every morning." She returned to her attention to the mirror and patted the concealer over the bags under her eyes.

"I overslept," he said. "I need to… What are you doing?" He looked stunned.

"Nothing."

She finished with the concealer and patted on some powder.

"You wear *makeup*?" Brady sounded incredulous.

She nodded and he huffed out a little laugh. "You sure can't tell."

She paused mid powder-pat and gave his mirror image a stony glare. "Gee, thanks."

"No, I didn't mean it like that," he said, eyes widening. "I meant…"

"It's all right. Never mind." Fortunately, the hurt and humiliation were quickly replaced by anger. She put away the other stuff she'd planned to use—eyeliner, mascara, blush—and turned around, leaning on the sink. She might as well let him see the hag he'd slept with last night. It was already obvious he was having second thoughts. "So you have to get going this morning, right? In fact, I bet you're already late."

He backed up, looking uncomfortable. "Well, actually…"

"It's not a problem, Brady. In fact, it's kind of a relief." She did her best to laugh, but it sounded hollow. "I sure didn't expect you to still be here this morning. Go on." She wished she hadn't put the makeup away, so she'd have something to do with her hands. Of course, they were shaking so badly she could hardly have applied eyeliner or mascara. But hey, then she wouldn't have had to watch Brady walk away, because she'd have poked her eyes out.

She needed to get him out of here before she started really feeling sorry for herself. God forbid she should embarrass herself by crying in front of him. She prided herself far more on her toughness than on her feminine wiles. She forced a smile.

"Go, Brady." She made shooing motions with her hands, forcing him to back away. "Go. I have stuff to do too, starting with that breakfast you thought was all for you. What are you hanging around for?"

"I'm not. I—okay." He looked puzzled, but he didn't waste any time striding out the door and out of her life. "Bye."

As the door swung shut behind him, she looked down at Dooley, who had watched their conversation like a spectator at a tennis match, his gaze swinging from one to the other. Now he looked longingly at the door and whimpered.

"I know, buddy. It was nice while it lasted." She sank down onto one of the benches at the kitchen table.

Dooley tossed out a little bark and ran over to his bed. Trotting back, he dropped a gift at her feet. He often did that, bringing her toys and sticks when he wanted to play.

But this time he'd brought her a sock. A man's sock.

She picked it up and laughed, thinking of Brady walking around with his bare foot in one boot. She hoped he got blisters.

"Good job, Dooley. Well done."

She lifted the dog into her lap. Hugging his furry body, she buried her head in his silky fur and gave herself the luxury of just a few tears before she looked up, wiped her eyes, and headed to the bathroom to wipe off that makeup.

Chapter 9

BRADY WALKED ACROSS THE RODEO GROUNDS TO HIS pickup feeling strangely deflated, as if he'd left something behind besides his sock.

It irked him that Suze thought he was some kind of love-'em-and-leave-'em cowboy gigolo. And for some reason, it bothered him even more that she'd lowered herself like that, giving herself to someone she believed didn't care about her.

No. Not believed. *Knew.* Because she was right, wasn't she? He didn't care about her. Not really.

Which made him a jerk.

Was he screwed up or what? He wanted to punch his own lights out for what he'd done to her.

And when had his ego gotten so big? He'd gone and assumed Suze was making breakfast for him, when he should have known she was the type that would eat right. No fast-food breakfast burritos for Suze. She had too much class for that.

He pictured her at her pretty little table, eating eggs and bacon and maybe some pancakes. And Frosted Flakes. His favorite. His stomach rumbled at the thought.

He found his pickup in the parking lot, which was starting to fill up with the sedans and minivans of today's fairgoers. Later on, it would be jammed with vehicles from rodeo attendees. Brady wasn't competing today; he'd blown it yesterday by riding a little too close to the edge and getting bucked off. But Suze would be racing. Maybe he'd go back and watch her later on. He started up the truck and headed over to his meeting at the Buck 'n' Bull Diner.

Dang it, he couldn't get her out of his head. Images from the night before flickered through his mind like an old movie, the frames flipping and changing in his mind's eye.

He saw Suze as she'd edged around the dance floor in the beer tent, trying not to be noticed. He saw her face lit by the lights from the midway, and saw it again reflected in an oil-slicked puddle on the asphalt.

He saw the wonder in her eyes as that falling star had streaked across the sky. But mostly, he saw her sprawled on the bed naked—beautiful, lost, and hurting.

He pressed the accelerator a little more firmly to the floor, figuring speed would force him to pay attention to the road. But the images just flickered a little faster, torturing him even more.

He walked into the diner praying he didn't look like he'd had a bad night—because the elation he'd felt from the great sex with Suze had been erased by her dismissal. It had hit him hard, even though he'd needed to leave. It *hurt*, dammit.

And Brady Caine was never hurt. Not by broncs, not by life, and definitely not by women.

He slid into a booth beside Cooter Banks. He and Cooter had endorsement deals with Lariat Western Wear, and the meeting was with the ad director. They'd been asked to scout around for a suitable woman to be the face of a new line of women's wear. The ad manager had suggested they check out rodeo queens, trick riders, and, in their words, "even" barrel racers.

Cooter had been testing out rodeo queens ever since, as if being good in bed was a stiff requirement for the job, when really the only thing stiff was between Cooter's legs.

Brady didn't think much of Cooter. Most successful rodeo cowboys grew out of the buckle-bunny braggadocio stage, but Cooter was still slavering over the sweet young things that followed the cowboys around like dogs scenting bacon. Cooter used women, and took advantage of the small-town girls—even the young ones. He was a player, the kind of guy Suze thought Brady was.

Actually, Brady wasn't much better.

Sure, he drew the line at underage girls and girls who'd had too much to drink. But he never got exclusive with women, never slept with the same one twice—for the most part.

By the time Brady got there, Red Sullivan, the advertising director, had already ordered coffee all around. Brady reached for the sugar packets and stacked three together, then tore them all at once and dumped them into his cup.

"Man, you like it sweet," Cooter said. His arch tone made it clear he wasn't just talking about coffee.

Brady ignored him.

"I hope you guys came up with some suggestions for me," Red said. "We've got a couple girls in mind, but I thought you gentlemen might have some insight into what kind of girl best represents Western women today."

"We sure do." Cooter slurped his coffee, which was apparently too hot to drink. Carefully, he poured some into his saucer, then lifted that to his lips and slurped it out of there.

Brady blanched. He hadn't had a mother until he was fifteen, but he'd learned better table manners than that in the foster care system. He glanced up at Red, who was watching with an expression of mingled amusement and horror. The man met his gaze and the two of them shook their heads.

"What?" Cooter said. "You think I don't know my Western women? I tell you, me and Brady here probably know more cowgirls than anybody you could ask. And I'm talking about knowing 'em in the biblical sense, right, Brady?"

Brady slunk down a little in his seat and pretended to be absorbed in something outside the diner's plate glass window.

"*Right?*" Cooter insisted.

"Speak for yourself, man," Brady said. "I don't think Red's looking for the one who'd be best in bed."

"Not at all," Red said. "I'm looking for a woman who represents the best of the West—a strong woman, a real role model. Of course, she needs to be a beauty too. Goes without saying."

He did a little slurping of his own.

Brady poured a couple creamers into his cup and stirred them, watching the white milk plume like clouds in a time-lapse video.

What was that song about "clouds in your coffee"? "You're So Vain," that was it.

That song probably described him. He'd been so vain,

so full of himself, that he'd just assumed Suze would fall at his feet, grateful that the great Brady Caine deigned to notice her.

Last night, it had seemed like he was right. But this morning…

"Brady?" said Red.

Brady pulled himself out of his reverie. "I'm sorry. I was thinking about something. What did you say?"

Cooter sniggered. "Thinking about some honey you had last night?" he asked.

Brady grabbed the edge of the table. If it hadn't been screwed to the floor, he probably would have overturned it onto Cooter's lap, hot coffee and all. But the resistance it offered gave him time to clear the rage that had bloomed in his mind like the cream in his coffee.

Cooter didn't know who Brady had been with last night. He wasn't insulting Suze. He was just being his usual disgusting self.

"I was just asking if you had a suggestion," Red said.

Brady nodded. Fortunately, he had a couple of other girls to recommend—both of them barrel racers. Brandy Hallister and Megan Wright were both pretty, strong, and talented. Not as pretty, strong, or talented as Suze, but then again, they hadn't thrown him out of their trailers either. As a matter of fact, they were the kind of girls who could stay friends with a man after a roll in the hay. He knew that for a fact.

In fact, Cooter had both of them on his lengthy list of suggestions. As he read off the names, he made it clear they'd all been conquests. He kept glancing up at Brady, as if he was checking to see if he was impressing him.

He wasn't.

"I gotta tell you," Red said. "We've checked out most of the girls you listed. Rodeo queens, barrel racers... Most of them already endorse other products. We want somebody new, fresh. Somebody different. And remember, we want to emphasize that Lariat clothing is for the strong Western woman. Do you guys know any ranchers' daughters who would work? Maybe a horse trainer?"

"I know a joke about a rancher's daughter," Cooter said.

Brady and Red both ignored him.

"Guess we'll have to keep looking," Red said. "I appreciate you guys' hard work."

"Oh, it was *hard*, all right," Cooter said.

"Shut up, Cooter." Brady tried to sound like he was joking, but he could tell from the anger that flashed in Cooter's eyes that he knew Brady meant it.

Well, Brady didn't really care what Cooter thought of him. Cooter was a jerk who'd never had an honest emotion in his life outside of vanity, pride, and lust. He loved to brag about how some sweet young thing kept calling him. He'd lead them on, then stop answering their calls once he'd gotten what he wanted.

Brady was better than that. Not much better, but he was working on it.

At least he and Suze had talked last night. She'd shared some of the problems she was having with her dad, with her finances.

Wait a minute.

Her finances.

This was a chance for Brady to prove himself, to be a better man than Cooter. Suze might have rejected him, shoved him out the door, but he had a chance to help her, and he was going to do it.

Red picked up the tab the waitress had dropped off and passed her his credit card. Sliding their lists of names into a binder he'd brought along, he started to stand up.

"Hey, wait a minute, Red. I got another one for you."

"Yeah?"

"Yeah. Suze Carlyle."

Cooter let out a big har-de-har laugh, slapping his thigh. "That stuck-up bitch? She won't give a man the time of day. I think she's a lezzy."

Brady gave him a tight smile. "She's not. Not that it should matter."

"She's not, huh? How do you know?" A slow smile spread across Cooter's broad face. "You get a piece of that, Caine? Shit, nobody I know's ever—"

Red slid across the vinyl bench seat and stood. "Shut up, Cooter."

Cooter shut up.

Brady slowly unclenched the fist he'd been preparing to drive into the side of the picture-perfect face that fronted Cooter's tiny brain, and took a deep breath.

"I've seen Suze Carlyle, Brady. I just don't know if she's got the look we want."

Cooter started to speak, then glanced at Brady and shut his mouth.

"That's because she's an athlete, not a model. She's a great person—just the kind of strong woman you're talking about. She dresses kind of sloppy, but I'm sure she'd change that if you gave her the deal. And that would attract a lot of attention. I mean, she's a two-time world champion, and she's always worn baggy jeans and men's shirts. If she started turning up looking great in Lariat's clothes, people would notice. I guarantee it."

"Hmm." Red tapped a pencil on the table, then wrote "Susan Carlisle" on Brady's paper.

"It's Suzanne, with a *z* and two *n*'s," Brady said. "And I think Carlyle is with a *y*. C-A-R-L-Y-L-E."

"Geez, you gonna marry her, Caine?" Cooter asked. "Seems like you know a lot about her."

Red ignored him. "Was her mother Ellen Carlyle?"

"Yup." Brady grinned. "And when she takes off that old hat and dresses up, she looks exactly like her mom."

Actually, he'd never seen Suze dress up. But he'd seen her naked, and he'd seen her happy.

Because for a little while, he *had* made her happy. And he'd discovered she had a beauty no other woman he knew could match.

Chapter 10

BRADY WAS SMACK-DAB IN THE MIDDLE OF THE BEST rodeo season of his life when he pulled into the Grigsby rodeo arena for a photo shoot two months later. It was nearly Independence Day, also known as Cowboy Christmas for the amount of money a cowboy could take in at all the big rodeos that weekend. If Brady was as successful at those competitions as he'd been this past weekend, he'd be on his way to the National Finals in Vegas for the first time.

Suze Carlyle might have thrown him out of her trailer, but she'd done him a big favor. He'd taken her advice and focused hard on his sport, and it was working.

Not that she'd noticed. Despite his newfound success over the past two months, she hadn't changed her attitude. Every time she saw him, she flipped that long, blond braid and tossed him a scornful glare.

Tucking in his shirt, he adjusted his belt buckle and everything else down there, wondering who his dance partner was going to be on this bright, sunny day.

Yesterday it had been a big, hammer-headed horse named Boondoggle who'd put a twist in his buck that had almost, but not quite, unseated Brady before the eight-second buzzer blessed the ride. That had gotten him into the short round, where he'd ridden Lindy Hop to a score of eighty-eight, the highest of the day.

The night before, he'd ridden Bad Whiskey. The

big paint had spun like the devil gone dizzy, but Brady
stuck to the saddle and found himself at the top of
the leaderboard.

His partner today would be from another breed altogether. No doubt Lariat had chosen some rodeo queen
for the photo shoot. Those cowgirls were so polished
and pretty, they made Brady feel like a dirty old bronc
who'd shown up at a dressage competition.

And today was the day he'd find out who they'd
chosen to represent their ladies' wear line. According
to Red, the company had run some focus groups and
discovered that Brady did well with their female demographic, so they'd decided to have him do a few ads with
whomever they'd chosen.

Cooter, fortunately, was out of the picture. Red had
pulled his contract soon after the three of them had
shared breakfast, and the word was that he'd made it
clear Cooter's crude comments were the reason why.
Lariat wanted role models to represent their brand—
another reason for Brady to clean up his act.

Despite his success with the female demographic,
Brady was a lot more nervous dealing with women
than with horses these days. The one-two punch of
Suze Carlyle's rejection and Cooter's illustration of
how crass a cowboy could be had made him rethink his
lifestyle. He was still easygoing Brady Caine, and he
still flirted with the girls—but he didn't take it into the
bedroom anymore.

Not much, anyway.

Women still went after him, even knowing they'd
be a notch in his bedpost, but he knew now that they
deserved a lot more than an eight-second ride and a tip

of his hat. Maybe someday he'd meet one that made him want to give more than that, and when that happened, he'd want to deserve her respect.

Grabbing the shirt Lariat had given him, he glanced around the trailer the company had provided just for this shoot. They'd gone to a lot of expense, that was for sure. They'd rented a small rodeo arena between Wynott and Grigsby, and they'd pulled in dressing trailers for both him and his female counterpart. He felt like a danged movie star.

The trailer was wall-to-wall mirrors, which made it painful to put on the shirt they'd given him. It looked like a refugee from Roy Rogers's dressing room, with six-inch fringe hanging off the front, plus pearl buttons down the middle and little bucking horses stitched on the pockets. Just in case some fool didn't get the message, it said "Saddle Up 'n' Ride" across the back in huge embroidered letters. If Lariat could have figured out a way to plug it in, they probably would have put neon lights on it.

He adjusted the collar and made a series of tough-guy faces at the mirror, but no matter how much he squared his jaw or squinted his eyes, he still looked like an idiot in the danged shirt. It was going to be a trial to walk the midway in it at Fort Worth, and worse yet to hit the beer tent. But his endorsement deal meant he had to wear their clothes in public, not just for photo shoots. He'd take the shirt with him and wear it at least three times in three different towns.

"You in there?" Stan Petersen, the photographer, stuck his head in the trailer and scowled. "You're worse than a woman. Put on the shirt and get out here."

"I'm coming. This thing's got more snaps and straps than my saddle."

Brady followed Stan out into the arena, tugging at the too-tight collar. The local 4-H team had been practicing all morning, so the loose dirt was rutted with swoops and swirls where horses had spun and turned. A few candy wrappers fluttered, trapped in the grass around the edge, and a young boy hurried around with a manure fork, cleaning up the inevitable mess the horses had left behind.

The late-afternoon sun was shining but the sky to the east was dark, making the white-painted bleachers and the cottonwood trees beyond them stand out in hard-edged relief. It was the kind of day that made the animals restless and gave the cowboys a sense of dread in their guts. There was no way to know if it was the threat of rain that charged the air or if it was something more—like a premonition of a ride going wrong. The possibility of life-altering injury always hung over the bucking chutes, making time spent in the arena stand out as sharply in a man's memory as the sunlit trees against the storm-dark sky.

This place was close to home, and it called up a lot of memories for Brady—good memories. If he closed his eyes and breathed a little of the dust blowing across the ground, he could relive the tight, tense moment when he tilted his hat down over his eyes, set his heels, and gave the nod to open the gate and start the dance. Eight seconds felt like eternity while a bronc leaped and snorted under your saddle. Meanwhile the crowd, so hushed and expectant just seconds before, churned and roared like a storm-stirred ocean.

It was a fickle ocean, though, with a nasty undertow. Everybody knew the spectators who cheered when you rode to the buzzer came as much for the wrecks as for the rides. A rodeo-goer could spin the story of a cowboy he'd seen crippled by a wild bull a lot longer than he could talk about watching some unknown ride to a high score.

"Where's our girl?" he asked Stan, who was fooling with his camera lens. The photographer, who hailed from the great Wyoming metropolis of Cheyenne, had never spun a rope or shoveled a stall in his life. But he and Brady had worked together before, and the two had struck up an *Odd Couple* sort of friendship. Stan knew how to make Brady look good in spite of the ridiculous clothes, and he worked well with the women they used.

Although they'd never had a female face of Lariat before, they'd often used rodeo queens and other women in the ads for the men's clothing. In Brady's opinion, they really did *use* them. For some reason, the company thought more men would buy their shirts if the girls crouched at a cowboy's feet like fawning dogs in their ads. Brady hated that part. It was undignified and disrespectful to women. He'd say something, but then there was a chance they'd cut off those fat checks that were filling up his special account—the cowboy equivalent of a 401(k).

At least Stan somehow managed to keep things light while he instructed bright, accomplished women to grovel at Brady's feet.

"She's late," Stan said. "I guess there's some problem with the makeup."

Brady glanced skyward and said a little prayer. Most

rodeo queens were pretty good people—emphasis on the *pretty*—but once in a while, they got one who thought the sparkly tiara on her Stetson made her the next heir to the Kardashians. "I thought we were using a barrel racer this time."

"We are. And she signed a long-term contract like yours, so she'll be in all the ads from now on." He flashed Brady a warning look that was only half-joking. "So behave yourself. This girl's a serious athlete. She won't fall for your cowboy shtick like all those rodeo queens do."

Brady couldn't help remembering one particular barrel racer who *had* fallen for his shtick. He'd thought Suze was falling hard, right into the clean white sheets in that deluxe Featherlite trailer. But the next morning had sure proved him wrong.

Luckily, there was no chance Lariat would choose Suze. He'd tried talking to Red about her again, but Red had shrugged him off, and Brady wasn't surprised. Suze hadn't changed since the night she broke his heart. She still rode like an avenging angel and dressed like a barn bum. She hardly ever smiled—never at Brady, of course—and he knew it was a challenge to see the beauty hiding under her beat-up old hat.

They'd probably picked Jeannie Sommers. He and Jeannie had burned up the sheets once too, and she'd been wild as a woman could be considering they'd had to whisper so his brothers, sleeping in adjoining rooms, wouldn't hear what was going on. Jeannie had walked away the next day with a wave and a smile, so he figured she was like him, a player. His brothers said she was trying to work some reverse psychology on him, but

Brady didn't even know how psychology worked when it was running forward. Maybe that's why whatever she was doing to him didn't work.

They might pick Brandy Lamar, though, or Trudie Banks. Both of them were unknown territory for Brady, but they both knew how to rock a short skirt and high-heeled boots on a Saturday night at the beer tent, and they knew how to smile, which was more than Suze Carlyle could manage.

Dang. He needed to stop thinking about that woman. He didn't know why she'd stuck with him the way she had.

"So who is it?" he asked Stan.

"Not telling," said the photographer.

"Jeannie Sommers?"

"Not telling."

"Brandy Lamar?"

"Shut up and put your tongue back in your mouth." Stan flashed him a grin. "I told you, this one's not going to fall for your cowboy charms. I can just about guaran-dang-tee it."

Brady grinned. There was nothing funnier than starched-shirt Stan trying to talk cowboy—and nothing Brady liked better than a woman who was a challenge.

Chapter 11

SUZE STARED STRAIGHT AHEAD, WILLING HERSELF NOT to cry while the stylist tarted her up for the second time in an hour. The stylist was a matronly woman who had announced, "I am Marta," and gone to work with mind-numbing dexterity, chattering to herself in broken English as she worked. When Marta was done, Suze had taken one look at the final result in the mirror and burst into tears — stupid, messy tears that spoiled her makeup and reddened her nose. Marta had made Suze a cold compress to ease the swelling under her eyes and patiently started over.

Suze was grateful that Marta didn't ask what the tears were about. Partly they came from hating the idea of posing for a fashion shoot. Partly they came from too much pressure at home, with her dad's health problems getting bigger and the bank account getting smaller.

But mostly, they came from that glance in the mirror.

She hadn't peeked while Marta did her work, but as soon as the stylist was finished, Suze had looked over her shoulder at the mirror and tried out a smile.

The image in the mirror smiled back, and it felt as if her mother had come back to life and was sitting across from her in some shiny, new looking-glass world. Suze reached out, but of course her hand hit cold glass, not warm flesh. Ellen Carlyle was still gone. And that was the real reason she'd cried.

That, and the realization that her father was wrong.

She *did* look like her mother. *Just* like her mother once she was prettied up properly.

Now, as Marta made her repairs, Suze considered the results. Watching the eerie resemblance build up gradually somehow made it easier.

"I look so—strange," Suze said. "Not like myself."

She thought of the photos that dotted the walls of the Carlyles' old farmhouse. There were dozens of them. Photos of Ellen running barrels on her famous horse, Tango. Photos of her posing with rodeo celebrities like Ty Murray and Trevor Brazile. There was even an oil painting of her and Tango some fan had painted. But the only photograph of Suze was a shot of Ellen holding a three-year-old Suze on Tango's back.

By the time she was sixteen, Suze had figured out she'd never live up to her father's exalted expectations or her mother's extraordinary legacy. She didn't like attention anyway, so she'd sunk into the anonymity of the plain-Jane look. She'd have stopped riding too, but she loved it too much to quit.

Now she realized that with a little effort, she looked eerily like her mother. What would her father's reaction be if she walked into the house looking like this? And why couldn't he see it?

It's too bad you didn't get your mother's looks.

Adding a touch of gloss to Suze's lips, Marta smiled encouragingly. "You ready?"

"Yes." Suze tilted her chin up, her father's voice echoing in her head, as usual. This time it wasn't one of his put-downs, though; it was a Carlyle maxim: *Carlyles don't cry.* "I don't know what hit me last time. I won't do it again."

Marta spun the chair around and stood behind it, fluffing Suze's hair so it flowed out from under her hat in a golden cascade of curls.

"You are beautiful girl," Marta said. "You look like star, yes?"

Suze was sure people would see through her disguise, but she wasn't about to say so, because she'd be criticizing Marta's handiwork if she criticized herself. The last thing she wanted was a reputation for being hard to work with. She'd never expected anyone would consider her model material, but now that lightning had struck once, she wouldn't mind if it struck again. The money Lariat offered was a revelation. They could ask her to wear a clown nose and she'd do it.

"I look wonderful. Thank you so much."

"Wait till you see with who you are sharing the shoot," Marta said. "You gonna be excited."

"Sharing the chute?" Suze felt a ray of hope cut through the clouds of dread. "Am I posing with a horse?"

It took a minute for Marta to understand, but she'd lived in Wyoming long enough to pick up a few rodeo terms.

"No, no, no. I mean the *photo* shoot, not the—what is it? The bucking chute?"

"Darn." Suze dared a slight smile. "I'd rather pose with a mean old bull than some stupid cowboy."

Marta laughed again. "He is quite a gentleman, and very handsome. Famous too. Trust me, you gonna be pleased. Any girl would be. And he asked for you special."

"He asked for me?"

"He was the one who suggested you to Lariat. So you see, he likes you very much."

Suze wondered who on earth it could be. She'd been worrying for days that she'd be posing with Brady Caine, since he was one of Lariat's frequent models, but there was no way Brady would ask for her. They'd managed to avoid each other since that night.

"I wish you'd tell me who it is," she said. "Give me some warning."

"It's a surprise. Now get out there and give him some swagger." The advice sounded comical in Marta's lilting accent. "Act confident and you *be* confident, okay?"

"Okay." Giving Marta's upraised palm a resounding smack, Suze straightened her shoulders and headed for the door.

"Remember," Marta called after her. "Swagger!"

—◦◦◦—

Brady watched the tall blond strut out into the arena and felt his heart do a double backflip as she rested her shapely self against the fence.

Who the heck was that? She was a drop-dead knockout, but he couldn't remember ever seeing her before. She wasn't Jeannie Sommers, and she wasn't Brandy Lamar either.

Surely he'd remember her, with that blond hair rippling down her back and that tanned, toned body. She reminded him of Suze, but...

But nothing.

She *was* Suze.

Shoot. Red hadn't seemed interested at all in the idea of Suze as a representative of Lariat's ladies' line, and that had been fine with Brady. Now he'd have to work with her, thanks to his overactive conscience. She'd avoided him so effectively since that night that he'd never gotten a chance to apologize, and now? Now it was way too late.

"Told you she was serious," Stan said.

"You weren't lying." Brady clutched his chest. "That girl's serious as a heart attack."

Stan wrinkled his brow with sudden concern as Brady took a step backward.

"We need Marta over here." The photographer gestured to a dark-haired woman standing at the rail. "We need you to work your magic again. Brady's looking a little pale."

Brady resisted the urge to swat at the makeup lady, who came over and fluttered around his face with blush and powder like some annoying, fashion-conscious insect. The only fashion he was conscious of was the kind that had transformed Suze Carlyle from barn bum to beauty.

"She is luffly, no?" the stylist whispered.

"She is luffly, yes." Brady glanced back at Suze and felt like he'd been felled by a hammer. *Wham!* Right to the forehead.

What the hell was going to happen now? She was staring at him, eyes wide, jaw dropped in surprise. But when she caught him looking, her whole attitude changed. Tossing her hair, she turned away, looking angry and proud and drop-dead beautiful.

Scenes from their night together rushed into his head and heart as if he'd dammed them up and the dam had broken.

Suze, lean and languorous, lying across the bed; her long legs tangled with his; her eyes, green as a summer lawn, glowing with happiness and humor. Those same eyes an hour later, shaded by her long lashes and sleepy with satisfaction.

Trouble was, the lawn had frozen over the next morning, and satisfaction had turned to something sour. So how was he going to make this shoot anything less than torture for the two of them?

People thought he was a ladies' man, but it was the ladies that made him one. He had no idea what he did that made them flock around him like crows to cracked corn. He usually kept things light. Teasing. But nobody teased Suze Carlyle, and here she was, coming his way. Her eyes were shining like they did before a race, when she was holding back her horse and waiting for the signal to start. He was surprised she was so excited about modeling.

Aw, hell. He had to talk to her, and all he could think to do was make some lame joke.

"Wow." He widened his eyes. "How'd they get you to do that?"

"Do what?"

"Dress like a girl."

She tossed her hair. Marta had apparently worked some magic with a curling iron, because Suze's straight, glossy stream of hair was coiling around her shoulders and framing her face in pale flames.

Brady had only seen her hair loose one other time. He had no problem pulling that picture out of his memory—Suze, naked on her bed, her hair fanning over the pillow while he…

Stop it. Just stop it.

She shrugged. "They asked, that's all."

She wasn't looking at him. He wasn't sure if she was being stuck-up or self-conscious. It was always like that with Suze. She was a bundle of emotions, but he was never sure which ones were on the surface and what was simmering underneath. She was one complicated woman.

Setting the Lariat cowboy hat she'd been carrying on her head, she adjusted the brim just so. Hot damn, she was gorgeous.

He managed an aw-shucks grin. "You wouldn't have dressed like that for me if *I'd* asked."

"Darn right." She leaned on the chute gate, resting her elbows on one of the metal rails, and shot him a look under her lashes that told him he didn't have a chance.

"So how'd they get you to do it?"

"They offered me money." She said each word separately, as if it hurt to say them, and the shine in her eyes intensified. He felt his heart drop in his chest. She wasn't excited. She was on the verge of tears.

Dang it, now he'd hurt her feelings. He'd known the answer to that question. And although he didn't think there was any shame in needing money, it apparently bothered Suze.

Maybe the teasing thing wasn't a good idea. He stole another look at her and stumbled back another step. Just her face was enough to knock a man sideways—high cheekbones, a straight nose, and that generous mouth, perfect for kissing.

Maybe he should piss her off as a form of self-defense. The Lariat outfit showed off every sweet, seductive curve, and there was a dab of shimmer on her lips that made him want to taste her. Her eyes had green depths like a pine forest, dark with secrets and shadowed with pain. Suze had never had it easy, but she still managed to look more strong than vulnerable. And her beauty was natural, with no special effects or fancy frills.

He gave her his best smile, hoping she'd remember she'd liked him once. "So what if *I* offered you money?"

"Not a chance." She finally looked at him, and the anger and hurt in her eyes nearly knocked him to his knees. What did she think had happened that night in the trailer?

He hadn't done anything wrong. It wasn't like he'd promised her anything but a night she'd never forget, though she apparently wished she could. Ever since, she'd stepped around him like she was afraid he might stick to the bottom of her shoe.

Maybe he should just pretend it hadn't happened.

With a dismissive toss of her hair, she strode to the center of the arena, stepping lightly over the cords that snaked all around the arena to power Stan's equipment. She stood there like an experienced model, her stance wide, her gaze commanding.

"Let's do this." She sounded like she was about to have a tooth pulled.

"Yeah, let's." Brady kept his tone bright. "Where do we start?"

"Let's see." Stan tapped his front teeth with his index finger, a tic that meant he was thinking things through, visualizing the finished photo and putting the elements together in his head. Brady hoped to God he wasn't planning his usual scenario, where the woman knelt at Brady's feet. Suze would never do that. Never.

She might be desperate enough to dress like a girl, but the woman had her principles.

Chapter 12

SUZE WATCHED STAN PETERSON DITHER OVER THE positions she and Brady should take for the photo shoot and wondered what the heck was wrong with the guy. Lariat might be peddling clothes for women now, but their big bucks came from menswear. They'd managed to convince Easterners who had a romantic image of the West that real cowboys actually tolerated shirts with fringe and all kinds of frippery. In reality, fringe could get caught in buckles and straps, and besides, all that fancy stuff looked plain ridiculous.

She knew when she'd signed on with Lariat that she'd be required to shed most of her dignity and half her clothes for the shoot. But what mattered was the money. She needed to keep that in mind, because this was the tough part—the part where she knelt at the feet of the male model who shared the shoot. And in this case, the model was the man she'd been avoiding ever since they'd burned up the bedsheets just months before.

That time, she'd lost most of her dignity and *all* of her clothes.

"Okay. Suze, I need you to stand over there." Stan gestured to a point just in front of a particularly rustic part of the bucking chutes, with their weathered wooden frames and rusting metal gates. "Brady, you go stand beside her. Not a hardship, right?"

Brady flashed Suze one of his blinding smiles. "Never a hardship."

It was a hardship for Suze. The truth was, she'd sooner stand beside a riled-up rattlesnake than get anywhere near Brady Caine.

But she needed the money, she needed the money, she needed the money. She chanted the words in her head like a mantra. Barrel racing was an expensive sport. You needed a great horse, who needed great feed and a nice stable and pasture. You needed a good-sized arena for practicing too. All these things made it essential to hang on to the Carlyle family ranch, and lately that had become a challenge. Her dad had mortgaged the place to pay off her mother's medical bills after her long fight with cancer, and now he had medical bills of his own. Suze couldn't go out and get a regular job to pay the bills, because her dad needed her to do the chores at home. Besides, she had to practice, and she was out rodeoing every weekend.

She won often, and brought home substantial sums, but it never seemed to be enough. That was the reason— the *only* reason—she was standing beside Brady Caine with her arms folded over her chest and her jaw clamped so tightly it hurt. She might have to stand beside him, but she didn't have to look at him.

Not yet, anyway.

"Okay." Stan looked a little worried. "What we need to do is soften up your look a little bit, Suze. Just— maybe unbutton your shirt a little."

She unbuttoned the top button of her shirt. "Like this?"

"Well…"

She unbuttoned another. "This?"

He gave her a charming smile and she unbuttoned a third, exposing a generous swath of her embarrassingly generous cleavage. Men liked big breasts, but Suze would have traded hers for a smaller set in a heartbeat. Normally, she wore maximum-strength sports bras to keep everything pressed in tight. But today the girls were on full display, and Suze was sure Brady was enjoying the view. She stood stiffly, chin high, jaw clenched.

"Do you two not get along, or something?" Stan grimaced and raked his fingers through his hair, making a matched set of cowlicks stand up like owl's ears. "We're looking for a little spark here."

Suze waited for Brady to say something teasing about how well they got along. She was sure he'd allude to their night together sooner or later, making sure Stan knew what a stud he was. But to her surprise, he just gave her an honest cowboy grin with no leering undertones.

"Sure," he said. "We get along fine, don't we?"

"Oh, yeah. Fine." She tried to smile back at Brady, but her mouth wouldn't cooperate. It felt stiff in the middle and shaky at the edges. She hated to think how it would look on film.

"Right. Well, we need to get this done," Stan said. "Brady, just do what you always do."

"Okay, but..."

"The pose. This is the introductory ad for our cowgirl line, so we're doing a modified version of the standby. So pose."

The photographer might've looked meek as a kid's pet hamster, but he was in charge of this shoot and

Brady knew it. Crossing his arms over his chest, he stood tall, shoulders back, chin raised. Suze had seen the pose in a half-dozen Lariat ads, so she knew what came next.

"Now, Suze, if you could just kneel beside him…"

In the eyes of Lariat Western Wear—and in the minds of most of the men she knew—men were men, and women were born to adore them. Gingerly, she rested one knee in the dirt and knelt sideways so the other leg bracketed Brady.

Brady glanced down. Instead of looking admiring, like he had when she'd first strolled into the arena, he looked horrified.

She braced herself for the joke, the sarcastic comment, the jab.

Instead, he reached down and grabbed her elbow, hauling her roughly to her feet.

"Hell no, Stan," he said. "We're not doing this. Not with *her*. No way."

Brady watched Suze stomp across the arena, her hands clenched at her sides, her blond hair bouncing with every stormy step. He'd obviously ticked her off.

It figured. Every time he tried to do the right thing, he made her mad.

He'd just been trying to protect her. Frankly, he'd expected her to protect herself, and he'd been looking forward to the fireworks when she told Stan that she wouldn't kneel at Brady Caine's feet if you gave her a million dollars. He'd have bet his last gold buckle on her refusal. Ever since that night in her trailer, Suze's every glance told him she thought he was lower than the prairie dogs that dug up her pasture—and for a rancher, nothing was lower than a prairie dog.

She must've really needed the money from this contract, and she was willing to do whatever was required to keep it. That was her choice, and he ought to have let her make it.

But he couldn't. He just couldn't. He knew how proud she was, and watching her kneel down like that—it was unbearable. He'd had to stop her. But instead of thanking him, she'd stormed off.

"What just happened?" he said to Stan. "I was trying to help."

"Who exactly were you *helping*?"

"Her. You too. If I'd known who you'd chosen, I could've told you she wouldn't kneel at my feet like those other girls. I mean, Suze Carlyle? She's got no reason to grovel."

"She was fine with it," Stan said. "You're the one with the problem."

Brady took his hat off and raked his fingers through his hair. "It's just that it's disrespectful," he said. "Especially with her. I mean rodeo queens, they don't mind. They know darn well they're part of the West's grand tradition of objectifying women. But Suze is an athlete. She deserves respect."

"Listen to you," Stan said. "The cowboy feminist, all up in arms about objectifying women. I didn't even know you knew words that big."

Brady flushed. "I must have heard it somewhere. Half the time I don't know what I'm saying." Brady gave him his aw-shucks grin. Who was he to mess with the legends of the West? He did his best to live up to expectations as the dumb cowboy bronc buster.

He sobered. "Bill taught me not to treat women like that, though." He thumbed over his shoulder toward the trailer that served as Suze's dressing room. "You think she's coming back?"

"I doubt it," Stan said. "Why would she?"

"So we can work things out. I think we should change the shot," Brady said. "Why don't you lay me down in the middle of the arena and let her trample me on her horse? Cowgirls would love to see that. Speedo's as famous as she is. Best-known quarter horse in the world."

"Brady, she doesn't think there's anything to work out. She thinks you just refused to work with her. Hell, that's what I thought too."

"What?"

"Brady, you said, and I quote, 'Hell no. We're not doing this with her.'"

"No, I said..." Brady ran the words over in his mind. Yep, that's what he'd said.

He took off at a dead run, following Suze's footprints across the arena. When he tripped on a light cord, he caught himself, then spun around to holler at Stan.

"Think of something different to do. We're not doing that dumb shit with the girl at my feet, okay? Not with Suze. Not in a million years."

He slowed, walking backwards to make sure Stan would hear what he'd really meant to say—and maybe Suze would hear it too.

"If you want," he said, "*I'll* kneel at *her* feet."

Chapter 13

MARTA HAD RETURNED TO THE TRAILER AND WAS FUSS-
ing around, cleaning the sink and setting her makeup
into a carefully organized carryall.

"Back so soon?"

"It didn't work out." Suze had intended to be brusque
and efficient, as if she had somewhere important to go.
That way, Marta wouldn't see how upset she was.

"What didn't work out?" Marta ran some water in the
sink to wash down a few stray hairs she'd trimmed from
Suze's 'do. "You didn't like the cowboy?"

"I can't stand the cowboy." To Suze's horror, her
bold words came out along with a rush of tears. "I can't
stand him."

Marta put her arm around Suze's shoulders and led
her over to a couch. As they sat down, she smoothed
Suze's hair back from her forehead in a motherly gesture
so kind it made Suze break down entirely.

"You know this cowboy?"

Suze nodded, unable to speak.

"You have a history?"

"Not really." Suze huffed out a mirthless laugh. "It
was over as soon as it started."

"So you don't want to pose with him? That is not
professional, dear," Marta said gently. "Is not right."

Marta was right, and Suze suddenly wished with
all her heart that the makeup artist would come back

to the ranch with her and be her stepmother. Marta wouldn't have to marry Earl Carlyle. Heck, she and Suze could throw him out. Because here was a woman who barely knew her, and she was offering the kind of wise, motherly advice Suze had longed for most of her life.

A fresh fountain of tears rose up, and Suze reached blindly for a tissue, patting the sofa and end table. "He didn't want to pose with me. He just kicked me aside like a—like a *dog*. I was kneeling at his *feet*."

Marta calmly rose and crossed the room for some Kleenex. She came back with the box.

"How could he not want to pose with you?" she said. "You are a beautiful cowgirl. And a champion, right?"

Suze nodded, blowing her nose so loudly she could probably be a champion at that too.

"He kicked you?" Marta asked. To her credit, she didn't sound the least bit skeptical.

"Metaphorically." Suze honked into a tissue one more time and set it aside. It was obvious that English wasn't Marta's mother tongue, so Suze rushed to explain. "That means not really, but sort of. He made me *feel* kicked." She sniffed, struggling to compose herself. "He might as well have kicked me with those fancy boots of his. I got his message loud and clear."

Marta patted Suze's arm. Somehow, the kind gesture gave Suze courage and her despair was driven out by a heady, white-hot anger that filled her up and burned like a dozen shots of tequila.

"He probably had a bet going with the photographer over how many buttons they'd get me to unbutton before I said stop." Suddenly remembering her state of undress, Suze pulled the front of the shirt closed with her fist.

"You know this?" Marta sounded shocked.

"No." Suze stared down at her boot tips. "It's probably not true."

Somehow, her rage flew out with the words, and she was left feeling as unsteady and deflated as one of those waving balloon men they put in front of car dealerships. Those things waved their arms around, all riled up, but they flopped down dead if anybody turned the air compressor off. She felt as if her anger was the compressor, and if she gave way to the tears rising behind her eyes, she'd lose all the backbone she'd ever had and flop on the floor, utterly deflated.

"It's not just about today." She leaned into Marta's warmth. The woman smelled like roses and powder—like a mother. "I fell for him when I was sixteen, but he wasn't interested. And then, just when I started to get over him, he—we—you know."

"You spent the night together."

Marta didn't seem the least bit shocked.

"I woke up the next morning and he was still there, sleeping with my dog. I mean, he was cuddling it, you know? It was the sweetest thing. I thought he was going to stay. It surprised me, but I thought he really cared, because he spent the night."

"Why did that surprise you?" Marta asked. "Of course he cares. He would be lucky to have you."

"Trust me, I'm not his type. And he proved it by running off the next morning, just as quick as he could."

Suze thought back to that morning and remembered him standing in the doorway of the bathroom, hanging on to the door frame. What had he said? She couldn't remember. But he'd been gone before she knew what had hit her.

"Why don't you tell him how you feel?" Marta asked. "It could be a misunderstanding. My husband and I, we have learned to talk of hard things."

Suze wanted to simultaneously giggle at Marta's phrasing and sob at the news she was already married, but she simply shook her head. "It's not a misunderstanding. I just need to get over it." She wiped her eyes with the back of her hand and sat up straighter. "I have to stop wishing and hoping for things I can't have, you know? Like him, and—and my mother."

"Your mother?"

"She died." Suze had gotten used to saying that to strangers over the years, but somehow it was hard to say it to Marta. Her throat ached and she felt like she might cry again.

"I'm so sorry," Marta said. "How old were you?"

"Ten," Suze said, swallowing the ache and clearing her throat.

"You have a lot of pain," Marta said. "You're young to carry so much here." She patted her ample bosom, apparently to indicate her heart. "You love this cowboy?"

"No. Well, sometimes." Suze stared down at her hands, knotted so tightly in her lap the skin whitened at the knuckles. "It doesn't matter. Any chance of a relationship went belly up that morning in the trailer. He was so anxious to leave…"

"That must have been painful. But can't you let bygones be dead?"

With her limited English, Marta had hit on

the problem more precisely than if she'd been a trained psychologist.

"I guess I don't want them to be dead. As long as I stay mad at him, I don't have to face the real reason we're not together."

"And what is that?"

Suze shrugged. "He just doesn't want me. He likes pretty girls—you know, the ones who dress up and go out to the bars after the rodeo."

"He likes them now. But a man doesn't marry those girls." Marta's smile bracketed her mouth in deep wrinkles. "My husband chased the girls too, but we knew each other from childhood. When he went looking for someone to settle down with, he chose me. We understood each other."

"I don't know. I think I need to get on with my life. The trouble is, he's always there, somewhere in the background." She smiled, remembering their first meeting. "He has this sort of rebel yell—a cowboy whoop that I swear only he can do. He did it the first time I met him, because I was riding fast."

"And he thought you were beautiful."

Suze thought back to that day.

Maybe Marta was right. Maybe Brady *had* thought she was beautiful.

She'd sure thought he was.

<hr />

She'd been riding around her home arena that day, practicing lead changes on Sherman, a big, beautiful quarter horse with a heart the size of Wyoming. Unfortunately, Sherman's brain was about the size of Rhode Island, so she was concentrating so hard on her horsemanship that she almost didn't see the three boys climbing the fence on the far end of the arena.

Once she'd noticed them, she'd thought about pulling Sherman to a stop, but then she'd have to talk to them. Back then she never knew what to say to boys. Especially bad boys—boys with reputations, like Shane, Ridge, and Brady.

Pretending not to see them, Suze had urged Sherman into a lope. He was a high-spirited horse who needed to be loped long and often, but that wasn't the real reason she gave him the gas. She'd known even then she was no beauty, but speed would blur her plain features, and with her long, blond braid streaming behind her, she made a pretty picture on horseback.

The first time she'd passed the boys, she'd snuck a look out of the corner of her eye. There was Shane, the tall dark one; Ridge, the quiet, muscular one; and Brady, the handsome, popular one. She had no idea what they were doing at the Carlyle ranch.

Normally she didn't ask Sherman for top speed during practice. She saved her best riding for the weekends, and it was only fair to spare her horse too. But that day, on her second circuit of the arena, she'd waited until just before she passed the boys to bend over the horse's neck and nudge his flanks with her heels, a move she thought of as lighting the afterburners.

The horse had stretched out his neck and lengthened his stride, his hooves digging into the soft dirt of the arena and tossing it behind him. The sheer excitement of speed felt so good, Suze had almost forgotten about the boys. As she passed them, two of them had simply stared, but Brady had let out an appreciative whoop so wild and heartfelt she would have tipped her hat if she could have done anything but ride—ride and try to still her hammering heart.

Her father stepped up to join the boys, along with their neighbor, Mr. Decker. Suze knew her dad wouldn't appreciate the way she was riding. She prayed he wouldn't embarrass her in front of the guys with a lecture on sparing her horse, or, worse yet, call her out for showing off.

"Cool him down," was all he said.

Contrary to popular lore, horses couldn't be "rode hard and put away wet." They needed to be walked until their hearts slowed and the blood cooled in their veins, until the tendons stretched and any chance of muscle cramps was gone.

As she walked the horse around the arena, Suze's mind was racing, struggling to come up with something to say to the boys when she finally had to stop.

Hello. Would you like something to drink?

Too formal.

Hi, how are you guys?

Too casual.

Hey. What's it like being the hottest badasses ever to hit Grigsby High?

Totally inappropriate.

She let the reins drop over the horn of her saddle while she worked the problem through in her head. She found social etiquette far more challenging than algebra or trigonometry. Fortunately, Sherman was a good boy, and slow-witted enough to walk himself around the ring for hours if she didn't tell him to stop.

She was startled out of her thoughts by a voice at her knee.

"Hey. What's it like being able to ride like that?"

She nearly fell out of the saddle. Either her horse had gone all Mr. Ed on her and learned to talk, or she was going to have a conversation with a boy.

She dared to look down.

Not just any boy. She was going to have to talk to Brady Caine. The handsome one. The one who'd let out that whoop.

She stared at him a little too long, and then she stared at him some more. Instead of his usual torn jeans and T-shirts, he was dressed top to toe in Western wear, all of it so new the creases were still in it from the store. Most guys looked like fools when they got all duded up, but Brady Caine wore his brand-new cowboy hat and Wranglers like he was born to be a cowboy.

Suze suddenly realized she was staring at him with her mouth hanging open. She looked as dim-witted as Sherman on his worst day, and no wonder. Every word in the English language had fled her brain like horses escaping a burning barn.

She swallowed, blinked, and finally said, "What happened to your clothes?"

Genius.

"I don't know. Irene prob'ly threw 'em away. She's Mr. Decker's wife. My—mother, I guess." He sounded like he was trying out the word, like he'd never had a mother before.

Maybe he hadn't. Suze knew he was a foster kid, with some kind of troubled past.

"They adopted us," he said. "The Deckers. Bill and Irene."

What would it be like to suddenly have a mother after being an orphan? It seemed like it would be wonderful, but this boy seemed to have trouble even saying the word.

Suze wouldn't. She'd be willing to call just about anybody *Mother*. Anyone who would help her navigate the confusing teenage world of relationships, makeup, clothes, and everything else the other girls seemed to understand without thinking.

"So this is my new look." He stepped away from the horse and spread out his arms. "It's what Mr. Decker says we should wear. What do you think?"

He looked great. Handsome. Manly, even—something none of the other boys in her school managed to pull off. But how could she tell him that? She struggled to find a response that wouldn't make her sound like an idiot. Maybe she should just twitch her heels into Sherman's ribs and pretend the horse was an intractable runaway.

"That bad, huh?"

"No." She realized she'd been staring at him with that goofball look on her face again. Old Sherman was an honor student compared to her. "No, not at all. You look great. I mean, good. Fine, I guess."

"Stop talking." With a good-humored grin, he held up his hands to stop her. "You went from 'great' to 'good,' to 'fine' in three seconds. By the time you get done, I'll be ugly as the ass end of that horse."

She couldn't help smiling, even though he'd sworn. He was so friendly, so funny, so...*nice*. And when she smiled back and her eyes met his, she could swear there was something there—a little *zing* of a thrill that actually felt mutual.

Ridiculous as it seemed in retrospect, that was all it took. From that time on, she'd been stuck on Brady Caine.

Now that she was older, she realized how foolish it was to think she'd ever mean anything to him. He saw her the way all the other guys saw her—as an athlete, one of the guys; as a girl who could ride, but couldn't dance or flirt. Not a girl you'd take to the movies or the skating rink or the prom.

There were guys who wanted to date Suze, but they were all like her—awkward, serious types who respected her abilities more than they craved her touch. None of them could touch Brady when it came to looks, and none of them talked to her with that easy, bantering charm.

With one quick conversation, one wild rebel yell, and one admiring glance, Brady Caine had spoiled her for all the other boys.

Chapter 14

MARTA HANDED SUZE ANOTHER TISSUE, JOLTING HER from her reverie. Suze patted her face, surprised to find it wet with tears.

"I'm sorry," she said. "I didn't mean to cry all over you. I need to get over this stupid fixation on a guy who barely knows I'm alive."

Marta patted her back gently. "You are very foolish."

"I know." Suze folded the tissue and gave her nose a final, undignified honk before tossing it in the trash. "It *is* stupid. Foolish. And mostly, I'm over him. It's just that he still lets out that yell once in a while, after somebody rides a rank bronc or gets away from a mean bull. I hear it all the way across the arena, and it brings me back, you know? To that day and how I felt—oh, never mind."

"You are not foolish to care for him," Marta said. "It sounds like you are alike." She stood and led Suze over to the makeup chair, spinning it so Suze could see herself in the mirror.

Oh God. She'd made a mess of her makeup—again. This woman seemed to have infinite patience, but it was embarrassing to be such a screwup.

Still, she couldn't resist pursuing the conversation, even though she knew it was unprofessional to get so personal with the makeup lady.

"I'm nothing like Brady," she said.

Marta lifted Suze's hair off the back of her neck and let it fall in graceful waves over her shoulders. "It sounds to my heart like you are the same," she said. "He has the whoop, you ride fast—you are alike."

Suze turned to look at the woman, amazed. She'd thought the exact same thing the first time she'd heard that wild shout from Brady. It was as if the wildness in him called to the wildness deep inside her. Every time she heard that yell, it reminded her of the kinship between them.

"You know, I think there is something in common between us, deep down," she said. "Maybe that's why I can't let go. I always felt like he could release my real self, you know? He did—just that once. He made me stop worrying about what other people were thinking and really live."

"Maybe you have to do that on your own," Marta said.

Suze nodded. "Maybe he's become an excuse. I don't know. But I need to get past it, that's for sure."

"You think about this," Marta said. "You race the horses, am I right?"

"Just one horse," Suze said, smiling.

"But you compete. You have to be first. Faster than everyone."

Suze nodded.

"It is your job to compare yourself to others when you ride," Marta said. "But in life, that is not a healthy way to think. In life, you can only do your best."

"I never thought of it that way," Suze said.

"In sport, you compete," Marta said. "In life, you live. And living is enough."

"Thank you." Suze did her best to drink the words

in, make them part of herself. Marta was right, although she didn't know that Suze's competitive nature had its roots in her childhood. Her father had always compared her—to other racers, to her mother—and she'd always come up short.

Marta began bustling around, gathering up her makeup supplies.

"What are you doing?" Suze asked.

"Getting ready." Marta opened what looked like a fishing tackle box and began to lay an assortment of brushes and sponges on the counter. "You're going back out there, correct?"

"Are you kidding?" Suze spun the chair to face Marta and made a scary face, making the woman laugh. "I went and ruined your makeup again. I look like one of those women who stays too late at the beer tent and ends up drunk, with their mascara all streaked."

"We can fix that," Marta said. "I can fix anything."

"I couldn't ask you to. I've given you enough trouble already."

"Pooh." Marta dismissed the notion with a wave of her hand. "Sit down, Suzanne. Let me fix you."

Suze sat down and closed her eyes while Marta ministered to her face for the third time that day.

If only it was that easy. If only Marta really *could* fix her.

But the makeup lady was right.

She was going to have to do it herself.

Once you gave yourself over to Marta for a makeup session, you were hers until she declared you complete. So

Suze was a helpless victim, trapped in the spinning chair like a fly in a spiderweb when someone tapped on the door a moment later.

"Come in," Marta sang.

The door was behind Suze, but she could see it in the mirror as it opened.

Brady.

She wanted to hide her face or crawl under the table, but Marta had her trapped, so she was forced to stare straight at his image in the mirror while her lashes were curled. She couldn't even close her eyes.

"Hey," he said, smiling ruefully. "I did it again, didn't I?"

"Did what?" Suze couldn't believe how her heart longed for him, even now. When he smiled like that, she wanted to believe everything was all right.

"I messed up. I do it every time I see you." He came over and rested his very fine ass on the counter, folding his arms over his chest. "The good news is, I had a witness this time, so I know what I did wrong. The last couple times, I was too dumb to figure it out, but Stan caught the whole thing. So at least I know what to apologize for."

"You don't have anything to apologize for." As Marta released her lashes, Suze started to shake her head but stopped when a mascara brush loomed large in her field of vision.

"She says you kicked her," Marta said, her voice steeped in motherly disapproval. "Misanthropically."

"Um...metaphorically, yeah." Brady looked down at the floor and bit his lips. Maybe he was smarter than he looked. Suze might be in love with the man, but she hadn't figured he knew any six-syllable words.

Maybe she didn't know as much about Brady as she thought.

"But, Suze, I swear to God, that wasn't what I meant." His eyes hardened, and his lips narrowed to a thin, grim line. "I hate the way Lariat does these ads, with the girls kneeling and all. I hate it, and I didn't want you to have to do it."

"Close your eyes," Marta demanded, and Suze obeyed. She felt a soft brush skimming over her face, over the nose, the cheekbones, the chin. She should feel self-conscious, letting Brady watch this, but she was never self-conscious around Brady. Lord knew he was never self-conscious around her.

A memory flashed across her mind—Brady naked in bed, his head resting on his crossed arms, that broad, tanned chest with sun-bronzed hair sketching a faint line over the bars of his abs and then down, down, beneath the sheets.

She tried to rub the picture out of her mind, but it wouldn't go away. Not even when she opened her eyes.

Fortunately, Brady didn't seem to notice she was picturing him naked. He was too busy talking his way out of the corner he'd talked himself into.

Brady actually talked a lot for a cowboy. She'd never realized before what a blessing it was. It gave a girl time to think.

About him. Naked.

"It's okay for the rodeo queens," he said, watching with interest as Marta stroked liner onto Suze's lids. "They like to pose sexy and all that. They're just happy to get their picture in a magazine." Marta turned back to her magic box, and he reached over and grabbed the arm of the chair, giving it a slight turn toward him so Suze was forced to look into his eyes. "But you're better than that."

She huffed out a little laugh. "Right. That's what you meant when you said, 'Hell, no, not with her.'"

"Exactly. That *is* what I meant."

His eyes were steady on hers, and she almost believed him. Almost.

Fortunately, Marta needed to stroke on another coat of mascara, so she couldn't look at him, which meant he couldn't work his wiles on her. Otherwise, she probably would have ended up forgiving him without even realizing what she'd done.

She'd once seen a nature documentary where a sparrow was hypnotized by a snake. That's how she felt when she was around Brady—like that helpless, hopeless sparrow, hypnotized by his brown eyes.

What happened to the sparrow if the snake slithered away—when it was left there, hypnotized and hanging? Did the little bird long for more? Did it pine away? Did it ever recover and live a normal life?

Or did it spend its whole life searching for the snake, even knowing it could kill?

Brady was still talking. "What I said was 'Hell, no, not with her.' As in, I refuse to do this stupid pose with a woman I admire and respect and—well, you know."

Marta was standing behind Suze, fluffing her hair. "I don't think she knows."

With the toe of his boot, Brady traced a line on the floor.

"I think you need to tell her," Marta said.

He took a deep breath and met Suze's eyes. Tell her what? She waited, a little breathless.

When he finally spoke, he didn't say what she'd expected.

"We're friends, Suze. Aren't we? We're at least that."

Oh God. She did *not* want to talk about this.

"Of course we are." She hated her phony, snappish tone of voice, but she couldn't help it. "I almost wrecked it after one too many beers, but we're still friends."

He shook his head. "You didn't—I had to—oh, never mind. Just promise me that if I treat you badly from now on, you'll say something. Don't just walk away."

She had *run* away, but she didn't correct him. "Sure. I'll tell you."

———ᴧᴧᴧ———

"There." Marta stepped back and waved a hand at Suze like an artist unveiling a masterpiece. "She looks beautiful. You think?"

Brady grinned. "I *know*." He held out his hand. "Come on. Let's get this done. I told Stan to think of something else—an action shot or something. I promise I'll make sure it's done right."

Suze didn't know how to respond. She took his hand without thinking and stared back, mesmerized by the faint gold starbursts surrounding the pupils in his brown eyes. His tone was so gentle, and there was so much heart shining in his eyes that every bone in her body told her to trust him.

But that's how it always was with Brady.

"Suze? Give me a chance, okay?"

She got the impression he was talking about something more than today's photo shoot—but maybe that was just wishful thinking. It was probably a line that had worked on six hundred other women. He had enough girls flocking around him to run clinical trials on which lines were most effective. He could do focus groups to determine what kind of sweet-talking worked on rodeo queens, what won over buckle bunnies, and what drew in the barrel racers.

Although she could save him the trouble on that last test. Everything he said worked on her—every single line, as long as he said it with that sweet, crooked smile.

She released his hand, shaking her head. He headed toward the door, then turned around fast, as if he just had to say one more thing.

"You need to know this." He looked up at the ceiling, as if searching for inspiration, then down at his boot tips. When he looked up, his eyes met hers and held her gaze. "You run rings around all the other girls, and not just on horseback," he said. "You're beautiful, you're classy, and you can ride like nobody I ever saw." He gave her a little shake, as if she wasn't listening. "Don't ever let anybody tell you different." His eyes never blinked, those gold flecks sparking in the sunlight. "Not anybody."

Chapter 15

STAN WAS ALL BUSINESS AS SOON AS BRADY AND SUZE returned to the arena.

"Suze? We're going to do an action shot."

Brady gave her a smug nod, and she grudgingly returned it.

"I want to do something authentically *cowboy*." Stan said the word as if it was a new concept he'd invented. "Brady suggested it, and I just got permission from the main office to do it." He turned to Brady. "Got to thank you for this, buddy. I'm so tired of that other pose, I could spit. They were designed by the marketing department and tested on focus groups, but I'll guarantee the focus groups were all middle-aged men with porn addictions. Now, thanks to you, I get to design the shoot myself. I'm thinking something with both of you on horseback. Moving fast, in stop-action. Can you rope?"

Both Brady and Suze nodded.

"Then you'll each need a horse and a rope. Use the fanciest tack you've got."

Brady grinned. "I'm a bronc rider, remember? My fanciest tack is a saddle that's not too tore up and trampled."

Stan shook his head. "Well, at least try to find something clean."

Suze laughed. "I'll loan you something."

"Thanks." She'd earned another Brady smile. Score.

"We'll meet back here in two hours and get started." Stan looked at Suze. "Don't worry. I'll call Marta back to do touch-up. You'll look fine."

"I don't know." Suze looked from Stan to Brady and back again, as if she was wondering what they were up to. Brady tried to look innocent, and then realized he actually *was* innocent for a change.

"What are you up to?" Suze asked.

"Nothing."

"Then why are you trying to pull that innocent act on me? Don't lie to me, Brady. I've seen it before."

"I know, but this time I actually *am* innocent."

She gave him a disbelieving stare.

"I know. I can't believe it either. I think you're a good influence."

Brady knew Suze needed the money from the shoot, so he knew she'd cooperate. But he wanted her to enjoy the experience, and he only knew one way to ensure that. She was the most competitive person he knew. If she thought this was a contest, she just might relax and have fun.

"If you need a few roping pointers, I'd be glad to help," he teased.

She tossed her hair and looked annoyed. "I can rope just fine."

He loved it when she tossed that golden hair, especially when it was all done up in swirls and curls, like now. He wanted to make her do it again.

"You sure?" He wrinkled up his forehead so he looked all earnest and serious.

Yep. That got him another hair toss.

"I was a roping champion in 4-H before you even knew how to ride a horse," she said.

He'd been hoping she'd bring that up. "Oh, yeah. What is it you rope in 4-H again? Puppies?"

Hair toss. "It's goat tying. You know that. They don't let us do calves, but I've roped them on the ranch."

"Goat-roping champion, huh? Well, that's pretty impressive, honey."

She turned to face him, and he realized his quest for hair tossing might have gone a little too far. Her eyes were narrowed to slits, and color had risen to her cheeks. She looked absolutely gorgeous—and mad as a cornered badger.

"Don't call me honey."

"Okay, darlin'."

She let out a noise like a cross between a mad chicken and a rodeo bull, and spun on her toes, stalking off across the arena toward the parking lot.

Stan looked up from where he was gathering cables, clearing a space for whatever "action shot" he had in mind. "That went well."

Brady grinned. "I thought so."

"I heard once you were a real ladies' man, Caine."

Brady leaned back against the fence, thumbs in his belt loops. "Yep."

"Well, if that was an example of how you romance the ladies, you've got a ways to go."

"I'm not trying to get Suze Carlyle into bed." Brady wasn't about to mention that had already happened. "I'm just trying to get her through this shoot. Trust me, she's beautiful when she's mad. And she'll play along just to prove she's a better roper than I am. Which she is, by the way. Way better."

Stan gave him a sharp, considering look while he

rolled up a length of cable. "If I didn't know you better, I'd say you actually liked this girl."

"But you *do* know me better. And, hell, I like 'em all."

Brady spit for emphasis, but he didn't spit much as a rule, and instead of landing in the dirt of the arena, the glob landed on the toe of his own boot.

"Smooth," Stan said. "Bet that really slays the ladies."

Brady shoved off the fence and pulled a cell phone out of his pocket. "I need to make some calls. Got to see a man about a horse. Or a couple of men." He squinted across the rodeo arena, where a dust devil had whipped up and was whirling in front of the bucking chutes like the ghost of a wild ride. "I just hope there's a decent animal left around here somewhere. Most everybody I know is in Fort Worth or Rapid City."

As a rough stock contestant, Brady didn't haul his own horses. Only the barrel racers and ropers did, and even ropers sometimes borrowed horses from the locals. The summer months were so packed with rodeos all over the West that a hardworking contestant could hit as many as three in one day. Brady was going to have to hustle if he was going to find a horse to ride. There were a couple at Decker Ranch, but they were old lesson horses, hardly animals he could put on the same page as Suze's Speedo. His brother Ridge had a couple of nice quarter horses in training, but there was no way he'd let Brady ride a client's horse.

He was starting to regret razzing Suze. If he couldn't find a decent horse, he wouldn't be able to rope anything. Not even a goat.

—∾—

Suze was just turning into the drive when Speedo, grazing in the pasture that bordered the driveway, lifted his head. His pointy ears swiveled like tiny radar dishes until they fixed on her, and then he flung himself into action, racing the truck to the turnaround in front of the barn. Patient as a faithful dog, he stood at the gate and waited for her.

Speedo was always calm, except at race time, when his personality transformed. Once he saw those barrels, he was laser focused and crazy for the win. Speedo loved running barrels like a Labrador loves fetching tennis balls.

Suze stepped up and rubbed the whorl of fur on his forehead.

"Hello, old man."

The nickname fit these days. His muzzle was beginning to gray, and it was a challenge to keep his famous blond mane looking good. She'd spent a fortune on horse shampoo and conditioners in the past couple months, and even more on vet bills to treat his various arthritic joints. The fast stops and tight spins of a professional rodeo horse were hard on an animal's body. She was going to have to retire him soon.

And then what?

That question kept her up at night. Though you could sometimes turn a mediocre mount into a pretty good barrel horse, you needed an animal with racing in his genes and running hardwired into his brain if you wanted to compete at the highest level.

That's why she was willing to do whatever Lariat wanted. A few more contracts like this one, and she'd have the money she needed to buy a new horse.

As she slipped a halter over the gelding's handsome head, she could almost feel her blood pressure dropping.

Sometimes she wished she could have a horse with her all the time, like a service animal. She felt so much better when she could just lay her hand on Speedo's warm neck, or cup her hand under his whiskery muzzle. Horses never judged you. They never implied you weren't good enough. Once they trusted you, they were yours, and you were theirs.

If only human relationships were that simple.

Remembering Stan's advice, she led Speedo over to the barn and cross-tied him in the alley. She grabbed a bucket with a big *S* on the front that was full of brushes and took her time polishing his coat to a high shine. His skin twitched under the brush, the way it did before a race.

"Hold your horsehair," she said. "We're not running today. Just posing pretty for a picture. You can do that, can't you, handsome boy?"

Speedo nodded as if he understood.

His blond mane was looking good, and she combed out the magnificent tail that streamed out behind him like a flag when he ran. Then she grabbed two prize saddles—one for her and one for Brady—and a couple of flashy bridles to match.

The truth was, Speedo didn't need much in the way of equipment. Once she was on his back, he'd go where she wanted if she just thought about it. The books said horses sensed slight, subconscious movements of the body, but it always felt like he was reading her mind.

"You're my equine psychic," she said. "Aren't you?"

Speedo stretched his neck out and nibbled on her shoulder.

"So how about if you predict how this shoot's going to go? Are we going to ride rings around Brady Caine and whatever pathetic old broken-down mount he manages to come up with?"

Speedo nodded again, stamping one front foot for emphasis.

Suze lifted a coil of rope down from a hook in the wall and held it out for the horse to smell.

"We're going to do some roping, okay, bud? Something different."

She'd roped on Speedo just a couple weeks ago, so she had no doubt he'd do fine. Horses who were so consistently used for one particular sport needed to be ridden for other purposes, or they'd go stale, doing their jobs by rote instead of using their minds. She and Speedo played all sorts of games, practicing pole bending and roping, as well as taking long trail rides into the open land around the ranch. Sometimes she'd take a rope on trail rides, so she could rope fence posts or drag old logs just for fun.

"We'll do fine today, won't we? We'll show Brady Caine who's boss." She patted his neck, then unclipped the cross-ties and led him to the corral.

"Don't you dare roll while my back's turned," she said. "I just need to hitch up your trailer and then we'll go. We're going to look like stars and perform like pros." She smiled to herself. "Brady Caine's going to swallow his tongue when he sees what he's up against."

Marta's words came back to her. *In life, you can only do your best.* Suze knew deep down that this shouldn't be a competition, but that was how her mind worked. She was so used to racing that everything became a quest to be the best.

"Marta's right. I'm being stupid," she muttered, more to herself than to the horse. "I need to stop worrying what other people think. And I don't need some man to back me up, either." She tossed her hair, and it felt so good brushing her shoulders that she did it again. She thought of the way Speedo would toss his head when she tried to hold him back before a race. "Just watch me, Brady Caine," she said to herself. "Just watch me go."

She meant it. She wasn't going to cry over Brady or let that careless grin give her heartache. If she wasn't good enough for him, that was fine with her. If you asked around, she wasn't good enough for anybody. Not for her father, who compared her to her perfect mother in everything she did; not for the other girls on the circuit, with their cliques and their boyfriends, their lip-gloss smiles and stylish clothes; not even for her mother, whose triumphant smile gleamed from dozens of photos around the house, her beauty and confidence a silent reproach. Sometimes Suze wondered what kind of woman would want pictures of herself all over her house and none of her own child, but she didn't like to think about the answer to that question.

Speedo gave Suze a playful nip, as if to remind her that she was good enough for him and she was good enough to win races. To all appearances, she took her wins in stride. But in her mind, she threw her success in the faces of everyone who doubted her.

Not good enough? How about this? And this? And this?

How about two world championships before I'm twenty-five? How about that?

But for some reason, she never could win quite enough races to make herself absolutely sure they were wrong.

Chapter 16

BRADY FISHED HIS CELL PHONE OUT OF HIS POCKET AND said a little prayer. It seemed like every able-bodied cowboy in the area had taken off for some faraway rodeo and taken his horses with him. His last hope was his friend Justin, who rode locally as a pickup man but didn't compete. Scraping riders off the backs of bucking broncos after the eight-second buzzer blared wasn't easy, and the horses used for the job were usually tall, handsome, and highly skilled.

Justin Brown was rarely serious, but he lived by the code of the cowboy, same as Brady did. Sure enough, he was willing to help a friend in need.

"Yeah, I can get a horse for you," Justin said as soon as he heard what Brady wanted. "What are you looking for?"

"It's for a Lariat ad, so he's got to be good-looking," Brady said.

"Is he going to have to wear one of those dumb-ass Lariat shirts? Because I don't mind loaning you a horse, but that would have the animal cruelty folks on my ass so fast, they'd have me naked on a street corner before I knew what hit me. Those shirts are so ugly, it's a crime."

"Very funny."

"Seriously, I've got just what you need. I can't get out there, but I'll have my little sister drive him out."

"Okay." Brady was starting to feel a little nervous. Justin might take this as an opportunity for a practical joke. "Remember, he has to look good. Don't send me some old nag."

"I promise, this horse is so purty, you'll probably want to marry him," Justin said. And before Brady could say another word, he hung up the phone.

"Hey, wait," Brady said into the empty air. "I'm going to rope on him. Make sure he's got some roping experience, okay?"

He shoved the phone in his pocket, disgusted with himself. Is that what it had come to? That he cared more about how a horse looked than what it could do? That was how careers got ruined.

He'd better make sure he wasn't turning out to be just as superficial as people thought he was.

Justin's shiny new F-250 pickup swung into the lot a half hour later, hauling a clattering rust bucket of a horse trailer behind it. The driver was barely visible above the truck's looming dashboard. All Brady could see was a high ponytail bobbing in the breeze from the open window.

Justin's little sister, Carly, had to be at least fifteen, or she couldn't have driven the truck. But when she slid out of the driver's seat, Brady thought she looked about twelve.

"Don't be mean to Dandy," she said, trotting around to the back of the trailer. "He's my favorite horse. And don't ride him too hard. He doesn't like it if you kick him." She turned to face Brady and held up one finger like a schoolteacher. "If your heels even touch his flanks, he'll blow up on you. Remember that."

"Okay. I'll remember." She was a cute kid, but Brady was starting to get a bad feeling about this. He'd wanted one of Justin's horses, not one that belonged to his little sister.

She pulled back the latch on the trailer, then stopped to offer more advice. "Keep his tail wrapped when he's not working, okay? He hates to have it brushed out, and besides, I want him to look his best. I'm so excited he's going to be in a magazine! Which one, do you know?"

"Not sure," Brady muttered. "Can we get him unloaded, please? I'm kind of in a hurry."

She had a few more words of advice before she opened the door. Dandy liked this, and Dandy didn't like that. Dandy needed leg wraps, and Dandy needed a wool saddle blanket, only wool. Before long, Brady felt kind of sorry for Dandy. But he felt even sorrier for himself.

By the time Carly finally let down the ramp, Brady was actually nervous. And he was never nervous. At least, not until today, which seemed destined to be the day of his first nervous breakdown.

The inside of the trailer was dark. After squinting into the sunlight on the pale dust of the arena, he could hardly see anything when he peered inside—just tiny Carly, hauling on a lead rope.

"He won't come." She pulled on the rope with every ounce of her ninety-three pounds, but the horse wasn't budging.

She rolled her eyes like only a teenaged girl could.

"First he doesn't want to get *into* the trailer, and now

he doesn't want to come *out* of it." After one final tug, she dropped the rope and stormed off, stamping her feet on the metal ramp so it clanged against the pavement. "Stupid horse."

Brady grabbed the rope before anything bad could happen. If Carly was Dandy's trainer, that might explain his reluctance to do as he was told. She'd given up before she'd tried anything but manhandling the animal—even though she was hardly big enough to manhandle a house cat.

Peering inside the trailer again, Brady caught sight of a narrow, dished face; a wide, long-lashed eye; and enough hair to top six or eight normal horses.

"What is this? Barbie's Dream Horse?"

"He's a purebred Anglo Arabian."

Brady was pretty sure an Anglo Arabian was a half-breed by definition, but he wasn't about to argue with Carly. She might stamp her foot again, or roll her eyes at him. Her temper tantrums were legendary.

The horse shrank back into the darkness of the trailer until nothing showed but the white rim around its rolling eyeballs.

"Come on, darlin'," Brady said. Women hated to be called that, he'd noticed, but horses usually loved it. He made a kissing sound and the horse took a step forward. Carly folded her arms over her chest, disgusted.

"He's a *boy*. Quit calling him 'darlin',' and he might do what you want."

Ignoring her, Brady stepped into the trailer and stood quietly, stroking the animal's neck. "Hey, sweetheart," he murmured. "Aren't you pretty?"

The horse was good-looking, all right. He couldn't

complain about that. But he probably should have stressed the roping angle a little more.

Like, maybe *mentioned* it.

He finally convinced the horse to take one step forward. Dandy flinched when his shiny black hoof hit the metal ramp, and a shiver ran the length of his body, from his tiny teacup nose to the root of his tail, which was tied up in a bag and topped with a bow. He was a beautiful animal, and probably valuable, but he spooked at the slightest thing. Brady could just see what Dandy would do if he tried to twirl a rope from his saddle.

"Just be real careful with him, okay?" Carly walked up to the horse and cupped his muzzle in her hand, giving it a kiss. "He's my big fuzzy-wuzzy sweetie, isn't he? He's my boogie-woogums."

Dandy took that single step back, hiding in the darkness of the trailer. Brady figured he was probably afraid some other horses had heard he was a boogie-woogums and would make fun of him.

"Quit calling that poor animal names," Brady said as he coaxed the horse down the ramp. "Bad enough you named him Dandy."

"Oh, it's *Jim* Dandy," she said.

"Great. I'll call him Jim."

"You can't. He's a show horse," she said. "You have to use his full registered name. He's Little Lula's Jim Dandy. See, his dam was Little Lula and his sire—"

Brady cut off the pedigree recitation. "How come you called him your boogie-woogums?"

"That's different."

"Right. And it's different when I call him Jim. You show him yourself?"

Carly nodded, beaming with pride.

"He win much?"

"He sure does." She looked as satisfied with herself as boogie-woogums, who had finally left the trailer and was standing at the foot of the ramp, squared like a stud horse posing for a marketing photo.

"What classes do you compete in?" If he could figure out the animal's strengths, he could probably find a way to make this work.

"Oh, just halter so far. I want to do Hunt Seat Equitation, but he's just too nervous. That's okay for showing at halter, though. I just have to jerk his head a little and he storms around and acts all fiery and wild. The judges love it."

"Yeah. That's great." He gave the lead rope a faint tug and the horse stamped his foot and rolled his eyes just like Carly.

Brady had seen some Arabian halter classes at one of the big stock shows. Some folks seemed to think that nerves strung tight as a sopranino banjo meant good breeding, and eyes that rolled around in their sockets like greased marbles were a sign of high spirits rather than imminent nervous prostration. As far as Brady was concerned, all it meant was that you had a horse you couldn't do much with. If you put old Jim in a calf-sorting pen, the horse would probably kill himself trying to climb the fence and get away from the bad, scary cows without penning a single one.

Brady had seen some terrific Arabians that could do just about anything, bred by responsible breeders who valued temperament over looks. Unfortunately, Dandy wasn't one of them.

For now, the horse stood quietly, the only clue to his temperament the faint shivers that rippled across his back. Watching him, Brady got a funny feeling.

"You ever ridden him?" he asked Carly.

"Nope," she said cheerfully. "But you don't care about that, do you? Justin says you're a bronc buster, so you can ride anything."

Brady winced. Broncs were bred for bucking. Horses like Jim couldn't be bucked out; it would ruin them for life. Then the *humans* would be bad and scary.

"My daddy rode him, though. Couple times."

"Well, that's good."

As he helped Carly uncouple the trailer from the truck so she could drive off on some mysterious errand, Brady wondered if Justin knew his sister wasn't staying to watch the photo shoot. He figured probably not, but hey, it wasn't his day to watch her, and Carly seemed like a sweet kid whose idea of rebellion would be going to Starbucks when she was supposed to be at the library. Since he was pretty sure Justin had stuck him with boogie-woogums on purpose, he'd let the guy look out for his own darned sister.

As Carly blew him a kiss and drove off, Brady looked at the horse, who was sneaking glances at him out of the corner of his long-lashed eyes, like a coy seventh grader at the spring dance.

Great. He was about to meet Suze and Speedo with a horse that acted like a teenaged girl—temper tantrums and all.

"Boogie-woogums, huh? Maybe I'll call you Booger."

The horse stamped one front hoof and thrust out his lower lip in a pout.

Chapter 17

WHEN BRADY GOT BACK TO THE ARENA, STAN NODDED toward a beautifully tooled prize saddle that was perched on the rail. A silver-mounted bridle was draped over the seat.

"Suze left those for you. You find a horse?"

"Sure did," Brady said.

"It's not some old nag, is it?"

"Nope. Definitely not."

Brady had left Booger in the trailer. The horse was ridiculously reactive, flinching at a candy wrapper, a stray leaf, even a plane passing overhead. When he tried to turn inside out at the approach of a fly, Brady had led him back to the dark, safe depths of the trailer.

"Really, Booger," he said to the horse. "You never saw a fly before? She must keep you in Barbie's Dream Stable."

The horse stamped his foot and rolled his eyes, but allowed Brady to saddle him and took the bit placidly. It was clear he'd done it before, and Brady wondered if Carly had the same sense of humor as her brother. Maybe she'd been teasing when she said the horse had barely been ridden. He managed to exit the trailer without any drama at all. Mounting was an issue, but Brady just shortened one rein, forcing the horse to spin in a tight circle that actually helped him swing into the saddle.

He warmed up a little, loping Booger up and down the alley, and discovered he'd guessed right; Booger had actually been fairly well trained, and as long as things were quiet, he performed pretty well. Once he'd been introduced to the rope, he even allowed Brady to throw a loop or two from his back without shying—much.

And he *was* pretty. There was no denying that. Hell, the dudes that bought the fancy fringed shirts would probably be more impressed by Jim Dandy's aristocratic profile and high-arched neck than Speedo's muscle and brains. The thought made Brady laugh out loud.

Booger, startled by the noise, arched his back and blew up. Bronc buster that he was, Brady could barely hang on as the horse pitched and yawed like a ship in a storm. He could swear steam came out of the horse's nostrils. He was like a cartoon horse, having a cartoon temper tantrum.

Once he had Booger under control again, Brady pushed the horse into a lope, letting him run out his nerves while Brady invented some creative new swear words to use on Justin next time he saw him. The horse performed far better at speed, even allowing a bird to flit up from the fence without so much as a flick of his ear.

"We'll do fine," Brady said, allowing the animal to slow. "We'll just keep you moving, okay, buddy?" He reached down and patted Booger's neck.

Big mistake. The horse reared up on his hind legs, then slammed his front hooves to the ground and took off running, only stopping after Brady forced him into a circle so tight he had no choice.

"Can we cut the drama?" Brady murmured the words as if they were endearments, knowing the horse read his tone but not his meaning. "Your little mistress might like that stuff, but I go for the strong, silent type. In horses, anyway."

He wondered how Booger would deal with flash-bulbs going off, Stan shouting instructions, and Suze and Speedo doing their best to outride and out-rope Brady. Hopefully Booger was one of those horses who liked to compete.

Brady petted the horse again and was relieved when Booger just bent his pretty head low so he could peer back at his rider. Brady could swear the horse smiled. It might have been an "I'm starting to like you" smile, or even an "I'm sorry" smile. But Brady was pretty sure Booger took after his teenaged mistress, and it was a "wait till you see what I'm going to do next" smile.

Suze was feeling good. She was high in the saddle on Speedo's back—the one place in the world where she felt completely at ease. She was fooling with her rope, getting the feel of it, while she chatted with Stan about photography. He was explaining the concept of aper-tures when Brady stormed into the arena on the back of a hurricane. His mount was a whirling mass of mane and tail, and it wasn't until he stopped that she managed to sort out the whirlwind into a very attractive but high-strung Arabian bay.

"Wow," Stan said. "Good job, Brady. That animal is *gorgeous*. This is going to be great." He glanced over at Speedo, then back at Booger. "They didn't have any more like that, did they?"

"Trust me, one's enough," Brady said.

Suze laughed. It was obvious that Stan knew as much about horses as she knew about apertures. One look at the quivering mass of horseflesh under Brady's borrowed saddle told her this was going to be a disaster.

"You shopping in the ladies' section now?" she called across the arena.

"Oh, yeah," Stan said. "It *is* more of a woman's horse, isn't it? How 'bout if you ride that one, and Brady rides Speedo, Suze? You'll look great on—what's his name?"

Brady was moving pretty fast, but Suze could still tell he was blushing. "Booger," he said.

"Booger? Stupid name for such a looker."

"Yeah, what's his full name?" Suze knew the horse had to have more of a name than that. The animal was definitely registered and probably had a name as long as her arm.

Brady just kept moving, loping the horse from one side of the arena to the other.

"So, Suze, what do you think?" Stan asked. "Can you ride that thing?"

"I could," she said. "But I think we should let Brady do it. I like the contrast: the macho man on the delicate little sissy horse, and the woman on the powerful take-charge racehorse. If you want to appeal to strong women, that's the way to do it."

"Yeah, I'll bet you like the contrast," Brady muttered. She wouldn't have heard him except that his circuit of the arena happened to take him past her at that moment.

"I don't know." Stan was looking from one horse to the other, tapping his teeth with his index finger the way he did when he was worried. "I'm afraid it won't look right."

"But my hair matches Speedo's mane," she said.

"Oh." He cocked his head and eyed her and Speedo. "You're right. That's kind of a nice effect."

Stan busied himself with a light meter, checking various parts of the arena. Brady passed him a few times. He'd toned things down a bit and was only trotting the Arabian, but Stan still looked annoyed and Suze couldn't blame him. "Can you hold up for a minute, Brady?" Stan asked. "You're making me dizzy."

"Okay." Brady reined in the horse, which stood quivering beside Suze and Speedo. Suze had gone through a brief phase as a little girl when she'd longed for an Arabian, but she'd known enough not to voice that desire around the barrel-racing arena. It was all quarter horses, all the time in her world. As she'd grown older, she'd fallen in love with the breed's dependability and athleticism, and now she wouldn't trade Speedo for all the Arabians in the world.

She started to ask Brady about the horse's lineage when a leaf blew across the arena. It flipped its way toward Brady and Booger, and judging from the way Brady was watching it, things were about to get entertaining. He turned the horse away from the leaf's trajectory, but it was too late; Booger had caught sight of it and was rolling his eyes so the whites showed.

A moment later, Booger leaped into the air, his four skinny legs pointing north, south, east, and west. The formerly graceful neck thrust sticklike from his body, his mane flew straight up in the air, and his tail did the same—but with more purpose as he dumped a steaming heap of panic onto the dirt. Suze was pretty sure his eyes turned into little pinwheels of fear before his back hooves hit the ground and he started walking around on his hind legs, waving his forelegs around and screaming.

Brady looked like the Lone Ranger up there. Fortunately he rode as well as any ranger, lone or not. The effect was actually kind of impressive, but Booger was the sort of horse who didn't know when to quit. He started bouncing down on his front legs and rearing up again, bouncing and rearing, until he finally reared himself ass over teakettle and lay kicking in the sun-warmed dirt like an overturned turtle.

The cloud of dust that formed as the horse struggled to rise parted occasionally to give Suze a few brief glimpses of Brady. First his hat flew out of the mix, and then she caught sight of a leg. It was still wearing its boot, which seemed like good news. Next was a shiny hoof, then Brady's arm, and then the boot again.

Finally, the bundle of grunting and whinnying and swearing and snorting straightened out and there was Brady, covered with dust, his fancy shirt torn and his hat trampled. But he still had hold of the reins. Beside him, the horse trembled like the aspen leaf that had started the whole thing.

Stan was standing protectively in front of his camera equipment, looking alarmed. "What just happened?" he asked.

"Brady's horse blew up."

"He exploded?"

"Sort of."

"Dammit, I didn't get any pictures."

At this point, Brady, Suze, and the two horses were all covered in a fine coat of dust. Stan had somehow escaped unscathed.

"Guess we'd better go clean up." Brady brushed off his seat, which bore an arena-dirt imprint that reminded Suze of a tractor seat.

"No, wait. I like this. We were looking for authentic, and I think we've found it here."

"You want me to get back on that animal?" Brady looked like he'd sooner ride a rodeo bull in his birthday suit than get back on Booger's back.

"He was doing okay before," Stan said. "What happened?"

"He saw a leaf."

Suze had to give Brady credit. A lot of cowboys would have been furious with the horse, and would have taken out their frustration by jerking his head around or worse. But Brady was doing his best to soothe poor Booger, and while she and Stan watched, he put his foot in the stirrup and swung back on board. He looked like he was about to ride to his own hanging, and Suze took pity on him.

"Long as Booger's moving, he's too busy to look around. And if he doesn't look around, he doesn't get scared and blow up," she said. "So let's figure out a path and stick to it. We wanted an action shot, right?"

After a little discussion, she and Brady began racing from one end of the arena to the other, occasionally waving their lariats over their heads. It was a lot more fun than kneeling at Brady's feet, that was for sure. Suze found herself egging Speedo on, pushing him to beat the surprisingly fleet-footed Arabian.

Then they changed it up, running full-tilt toward each other and veering off just in time to avoid a collision. Brady had been worried this would be too much for

Booger, but the horse took it all in stride—as long as he kept moving. Suze loved it. It was like playing chicken on horseback, and she made darn sure it was always Brady who turned chicken.

Still, watching him pound toward her across the dirt of the arena, his eyes intense as a hawk's as he crouched over the horse's neck, gave her the willies—the good willies, the ones that start in your chest and shimmer all the way down to your unmentionables.

As Brady passed her for the tenth time or so, he gasped out, "Let's get back to running together. I'm worried this guy won't turn when I tell him to."

"Chicken?" Suze grinned.

"On this horse I am."

Suze could understand that. In fact, it was probably a smart and safe decision. She had a tendency to try to prove herself. It had gotten her in trouble a few times, and she had the scars to prove it.

At the end of the arena, she stopped Speedo and waited for Brady to catch up. Speedo had caught the spirit of the afternoon and kept prancing in place like he was gearing up for a race.

As soon as Brady reached her, she spurred Speedo into action and the two of them took off at top speed, their horses churning up dust, their ropes whistling in the air over their heads.

After a few more shots, Stan waved them to a stop. Brady climbed down and held the reins, stroking Booger's neck in a gentle, almost tender way that made Suze feel flushed and warm.

"I'm not quite getting what I want," Stan said. "It's just two people riding, you know? No excitement. How about some stops? You know, those sliding stops the cowboys do?"

"Those are reining horses," Brady said. "Speedo might be able to do it, but Booger isn't going to give you a flashy stop. He's just not made for it."

Suze grinned. "Scared?"

"No." Brady didn't look very happy. "With my luck, I'd snap one of his skinny legs. I hate to think what Carly's dad paid for this horse."

"You're chicken," she said.

"I'm sensible, that's all."

She laughed. She couldn't help it. Brady was the least sensible person she knew. She also figured he was probably the most competitive person she knew. Being the youngest of three brothers, he'd always worked twice as hard as the other boys to keep up.

If she made him a dare, he'd do it.

Chapter 18

Suze thought about pushing Brady a little harder, risking a little more just to prove herself, and decided it was a bad idea—not so much for her as for Speedo.

"I'd just as soon not do any hard stops," she admitted. "Speedo's getting older, and it's hard on his legs."

"I've got it!" Stan's eyes widened, and he snapped his fingers. "How 'bout a shot of you roping each other?"

"What do you mean?" Suze asked.

"You ride toward each other, just like you were." Stan came out from behind his equipment and walked to the center of the arena. The dirt was stirred up into humps and ridges, but he managed to scrape a recognizable X into it with the heel of his shoe. Then he stepped to the side about three feet and made another X.

"You ride toward each other, and when you hit these X's, you rope each other. Just throw a loop up and let it drop over the other person's head."

"Are you crazy?" Brady asked.

"Like a fox," he said. "It'll be a million-dollar shot."

"Do you know how challenging that is? Most riders I know couldn't do that. And even if we could, it's too dangerous."

"I can do it," Suze said. She couldn't stop smiling. The trick was dangerous, but not if you timed it right.

All you had to do was drop the rope as soon as the loop settled and nobody would get hurt.

Best of all, since she had the more dependable mount and had actually done it before, she was likely to succeed in roping Brady, while the chance he'd rope her was slim to none. She could see it now: a photo in a nationally distributed magazine of Suze Carlyle roping fabled bad boy Brady Caine.

"I think you're chicken," she said.

Brady fixed his eyes on hers. "You really want to do this?"

She grinned and nodded, feeling reckless and strong and happy. This was almost as good as sex. The photo would be great, she'd get more modeling endorsements, and the money would pour in. She'd get up-to-date on the mortgage and add enough money to her barrel horse fund to get a really spectacular partner worthy of traveling in Speedo's hoofprints.

"Come on, let's go." She gave Brady her best pleading, sweet-thing face. "Please? I need this ad to be really great, Brady."

When he didn't respond, she made a very slight flapping motion with her elbows and clucked softly. "Chicken," she whispered.

Brady looked down at his boots, kicked up a little cloud of dust, and sighed.

"All right."

With no further discussion, he climbed on Booger's back. Booger seemed to be calming down, but as he and Brady crossed the arena, the horse suddenly let loose with a quick bout of crow hopping and a couple of high equine screams.

"What was that?" Suze asked.

Brady shrugged. "I think he saw an ant."

—◦◦◦—

Brady knew he was being an idiot. The trick was too dangerous. He really should stop it, but nobody called him chicken.

That was what his brothers had called him, back when they'd been three teenaged foster kids thrown together into a loosely stitched family by location, circumstance, and the dedication of an old rancher named Bill Decker.

At the time of their adoption, Brady had been barely fifteen. His soon-to-be brothers, Ridge Cooper and Shane Lockhart, were sixteen, and they never let him forget they were the older brothers. The three of them had learned to get along, even to love each other. But as the youngest, Brady had been the brunt of every imaginable practical joke, the loser in every game, and the last to learn the daring stunts his new brothers dreamed up.

He'd also been the most timid of the three, though no one would guess that now. He hadn't been kidding when he'd told Suze he was sensible.

And if there was one word that reverberated from his childhood, one word he never wanted to hear again, it was *chicken*. He'd heard it from his brothers over and over, when his caution had overruled his bravado, his prudence had won over his flair for drama, and his sensible side vanquished his desire to impress them. They'd teased him with the same act Suze had, flapping their arms like wings and clucking.

Chicken.

Suze might as well have pushed a green button that said "go."

The stunt was stupid. The stunt was dangerous. But the stunt was going to happen.

He loped Booger around and around the ring. He'd have liked to practice his roping a little, maybe catch a few fence posts. Actually, what he'd really like to do was to catch Stan in a few loops. Around the neck. Rope him, throw him, and truss him up.

Then he'd serve him up to Suze and see how she liked that for chicken.

But that was fantasy. Reality was a crazy horse, an equally crazy woman, and a photo shoot gone nuts. Sighing, Brady headed for his side of the arena, coiled his rope loosely in one hand, and nodded his head to signal that he was ready.

Suze nodded too, and then the two of them were off, galloping toward each other at top speed, ropes twirling in the air as they got closer, closer, closer...

The ropes were thrown. The loops floated, floated, dropped, dropped, dropped...

...and missed.

Both landed far off the mark, and the two riders sheepishly reeled them in without looking at each other.

"Try it again," Stan said.

They did.

They thundered across the arena, getting closer, closer, closer...

Brady threw too soon. His rope lashed out and smacked Suze in the face before she even had a chance to build a loop.

He tensed up, horrified. Fortunately, Suze was

laughing, unhurt. In fact, her eyes were glistening, her face shining. This was all good fun to her. It hadn't even occurred to her that the stunt could go wrong.

Maybe that's why she was a world champion while Brady was still short of that mark. Maybe her reckless courage was the difference, rather than focus or dedication.

This time, he'd go for it. No hesitation, no caution—just ready, aim, throw.

They started toward each other again, and this time Brady knew he'd succeed. His vision narrowed until all he could see was that blond head of hair flying toward him. He barely heard the thudding of Booger's hooves, or the yell Suze whooped out when Speedo's muscular hindquarters threw him into a full-on run. All he could see was Suze, coming toward him, closer, closer—as his rope twirled, spun, then dropped, dropped…

Got her.

As the rope settled around her shoulders, he did what he always did when he scored. He threw back his head and let out a holler that was part rebel yell, part cowboy yodel, and part shout of triumph.

That's when Booger blew up for real.

Chapter 19

As long as Suze lived—which might not be long, judging from how she felt—she'd remember the *clang* that reverberated through the entire arena when the back of her head hit the top rail of the bucking chute. It sounded like the bell for a boxing match.

But did the bell mean the match was starting or ending? As she stared up into the cloudless sky, she felt like it was very important to know that. Because while she knew for sure that everything in her world had changed with that bell, she'd really like to know if it meant her old life was ending or if something new was beginning.

She didn't want a new life. She liked her old one—or at least she did now.

"Stay with us, hon, stay with us."

Who was that? Brady? She squinted at the face that loomed over her. *Nope. Not Brady.*

The edges of her vision dimmed. Maybe she was dying. She didn't want to, but then again, she might get to see her mother if she did.

And why should she stick around? Her father was a mean old bastard who couldn't see his daughter past the shadow of his late wife. They were so deep in debt they were drowning, and he expected her to save them somehow. And she had a ridiculous, unrequited crush on a cowboy who had probably just killed her—and had celebrated with the wild rebel yell of victory she'd heard just before that bell went off.

Lying on the soft dirt of the arena, staring up into that blue Wyoming sky, those problems didn't matter, because all she could think about was waking up every morning to see gray dawn steal over the prairie, reflecting light from an invisible sun that tinted the horizon silver, peach, and gold. She thought about the rattle of feed buckets and the answering nicker of her horses, the rustle of hay flakes, and the soft, rhythmic munching of the animals. She thought of all the little things she loved: the mingled scents of leather, horse, and hay; dust motes dancing a tiny cosmic hoedown in a slant of light; and the way the barn's rafters rose like the bones of some enormous animal or the roof of a great cathedral. She realized how much it meant to be whole and healthy, to be able to ride tight circles around a bunch of rusty old barrels faster than any girl in the world. And she thought of Speedo—her best friend, her partner, her horse.

She lifted her head, struggling to see something other than sky. The sunbaked arena shifted in and out of focus, as if she were on some kind of drug. Lights flickered at the edge of her vision, and her head felt hot. Too hot. Then the light faded and she couldn't see anything but shadows. Everybody seemed to be mumbling. Why were they mumbling?

She asked them if Speedo was okay and they wouldn't answer. She asked them again, but they just ignored her while they worked on her leg or her arm or some other body part.

They kept hurting her, but that didn't matter. She

needed to know if Speedo was okay, and they wouldn't tell her, so she started screaming his name, over and over. Her voice rose into the serene blue of the sky, harsh and hoarse and desperate, and still nobody answered.

It wasn't long before she wore out, and the screams turned to whimpers. Maybe they gave her something, a sedative. She didn't know.

Didn't know anything…

———◦∾∾∾◦———

Brady would give anything, everything, for a do-over.

He'd had that feeling before after making the wrong move on a bronc, or saying something clumsy and hurtful to a woman. But this time it was stronger. He would honestly give his own life to change one second of the past: the second when he'd thrown that rope.

Or better yet, the second he'd held on to it. That single ill-advised second had let the rope go taut and pull Suze off her speeding horse, and it had flung her into the chute gate.

A do-over.

There had to be a way to make that bargain. Didn't people sell their souls to the devil? He'd gladly burn in hell for what he'd done to Suze. In fact, he deserved to.

So where the hell was Old Scratch when you needed him?

The incident ran through his head over and over, like a video on an endless loop. Booger had acted up the second things went sideways. He'd bucked, crow hopped, and danced a terrified tarantella while Brady's rope pinned Suze's arms to her side. Everything would have been fine if Brady had just let go of the rope, but he'd been so focused on the frightened horse that he'd forgotten to drop it.

At that point, the video in his mind dropped into slow motion. The rope jerked Suze off her horse and launched her toward the chute gate. His palm bore a stinging memento of the rope burning through his grip.

He didn't know if Suze had screamed. She must have, but the sound got mixed up in his own idiot yelp of—of what? Victory? Triumph? Terror?

How about sheer, unadulterated stupidity?

He knew one thing for sure: the sound of a healthy body striking unyielding steel would reverberate through his mind for the rest of his life. That sound was the end of one life and the beginning of another—for Suze and for him, because whatever happened, however she felt about him, he owed her.

If she was even alive.

Someone—Stan—was patting his shoulder and muttering incoherent words of comfort.

"Not your fault…just an accident…could have happened to anyone…it was the horse, it was the wind, it was nobody's fault…"

"Stop it." Brady glanced over toward the EMTs. If it weren't for the frantic way they hovered over Suze's prone body, Brady would think the worst. "It was my fault."

"It was my idea," Stan said. "And Suze wanted to do it."

The fog in Brady's mind suddenly disappeared. He could feel himself coming out of what must have been a state of shock. His face heated, and with that heat came anger.

He smacked Stan's hand off his shoulder and spun to face him. "Don't you dare say one more word that even comes close to blaming Suze for this. Not now, not ever."

"Of course not. It wasn't anybody's fault. But I heard you, man. You tried to talk her out of it."

Brady clenched his fists and took a step back—not to create a safe distance between himself and Stan, but to give himself room to throw a really effective punch. He'd just started to raise his fist when he heard Suze moan. It was a soft sound, so low he almost missed it, but it was something.

He spun away from Stan and headed for the spot where Suze lay, dropping to his knees and skidding toward her in the soft arena dirt.

"Suze? Hey, Suze?" He looked at one EMT, then the other. "Did you hear that? She said something. I heard her."

"We heard her. Don't crowd us, okay?"

Brady half stood and backed away.

"Why is she on that board? Why did you put that thing around her head?"

"It's just a precaution. With head injuries, you have to stabilize the patient."

Brady wanted to scream that this wasn't "the patient"; this was Suze, Suze Carlyle, a woman who'd been barreling toward him just moments before, her rope twirling over her head. She'd been so alive in that moment. Surely that life would sustain her in spite of what had happened.

Surely it would.

The EMTs lifted the gurney and legs unfolded from

beneath it. They rolled it through the alleyway between the bleachers to the ambulance. Brady followed, with Stan trotting behind him.

"Is she going to be okay?" Brady asked.

The tech shrugged.

Just then, Suze's eyes flipped open, like the eyes of a doll. Her pupils were tiny, her expression frantic as she tried to turn her head and look around.

"I'm here, Suze," Brady said. "I'm here, and I'm not going anywhere."

Her gaze darted around, searching for something. And that's when she started to scream.

"*Speedo! Speedo!*"

"He's fine," Brady said. "Speedo's fine. I'll take care of him, okay?"

But by then the gurney had slid into the ambulance, and he knew she couldn't hear him anymore.

"Can I ride along in the ambulance? I'm a…friend, and I—I'm really concerned."

He'd almost told the techs that he'd caused the accident. Stan had put his hand on his shoulder just in time. He felt bad about slapping it away earlier. He'd apologize. He would. He just had more important things to do right now. He could still hear Suze calling Speedo's name.

"I need to tell her, her horse is okay. Somebody tell her that, okay?"

He shoved through the crowd of EMTs as the doors closed, muffling Suze's cries.

"Can I ride along?" he repeated.

The tech turned. "Are you Brady Caine?"

Brady nodded. "Did she ask for me?"

The tech looked at him as if he was just another pile of horse leavings in the dust of the rodeo arena.

"Tell you what," he said, "she's only been conscious for thirty seconds or so. Normally, during that time, people say stuff like *tell my mother I love her*, *make sure my kids are okay*, stuff like that."

Brady didn't bother to tell the guy Suze didn't have a mother or kids. The man was clearly making another point.

"She didn't say any of that stuff. She said, and I quote, 'Keep Brady Caine the hell away from me.' So, no, you can't ride along."

Chapter 20

THE EMERGENCY ROOM AT CHEYENNE REGIONAL Medical Center was a hive of activity, with bells ringing, nurses padding to and fro, and harried-looking doctors striding with the kind of self-importance only doctors can pull off.

"Excuse me." Brady nodded politely to a pleasantly plump woman at the counter. Her head was bent in concentration as she tapped at a computer keyboard. "My girlfriend is back there. I wondered if I could…"

"Family only." The woman spoke with all the animation of the Terminator and continued to stare at the keyboard.

Brady held his hat to his chest and turned on the smile that had won the hearts of half a dozen rodeo queens, but the woman continued to type. "Could you maybe just tell me how she's doing?"

"That information is for family only." Deft and efficient, her fingers danced over the keys. She still didn't look up.

Maybe he needed to take a more personal approach. "Whatcha working on, hon?"

She finally looked up. Her snuggle-bunny figure and teddy-bear scrubs had led him to expect a cute little country girl, but her skin was pale as wax, and her eyes were bordered in an odd combination of dark liner and glitter paint that made her look like a cross between Cleopatra and Elvira, Mistress of the Night. He half expected fangs, but her teeth were actually a little smaller than normal and set slightly separated in her gums, like the tiny teeth of a child. Somehow, that seemed more ghoulish than fangs.

"What I'm working on," she said, "is confidential." She pulled a few pages out of a printer, tapped them on her desk to align the edges, and slipped them into a folder. "Now, can I do anything else for you?"

"No. No, forget it."

He felt like he'd fired his entire arsenal and it had simply bounced off the protective layer of Goth she wore like a suit of armor. Backing away from the desk with his hat in his hands, he sat down on one of the plastic chairs in the waiting area. The chairs had once been white, but hundreds of waiting family members had scratched dark scars in them with the rivets on their Wranglers.

Brady had been here before—once when a bronc rolled over on his brother Ridge, and once when a buddy had an unfortunate encounter with a Brahma bull. But though he'd been anxious both times, they were nothing compared to this. The fluorescent lights seemed to flicker, and he was afraid he might throw up.

Maybe if he did, they'd take him back there as a patient. He tried thinking about a really terrible Mexican dinner he'd had once in Amarillo, but though the memory made him feel a lot worse, it didn't quite do the trick.

Setting his hat on the chair next to him, he rested his elbows on his knees and ducked his head to rake his fingers through his hair. What the hell was he going to do now? He couldn't leave Suze, but there wasn't much point in being there if no one would tell him how she was.

"Little brother? You okay?" The voice was deep and familiar.

"Shane." Brady slapped his hat back on, lurched to his feet, and stepped into his eldest brother's arms in a shameless display of relief and gratitude. The embrace lasted mere seconds before the two of them backed off, glanced around the room to see if anyone was looking, and switched to more manly displays of affection that ended with the two of them standing side by side, heads bowed. Shane put his hand on Brady's shoulder and squeezed.

"How is she?" Shane asked.

"I don't know. I can't get past the guardian of the gates over there." Brady gestured toward his nemesis.

"You're kidding. Brady Caine can't charm his way past a woman?"

"Nope." Brady scuffed his feet, still staring at the floor. "She's too smart to fall for my shit. I mean, what have I got? I'm a cowboy. Buckle bunnies love me. But there's not much going on under this danged hat."

He took off the offending hat and flung it on the floor. It slid over to the reception counter and slapped into the paneling. The receptionist paused in her typing just long enough to toss him a disapproving glare, then returned to her task without the slightest hitch in her rhythm.

"I don't know," Shane said. "You're pretty funny, and she looks like she could use a laugh. You try teasing her? See if you can get a giggle out of her?"

"She look like the giggling type?" Brady asked.

Shane ducked his head to get a look at the girl's face and shook his head. "Nope."

"See? I'm telling you, I got nothing." Brady dropped into one of the hard plastic chairs like he'd been shot. "This whole thing's taught me to take a hard look at myself. I'm nothing but a good-time cowboy. A god-damn punch line."

Shane bent down and picked up the hat, setting it beside him as he sat down beside his brother. "You're way more than that."

"Am I?" Brady gave his brother a hard look, and Shane couldn't hold it. "You said it yourself once. I'm wasting what God gave me on buckles, babes, and beer." He walked over and picked up the hat. "You know why she's back there?" He waved his hat toward the double doors. "Because I'm not man enough to admit it when I'm outmatched. I knew I couldn't pull off that stunt, but I wouldn't admit it. And now she's hurt. Bad. Because of me." He returned to his chair, mashing his hat down on the chair beside him, crushing the crown.

Shane put a hand on his brother's back and stayed silent. That was one of the things that made Brady glad to have him for a brother. Shane knew when to keep his mouth shut, which was most of the time. He could be bossy, and as the oldest of the three foster brothers, he could be stern. But he cared, and he was kind.

Luckily for Brady, he was family—by the grace of God, Bill Decker, and the Wynott Home for Boys.

The two men sat silently under the yellowed lights of the waiting room, watching an orderly dance a mop down the adjacent hallway in a slow, swirling tango.

Suddenly Brady leaped to his feet. "Speedo," he said. "Goddamn it, I forgot about Speedo."

"Suze's horse?" Shane pulled his brother back into the chair by his shirttail. "Quit worrying. Ridge put him in a stall at the rodeo grounds for now. He didn't have a trailer or he'd have taken him home to the ranch or over to Suze's."

"Thanks, bro." Brady put his hand on his brother's shoulder and squeezed. "I'll pick him up later. Soon as I've seen Suze."

"Take Ridge with you," Shane said. "He said that animal's a real handful."

"For anybody but Suze, I guess." Brady glanced at his watch. "I should probably go get Ridge and haul the horse home," he said. "He's probably nervous, being alone in an unfamiliar place."

"Yep."

Brady looked longingly at the double doors that barred him from the treatment area. "I just want to see Suze first."

"Does she want to see you?"

Brady shook his head. "Probably not."

"Maybe you should take care of the horse, then."

When a doctor stepped out of the double doors, Brady lurched to his feet. The doctor never shifted into a trot, but he somehow passed the orderly and his dance partner and disappeared around a corner before Brady could say a word.

"I'll get the horse later," Brady said. "They have to let me in eventually."

"Do you want to see her for your sake or for hers?"

Brady sat down and sighed, feeling about as lost

and hopeless as he'd ever felt in his life. Glancing at his face, Shane rose and went over to the Goth girl. Bending his dark head over the computer monitor, he managed to engage her in a whispered conversation. At one point, the two of them both looked at Brady. He tried to look like a responsible party. Normally, he was just a party—a walking party, in boots and a hat. That was Brady Caine.

The woman talked to Shane a little longer, then gave him a ghoulish smile. Her lipstick was practically black. It made her teeth look nice and white, but it had the same effect on her complexion. Brady was going to have scary clown dreams tonight for sure.

Shane raised his eyebrows, obviously asking a question. The Goth girl nodded twice, in a way that made her head seem completely disembodied from the rest of her.

Scary puppet dreams, maybe.

Shane walked back to Brady. "She says you can go on back there. Just don't tell anybody she saw you. Don't even tell them you saw her. She'll say she was making copies and you must have slipped by her."

Brady stood and put his hand on Shane's shoulder, bowing his head. "Thanks, man."

Shane gave him a little shove. "Just *go*. And then take care of that horse."

Glancing left and right, making sure the mop man was gone, Brady strode toward the double doors, smacked them open, and slipped through.

Chapter 21

BRADY FOUND HIMSELF IN A HALLWAY LINED WITH cubicles, each containing a cot and an assortment of beeping, blinking medical equipment. Most of the curtains were open, revealing empty cots, but a few were occupied, the patients hidden by drawn curtains and hushed voices.

How the hell was he going to find Suze? He needed to hurry. Shane was right; she'd want him to rescue the horse first. But he had to know if she was okay.

He edged back the first curtain and peered inside.

A woman lay on the cot, staring unseeing at the ceiling. An elderly man sat on a chair beside her, holding her hand while he rested his forehead on the edge of the cot and stared down at the floor.

Wincing, Brady let the curtain swing closed. He felt like he'd intruded on a moment as private as lovemaking.

The next two carrels were unoccupied. When he pushed back the curtain that hid the fourth compartment, an elderly woman propped herself up on her elbows. She had sparse apricot hair organized in neat swirls over a shiny pink skull, and wore cat-eye glasses with bright red frames.

"Well, now, look at you," she said. "Did I die and go to heaven?"

"No, ma'am," he said.

She slumped back down and rested her head on the

pillow. "You got that right. In heaven, the good-lookin' cowboys don't call me ma'am."

Brady smiled. "What do they call you?"

She smiled. "They call me sweetheart." She turned sharp eyes on him and scanned his clothes top to bottom. "You're dirty."

"Been in a wreck."

"You remind me of my husband. He was a rodeo cowboy." She smiled at the memory, staring at the ceiling. "He'd get dirty like that, and I'd make him clean up before I'd let him touch me." She sighed. "We were married almost sixty years."

"You must have married mighty young," Brady said gallantly.

"I was seventeen," she said. "We had a little ranch. Raised three kids." She shot a sharp look at Brady. "You got kids?"

"No, ma'am."

"What're you waiting for?"

He smiled wryly. "A sweetheart like you, I guess."

"You got one in mind?"

He shook his head. "Not yet."

She propped herself up on her elbows again. "Why not?"

Brady shrugged. "I like 'em all. It's hard to choose."

She lay down again. "You haven't met the right one yet, then. You'll know her the minute you see her."

Brady had a flash of memory, bright as the fluorescent-lighted corridor. In it he saw Suze riding around her home arena, bent over her horse's neck like an avenging angel bent on destruction. The moment she'd rushed past him on that hot summer day, something inside him changed. A part of him grabbed that image and held on tight, and he was pretty sure it was his heart.

It sure as heck wasn't his brain, because anybody could see Suze Carlyle was too good for the likes of him. Baggy pants and untucked shirts couldn't hide class and talent.

"What if the right one doesn't even like you?" he asked.

"Then you set your mind to proving her wrong," the woman said. "Show her you're deserving of her respect."

Now that Brady thought about it, he realized he'd never done a danged thing to earn Suze's respect. He'd just kept on being the same empty-headed, charming cowboy he'd always been, and expected her to eventually break down and admit how lovable he was.

"I'll try that." He moved toward the hallway, but the woman looked scared for the first time since he'd seen her.

"Don't go," she said.

He couldn't leave her there alone. She seemed like a nice old lady, with a sort of wisdom about her. He sat down. "How are you feeling?"

"Not so good," she said. "I got a bad heart, and I guess it'll kill me. But it's okay. It's my time. I've done what I needed to do on this earth. It's time to stir up some trouble in heaven."

"I bet you will."

He needed to go find Suze. He needed to go get Speedo. But he couldn't leave this woman, even though she made him uncomfortable. The sharp eyes behind those outlandish glasses saw right through him.

"Young man?" She sat up, popping upright so

suddenly Brady would have fled if she hadn't reached out and grasped his hand in a surprisingly powerful grip. Ranch work made a woman strong as most men, and she'd apparently done her share.

"I need to tell you about dying," she said.

Brady wasn't sure he wanted to know about that particular topic, but she wouldn't let him loose.

"It's not so bad except for the regrets," she said. "And I've only got one." Her voice was a little slurred, as if she was getting sleepy.

"What's that?"

"I wish I hadn't asked that man of mine to clean up before he touched me. Wasted too much time." She lay back down on the bed and the sharp eyes softened. He could see that she'd been beautiful once. Still was, actually.

"Him touching me was the best thing in my life, and I wasted precious moments," she muttered to herself. "Precious, precious moments."

She closed her eyes and seemed to drift into sleep. Her grip on his hand eased, and then she let go altogether. She seemed safe, so Brady pulled the curtain shut as quietly as he could and moved on down the line.

He passed three more empty cubicles before he found Suze. She was either sleeping or unconscious, lying eerily still while a little dark-haired nurse bustled around her, checking various machines that beeped and booped, blinking like sparkling party lights. The lights, along with the noise and bustle, made the cubicle seem strangely festive.

But there was nothing there to celebrate. He'd never seen Suze so pale. All the animation was drained from her face. That was her body, there on the cot. But there wasn't any other sign of the Suze he knew.

He wished to God she'd sit up and yell at him or tease him, or something. Anything—just so he'd know she was still in there.

———

Suze lay as still as she could. There wasn't a single part of her body that didn't hurt, and everything hurt even more if she tried to move.

She'd checked already to make sure she wasn't paralyzed. It had been an agonizing process, wiggling her fingers and toes one by one, turning her head and twitching each arm and each leg. It felt like everything except her head was broken. The doctor had run down the list of injuries, but she couldn't remember what was broken, what was sprained, and what was just torn or bruised.

She couldn't remember how it had happened, either. The last thing she remembered before waking up in the hospital was flying, and that made everything seem like a dream. She'd flown along for quite a while before hitting some kind of obstacle.

And now she was in the hospital, and someone was beside the bed. It was probably her father, and he was probably mad at her. She'd paid entry fees for rodeos from Fort Worth to Billings, but she wouldn't be running barrels for a while. Not like this. Her heart ached as bad as any of her broken parts when she thought of Speedo, of how he'd miss her. She wouldn't be able to work with Bucket, her second-stringer, either.

Worst of all, she'd promised herself this would be Speedo's last rodeo season. He was getting old, and arthritis was taking its toll. She'd need to go to the Finals again to win enough to buy a new horse, and that was probably impossible now. Bucket wasn't ready and probably never would be. He was a good horse, but not a great one.

Now she'd be missing income, and she'd have her own medical bills as well as her father's. She didn't know how she was going to shovel herself out of this hole. She didn't even know how she was going to get Speedo's stall shoveled out. Her dad would have to get out of his chair and miss a few *Bonanza* reruns for a change. He'd never been a horseman, but he was all she had.

Well, it would do him good. But it wouldn't help her any to hear him complain about it. She kept her eyes closed and stayed as quiet as she could.

"I'm so sorry. So sorry. You can't imagine…"

The voice cracked in the middle, and it was so soft she could hardly hear it. It was a male voice, but it didn't sound like her father. For one thing, he wasn't big on apologies.

"You know I'd trade places with you if I could."

It definitely wasn't her father. He'd never volunteer to take on anyone else's pain, either. He was too busy complaining about his own.

Whoever it was reached under the blanket and took her hand.

That settled it. This was definitely not her father. He never touched her if he didn't have to, and she was sure her father's touch wouldn't send swirls of warmth through her veins, swirls that turned into butterflies and hummingbirds that fluttered in her heart—and down below too.

Maybe it was a doctor. A sexy doctor who would fall in love with her, marry her, and solve all her problems while he patched her up good as new.

"Oh God, even your fingers got hurt."

She snuck one eye open just the slightest bit, hoping to catch a glimpse of her visitor without giving herself away. But he was sitting slumped in the chair, his head bowed, and without a better angle, she couldn't really tell who it was. He had nice brown hair, though, thick with just a touch of sun-kissed gold.

She doubted he was a doctor. If a doctor got that upset about somebody's fingers being hurt, he'd never make it through the day—especially during rodeo season, when the doctors here had to glue the cowboys back together after they'd been taken apart by the bucking bulls.

She closed her eyes and enjoyed the feeling of the gentle hand holding hers. Maybe she had a boyfriend and the knock on the head had made her forget. She tried to remember if she'd kissed anybody lately, but the only man she could think of was Brady Caine, and you'd never get Brady inside a hospital. The nurses might tempt him, but hospitals weren't fun, and they didn't sell beer.

"It'll probably be a while before you can do much." The voice had a tremble in it now. "A long while. I'm promising you, Suze, I'll work for you every day. Day and night, if you need me, until you're back the way you were. Back in the saddle, okay? This was my fault, and I'm going to make it right."

She edged her eye open again just as her visitor looked up.

It *was* Brady Caine.

She must be dreaming.

"You can depend on me, Suze."

She closed her eye, praying he hadn't seen that she was awake and trying not to laugh. Because what a bunch of bull that was. Nobody could ever depend on Brady Caine.

Now he'd stood up, and he was stroking her hair. *Stroking her hair.* The last time he'd stroked her hair...

She felt herself blush despite the pain.

"How's she doing?"

That was a new voice.

"I don't know, Doc. She looks kind of pale."

Another hand held hers, feeling her pulse. No butterflies, no hummingbirds. Why couldn't the doctor make her feel those things, instead of Brady? She didn't want anything to do with Brady's butterflies, or his hummingbirds either. They were probably carnivorous or something.

"Tell me again what happened," the doctor said.

Brady launched into a horrific story where, for some stupid reason, he'd roped her and pulled her off her horse, flinging her into a chute gate.

That's what had happened?

She was starting to remember now. The strangest pictures flashed through her mind. A candy wrapper fluttering in the weeds at the edge of an empty arena. Brady playing *Hi-ho, Silver* on some crazy horse. An Arabian.

That couldn't be right. Brady wouldn't be caught dead on an Arabian. She must have been dreaming about that part. It was a really weird dream. She remembered getting made up, looking in the mirror and seeing her mother staring back.

Or had that really happened? It felt like one of those memories that was etched so deeply you knew you'd never forget that flash of a moment, what you saw, what you felt.

So part of this was a dream, and part was real. She needed to figure out what was what, but from what he was saying, one thing was for sure: Brady Caine had gone and ruined her life again.

Damn it, he did that every time he came near her. That night in the trailer—he'd stolen her heart, and for a few happy moments she'd believed in him. Believed he'd cared, believed he'd told the truth, believed he'd wanted her for more than one night.

In the morning, reality had returned, and she and Dooley had watched him walk away. But it had been a hard dream to let go of, and her heart still hadn't recovered.

And now...

She sat up, which just about killed her. Forty-'leven different bones and joints screamed out in agony, but she set her jaw and didn't make a sound until she could see eye to eye with Brady.

All the pain was worth it to see his tanned face turn white.

"Suze," he said. "You're—"

"I'm damn near killed," she said. "Get the hell out of here, Brady. And don't ever, ever come near me again."

Chapter 22

BRADY STEERED HIS TRUCK DOWN THE ENDLESS RAMPS of the hospital parking garage. He'd had to park at the top, which meant the cab was hot enough to bake biscuits, and he'd had to put his bronc saddle in the cab, so it smelled like horses, arena dirt, and sweat.

Following Shane's orders, he stopped at the ranch and picked up Ridge on the way to the rodeo grounds. The two of them hooked up a horse trailer and hit the road to rescue Suze's horse.

"So old Speedo gave you trouble?" Brady asked.

"Sure did." Ridge shook his head. "That horse was riled up like a bronc in a chute. It was all I could do to get him into a stall. And that critter of Justin's?" He shook his head. "That horse needs psychotherapy. Bad. I hope Justin's picking him up himself."

"He probably already did," Brady said. "How'd you know to get 'em, anyway?"

"I didn't. Stan called and told me what happened, so I went to the rodeo grounds while Shane hit the hospital. He guessed right, I guess. By the time I got to the arena, you were gone, and Stan was trying to deal with two crazy horses. That guy doesn't know the front end of a horse from the back, does he?"

Brady almost laughed. "No, he doesn't."

"Anyway, taking care of the horses seemed like the only way to help."

"Well, it's a good thing. I was so worried about Suze I forgot all about 'em." Brady drove along in silence for a while, his eyes on the road, his mind on Suze.

Ridge gave him a speculative glance. "You're beating yourself up about this, aren't you?"

"Wouldn't you?"

"Probably. But I'd be wrong. It wasn't your fault, little brother. From what I heard, the whole thing was Stan's idea. Suze can probably sue Lariat for everything they've got."

Brady felt himself go pale. "It wasn't Stan's fault. Wasn't anybody's. We all agreed on what we'd do."

"There." Ridge sat back, satisfied as if he'd solved all the world's problems. "You said it yourself. It wasn't anybody's fault."

"But I held on to the rope," Brady said. "Booger blew up, and I forgot about the rope. I held on a second too long, and it pulled her out of the saddle."

"Booger?"

"Justin's horse. His little sister's horse, actually. That was my first mistake. I never should have used that horse."

Ridge didn't speak for the rest of the ride. He was always quiet, and not much for small talk, but Brady knew there was another reason for his silence. He probably hadn't heard the whole story until now. Now that he knew Brady really was at fault, he didn't know what to say.

The rodeo grounds stood empty in the summer sun, though Brady would have sworn he could hear the roar of past crowds riding the wind as they headed for the area where contestants kept their horses.

"Shoot." Ridge rubbed the back of his neck, tilting his hat forward. "I could've sworn this was the stall."

"Hope you didn't lose him," Brady joked. "Hard to misplace a sixty-thousand-dollar horse."

"He must be around the other side."

They walked past the row of empty stalls and down the next row that backed up against them.

No Speedo.

They backtracked to the first row of stalls. Nothing had changed. No horses occupied the rough wooden enclosures.

Brady had never noticed how quiet a Wyoming summer day could be. A few grasshoppers clicked in the grass, and a few crows called in the distance, but other than that, it was him, his brother, and the wind.

"He's not here," Ridge said.

Brady peered into the stall where Ridge said he'd left the horse and felt the bottom drop out of his already shattered world.

"Here's his saddle and blanket," Ridge said. "His bridle. It's definitely the right stall."

The two cowboys stood there in the hot sun, staring at the ground. After a while, Ridge bent over and traced a line in the gravel and dirt with one hand. "If I'm not mistaken, somebody let down a ramp right here." He pointed to a spot just beyond it, where the gravel was heaped in random piles. "And there was a little set-to right there." He stood, brushing the dirt off his hands on his thighs. "Somebody took him."

Brady felt like someone had punched him in the gut. For a moment, he couldn't breathe.

Speedo. Gone. Stolen.

"You think Justin picked him up? Maybe he thought he was doing you a favor."

"Justin's got a one-horse trailer," Brady said. "There's no way he took him." He looked hopelessly up and down the row of stalls, praying that Speedo would miraculously appear. "Why would anyone take him?"

"You said it yourself." Ridge stroked his chin, staring into the empty stall. "That's a sixty-thousand-dollar horse. More, probably. We better hope it was Suze's dad that picked him up, though I don't know how that could've happened. You and me are the only ones that know he was here."

"Apparently not," Brady said. "Somebody else knew." He looked down at the ground, where the signs of a struggle were obvious now that Ridge had pointed them out. "I sure hope it was a friend."

Chapter 23

EARL CARLYLE TOOK A SLOW SIP OF COFFEE AND LET out a satisfied sigh, then lifted his mug in a silent toast to his wife.

"Nothing like a good cuppa joe in the morning," he said. "Isn't that right, Ellen?"

She smiled. She always smiled. She was trapped in a weird smiling limbo, frozen in photographs, forever young, forever happy, forever gone.

Suze's little dog trotted into the kitchen and sat down a few feet away. Earl could tell the dog was staring at him through his curtain of hair.

"Quit looking at me," he said. "I know it's just a picture. But it doesn't hurt anybody for me to pretend a little, does it?"

The dog cocked his head as if he didn't understand.

"You wouldn't get it. You're not human." Earl said. "So go 'way and leave me alone. Damn dog." He turned back to the photo of Ellen he'd propped up in front of his plate. "I tell Suzanne every day how pretty you were. I tell her how smart you were, how successful. She still loves her mama."

He couldn't stop a little bitterness from creeping into his tone. He'd never told his daughter everything about her mother.

There was no reason to. A girl needed a mother she could look up to.

"I did it for you, Ellen." He lifted the cup in another silent toast to the framed photo. "You never asked for anything else."

The truth was, Ellen hadn't needed anything else. She was the most self-possessed, independent person he'd ever known. Some women leaned on a man; some worked side by side in partnership. But Ellen ran on ahead, shouting, "Watch this!"

It had driven him crazy. Women were supposed to be fragile. They were supposed to *need* a man once in a while. But Ellen had never needed him, not a day in her life, until she'd gotten sick. Cancer had destroyed her, bit by bit, and watching her die had just about destroyed him.

He looked down at the dog, who was performing some sort of doggie maintenance on his hindquarters.

"Stop that," Earl said. "Stop it, and tell me what I'm supposed to do about Suzanne."

Dooley stood up, shook himself, and walked away, tossing Earl an aggrieved look. So much for animal wisdom.

Earl knew he'd almost lost his daughter yesterday. She was all he had in the world, and the doctors said she could have died from her head injury. Even now, they didn't know if she'd fully recover.

And yet he felt numb. He knew he ought to be beside her, but he couldn't bear to set foot in that hospital. Ellen had died there, surrounded by machinery, tended to by kind strangers with faces he couldn't recall.

Watch this!

He'd watched her, all right. He'd watched her die, just as he'd watched her live. He was useless as ever while she lay there in that hospital bed.

He was sure Suze understood that he simply couldn't stand to go there. Too many memories.

A rap on the door jolted him out of his reverie. Dooley tore through the hallway and leaped at the door once, twice, three times. The damn dog was made of springs and rubber bands. Bouncing and yapping, yapping and bouncing. When nobody was home to watch him, he jumped up on the kitchen counters and ate anything he could find. Loaves of bread, bags of bagels, packages of Oreos—they all went down Dooley's gullet. And they all came back up later, usually on the furniture.

The dog continued to yap while Earl shoved his chair back from the table. Grunting with effort, he straightened his knees and got his feet working. "I'm coming, I'm coming," he grumbled.

Who the hell came calling this early in the morning? A man didn't even have time for breakfast with his wife before the world came rushing in and ruined everything.

—∿—

Brady stood on the doorstep, waiting for Suze's father to get around to answering the door. His teeth were clenched together so tightly it hurt, and a muscle was twitching in his jaw.

He'd spent hours the night before calling everyone he knew who'd ever had anything to do with the Grigsby rodeo. No one had seen Speedo. Then he tried local cowboys and cowgirls. No luck.

The horse was gone.

What the hell was he going to do? Suze's injuries were nothing compared with losing that horse.

All animals were important to people who cared

about them. All of them had distinct personalities, idiosyncrasies, and, in Brady's opinion, souls. But some were more special than others. Speedo was one of those—the horse of a lifetime. For Suze, he was more than a pet, more than a partner. He was her soul mate. Half of her heart.

Somehow, Brady would have to find the horse. And somehow, he'd have to hide the problem from Suze until he did. He had a trusted team of cowboys and cowgirls in three counties looking for Speedo. With a distinctive heart-shaped blaze on his face, he'd be hard to hide.

Meanwhile, Brady wasn't leaving anything else to chance. Suze might want him to stay away, but he'd headed for the hospital next and discovered no one had been to see her since she'd thrown him out the previous afternoon. No one had been there to answer the doctors' questions about her past health issues. No one had sat by her bed, held her hand, soothed her pain, distracted her with jokes, or cared for her. No one had brought her magazines to read or clothes to wear. Nobody. She'd lain there, forgotten and abandoned and probably in pain, all night. Alone.

He knew her father had been notified. The old bastard just hadn't bothered to go.

Brady slammed his fist into the door again. Earl Carlyle would hurry if he knew what was good for him, because the longer Brady waited, the hotter his rage burned. When the door finally opened, he had to consciously take in a few slow breaths so he wouldn't use that same fist to smash in the man's face.

Looking at Earl Carlyle, he realized it wasn't worth it. The man looked like a plant that had gone too long without water. His posture was bent from arthritis and his face was lined by sorrow; his eyes drooped, and the corners of his mouth turned down in a permanent frown. His hair, still dark, was sparse, and his efforts to combat encroaching baldness with a comb-over were futile.

Maybe it wasn't water Earl needed; maybe it was fertilizer. Maybe he needed someone like Brady to give him some shit about how he treated his daughter.

Through clenched teeth, Brady asked, "What are you doing, Earl?"

"Having breakfast with my—having breakfast." The old man lifted his chin, asserting some dignity. "Not that it's any of your business."

Behind him, Suze's little dog was bouncing like a kid on a pogo stick. The old man started to swing the door shut, but Brady smacked his open palm against the wood and shot the man a look that would freeze a bird in midflight.

"You going to see your daughter after breakfast?"

"None of your business."

Dooley rushed out the open door and circled Brady, yapping like he was possessed. Brady knelt and petted him, but nothing quieted the dog until he picked him up.

"You fed her horses yet?" Brady knew the answer to this one. If Earl had been out to the barn, he would have realized Speedo was missing, and he'd be in a panic—not because he cared about the animal, but because the horse was worth money.

"I'll feed 'em when I'm ready. And those are my horses much as hers, young man."

Brady narrowed his eyes, but it was hard to look

tough when you were holding a hairy little mutt in your arms. "When's the last time you had anything to do with 'em?"

Earl turned away, grumbling something about them reminding him of his wife. That was his answer for everything. Supposedly he'd been crazy in love with Suze's mother, but the way he shied away from anything that reminded him of her, you'd think the time he'd spent with her had been the worst years of his life, a trauma he couldn't bear to think of.

No doubt her illness and death had been just that—a trauma. But from what Brady had heard, Ellen Carlyle had only lived a few months after the diagnosis, so it wasn't as if she'd lingered for years. They'd had plenty of happy times on horseback, and you'd think he'd want to remember those.

"I've got Speedo at my place," Brady said. The lie almost choked him, but it had to be told. Brady would get the police involved if the horse didn't turn up soon, but for now he was doing his own detective work. "Tell you what." He stepped into the house past the old man without asking for permission, shedding his Carhartt jacket and hanging it on a hook beside the door. The rising sun was beginning to warm the Wyoming plains and gild the grass with gold, but that wasn't why he hung up his coat. He was staking his claim, letting Earl Carlyle know that he'd come to stay.

Glancing around the house, he saw chaos—dirty dishes stacked high in the sink; floors smudged and dirty; junk on the stairs that looked like it had been dropped midclimb. He knew Suze wasn't home much, and no wonder. He'd seen how neat she kept her trailer, and doubted she could stand to live in the pigpen her home had become.

It would have to be cleaned up before she came home, that was for sure. It would probably be a long time before she could climb stairs, but still, all those tripping hazards should be cleaned off the steps. And the dishes needed to be washed, and the floors mopped.

Looking at Earl, Brady had a sinking feeling he knew who was going to get stuck doing all that housework. He might as well buy an apron and a stock of Swiffer refills right now.

Maybe he could let the dog mop the floor. Dooley looked like a mop, after all. But he probably shed more hair than he picked up.

"You got a sister, Earl?"

"Nope. Only family I had was my wife," Earl said.

"And your daughter."

The old man didn't respond, just stared at Brady. "What do you want, son?"

"I'm not your son," Brady said. "But I tell you what. I'll take care of the animals so you can go see your daughter."

Earl looked at him from under heavy brows. He'd reached that point in old age where men's eyebrows went all wild and scraggly.

"Don't tell me what to do," he said.

Brady felt a stab of compassion for Suze, even beyond what he'd felt at the hospital. How did she live with this day after day? Her injuries were a temporary condition, but she'd dealt with her father all her life. Surely there was some way to make the man see what he was doing to the one person he had left to love.

"You know what she's feeding the horses these days?"

"Hay, I s'pose."

Brady wanted to wipe the smug smile off Earl's face. "Supplements? Grain? Anything?"

Earl shrugged. Disgusted, Brady left him standing in the hallway and headed for the barn, slamming the door behind him.

Once he'd entered the shadowy realm of the barn, Brady's anger faded. This was his world even more than the rodeo ring. He'd loved barns from the first day he'd arrived at Decker Ranch. The rough-hewn wood, the smudged windowpanes draped with cobwebs, the high hayloft where a boy could sit and dream in the sweet-scented dark—the barn at Decker Ranch was a cathedral to him, a symbol of the new life he'd been granted when the Deckers had found him and his brothers and given them a home. Somehow, all barns had taken on that same spirit for him. They calmed his soul.

He could hear Suze's backup horse, Bucket, stamping with impatience. Apparently the only thing that would calm *his* soul was breakfast.

He was probably lonesome too. Horses were herd animals, and they needed company. With Speedo gone, there was a good chance Bucket would go off his feed.

"Bucket." He kept his voice low and soothing. "'Bout time to eat, isn't it, boy?"

He put a few flakes of hay in the horse's net, then rinsed and filled the water buckets at the outside tap. He noticed Earl Carlyle's car was still in the drive, and he could hear the squawk of a television drifting from the house. Breakfast was over, but there was no telling when visiting hours at the hospital would start. Or if they'd ever start for Earl.

Brady hung the water bucket back in Bucket's stall and found a well-stocked tack room at the back of the barn. It boasted an entire wall devoted to plastic bins that held grain and supplements, and above them was a whiteboard, the kind you saw in corporate board-rooms. Suze had inked each horse's proper ration under its name.

Now why couldn't Earl Carlyle have told him that? Did he not know? Did he *never* come out here?

Brady hung around until Bucket was finished with his breakfast, biding his time by restocking the stack of hay bales Suze kept near the horse's stalls. Tossing the big bales from the loft and lugging them into the alleyway helped him work up a healthy sweat—always a good way to start the day, in his opinion. As he took off his hat and wiped his brow, he admired the tidiness of the barn. He'd have to work hard to keep the place up to Suze's standards, but he was determined to do the job right.

He turned Bucket out into a small corral beside the barn and leaned on the gate for a while, chewing a green stalk of timothy and watching the horse relax in the morning sun. It was hard to think of Suze spending this blue-sky day trapped in the fake fluorescent lights of the hospital.

But maybe it would be a good day for her, in a way. Maybe once her father saw his only child there, so small and frail among the lifesaving machinery, he'd find the heart he'd mislaid when his wife had died. Maybe the two of them would talk—really talk. That could make this all worthwhile for Suze.

Aw, who was he kidding? That kind of thinking might make him feel better, but there was nothing good about the accident, and wishing wouldn't make it so.

Besides, Earl Carlyle's truck was still in the driveway.

Chapter 24

Suze woke reluctantly to the poking and prodding of a nurse who said she was "taking her vitals."

Yeah, she was taking her vitals, all right. *Sleep* was vital, and the nurse was taking it *away*.

Suze took some medication and said she felt okay, which was a lie. When the nurse left, she lay in the half dark, listening to the sounds of the hospital waking up—a faint blend of voices from the nurse's station down the hall; the soft squeak of nurse's shoes up and down the hallway; her own breathing, steady and slow but ragged with pain.

She stared up at the ceiling. She hated sleeping on her back, but with all the tubes coming out of her arms and the bulky brace around her neck, it was the only choice she had. They'd said the neck brace was a precaution, as she hadn't actually broken anything there. She felt like she'd been put through a meat grinder and pounded into patties, but they said her injuries were mostly sprains, strains, and torn ligaments. The only thing broken was one foot, her wrist, and some fingers. Her ankle was sprained, but that wouldn't be a problem. She'd be back in the saddle in no time.

She flicked through all the television stations, but she hated *SpongeBob SquarePants* and wasn't too fond of the Kardashians, either. For a while, she watched a mixed martial arts fight on Spike TV. The fighters were women, and she settled on that. Maybe she'd pick up some tips to use when she got a chance to beat the crap out of Brady Caine.

—⁂—

Brady finished with the horses and looked around the Carlyle place for something else to do. He'd go hunt for Speedo if he had any idea where to look, but he'd have to count on the cowboy network for that. Meanwhile, he'd lose his mind if he didn't get busy.

If Earl didn't go to see his daughter, he'd lose his temper. Or, more likely, he'd go to the hospital himself. Suze had made it clear to Brady that she wanted him to leave her alone, but he'd tried that once before, after the night of heaven they'd spent together. He'd regretted it ever since.

With age had come wisdom, and he realized now that she'd completely misunderstood his reason for leaving. She thought he'd gotten what he wanted and didn't care about her anymore. She thought she was nothing more than a notch on a bedpost.

He wasn't sure where she fit into his life, but she was more than that. She'd burrowed deep into his subconscious from the moment he'd first seen her.

He leaned against the hitching post in the sun, watching the house for signs of life and pondering the fact that this was his one chance to show Suze he was something more than some jerk who lured women into bed and then walked away.

The sun felt good on his face, and he could smell sage on the breeze that stroked his cheek. There were acres of wild country beyond the Carlyle house, acres that had never been tamed. It would have been better for Earl Carlyle if it had all been cleared and turned to pasture, but Brady loved the wildness of it, the toughness of the rocky land and the twisted trees that managed to grow from the sandy soil. Oddly enough, the trees reminded him of Earl. There was a toughness about the old man that made it seem like he could survive anything. So why was he so weak in the face of his grief?

Brady plucked a daisy from the tangle of flowers that grew alongside the fence. It was wildflower season, and there was a festival of color hidden in the tall grass. Asters showed their shy faces in the shady spots, while dame's rocket grew even where the sun had baked the soil brick hard.

This was Suze's world, when she wasn't on the road. Every morning and every evening, she smelled this sweet-scented air and listened to the grasshoppers clicking in the tall grass. She carried buckets to the rusty faucet by the barn and checked the fence along the weedy pasture.

He looked down at the daisy smiling up from his work-worn hand. It didn't look like Earl was going to go anywhere today, and Suze wouldn't be happy to see Brady arrive in his place. But she might welcome a little piece of her ranch, since she was trapped in the sterile world of the hospital. Those harsh white lights, the gleaming linoleum floors—it was all so artificial.

Half an hour later, he had a healthy fistful of wildflowers picked, and they were even arranged in some sort of order, with the little ones around the edge and the big, showy ones dead center. He found a length of twine in the barn and wrapped it around them, then fumbled the ends into a sloppy bow with his big, clumsy fingers.

Pleased with his work, he climbed in his truck and did a quick and very noisy K-turn in the turnout, raising as much of a dust cloud as he could. As he sped down the drive, he could see the dust billowing up behind him. He pictured it settling on Earl Carlyle's shiny pickup and smiled at the thought of the old man cussing up a storm while he cleaned off his vehicle.

Hell, Earl probably wouldn't bother. The old man was such a do-nothing stick-in-the-mud, he'd probably leave the dust. Brady was surprised there wasn't a layer of it on the man himself.

———~~~———

"Well, look at the pretty flowers. Are those for me?"

The woman manning the nurse's station on Suze's floor was just pretty enough to make Brady stammer, and he felt his face flush even as a response rose to his lips.

"If I'd known you were here, I would have picked more, ma'am."

The nurse laughed. "You were doing okay until you called me ma'am."

"Sorry, ma'am." Now he was really blushing.

An older nurse behind the counter shot him an appraising glance over the wire-rimmed reading glasses perched on the end of her nose. When she spotted the flowers, she broke into a smile wreathed in wrinkles.

"Well, who are those for, young man?"

"Um, Suze Carlyle?"

"Oh, that poor girl. She's in room 320," the older

nurse said. "But, Charlotte, why don't you find something he can put them in? He doesn't get them in water, those flowers won't last an hour."

"I guess I should have thought of that," he said.

The younger nurse—the one he'd called ma'am— examined the bouquet, touching a daisy at the edge that already showed signs of wilting.

"We've got some vases in the break room," she said. "People are always leaving them behind. Come on, we'll find something."

Two more nurses were in the break room, finishing up early lunches or a midmorning snack. Brady was touched by their determination to make sure Suze received a proper bouquet. They searched the top cabinets over the room's small sink and microwave, putting half a dozen vases on the counter for him to choose from.

"I think that one," Brady said, pointing to a simple but graceful vase of clear glass.

"But what about this?" One of the women turned around with a cobalt-blue number in her hands and displayed it with all the grace of a game-show hostess. "This would show off the blue in those asters."

The discussion went on, with Brady patiently clutching his bouquet. He might get on well with women, but he never felt like he truly understood them. To him, any of the vases would have been fine, but if these women thought it was important, Suze might think so too. Although she was the least girlie woman Brady knew.

They finally settled on the clear vase he'd chosen originally. With much fussing and a little fighting, it was filled with water. The baling twine was untied, and the flower arranging symposium began, dominated by the first nurse he'd spoken to. In her teddy bear scrubs, with her perky ponytail bobbing with every move, she reminded him of a kindergarten teacher.

"Did you pick these?" she asked.

He nodded. "Sure did. From her pasture. I thought she'd like a little bit of home."

"Did you hear that?" She fairly squealed the words to the others. "He picked them himself. Said she'd like a little bit of home."

The older nurse beamed at him. She had a nice, honest face, and a wide smile that made him feel blessed somehow.

"That *is* sweet," she said. "My Harley thinks a dozen red roses is all a woman wants. I appreciate it, but I wish he'd put more thought into it."

Brady hated to think he'd got Harley into any kind of trouble. "He's probably a hard worker, though," he said. "It's hard for a working man to find time for picking flowers. I'm just a saddle-tramp rodeo bum, so it's easy for me."

She beamed again, and he thought Harley might get lucky tonight.

"I knew it." The teddy-bear nurse had thin, artistic fingers that deftly arranged the flowers into a shapely bouquet. "I knew you were a real cowboy. I told Alice. Didn't I, Alice?"

Another nurse, dressed head to toe in *Toy Story* characters, nodded agreement. "You called it, Annie."

Annie handed Brady the vase. It looked like a bouquet from the best florist in town. She gestured with the baling twine and he held out the vase. Carefully, she retied it around the outside of the arrangement, finishing it off with a perfect, multilooped bow that added just the right rustic touch. Brady hadn't realized how crude the original bouquet was. This was more the effect he'd been going for.

"Where'd you learn to make 'em look so pretty?"

"I don't know." She shrugged and gave him a shy, sideways glance. "I just like doing stuff like this."

"Well, you're good at it. Thank you."

She smiled at him, her face suffused with a very becoming blush. "You're welcome."

Aw, shoot. Things were starting to feel uncomfortable. She was a nice girl, but Brady wasn't looking for a girlfriend, that was for sure. He had more important things to do.

Like finding a missing horse.

"Are you a friend of Suzanne's?" she asked.

"You'd have to ask her about that. I suspect she'd say no right now, but I've always thought of us as friends."

"*Just* friends?"

He looked down at the shiny white floor and thought about lying, just to keep himself out of hot water. But as he stared down at the nurse's hot pink Crocs, he knew the lie would follow him into Suze's hospital room and make all kinds of trouble. He shook his head.

"Just friends," he said. "Suze wouldn't have it any other way."

"Oh." She thought a moment. "Would you?"

Brady was surprised at the answer that rose to his lips. "Yeah." He looked her full in the face and smiled. "Yeah, I would." He looked at the other nurse, the one who wanted wildflowers from her Harley. "Room 320, you said?"

She nodded, and Brady headed down the hallway. When he reached room 320, he paused, sucking in a deep breath. Oxygen gave you energy; deep breathing was calming. And he had a feeling he'd need all the energy and calm he could muster to face Suze.

Chapter 25

SUZE LOOKED LONGINGLY AT THE PLASTIC PITCHER beside her bed. She'd tried to manage a drink of water on her own, but her splinted wrist wasn't strong enough to hold the mug and she ended up pouring half a cup into her lap. She wished a nurse would come and check on her. She'd dropped the call button while she was trying to pour the water. You'd think they'd notice she was kind of quiet, but they probably thought she was asleep.

Like that was going to happen. She'd spent the night racked with pain, relieved only by ibuprofen. She'd refused the stronger drugs the nurses offered; she kept her body clean and never took anything stronger than an aspirin. She was starting to reconsider that policy as she lay in bed throbbing from head to toe, her only entertainment the sharp pains that sped through her nerves to emerge in various locations—her wrist, her knee, her neck, her ankle, her foot.

Where was the doctor? Weren't they supposed to do rounds in the morning and check on their patients? They did on *Grey's Anatomy*. Maybe Dr. McDreamy would show up and ease her pain with his sympathetic eyes and perfect hair.

Yeah, right.

She didn't want a doctor anyway, or even a nurse.

She wanted her dad.

She felt tears rising, threatening to overflow, and

blinked them away. It was okay to cry from the pain, but tears of self-pity were not allowed. Not in her world.

When she finally heard footsteps outside her room, she smoothed her hair, grateful for any kind of distraction. She'd been flicking channels all morning, restlessly rotating through inane cartoons and even more inane reality shows. She'd tried a news channel, but it was even worse, with talking heads screaming at each other about food stamps and farm subsidies.

She was expecting a nurse to take her vitals again or maybe, just maybe, her father. So she was stunned into silence when Brady entered, followed by the floor's entire nursing staff.

Funny, *he* didn't have any trouble getting a nurse to help him.

"Hey." He set a vase full of flowers on the table beside her bed and sat down in the plastic chair provided for visitors. "Thought you might like a little bit of home."

She wanted to tell him to get out of her room. The whole incident in the rodeo arena had come back to her now, and she knew it was Brady who'd landed her in the hospital. She might have urged him, even dared him, to do the stunt, but he was the one who'd held on to the rope a second too long. If he couldn't do it right, he should have said so.

She wanted to tell him she never wanted to see him again. She wanted to ask him how he had the nerve to come here after what had happened, and she wanted to grab that vase of flowers and throw it at him, water and all. But she couldn't throw anything at him with all the nurses watching, their hands held prayerfully together as though they expected some romantic scene to play out.

So she burst into tears.

It must have been something they put in her IV, because Suze was *not* a crier, and these were big, fat, hot tears that wouldn't stop no matter how much she hiccuped and swallowed and choked. Huge sobs wracked her chest, making her bruised ribs ache. She hated herself for them. Her dad said tears were for sissies, and she was *not* a sissy.

So how could she cry in front of Brady Caine, of all people? Literally, figuratively, every way you looked at it, Brady had bashed her to bits. He'd broken her heart and bruised her body. It was hard to face him laid out in a hospital bed, helpless as a newborn calf. It was even worse to have to lie there and mop her streaming eyes while he handed her tissues.

She finally got ahold of herself and sniffed, then wiped her nose on the arm of her hospital gown. Now *that* was attractive.

The gaggle of nurses that had followed Brady into the room finally figured out they weren't going to get the warm fuzzies they were hoping for and left.

Suze plucked self-consciously at the neck of her hospital gown. The thing was hideously uncomfortable and the ultimate enemy to modesty. Half the time it gaped in the worst possible places, and the rest of the time it wrapped around her like a mummy's shroud and wouldn't let her move. The ties at the back kept coming undone, and she couldn't tie them herself, so right now she was barely covered. If it weren't for the sheet, she'd be practically naked.

Why were hospitals so determined to make you feel helpless? Weren't they supposed to make you feel *better*?

She let out a particularly loud and unfeminine *honk* into one of the tissues Brady had handed her and shot him a glare, daring him to comment. He smiled gently, his brown eyes soft and caring, and she hated him even more for being the only person she could ask for help.

"Could you do something for me?" she asked. Crying had stuffed up her nose and it came out "subthing."

"I'd do just about anything for you," he said.

The nurses had apparently left the room, but she could swear she heard a collective sigh coming from the hallway. Yeah, they thought it was all romantic that he'd said that. But they didn't know what he'd done. They didn't know he was the reason she was here.

"Go to my house and ask my dad to pack up some of my clothes, okay? And maybe some shampoo. I don't like the kind they have here."

"I can go get it for you."

Right. That was all she needed—Brady Caine going through her panty drawer.

"No. Just ask my dad."

"Okay."

"And tell him to bring them here, okay? You don't need to be running back and forth. My dad and I can take care of ourselves."

He paused, as if he had something difficult to say, but then he just nodded. "Okay."

She looked back at the TV and flicked the channel, then stared up at a reality show as if Khloé and Kourtney held the keys to the universe. She had the sound down on the TV, so the room was quiet except for the hum of the machines that were keeping track of her heartbeats or whatever.

Brady didn't seem to mind being ignored. He just sat there with his dirty old hat in his lap and watched her like she was some kind of exotic bird. His pose was relaxed, his eyes bright and interested. She'd have thought he didn't care about anything if it wasn't for the way he twisted the hat in his hands, rotating it around and around.

"How's Speedo?" she asked.

"Fine." He spun the hat faster. "He misses you. So does Bucket."

"I know." She thought of her horses and wished she could somehow teleport herself to the corral outside the barn. She'd lean against Speedo's solid side, resting her head on his sun-warmed fur, breathing in his musky scent.

"I'll take care of 'em," Brady said.

She must look terrible. He was too polite to look at her bruised face, and spoke to the wall beside her. She nodded, swallowing hard. Her throat still ached, as if she was going to cry again.

She was *not* going to cry again.

A sudden thought struck her, and she forgot about the pain. "You didn't put Bucket in the big pasture, did you?"

"Nope. He tried to convince me that was where he was supposed to go, but I knew he was lying. Judging from what you're feeding him, that grass is way too rich for him. I put him in that little corral beside the barn."

She almost smiled at that. He was right. Bucket was an incorrigible liar. Whenever she took him on the road, he'd lean out of the trailer and try to convince passersby they should feed him all kinds of terrible things, like ice cream and beer and French fries. When he didn't want to work, he'd fake lameness so convincingly that she once took him to the vet for nothing.

She reached over and touched the flowers, feeling the warmth of her home pasture lingering on the blooms.

"Those are actually from the horses," he said. "Bucket helped me pick 'em this morning, from around the outside of the corral."

She knew he wasn't making that up. Bucket would have followed him all around the corral, getting in the way, while Speedo would have kept his distance and his dignity by watching from the shade under the cottonwoods.

The tears were coming dangerously close to the surface. She'd give anything to rest her face against Speedo's warm neck and tangle her fingers in that platinum mane he was so famous for. She missed silly, affectionate Bucket too, and the cool patch of grass under the tree in the pasture, and the peace of the dimly lit barn. She didn't know if the scent of the flowers was making her homesickness better or worse.

She also didn't know how she'd manage to take care of her horses if she ended up in the hospital for long. Both of them needed to be worked, or they'd lose condition. And her father hadn't done that kind of thing since last year, when she'd won her second championship. Maybe he figured she ought to be able to do everything herself now that she was a two-time champ.

Not that that made any sense.

She'd have to hire somebody. But who? And with what? All her winnings went toward the mortgage and her dad's medical bills. If she hired someone to help with the ranch, she'd probably end up going broke and losing it.

Losing the ranch her mother had picked out was unthinkable. Her father had told her over and over how he'd thought the house was too old, the land too rough, but Suze's mom had fallen in love with it and had to have it. That made it sacred ground for Suze.

She felt a tear slipping down her cheek and dashed it away.

"I'll bring you some clothes, then, or send 'em with your dad," Brady said. "You want some magazines to read?"

She nodded, biting her lip. She wanted to tell him to leave her alone, but nobody else was volunteering to help her. Apparently the man who'd put her in the hospital with all these injuries was the best friend she had right now.

How pathetic was that?

Brady left Suze's room an hour later. She'd finally fallen asleep, but he'd sat there awhile, wishing he could somehow trade places with her. It would have been kind of funny if Suze had roped him and dragged him off his horse. His brothers would take care of him, and his only trouble would be the teasing he'd have to endure.

He plucked a daisy from the flower bouquet and laid it on her pillow as he left, hoping the little reminder of summer sunshine would be the first thing she'd see when she opened her eyes.

He paused as he passed the nurses' station and tipped his hat to the little nurse who'd been so eager to help him with the flowers. The manners Bill Decker had drilled into him wouldn't let him leave without thanking her, but he planned to skedaddle as soon as he'd said the words. He didn't want to discuss how Suze had welcomed him—or rather, failed to welcome him.

"Thanks for your help," he said. "I sure appreciate it."

"*She* didn't seem to appreciate it."

"Sure she did. She just isn't feeling good."

"Well, I thought she should have been nicer to you."

There was an undercurrent beneath her words that made Brady uncomfortable. He wondered where the other nurses had gone. First there was a whole herd of 'em, and now there was nobody else around.

He wondered if they'd done it on purpose. He'd noticed women could be sneaky that way.

He rested his forearms on the counter, folding his work-roughened hands together. These women had the power to make Suze's life miserable. He had to set the record straight.

"I'm surprised she'll talk to me at all," he said. "I'm the reason she's here. There was an accident, and I screwed up and got her hurt. So if she's not nice to me, it doesn't mean she's not a nice person. It's just what I deserve."

"Oh." The little nurse still looked at him like he had a halo on instead of a cowboy hat. He hated that. It was so hard to convince some of these girls that he wasn't who they thought he was. All those romance books and Wild

West movies made rodeo cowboys seem wild and glamorous, when really he was a bum who barely worked for a living and spent half his spare time in bars and the other half in bed with women he barely knew. He was no hero, and this girl needed to know it.

"I lassoed her and pulled her off her horse," he said, his eyes steady on hers. "I didn't let go of the rope in time and she got flung into a gate. She could have died because I messed around and screwed up. I've been a cowboy all my life. I know better, but I was trying to prove something."

She glanced away, and he waited until she looked back at him before he said more.

"That's why she doesn't want to see me or talk to me. Got it?"

The nurse nodded. Her eyes were wide now but a little less warm. *Mission accomplished.*

He stepped back shoving his hands in his pockets.

"You'll take care of her, won't you?"

She nodded.

"Good care?"

She cleared her throat. Evidently his admission had shocked the voice right out of her.

"Sure," she finally said. "We'll take the best care of her we can."

"She's not always easy," he said. "But she's got good reasons to be tough, and underneath it all she's—well, she's a sweetheart." He glanced around, as if listeners might be lurking in the hallways. "Just for God's sake don't tell her I said that."

Chapter 26

BRADY GOT BACK TO THE CARLYLE RANCH WELL AFTER lunchtime, but nothing had changed. Earl's truck still sat in the driveway. Standing at the front door, Brady could hear the television running.

He didn't bother to knock this time, just walked in, passing through the cluttered sun porch and into the front hall. Earl, alarmed, almost got out of his chair when Brady walked into the living room.

Almost.

"Suze needs some clothes and things packed up," Brady said. "She needs you to bring 'em to her soon as you can."

He needed to get Earl moving. Once he knew someone was taking care of Suze, he could start the search for Speedo in earnest. Anybody who owned a horse trailer and knew the way to the rodeo grounds knew how famous Speedo was, so they probably had the horse hidden somewhere. He planned to check a few abandoned barns in the area.

If that didn't work, he'd do some networking in the cowboy bars and tack shops. That would get the word out. Sooner or later, Suze would find out he'd been lying to her, and that Speedo was gone, maybe for good.

He didn't even want to think about how much that would hurt her.

Earl still had his eyes glued to the television. He seemed determined to ignore Brady, who sighed and headed for the kitchen. Lifting the dirty dishes out of the sink, he squirted in some dishwashing soap and started the hot water.

"She's there in the hospital with nothing but one of those cotton gowns they give you," he called to Earl. "You know, the ones that open in the back."

Earl didn't respond. Brady shut off the tap and tossed an assortment of glasses into the water. Glasses, then silverware, then plates, then cookware. That's what Irene Decker had taught him.

"Do you want to know how she's doing?" he asked Earl.

"I know how she's doing." Brady could barely hear the old man's mumble.

"How?" Brady scrubbed at a glass with a sponge. "Did you call?"

"Didn't have to," Earl said. "You just told me she asked for her clothes. Guess it can't be too bad."

Brady set the glass down and rested his hands on the counter, breathing hard and deep. He'd had bronc rides that were a Sunday drive compared to a conversation with Earl Carlyle.

Rinsing the glass and placing it in the dish drainer, he headed back to the living room. "You want me to go up and pack your daughter's skivvies for her?" He took another step into the room. "You want me going through her things? Because I can tell you one thing: she doesn't want me doing it."

Earl just waved him away.

Brady couldn't help himself. He strode in and flicked

off the TV. Standing in front of it with his arms crossed, he tried again.

"I'm going to be going through her underwear, Earl. Her bras and panties. Private stuff."

"I don't want to go through them any more than you do." Earl picked up the remote and turned the television back on as if the matter was settled. Brady wanted to rip the remote out of Earl's hand and smash it on his hard old head, but instead he leaned over and unplugged the set.

"What the hell's the matter with you? How can you sit there in your damn chair and sulk while your daughter suffers? Your wife's gone. I'm sorry. I'm sure it was a terrible loss. But she left you a beautiful daughter who needs you."

"I've done enough for that girl. I've given her a good home."

Brady spun toward the stairs so fast he never knew for sure if he kicked out on purpose, but his boot hit the wall hard enough to hurt. He hauled himself halfway up the stairs before he turned to see if his words had had any effect.

Earl had apparently plugged in the TV, because he was sitting placidly in his chair, engrossed in some old Western as if nothing had happened.

Sighing, Brady started up the rest of the stairs. He knew Earl wasn't entirely to blame for his attitude. Folks said Ellen's death hadn't just broken his heart; it had caused it to wither up and die. Some people grieve a long time, but Earl wasn't really grieving anymore. It was more like he'd died when his wife did and was just waiting for somebody to haul him off and bury him beside her.

The stairway wall was lined with pictures of Ellen, arranged so that climbing the steps was like watching her life run backward. At the bottom were pictures from just before she died. There were photos of her rounding the barrels on her famous horse, Tango, and photos of her in full parade dress. There was even a picture of her riding side by side with six-year-old Suze.

As Brady climbed, Ellen got younger. Suze appeared in one picture as a toddler, but then she disappeared and it was all about Ellen. Ellen and Tango, running the barrels at dozens of rodeos, in dozens of towns all over the West.

When he got to the top, it was like going full circle. There was Ellen as a six-year-old, already running barrels; Ellen as a toddler on the saddle of a handsome quarter horse; and Ellen as a baby in her own mother's loving arms.

He couldn't help thinking those pictures should have been of Suze. She was every bit as accomplished as her mother, yet the only picture of her was one where her mom was also present. It seemed backward for a parent to be immortalized there, instead of a child.

Brady had never known what happened to his own mother. For all he knew she was still out there somewhere, but he'd entered the foster system at age five and barely remembered her face.

But he thought of Irene Decker every day. She'd passed away just two short years after she'd adopted him and his brothers, but they'd all loved Irene with the deep, desperate love of boys who'd been motherless too long. Bill, of course, had loved her most of all. He'd memorialized her in an aspen grove on the ranch, decorating it with the tiny wind chimes Irene had loved. Brady still bought trinkets for the Chime Grove on occasion. So did his brothers.

There were only a few photos of Irene around the ranch house, and almost all of them were from the two years she'd had the boys to love. They'd always felt they were the heart of the household. Wherever they'd come from, they were now the next generation of Decker Ranch cowboys, and that made them matter.

Brady snapped out of his reverie and stared at the door to Suze's room. It was a plain white door, the same as all the others that lined the hallway. But by opening it and entering, Brady felt like he'd stepped over a line—a line Suze wouldn't have wanted him to cross.

—◦◦◦—

Although Suze had lived in the same house all her life, her bedroom was sparse and impersonal, as if she were only a temporary resident. There were hardly any pictures on the walls, and plain, sheer curtains hung limp at the window. The bed was neatly made, covered by a quilt that appeared to be the most personal thing in the room. It was made from squares of denim, probably taken from old blue jeans. Some squares were dark blue, some worn almost to white. Brady was glad it was there, figuring it probably warmed Suze's heart as well as her body as she slept.

The closet, which was standing open, contained a few clothes, neatly hung. In Brady's experience, women's rooms usually looked like war zones where a bomb had exploded, spraying shoes and scarves instead of shrapnel. But in Suze's room, everything was neat, everything was clean, and hardly anything was personal.

Well, that just made his job easier. The fact that the room had no more personal touches than the average hotel room made him feel less like an invader.

He didn't see anything like a suitcase, but there was a gear bag on the floor—the same kind he used for his own rodeo equipment. He removed a few horsey items—some brushes, a hoof pick—and then stared down at some knitting needles that trailed a length of neatly woven yarn. Somebody was obviously in the middle of a craft project. Suze?

She was hardly the knitting type, but who else could it belong to? If it was hers, it would give her something to do. He left it in the bag and opened a bottom drawer on her dresser.

Inside, he found a neat stack of nearly identical Wranglers. He grabbed two pairs, and added a couple of T-shirts from another drawer. The next drawer contained socks. He knew he was getting closer and closer to the skivvies. He threw a few pairs of white athletic socks into the zippered maw of the gear bag, then noticed a pair of fuzzy white socks with kitten faces at the back of the drawer. They must have been a gift from somebody, because he sure couldn't see Suze buying them. Grinning, he put them in the bag. They'd either make her laugh or make her mad. Either one would give her system a jolt, and that was probably a good thing.

The middle drawer held a neat stack of pajama pants and some cotton tank tops. That was what she'd need most in the hospital, so he chose one pair of pants with little horses all over them, and another pair with flowers he hoped would remind her of home. He did his best to match a couple tank tops to each pair of pants and shoved them in the rapidly filling bag, doing his best not to picture Suze in those outfits, her long legs curled beneath her, the tank top showing off the parts of her he was trying not to think about.

He knew what he was going to find in the top drawer. He reached his hand out to open it, then jerked it back as if he expected it to be filled with rattlesnakes.

It might as well be. Suze might dress like a farmhand on the outside, but he knew her baggy T-shirts and comfort-fit jeans hid a body fit for a Victoria's Secret model. He'd be reminded of that body, and the night he'd discovered it, as soon as he opened the drawer.

Ah, what the hell. It was just underwear. A little silk, a little lace—what harm could it do? Taking a deep breath, he opened the drawer and tried not to feel like a pervert.

The almost compulsive organization of the rest of the room didn't apply to this drawer. It was a festival of textures and temptations. Scruples forgotten, he buried his hands in the heap of silk and lace pretties, sifting the delicate fabric through his fingers.

He pulled out a strip of lace and found himself holding an electric yellow thong; he tugged at a bit of elastic and found himself holding a bright red bra that was clearly designed to lift and support the generous breasts he remembered. He missed those breasts—missed them with an ache that was just about killing him now.

He'd hoped to just grab something and run, but she wouldn't be wearing thongs and push-up bras in the hospital. She'd want something comfortable. Practical.

Maybe he should go shopping, because he wasn't finding anything remotely like that here.

He finally settled on a white bra and matching panties that would have been fairly conservative if they hadn't somehow brought the image of a naughty schoolgirl to mind. Rummaging around for a second set, he pulled out one tempting fantasy after another, but nothing fit for the hospital.

He lifted the last pair of panties out and held them up to the light. Not bad—blue with lace panels connecting two triangles of fabric. At least the triangles were big enough to cover something more than a postage stamp.

In fact, they were big enough to cover a photograph that was sitting at the bottom of the drawer. Brady picked up the old picture and stared.

It was a candid shot of Suze and a cowboy at a high school rodeo. She couldn't have been more than sixteen in the picture, and the cowboy was about the same age. Suze sat on the top rail of a fence. Her booted feet rested on a lower rung, and one leg of her jeans was hung up on the top of her boot. That always seemed to be the case with her. It was as if she was in such a hurry to get to the horse that she couldn't even dress properly.

It was an actual rodeo though, not practice, so she was wearing a regulation long-sleeved Western shirt and a white straw cowboy hat. The cowboy was dressed to compete too, in Wranglers and a bright, striped shirt. They would have looked like a couple of dudes except that the two of them were covered from head to toe with streaks and splotches of rich brown Wyoming mud.

Suze was smiling down at the cowboy, who had jokingly grabbed one of her legs as if he was going to pull her off the fence. He was grinning into the camera like a fool. Anyone looking at the photo would have known it had been taken on a good day, just from the smiles on their faces.

Brady knew it had been taken on a good day because he was the cowboy in the picture, and he remembered that Kodak moment.

It had been as good as a moment could be. Precious, like the lady in the hospital had said. It had rained on and off all day, but the sun broke through the clouds in that moment and made it feel blessed.

He looked at the photo more closely. Suze's face was in shadow under the brim of her hat, but her expression wasn't hard to read. She wasn't looking at the camera; she was looking at Brady. Her lashes, always surprisingly dark for such a fair-skinned blond, rested on her cheeks, and her smile was—fond. Affectionate. It was obvious that she was happy to be with the man in the picture.

Man, hell. That was a boy. A boy who was too stupid to know how lucky he was. Too stupid to know that heaven was right there, literally in his grasp.

The picture was taken Brady's sophomore year. He'd been so impressed by Suze's mad gallop the first time he met her that he'd joined the rodeo team first chance he got. He'd fallen as hard for Suze as he had for the sport, but nothing came of his boyish infatuation. Suze was focused on riding, not romance, and there were lots of other girls willing to take Brady's raging hormones for a test drive.

He covered the picture up with a few more pairs of panties. There had been a time when he and Suze might have stayed friends, even become lovers. Hell, if he'd dated her back then, they'd probably be engaged by now. Maybe even married.

Not too long ago, that thought would have given him the willies. But as he looked around Suze's stark, cheerless bedroom and thought of how sad and vulnerable she'd looked in the hospital, he wished he'd made some different choices since the day that photo was taken. Because he'd been telling the little nurse the truth: Suze was, deep down, a sweetheart.

He stuffed his selections into the gear bag and zipped it up, wondering why she'd kept that photo. Did she feel the same way he did—as if that moment could have changed their lives? Did she wish it had?

Maybe she had once. But now that he'd put her in the hospital with multiple injuries, he doubted she felt that way anymore.

Chapter 27

Suze lay in bed, like she'd been doing all day, and wondered when she'd be able to go home. She didn't want to stay in the hospital, but what the hell was she going to do once she got back to the ranch? She doubted she'd be able to walk. Even now, just resting there, her right ankle throbbed so hard it felt like a bomb about to explode.

She thought about asking the nurses for some pain medicine. The pills might knock her out and help her stop worrying.

Holy crap. That thought sounded so much like a drug addict, she'd better renew her promise to herself—a promise to use as little medication as she could, no matter what the doctors said.

She just wished she had something to do—a magazine to read or a book, or her knitting. She'd always thought knitting was an old-ladyish thing to do, but the fact was it made the miles go faster when her dad was driving her to rodeos, and helped while away the long nights between performances. Her mother had taught her to make scarves, and she'd made so many, she'd almost run out of people to give them to, even though she passed them out to every competitor, rodeo clown, pickup man, and announcer she met along the rodeo road. She really ought to learn to make sweaters or something, but there was something pleasurable about replicating the pattern her mother had taught her, over and over, in yarn of various weights and colors. It felt like a connection, a skein unwinding through the years that joined the two of them together.

But her knitting was at home in her gear bag, and she had nothing personal here at all—nothing but Brady's bouquet of flowers, which had brought her more pleasure than she'd ever tell him. She picked up a daisy that had somehow fallen on her pillow and brought it to her face. Daisies didn't have much smell, but she caught the grassy scent of her pasture, the high notes of the sunshine that had nurtured it, and the low, dark notes of the earth where it had grown.

She'd just begun to drowse a little, the daisy clutched in her fist, when footsteps and the gentle *whoosh* of her door opening alerted her to a visitor.

Finally. Her dad.

She opened her eyes to see Brady. Again.

She shoved the daisy under her pillow.

"I brought you your stuff." He still couldn't stand to look at her. She must be a real horror. "Some pj's, jeans, and T-shirts, and, um, other stuff."

Surely Brady Caine wasn't blushing? He was. Over what? Her underwear?

It wasn't like he hadn't seen it before, and lots more like it on other women—although she did have a liking for pretty underwear, and kind of collected sexy bras and matching panties. If she was competing, she wore a sports bra. Otherwise, her pretty underthings made her feel like something about her was pretty, at least.

"Where's my dad?" she asked.

"He was, um, busy."

"Yeah right," she said. "Let me guess. There was a *Bonanza* episode on he'd only seen sixteen times."

Brady sighed and sat down in the chair beside the bed. Taking his hat off, he raked his fingers through his hair and finally looked at her.

Suze had run her fingers through that thick hair once. Suddenly she had the urge to do it again. A picture flashed across her mind of Brady laying his head in her lap, of her stroking that soft brown hair while they both fell asleep to the clicking and humming of the medical machines. The thought made her eyelids droop, and a wonderful feeling of peace came over her.

She shook her head, hard. Where had *that* come from? She definitely needed to knock that picture out of her head, and fast.

She'd had thoughts like that about Brady since she was fifteen years old. She had no idea what it was that attracted her so strongly to this careless ladies' man of a cowboy. She believed in working hard, in taking things seriously, and Brady never worked a day he didn't have to. She trained hard and thought harder, strategized and drilled her horses; Brady just hopped on a bronc and hung on. He had so much natural ability he'd never had to work at it.

She still wondered what would have happened if she'd been nicer to him after that night in the trailer. Or if she'd pursued him a little harder back in high school, before he started catting around so much.

It was probably just as well she'd never learned the answer to that question. Whoever ended up in a relationship with Brady was bound to be miserable. He was a prime candidate for one of those off-kilter relationships where one partner does all the loving and the other partner is so busy dazzling the rest of the world that they don't have time for their partner. Because Brady was a dazzler. He couldn't help it.

She'd seen that kind of relationship in her own parents. She'd never understood their fights when she was little, but as she'd grown, she'd realized that her father was no match for Ellen Carlyle. The woman was like a Fourth of July sparkler, blazing so brightly she left the image of her white-hot beauty burned into the eyes of everyone she met. Suze's father had been a stabilizing influence, a support, almost a servant. Even as a child, Suze knew that wasn't what she wanted for herself.

"What's wrong with your dad, anyway?" Brady asked. "He's not the only person in the world who ever lost somebody. Why can't he get over it?"

"I don't know." Suze shrugged. She wasn't about to get into that with Brady. "What did you bring me?"

Brady shifted in his chair and cleared his throat, obviously uncomfortable. "Some pajamas," he said. "The pants and tops to match, and some jeans and T-shirts. Socks too."

"Is that all?"

He nodded, staring at the floor.

"Didn't you bring me any underwear?"

A ruddy flush started at the back of his neck and suffused his tanned face. Best of all, it turned the tips of his ears bright pink. "The red one and the white one," he blurted.

She'd have to keep in mind that the red one and the white one were apparently winners when it came to embarrassing Brady Caine.

The thought made her giggle, and that felt so good she loosened the reins on her laughter and let it fly. Brady looked stricken for a moment, but then, good-natured cowboy that he was, he joined in. The two of them struggled for control, but every time Suze managed to quit laughing, Brady would catch her eye and she'd start up again.

It felt good. After all the stress and tension of the past two days, she needed to let loose with some kind of emotion, even if it was a totally inappropriate one.

They finally wound down, slowing to little spurts of laughter here and there, with longer and longer intervals in between. When Suze finally recovered fully, she was stunned to find she'd taken Brady's hand at some point. Or had he taken hers? It was hard to tell, but she quickly disentangled their fingers and looked away, embarrassed. The air practically hummed with sexual promise, and images from their one night together flickered through her mind. The images moved from past to present, and she imagined Brady taking her now—climbing on the bed, kissing her, tugging at the tie on her hospital gown...

How could she shut this down?

"I wish I could help my dad somehow," she said.

That was one thing her father was good for, anyway. Bringing him up could slam the door on any kind of merriment in two seconds flat.

"There's got to be a way to get him back to the real world," he said. "You're going to need him, and right now he's no help at all."

She nodded. There was no point in disagreeing.

"I know he loved your mom, but it's been ten years. If he was trying to crack a Guinness record, he's probably already done it." He scratched his head, staring out the window as if the answer might be written on the clouds. "Why can't he get over her?"

She'd mulled that problem over so many times she thought she'd considered every aspect of the problem, but she'd never talked to anyone else about it before, mostly because she thought their family dysfunction was a secret. There was no hiding it from Brady, though. Not now. Heck, she couldn't even hide her underwear from him.

"He must have loved her so much." Brady's voice was soft, his tone wondering, as if he couldn't comprehend that kind of devotion. He probably couldn't. After all, she didn't think he'd ever had a relationship that lasted more than a week.

"I guess so. But you know, it's funny. I don't think their relationship was that good," she said. "Maybe he feels like he didn't love her enough, so he's making up for it now."

Brady looked puzzled. "That doesn't fit with what I've heard. Everybody says he was crazy about her, as in love with her then as he is now."

"Who's 'everybody'?" Suze asked.

Brady shrugged. "You know. People around town."

"People around town talk about my family?"

He grinned. "Well, yeah. That tends to happen when you have two generations of world champions."

Suze shrugged. "It's just barrel racing."

"This is the West. People care about barrel racing."

"Then how come it's always the last event at every rodeo? And how come everybody's always getting up to leave before our first competitor gets out of the gate?"

Brady looked down at the floor, kicking idly at the leg of his chair. He evidently didn't have an answer, because he changed the subject. "Did they ever fight?"

She laughed a short, hard laugh. "Oh, yeah. They had some real barn burners."

"About what?"

She shrugged. "I don't know. I was a little kid. He was jealous, I think."

"No wonder. She was beautiful."

"I know." She didn't want his pity. She didn't want anyone's, so this was what she always said—that she didn't remember her mother, so she didn't miss her. But it didn't really work that way. Not remembering her mother only made Suze miss her more.

"You look just like her," he said. "You'd think he'd be happy that she left him something so—I don't know, such a piece of her."

Suze stared at him, incredulous. "Have you *seen* my mom? The pictures of her? She looked like a movie star."

He grinned. "Have you *seen* yourself? The way you looked for that photo shoot?"

She had seen herself, and the mirror image of her mother, looking back at her in the makeup trailer. Maybe she really did look like her mom, but only if she piled on the makeup and frothed up her hair to unnatural heights. Beauty didn't come naturally to her the way it had to Ellen Carlyle.

That was what her father said, anyway. And he was the one person she could count on to tell her the truth.

Too bad she couldn't count on him for anything else.

Chapter 28

As he watched Suze pluck at a loose thread on the thin hospital blanket, Brady felt like his heart was going to swell out of his chest. Something right behind his eyes burned, and his throat ached.

He wondered if Suze realized how alone in the world she was. He hoped not. With her mother dead and her father consumed by grief, she'd thrown herself into barrel racing so hard she probably didn't have time to think about anything else. Her success had left her without any friends close enough to call on at a time like this.

Brady knew there were plenty of cowboys who'd be happy to spend some time with Suze Carlyle, but she was shy to the point of seeming rude. He was one of the few people who'd managed to get through her stubborn reserve to see the woman inside.

And he was probably the last person she wanted to ask for help. He didn't know what he'd done or said that night in the trailer, but something had gone wrong and ripped her trust away. The accident at the photo shoot was just ugly icing on a cake that had already collapsed. It gave her a reason to hate him that she could actually talk about.

And yet they'd been chatting almost like friends. He wondered why, and Brady didn't do a lot of wondering. He liked to ask his questions straight out and get answers right away.

"Why are you even talking to me?"

Suze yawned, patting it down with one hand. She tried to stretch with the other arm, but a wince put an end to that.

He winced with her, feeling every bit of her pain, every twinge, every ache, every tender bruise. Because it was all his fault.

"I'm too tired to be mad," she said.

If that was the case, he should make sure she didn't get any sleep.

That thought led to other ones, thoughts about how he could keep her awake. What would happen if he bent over the bed and kissed those full lips, caressed her shoulder, and tugged at the string of that hospital gown? He knew how to tease her and touch her just right, and he'd kept her up all night once before.

He wiped those thoughts out of his mind, hating himself just for thinking that way. Suze was going to be tired for a very long time, but it was his job to make that time as short as possible. If she still wanted to throw him out of her life at that point, that was her right.

"Listen," he said. "I want you to know something."

She rolled her eyes. "This sounds way too serious."

"This is a serious situation." He gestured toward the bed, with all its attendant medical gear. "And it's all my fault. If I hadn't screwed up, you'd be out in the arena with Speedo today, running drills," he said.

She looked over toward her nightstand. At first he thought she wanted a drink of water, but then he realized she was looking away from him to hide a tear. She managed to blink it away and looked back, brushing her cheek as if wiping the hair out of her eyes.

He started to reach for her other hand, then looked down at the splints on her fingers and thought better of it. She didn't seem to have any one life-threatening injury, and he was glad of that. But he'd somehow managed to hurt just about every part of her one way or another.

He cupped her hand in his instead and lightly touched the broken fingers.

"It's going to take time for this to heal."

He stroked the inside of her wrist, following the faint tracery of blue veins that branched like tiny rivers under her pale skin, gently pressing a bruise that looked suspiciously like the imprint of a fence rail.

"And this." He brushed his fingers across an abrasion near her elbow. "And this. And until every bone, every bruise, and every sprain and strain is cured and you're back in the saddle good as new, I'll do anything you want. I'm going to be there for you every minute of every day. You don't have to worry about a thing, okay?"

"No. Not okay." She pulled her hand away. "I'm sure this surprises you, but I don't want you around all the time, Brady." She let out an unconvincing laugh. "I'm not like most women, you know."

"Do I ever." He smacked the crown of his hat, which was sitting in his lap. He hit it harder than he meant to, crushing the felt and practically turning it inside out. "I know you're an independent cuss," he said. "I'm the same way. I guess it's a cowboy thing."

"I'm a cow*girl*."

"You don't ride like a girl," he said. "You're as cowboy as any of us, and you know it."

"Is that supposed to be a compliment?"

"It's more than a compliment; it's a membership in the club. When bad things happen, cowboys stick together. You're going to need help, and I'm right here to give it to you."

She could hardly argue with that, though she looked like she wanted to. Then, suddenly, her eyes narrowed.

"Did you say you'd do anything I want?"

He nodded. "Sure did. Until you're good as new."

"Good," she said.

Brady felt a whoosh of relief. He needed to help Suze—partly to cleanse his soul because of the mistake he'd made, but also because he was realizing, more and more, that she needed someone and that someone ought to be him.

"So I get to order you around, right?" she asked. "And you have to do what I say."

He didn't like where this was going, but he had to nod.

She stretched out her arm, pointing at him like a queen commanding her subject.

"I, Suze Carlye, order you, Brady Caine, to leave me the heck *alone*."

She smiled and whisked her palms together as if she was brushing off dust. "There. Done. Thanks for being such an obedient slave. Now go away."

He stood and caught a flash of fear in her eyes. It faded as fast as a campfire doused with a bucket of water, but for a second it had burned brightly.

They both knew she needed help, and they both knew she had nowhere to get it.

"That's the one thing I won't do," he said. "I'm not leaving you. I won't get in your way, and I'll try to stay out of your sight if you want me to. But I'll take care of your horses, and I'll make sure they get worked. I'll keep your barn clean. I'll even cook and clean. Whatever you need."

"You can cook?"

"No." He grinned. "But I'll learn. It might not be so good at first, but when I want to learn something, I learn fast."

"Really? Like when?"

Dang. He couldn't think of a single occasion when he'd worked really hard to learn something. Rodeo had come easy, so he hadn't bothered with the subjects in school that didn't interest him. Math and science had been his favorites, so he'd done okay. English? Social studies? Not so much.

"Everybody needs something to work at, Brady. A challenge. For me, it's riding and always learning to ride better. For my dad, it's getting over my mom, I guess. But I don't know what your challenge is."

He was starting to think *she* was his challenge, but he didn't want to say that. Besides, the question deserved a thoughtful answer. What was he supposed to learn in this life? Which one of his many flaws did he need to work on first?

"Probably personal relationships," he said.

She gave him an almost comical look of disbelief. "Are you kidding? Everybody loves you. The whole freaking world is your friend. You've had more personal relationships in the past five years than most men have in a lifetime."

Ouch. That stung.

"But they never last," he said. "I know how to get

people to like me, how to have a good time. That's all. I don't know how to really talk to people about deep stuff. I don't know how to make anything last."

"That's for sure," she muttered.

Ouch. That stung even more.

He thought about what he'd said about the deep stuff. He'd heard some TV psychologist say that exchanging secrets was the way to make people trust you. Maybe that would work on Suze.

He put his hat on his fist and set it to spinning, watching it teeter and whirl so he wouldn't have to look at Suze while he talked. "When you're a foster kid, you learn pretty quick that you shouldn't get attached to people. Or at least, you *should* learn it quick. I was a slow learner."

Suze didn't say a word, but when he glanced up, her eyes were on his and she'd gone still, like a deer listening for the telltale snap of a twig in the forest.

"I was a problem kid." He set the hat spinning the other way. "Always getting in trouble. But I tried. I really did. I wanted a family so bad, you can't even imagine."

Suze gave him a gentle smile. "They're not always all they're cracked up to be, you know."

"Yeah, I know that now, but I sure didn't know it then. If your dad would've had me, I'd have done anything for him."

That probably wasn't the smartest thing to say. The silence from Suze was deafening, and he felt like the temperature of the room had dropped a degree or two. But he kept on talking. Kept on trying.

"So I learned to make people like me. I thought some family would adopt me if I was cute, you know? And if

I did everything they said. And if I stayed cheerful all the time, no matter what."

Those last words took him by surprise. He'd always thought his positive attitude was something to be admired, but maybe it had its roots in something less than healthy. He'd have to think about that later. Right now, the words were spilling out like water from a faucet. He wasn't sure he could stop if he wanted to. It was a strange sort of relief to confide all this in Suze, even if she didn't care.

"So I might seem like I know how to make friends, but that's where it ends."

"That's not true," she said. "You know how to keep them too. You're still friends with half the girls you slept with."

"Well, yeah." He stopped spinning the hat and set it on his knee. "I still like them. I just don't know how to go any further, you know? I put on the brakes every time."

She should know, he thought. She'd had direct experience with his inability to keep a relationship going past a one-night stand. Hadn't he walked away from her the morning after without telling her how much the night had meant to him? How different it had been than the rest? It had been amazing to talk, to really share, and then the sex—well, it had been mind-blowing.

In retrospect, there were so many things he could have done—told her where he was going and why. Told her how he felt. Or even called and delayed the meeting.

But no, he'd walked out the door, telling himself the meeting was important, when the truth was that he was scared stupid of the feelings she'd called up in his heart.

Those feelings had seemed perfectly safe when they'd been tumbling together in the same bed, but in the light of day, it was different. When you loved people, they had the power to hurt you.

"I guess being in the foster system must have been hard on you, Brady," Suze said slowly. "I never really thought about that."

He felt the old familiar squeeze, like a fist around his heart, and changed the subject as fast as he could. "Naw, it was all right," he said. "But what do you say? Are you going to let me help you?"

She stared down at the hem of the sheet, shaking her head. "You don't have to."

"Who's feeding your horses?"

"My dad, probably. He takes care of Bucket when I'm on the road."

"He do a good job?"

She faked interest in something outside the window and didn't answer. Since her view consisted of a brick wall, he knew she was just avoiding his gaze.

"He didn't feed him last night or this morning, and he had plenty of time to do it." He knew the words were harsh, but she needed to hear them. If he didn't know how much the horses mattered to her, he might have let her keep her illusions that her father gave a crap about her, but she'd never forgive herself if something happened to Bucket.

Or Speedo. Shoot, he shouldn't have brought up the horses.

"What about Speedo?" she asked.

"Oh." It took him a second to think of something to say that wasn't a lie. "My brother Ridge picked him up."

Ridge *had* picked up the horse and put him in a stall. And that was the last anybody saw of him.

"I guess that's good," she said. "Ridge is a good horseman." Her brows arrowed down, and he braced himself for another question about Speedo, but she surprised him. "How do you know my dad didn't feed them?"

"Because I did."

"So why are you bothering to ask my permission, if you're just going to do what you want anyway?"

"I couldn't risk letting the horses go hungry. Would you have wanted me to risk that?"

She was silent.

"I'm sorry, Suze, but your dad isn't going to do it. I will," he said.

She looked up at him with red-rimmed, glossy eyes, not even bothering to hide her tears. "Just don't go in the house, okay?"

How did she think he'd gotten her clothes? He'd already seen the pile of unwashed dishes, the mess in the living room. But it didn't seem right to remind her. The less said, the better.

She tugged at a thread on the sheet, and he noticed she'd pulled quite a bit of it loose. She must have been working on it awhile.

Setting his hands on his knees, he stood. "I've got to go. I'll stop back tomorrow to see what else you need."

She shook her head mutely. Now that he was standing, she looked terribly small and helpless in the big, white bed under the glaring hospital lights. He wasn't used to seeing Suze look weak. He doubted anybody was.

"I brought you some magazines. Here." He pitched

them on the bed beside her. *Western Horseman*, *Quarter Horse Journal*, and one more. He topped the pile with a copy of *Cosmo*.

"Brady!" She blushed. The headline, written in hot pink letters across the top, was "Ten Orgasmic Moves He'll Never Forget!"

"Well, I don't know what you girls read. Everything else looked too old-ladyish. He looked her dead in the eye, making sure she was paying attention. "I'm not saying you need any help in that department, okay? I just thought it looked like—well, I thought it looked like fun." While she was trying to figure out how to answer that, he tossed two more magazines on the stack. "I grabbed a word search and some crosswords too. Don't know if you like that kind of thing."

"Oh, I love them." She picked one up with undisguised delight. "I love word puzzles. Thanks."

He reached behind her head and fooled with the lights, then hooked a cord around the bed rails. He was careful not to look at her while he did it, but he was close enough to smell her hair. "There's a switch on that cord that'll turn the reading light on and off. You want the big light off?"

She nodded and he went over and flicked off the overhead lights. Now the room was lit only by a bar of light over Suze's bed. It sparked gold off her blond hair and shadowed her face, accentuating the high-cheekboned Scandinavian cast of her features.

Pausing in the doorway, he shoved his hands in his pockets. The darkness made the room seem like a world apart, an intimate place where only the two of them mattered. Suddenly, to Brady, the two of them mattered a lot.

"You still mad at me?"

"Yes. No. I don't know."

"Be mad," he said. "Be you. Please. Don't let this change who you are." He clutched his hat to his chest so hard he crushed the crown again. He needed to engrave this picture of her, hurt and helpless, on his heart, so he wouldn't fail in the task he'd set himself. "I could stand just about anything, but I couldn't stand it if you changed." He shot her a sheepish smile. "Besides, the thing I'm supposed to work on? That big challenge? I think what it really is, is you."

"Brady, no."

"Why not? I've messed up every time I've been lucky enough to be around you. Every single time. I don't want things to be this way. I want us to be friends." He looked down at his feet, then lifted his eyes to meet hers and locked on. "Maybe more than friends."

Chapter 29

SUZE GLANCED WILDLY AROUND THE ROOM, SEEKING out something to throw at Brady. She needed to stop him before the conversation entered dangerous territory. Unfortunately, the only thing she could reach was a tissue, which fluttered uselessly to the floor about three feet short of its target.

"Don't be ridiculous," she said.

"Why not?" He moved toward the bed and sat down near the end, carefully avoiding her feet. "Don't you remember that night? We're great together, Suze. More than great. We were—"

Desperate now, she interrupted him with a laugh—a harsh laugh, so cold she wondered if she'd been suddenly possessed by a Disney villain. "I know very well what that night was all about, and I have no problem with it," she told him.

"Really?"

"Really. There was an attraction there. We didn't expect it—I mean, I sure as hell didn't—but once we felt it, well, the itch needed to be scratched, right? Why let it aggravate you when you can make it go away and have fun doing it?"

"So that worked for you? The itch went away?"

Up until now, she'd managed to look him in the eyes when she spoke, but now she picked up the top magazine and pretended to flip through it rather than look at him.

The only trouble was, the top magazine just happened to be *Cosmo*, and the first article she came to was entitled "Most Embarrassing Moments." Maybe she should submit hers: reading a magazine with a blazing headline about orgasms in front of the man she was trying to discourage from—well, from giving her blazing orgasms.

"Sure," she lied, dropping the magazine a little so the cover wasn't staring him in the face. "The itch went away."

"Because I have to tell you, I was kind of surprised you didn't have anything to say to me the next morning."

She flipped to another page, pretending to be absorbed in the magazine but feeling her face redden. She'd read *Cosmo* once before, since she was smack-dab in the middle of their "fun, fearless woman" demographic. But according to the magazine, that meant she was interested in three things: orgasms, shoes, and driving men crazy with lust.

She liked orgasms as much as the next girl, but there wasn't a single article about quarter horses in the whole magazine.

"I bet you were surprised," she said. "And relieved too. I talked your ear off the night before, didn't I? You were probably thinking, *just shut up and do it*."

He had the decency to look outraged. "I wasn't thinking that."

She smiled—or rather, she stretched her lips out and struggled to make the ends tip upward. Now she probably looked like a clown possessed by a Disney villain. The more she faked it, the scarier she got.

"Brady, you don't have to explain. I mean, I know who you are."

"Do you?"

"Sure. You're Brady Caine. You need me to explain that?"

"Yes."

"You're a good-time cowboy who rides broncs for fun and women for pleasure." She remembered their conversation about finding meaning in life, and she knew each word would wound him. But they'd also drive him away, as surely as a gun pointed at his family jewels. "Your life is all about beer, buckles, and babes."

"So you figure you were just one of the babes."

"I *know* I was one of the babes. Look, I know you're feeling all guilty and stuff right now. I can see how the accident would make you feel like you have to take care of me, and if that's what it takes to make you feel better, go ahead." She tossed the magazine to the foot of her bed. "But do it from a distance, okay? You and me together—it never ends well."

Brady reached Decker Ranch just as the sky was shifting from blue to pale silver, giving the cluster of aspens by the corner of the house a skeletal glow. Parking his Silverado in the drive beside his brothers' trucks, he jogged up the front steps and into the hall, slamming the screen door.

"Hey," he said to Shane, who was standing in the kitchen with a dish towel thrust through his belt. The flowered towel blended strangely with Wrangler jeans and workingman's shirt. Shane was foreman of a ranch up north of Wynott, and rode herd over fifteen or more cowboys and thousands of purebred Black Angus cattle, but he was as at home in the kitchen as he was in the saddle.

"I think that's the first time you've ever walked into this house without asking what's for dinner," Shane said. "You must have something on your mind."

"Just a little."

"Good. You got a plan?"

Shane knew about what had happened to Suze Carlyle and who was responsible. Brady figured everybody in the county did. Everybody in the state, maybe.

"Sure do." Brady took the stairs two at a time. "I'm going out there to the Carlyle place tonight to take care of her horses and stuff. I'll be doing that until she's better."

"What about the horse?"

"Speedo?"

Shane nodded.

"I'm heading out tomorrow to check every abandoned barn I can think of. Somebody probably hid him, so I figure that's a good bet."

"It's a thought," Shane said. "There are enough places on the back roads to keep you pretty busy."

Brady nodded. "Busy is good right now. I keep reliving that accident in my head, thinking what I could have done different."

"The key word is *accident*," Shane said. "It's not like you *meant* to hurt her."

"That's for sure."

"So does Suze approve of you going out to her place? I mean, she threw you out of the hospital."

Shane wasn't given to displays of levity, but the corner of his mouth was twitching and Brady was pretty sure he was holding in a laugh.

"She did. But I was just there, and we made up."

"So she approves of this? Of your going out there?"

"I told her I was going."

"That's not the same thing, and you know it."

Brady spread his hands helplessly. "There's nobody else to help her. Her dad's useless, and she doesn't have any other family. You know what that's like. So do I."

Shane nodded. "Ridge talked to Sierra about sending one of the kids over."

"What's a kid going to do for her?"

"Help with meals, maybe. If she's really laid up, he can fetch stuff for her. That kind of thing."

"Well, tell her to send the toughest kid she has. Earl Carlyle hasn't grown a heart anytime in the last ten years. He's still as ornery as God could make a man."

"Why can't *he* help Suze?"

"There's some kind of trouble between them, I think. He hasn't even been to see her yet."

"You're kidding."

"Nope. I had to go pack up her clothes and stuff. He wouldn't do it."

Shane looked down at the floor and shook his head. "That girl deserves a way better life than she's got."

"She sure does," Brady said.

"You going to make sure she gets it?"

"I'm going to try. It won't be easy, since she can't stand the sight of me. But I'll manage somehow."

Shane stared at Brady a long time—long enough to make Brady uncomfortable. His oldest brother saw deeply into people, into their hearts. Maybe it was because he'd experienced so much, so young. Though he'd grown up a foster child, he'd been an exemplary student and athlete in high school—until he got his girl-friend pregnant their junior year. Shane had proposed marriage, but she'd taken off the day after graduation. He'd never even seen his son, who would be almost six years old by now. So he knew about mistakes, and he knew about heartache.

His expression was a combination of compassion, surprise, and maybe approval—something Brady rarely got from Shane.

"Hell's bells," Shane said. "You just might be starting to become a decent human being."

"Yeah, well, I'd better."

Brady strode down the stairs, enjoying the sense of purpose he felt and resisting the temptation to turn around and look—even though he was pretty sure that finally, he'd earned a look of respect from the brother he most admired.

Chapter 30

FOR THE NEXT FEW DAYS, BRADY'S LIFE TOOK ON A new sense of order. Normally, he was on the road chasing rodeos ninety percent of the time; when that was out of season, he spent his days tormenting his brothers and his nights raising heck at the local bars. Lately he'd turned it down a notch. He wasn't sure why; he wasn't getting old, and he sure as hell wasn't growing up.

Or was he? He'd always resisted that notion. Growing up had always looked like a lot of work. But taking care of Suze wasn't work, somehow.

Maybe, in order to grow up, you needed to learn how to love. Once you loved someone, you didn't mind being responsible, because you wanted to take care of her. Make a home for her. Be worthy.

At any rate, he was up with the sun every day, rolling out of bed at dawn to head out to the Carlyle place to take care of Bucket. Then he'd hit the road, searching every place he could think of where someone might hide a stolen horse that was too famous to be seen in public.

Late in the afternoon, he'd go home for a shower and then visit Suze. Her moods were all over the map. Sometimes she seemed almost starved for company, and she'd pay rapt attention while he detailed his work with Bucket. Unfortunately, she'd begged him to bring Ridge sometime, so she could talk to him about Speedo. Somehow, Brady managed to stave off her inevitable discovery that the horse was missing. Right now, the knowledge wouldn't do her any good—at least, that's what he told his conscience.

Some days, she turned her face to the wall and told him to go away. At first he assumed that attitude was well-deserved anger toward him for his part in the accident, but lately he worried that it was pain or, worse yet, depression that made her unwilling to talk.

After visiting Suze, he'd run little errands, picking up anything she asked for and quite a few things she hadn't. She went through most of Bill Decker's collection of old horse-training manuals, along with a few trashy magazines Brady threw in for fun. Once he turned up with a set of pajamas he'd found at Kohl's, flannel ones with horses on them. That had been one of her bad days, and he'd thought maybe the gift was too personal, but the next time he visited she was wearing them. Neither one of them said a word about it.

In between, Brady made occasional forays into the Carlyle house, trying to get Earl to go visit his daughter. He'd originally planned to stay away from the old man, but it turned out to be a good thing he didn't; Suze had apparently been the housekeeper in the family. Brady wound up washing a pile of dishes and cleaning the bathrooms, but he drew the line at doing the old man's laundry. Suze's he was happy to do. She had pretty things to look at. Doing Earl's would be gross, and besides, something had to get the man out of that chair.

Finally, the day of Suze's release came. Brady stayed late at the house the night before, cleaning things and tidying up so the place looked warm and welcoming. He even made another wildflower bouquet for Suze's room.

He wished he had time to do something about the front porch. The screened-in area seemed to have been added to the house as an afterthought. It would have been a nice place to sit on a summer afternoon, but it was full of lumber, old windows, and other evidence of Earl's pack rat ways.

Brady wondered if the old man planned to build something, or if he just hated to see things go to waste. He could understand both urges, but the stuff belonged in the barn, not the house. He sure wouldn't want people to see all that crap before they even made it to his front door.

He'd fix it sometime. Sometime soon.

But right now, there were more important things to do. Like inform Earl that his daughter was coming home.

"Suze comes home tomorrow," Brady said. "You excited?"

The old man grunted. Up until that night, his plan seemed to be to ignore Brady as much as possible. Brady figured it worked out well that way for Earl; he never had to make excuses for the piles of dishes in the sink or thank Brady for taking care of his mess if the two of them didn't speak. But on hearing Suze was coming home, he finally roused himself enough to get out of his chair and come to the door.

"I want to go with you to pick her up." Earl's voice was gravelly from disuse, and he looked fierce as he spoke, gazing up at Brady from beneath dark, unruly eyebrows. His eyes were startlingly like Suze's if you ignored the network of wrinkles that surrounded them.

Brady glanced out at his truck. "I've got a two-seater," he said. "I don't see how that can work. She can't cram in there with two grown men. Not with her crutches and all."

"Well, then." Earl gave him a hostile look that seemed to signal the start of some war Brady hadn't realized was brewing. "I'll go get her myself."

Brady groaned to himself. He'd hoped to take Suze home, if only so he could listen in on the doctor's final instructions. Suze always waved him away when he asked about doctor's orders, even when she was in a good mood, and she never allowed him to stay in the room when the doctors made their rounds. What little he knew came from eavesdropping.

There was a broken wrist, he knew that. And her left leg was a mess, with damage to the tendons in the knee and ankle, and a break in the foot. She wouldn't be able to walk on her own for a while, and she'd suffered some nerve pain along with her broken bones and bruises.

That was the part that bothered him the most. Irene had suffered from MS, which included a lot of nerve pain. He didn't know much, but he knew that once nerves were damaged, they took a long time to heal—and sometimes they never did.

He also knew the pain could be excruciating. Once in a while, Suze would rock back in the bed, crossing her arms over her chest and squeezing her eyes shut. He knew that meant the pain was bad, and there was nothing in the world that made him feel so helpless. There she was, suffering because of him—and there wasn't a thing he could do about it.

"I can pick her up," he told Earl. "She'll need help getting into the house."

Earl shot him a hostile glare. "We'll be fine. We don't need your kind of *help*." He rose from his chair. "I wouldn't want to *sit in my damn chair and sulk* while you weasel your way into my daughter's life. We can take care of our own selves."

"Since when?" Brady said. "I went through her underwear almost a week ago, Earl. She's been in the hospital five days. You never bothered to go see her, never even sent flowers. Now she's coming home, and all of a sudden you give a shit. What happened?"

"I had enough of you, that's all," Earl said. "I want you out of here."

Brady gave him a hard stare. "I'm the only one that's done anything for her. How do I know you'll take care of her?"

"You don't," Earl said. "You don't know anything about us."

Brady clamped his mouth shut, determined to keep his temper under control. The only way to do that was to leave, so he stepped out into the night, slamming the screen door behind him.

"And another thing," Earl called after him. "Bring that horse back, you hear? That animal's valuable. I don't want that brother of yours messing around with him."

--- ⚬⚬⚬ ---

Suze sat on the edge of the hospital bed, wondering why Brady was so late. He'd said he'd pick her up once the doctor signed the release forms, and that had been done two hours ago. Since then, she'd taken some half-serious ribbing from the nurses, who said she ought to treat her handsome cowboy better if she wanted him to show up on time. As usual, Brady had managed to charm every female in the place.

Except her.

He'd come close. He'd softened her up considerably that first day, and his jokes and tales of Bucket's and Dooley's misdeeds made her smile in spite of herself.

It wasn't easy to hold on to her anger, but the accident had been Brady's fault. He'd been as careless with her safety as he was with everything else—his talent, his own safety, and the hearts of the women who loved him.

The door opened, and she looked up fast, trying not to smile for Brady and utterly failing. But it was just a nurse, the young one who always wore juvenile scrubs with teddy bears and clowns on them. She seemed to have even more of a crush on Brady than the other girls, and sometimes Suze sensed a whiff of jealousy under her cheerful professionalism.

"Your dad's here to pick you up," the nurse said. "Guess the cowboy's not coming after all."

The professionalism slipped as the little nurse shot Suze a triumphant glare and spun out of the room, leaving her alone with her dad, who shambled in pushing an empty wheelchair.

"Can you get yourself into this thing?"

It figured. He hadn't seen her in a week, not since the wreck, but there was no "Hi, how are you?" no "What can I do for you?" It was all about how much—or better yet, how little work he'd have to do to care for the daughter he could hardly bear to look at.

She'd always thought it was because she was such a disappointment—a plain daughter who looked nothing like her lovely mother. But after that glimpse in the mirror, she knew different.

She really did look like her mother. So why wouldn't her dad look at her? Why wouldn't he love her, like other dads loved their daughters?

Fortunately, an orderly turned up and helped her make it from the bed to the chair. He was good at his job, and the transition barely hurt at all. She set her crutches across her lap and off they went.

They headed out of the hospital to the smiles of the staff, Suze in the chair, the orderly pushing, and her father shuffling alongside. Suze looked down at his feet.

"Dad, you're still in your slippers."

"They're comfortable."

She told herself not to ask about Brady, but she only managed to wait until they got into the elevator.

"Where's Brady?"

"Don't know," her father said.

She sighed as the elevator began its descent. This had to be some kind of record. Five minutes—less than five minutes—and they were already annoyed with each other.

"You must have talked to him, Dad. He was the one who told you I was getting out, right?"

"We don't need him," her dad said.

Oh, great. Her father always liked to play the part of the independent old cuss, even though he rarely did anything for himself. He didn't even make his own meals unless Suze was away, and making the meals was the limit of his involvement—cleaning up after himself was apparently too much to ask. She always arrived home to find every dish they owned in a filthy pile on the kitchen counter, and the garbage heaping with half-eaten Hungry Man meal trays.

She kept her mouth shut while he wheeled her across the lobby. When they reached the double exit doors, her dad turned to the orderly.

"We can take it from here."

Suze almost corrected him but swallowed her protest. She could probably get up into the truck with just a little bit of help from her dad.

"Okay." The orderly set a stack of paperwork in her lap. "The wheelchair and crutches are yours to keep. They'll bill your insurance."

"I'm sure they will," her dad muttered. Since he'd retired as a CPA, he'd done freelance work helping seniors deal with insurance companies. He spent a lot of time barking into the phone, haranguing insurance reps. It was the perfect job for a crotchety old man who still had his wits about him—and his temper too.

His truck was parked in the roundabout reserved for emergency room drop-offs and patient pickup. He wheeled her to the passenger side, opened the door, and stared down at her. Judging from the expression on his face, this was the first time it had occurred to him that things might be a little tricky.

Chapter 31

"WE PROBABLY SHOULD HAVE KEPT THAT GUY around," Suze said, thinking of the orderly.

"We don't need him. Goddamn cowboy," her father growled.

She'd been talking about the orderly, but his response made her wonder what he'd said to Brady. Maybe he'd run him off. She felt that little clutch of fear again, but she did her best to ignore it. She'd manage. It would just take her a little longer to get things done.

"Just give me your hand," her dad said.

As she struggled to lever herself out of the wheelchair, she wondered how long it had been since she'd held her father's hand. His skin was dry and papery, but he was surprisingly strong. That was a good thing, because Suze was surprisingly weak. Spending five days in bed hadn't done a thing for her muscle tone. She felt like a human gummy bear.

The other surprising thing was how much it *hurt*. She noticed joints and muscles she hadn't known existed, mostly in her lower back. As she tried to stand, it felt like a dozen tiny cattle prods were being thrust between her bones, and it was all she could do to keep from crying out in front of her father.

By the time she was settled into the seat of the truck, sweat beaded her forehead and she had to clench her teeth to hold back the sobs that had built up at the back of her throat.

Cowgirls don't cry. Cowgirls don't cry.

She'd heard that refrain over and over, at every rodeo and every practice session. It was her father's mantra. He claimed he'd gotten it from her mother, but Suze didn't remember her mother ever saying it. In fact, she remembered her mother holding her while she cried about some slight from a schoolmate. The hurt was long forgotten, but Suze held tight to the memory of her mother's warmth, the way she'd held her across her lap like a baby, even though Suze had been nine and therefore a "big girl." Her mother had probably been sick then, but Suze hadn't known it. If she had, she would have held on a little longer and cried a whole lot more.

The drive home should have been a treat, despite the rattling of the crutches in the truck bed and the banging of the loose tailgate. Suze hadn't seen anything but the four walls of her hospital room for over a week, except for occasional forays to luxurious destinations like the X-ray department and the blood lab, so everything looked new to her, even her dad's dusty, old truck.

Most people wouldn't consider Wyoming a desirable destination, but Suze had always felt she'd been born right where she belonged, in a tough land for tough people. Even the wildlife was tough—pronghorn antelope, fast as any racehorse; jackrabbits, with hind legs that scissored like robotic springs; prairie dogs, with their whistled code of warning protecting them from the only predators that managed to eke out a living in the rocky outback: coyotes, mountain lions, and men.

Lack of water made even the flowers of Wyoming

tough, but a series of recent rains had fed the rivers and creeks, and worked their way into the hard-packed Western soil. Drought had plagued the area for the past three years, and it seemed like the earth had been saving up its bounty so it could explode all at once when the rains finally came.

At the roadside, pale lupine and sunny yellow ragwort vied for space with asters and coneflowers. Stands of penstemon in the coolest shade of blue imaginable softened the harsh edges of a gate, while Indian paintbrush decorated the grass with brilliant streaks of red. The sight lifted Suze's spirits. A little rain had fallen in her personal world too, but maybe she'd find a positive way to use it, just like the dry, stubborn prairie.

"So you said you talked to Brady?" she asked her father.

He grunted. It was a yes grunt. Suze knew this from years of practice interpreting his unwilling communications. She knew she'd end up playing a long and frustrating game of twenty questions if she stuck to queries where he could answer yes or no.

"What did he say?"

"Something about your underwear. You need to stay away from that boy."

"Dad, he's not a boy, and I'm a grown woman. You don't get to decide who I spend my time with anymore."

"Well, I told him we don't need him around."

"Then how are we going to manage?"

"Same way we always did."

"Dad, did you hear the doctor?"

He grunted, a noncommittal grunt this time, so she repeated the surgeon's terse instructions.

"I need to rest with my leg elevated for the next two weeks, at least. After that, *if* my ankle looks better, I can walk a little, but I'll still have a cast, and I'll still be on crutches for another four weeks, at least."

Her father didn't respond, so she continued.

"The more I try to walk now, the longer it'll take for my ankle to heal. It's possible it might never heal enough for me to—enough for me to do the things I'm used to."

She couldn't repeat what the doctor had really said, which was that there was a very good chance she'd never be able to ride again. Her left leg was the problem. Both ankle and knee were destroyed, with torn and sprained ligaments and torn cartilage. The knee had been repaired with surgery, but the ankle needed time to heal. An ankle might seem like a small and inconsequential body part, but it actually bore much of a rider's weight, and acted as a springy shock absorber. It also worked like a lever, lifting her when she rose in the stirrups, and lowering her when she got down and dirty in the turns. Even at a sedate walk on horseback, the ankle was flexed.

"I can't get out to the barn right now, Dad, so I'll have to count on you for the next two weeks to take care of Bucket. I guess it's best to leave Speedo with Ridge." She blinked back tears. "He'll take good care of him."

Her dad's face was set in a stony frown. "I want that horse back here where he belongs. He's worth money."

"He's not your horse, Dad, so you don't get a say."

Suze had bought Speedo with her rodeo winnings. Her father hadn't contributed a dime to any part of her riding endeavors, ever. She'd begged Irene Decker to give her lessons in exchange for helping around the barn when she was little, and up until she turned fourteen, she felt more at home at the Deckers than at home.

Then the boys came, and everything changed. Her father forbade her to go anywhere near "that riffraff." Irene loaned her an old but wise gelding, and she started rodeoing to earn money. Then she bought Sherman, and by the time she was sixteen, she was bringing home more money than her father.

"I know you don't like Brady, but I don't know how else we're going to survive," she said. "You heard the doctor. I can't walk. And you can't take care of everything—not with your arthritis."

Her father jerked the truck to the side of the road and slammed on the brakes, skidding to a stop in a spray of gravel. The car behind them veered around them, horn blaring, but her dad turned to face her as if nothing had happened.

"That boy did this to you." He stabbed his finger in the air inches from her face. "He was stupid and careless, and he's responsible for what happened. I don't want him around, you hear? He's a menace."

"It was an accident, Dad. He didn't do it on purpose."

"He did it though, didn't he?" Her dad squeezed the steering wheel with white-knuckled hands and stared straight out the windshield. "Don't know what he's thinking, coming around like he does. Acting like he's doing us some kind of favor. Acting like everything's my fault, when he's the one that messed you up like this." He turned to face Suze again, his bony finger pointing at her face. "You keep away from him, you hear me? He's not allowed in the house."

Suze bit her lips almost hard enough to draw blood,

trying to keep her anger reined in. But like an angry bull, it burst through her barriers and launched itself at her father.

"Don't you get it, Dad? There's *nobody* to help us. He's the *only one*." She paused to blink back tears— hot, angry tears of rage, not sorrow. "You think I want him around? There are a million reasons I never want to see Brady Caine again as long as I live. You don't even know…"

She stopped herself before she gave away too much.

"You don't even know all the reasons I don't want him around, but he's the only one who's willing to help us."

She couldn't hold back the tears any longer. Sobs erupted from some deep well inside her, a place she hadn't been to since her mother died. Back then she'd felt like she'd lost everything, but she'd been wrong. She'd lost her mother, but she could still ride. Riding was her source of solace. No matter how much she missed her mother, no matter how hard life got, it gave her peace. She belonged in the saddle, and riding let her escape the dry, loveless world where she and her father lived alone and apart, shar- ing the same house but as distant as if they lived in separate countries.

Now she'd lost even that. She could no longer escape to the freedom of riding, the thrill of racing.

"I *have* to get better, Dad. I have to be able to ride." She decided she should put it in terms he'd understand— terms that affected him personally. "If I can't ride, I can't win. And if I can't win, I can't pay the mortgage."

He cleared his throat, and she thought she might

be getting through to him. He was still staring straight ahead, but his eyes were moist. Suze had never seen him cry about anything, but she'd seen him get this same expression when he looked at photos of her mother.

Maybe he did love her. Maybe he'd take care of her through this rough patch. Maybe it wasn't too late to learn to care for each other, even love each other.

She reached over and put her hand over his.

"Either you have to do everything, help me with *everything*, or you have to let Brady do it. The two of you are all I have, so one of you has to step up. And I'm hoping it'll be you."

His hand loosened its hold on the steering wheel and turned over to grasp hers. It was a weak grip, but it was as close as her father had come in a long time to saying he loved her.

As they sped up the drive to the ranch, Suze smiled to see wild sunflowers rioting along the fencerow in a tangle of happy blooms. Brady's last bouquet had been mostly sunflowers, balanced with a selection of grasses in various textures and colors.

Her father reached over and patted her leg. She did her best not to wince at his tentative display of affection, but every part of her body hurt, and patting was the absolute wrong thing to do.

She didn't care about the pain, though. It was gone in an instant, and in its place was a feeling of warmth she'd been missing for the past ten years.

Maybe her injury would turn out to be a blessing in disguise. She and her father would be forced to work together, to solve problems and make their lives work in a new way—together.

Maybe they could even talk about her mother.

Suze longed to hear stories about her mother, to learn who she was, what she was like. Suze's dad offered her as a role model for Suze to live up to, but she never succeeded because his version of his late wife was some kind of sexy, beautiful saint who could do no wrong. Suze was never as pretty, as strong, as hardworking, or as successful as her mother.

The only other time Earl talked about Ellen was when he was making excuses. He couldn't feed the horses because being in the barn reminded him of Ellen. She'd hoped he'd come to the hospital, but she had no doubt he'd said it reminded him of Ellen.

He wasn't giving her much to work with. Truth be told, she was starting to hate hearing her mother's name.

If nothing else, they needed to do something about her father's grief, which had never wavered. Once his wife's funeral was over, he and Suze had retreated to their separate corners like prizefighters and nursed their wounds. She'd been only ten, but he'd never asked her if she was okay. In fact, she'd worried at one point that he'd forgotten about her.

She'd never really forgiven him for that. Maybe now they could talk about their loss. Maybe sharing their feelings would somehow help her father. The bruises and broken bones would all be worth it if she could mend the broken bonds between herself and her dad.

She watched the crooked fence posts of home flash past, one after another after another. She'd never noticed before how the ranch was hidden from the road. Not consciously, anyway. But today, as they turned down the long dirt driveway, it seemed as if the world opened up just as they rounded the last curve and revealed the center of her universe.

Most people probably would have thought it was a sorry world to hang your old cowboy hat on, but she loved the few beleaguered buildings that huddled at the end of the drive. Most of the ranch had suffered the insults of Wyoming's hot, dry summers and brutally cold winters for over a hundred years. The house they lived in was newer. It had been built back in the fifties. But the original homestead, along with the barn and assorted outbuildings, dated from the early nineteen hundreds.

She and her father did their best to stay on top of necessary repairs, but necessary was the key word. They were too busy and too poor to do more than keep the place from falling down, so if a board got replaced, there was a good chance it wouldn't match the boards around it. Just a few weeks ago, when they'd decided to replace a window in the barn, they'd scavenged a used one from a stack on the front porch. Earl kept a wide assortment of lumber and other junk there, squirreling away anything he thought might come in handy. It wasn't unusual for him to ask fellow ranchers embarrassing questions like, "Are you using that old screen door out there?" or "You mind if I take that stack of pallets that's been setting beside your barn for so long? No point in letting good wood go to waste."

So the house and barn had a funky, jerry-rigged look, and there probably wasn't a truly straight line or square corner on the place. But it was home, and there was nothing like it. After almost a week away, her love for the place hit her like a punch to the solar plexus, taking her breath away and reminding her of her greatest weakness.

If she'd been able to walk away from the place, she'd be living a very different life now. She could have used her winnings to buy a little house on a few acres, like so many of her fellow competitors had. Her dad had never done much for her. She could have walked away without much more than a faint twinge of guilt.

But this was the place they had lived with her mother. The place where Suze's few, vague memories of being part of a happy family took place. It was too precious to leave behind. So she'd stayed.

Now they were in danger of losing it all. Her stay in the hospital had undoubtedly cost a fortune. The two of them had a catastrophic health care plan with a sky-high deductible—so high they might have to take out a second mortgage on the place. If they could even get one.

She couldn't think about that now, though. Not when Bucket stood in the corral beside the barn, waiting for her. When she stepped out of the truck, the horse let out a soft nicker that told her he'd missed her, and invited her to come over and rub his velvety muzzle.

But by the time she made it out of the truck and into the wheelchair, she was sweating from the pain, and it seemed like every part of her body ached. When her father pushed her toward the house without asking her where she wanted to go, she didn't have the energy to protest. She'd have to boss him around enough in the days to come. She wasn't going to start any sooner than she had to.

Just this once, Bucket would have to wait.

Just this once, she'd put herself first.

Chapter 32

CLIMBING THE STAIRS WAS A PAINFUL AND HUMBLING experience for Suze, as well as a difficult one. It was painful because of that zinging pain in her back, and humbling because she finally had to ask her father to help her stand once she got to the top. The difficult part was avoiding Dooley, who thought they were playing some kind of game. He'd rushed up and down the stairs about a million times, panting happily as he welcomed her home over and over.

Her original plan had been to set herself up on the sofa in the front room. Then she'd be able to use the crutches to get to the kitchen, and with a little help she might be able to get outside and enjoy the nice weather.

She'd lasted about an hour before her father's grumpiness, combined with his incessant *Bonanza* reruns, chased her upstairs. She wanted to ask him to turn the danged TV off, but she couldn't bring herself to do it. Lying on the sofa, watching him watch Ben Cartwright and his boys struggle through all their troubles as if the plot of the episode held some key to existence, she realized something might be seriously wrong with her dad.

But things were getting better. She'd almost cried when she saw how much housework he'd done while she was gone. She knew he hated washing dishes and dusting—"women's work," he called it—but there wasn't a single dirty dish in the kitchen, and the old oak table gleamed in the Pledge-scented air. It must have taken two or more full days of work to wash the window curtains, shine the appliances, and clean the floors and even the windows. You knew a man really cared when he cleaned for you.

"Wow, Dad," she'd said. "The place looks great."

He'd only grunted.

Once she reached her room, she threw herself onto the bed—creating a whole new series of aches and pains—and fell into a deep, dreamless sleep. After all the sleepless nights and broken dreams she'd had in the hospital, she slept like the child she'd once been, like a woman with no worries.

And that was something she hadn't been for a long time.

When she woke up, it was well past four in the afternoon and she had a raging headache as well as a rumbling belly. She opened her mouth to call her dad, but nothing came out. Sure, it was her first day back. Sure, she was legitimately hurt and needed help. And sure, he was her father.

But calling her father for help just wasn't something she could do. He'd never been the one she called. Never. That had been her mother. And after her mother died... then she'd helped herself.

She crutched her way to the top of the stairs, then glanced around as if someone might be watching. The house was quiet. Maybe her dad was napping.

Finally, she sat down on the top step, set her crutches beside her, and gave them a push so they careened down the steps and clattered on the tile floor of the foyer.

Bumping her way downstairs on her bottom, she sacrificed dignity to practicality and joined them.

It hurt. It hurt her ankle, her back, and whatever nerve did that lightning-bolt thing that ran down her leg. She was sitting on the bottom step, panting and trying to ignore the pain, when Brady's voice jolted her back to the real world.

"Hey, Sleeping Beauty. You're up." He frowned. "You're also down. Why didn't you just call?"

"I didn't know you were here."

Struggling to cover up her undignified position, she leaned the crutches against the wall and pretended to be sitting casually at the bottom of the stairs, as if she did it all the time. Brady surely didn't believe that, but he just looked down at her and smiled, resting his elbow on the newel post. Dang, he looked hot—in the literal and figurative sense of the word. His skin glistened with sweat wherever it wasn't covered in dust. He'd traded his cowboy hat for a ratty baseball cap sporting the Cabela's logo, and he carried a rag in one hand. An extremely dirty rag.

"I've been cleaning. You got any more of these?" He waved the rag in the air.

Still sitting on the bottom step, she gaped up at him. "In—in the kitchen. The bottom drawer, next to the sink."

She hated it when anyone looked down on her—she much preferred looking down on them from the back of a horse—but she didn't have the strength to stand up without resorting to an ungainly climbing of the newel post. So when he held out his hand, she took it and let him hoist her to a standing position.

She didn't look at him while he did it. It hurt less that way.

"You got hungry, didn't you?" He started for the kitchen and she stumped after him, cussing silently with every painful step. "Sorry. I would have made you something earlier, but you were asleep. Then I got busy, and...shoot, I should have checked on you again sooner. Time got away from me."

"It's okay."

She wondered what he'd been busy doing. She scanned him again and decided that whatever it was had to be dirty work, because his face, his arms, his clothes—even his shoes—were covered with a fine layer of gray dust.

She crutched her way into the kitchen and leaned in the doorway, unable to go any farther.

"What do you want?" Brady asked.

"I'm going to make myself a sandwich," she said.

"Can I have one?"

She couldn't say no without sounding childish, so she nodded.

Brady was wearing a T-shirt so worn it was nearly transparent where it spanned his shoulders and chest. As he washed up and then explored the kitchen, bending over to open one cabinet, then reaching up to check another, he put on quite a show of male anatomy. Once he'd found bread and peanut butter, he scanned the refrigerator for jam. The cold white light from the open door lit the faint dark stubble that shadowed his jaw, and made his strong profile stand out in harsh relief against a backdrop of pickles and barbecue sauce.

Suze had never thought a man making a sandwich

could turn her on, but she was starting to feel kind of squirmy inside.

Shut it down. You couldn't do anything if you wanted to. And you don't want to. You don't.

She forced herself to remember the accident, the feeling of the rope tightening around her body, the wild whoop of triumph she'd heard before she passed out.

"Strawberry or grape?" he asked.

She reached for the grape. "I'm making my own."

She could feel his gaze on her as she slapped the peanut butter onto the bread with vicious slashes of the knife.

"What did that bread ever do to you?" he asked.

"The bread?" She tossed the knife in the sink, letting it clatter against the white porcelain. "Nothing."

She shot him a hard glare, but he didn't seem to notice as he spread his own jam, smiling slightly.

Smiling. After what he'd done to her.

She slapped her sandwich together and sliced it in half. "There," she said, leaning against the counter. "I'm fed. You can go now."

"You throwing me out?" He gave her a rueful smile that took all the starch out of her resentment.

"Once you eat that, yeah. Okay?"

"Okay."

He ate far more politely than she did, but then he probably wasn't as hungry. In the hospital, she'd eaten stuff like hot turkey sandwiches draped in gelatinous gravy and served on white bread that reminded her of memory foam. Peanut butter and jelly had never, ever tasted so good. She wasn't going to tell Brady, but as soon as he left, she was going to make herself another one.

He finished up and started cleaning up. Dang it, she should have done that so he couldn't.

"What time do you usually do your evening feed?" he asked.

She sighed. It was a cruel quirk of fate that had allowed him to take away her livelihood, her mobility, her everything, and then be so darned nice to her she couldn't even work up a good head of resentment.

"Around six."

He gave her his famous grin, along with a sloppy salute. "I'll be here, boss. Consider it done."

She opened the fridge and got out the milk jug, then realized the glasses were in a cabinet halfway down the counter. It was amazing how complicated life got when every move you made hurt. Pressing her hands on the countertop, she closed her eyes, willing herself not to break down.

"Thanks, Brady." She squeezed the words from a tight, aching throat as she opened the cabinet above her, rummaged around as if she was looking for something else so she could hide her face.

"Don't thank me." Brady gave her a carefree grin as he headed for the door. "I got you into this mess, and I'll help you through it as best I can." He sounded a little choked up himself, and she resisted the urge to look at him. The last thing she needed right now was an emotional moment with Brady.

Not that it wasn't tempting. If she let the tears flow, he'd let her rest her head on his strong chest and cry into his shirt. It would feel warm, comforting, and sweet.

And who knew what it might lead to?

She pictured him carrying her upstairs, Rhett

Butler–style. She imagined the feel of his strong arms surrounding her, supporting her, and she tilted her head ever so slightly to one side, imagining she was leaning against his powerful shoulders. When they got upstairs, he'd lower her gently to the bed, and then—then…

Then nothing.

She didn't stop staring at the contents of the cupboard until she heard the door close behind him.

Her nerve endings had apparently been waiting for him to leave too, because they immediately jumped to life, with stabbing pains, shooting pains, and every other kind of pain there was. Her ankle was throbbing with every beat of her heart, and her heart was pounding, struggling to pump out enough energy to overcome the urge to call Brady back so she could fall into his arms and cry.

No. That was wrong. She should want to scream at him until her throat was scraped raw.

Why hadn't he let go of the rope? Why had she let him into her trailer and her heart on that hot summer night? Why did he have to be so damned charming, so damned nice? And why did he have to be the only person who would help her?

It wasn't that she didn't have any friends. It's just that they were all barrel racers, and they were busy scooping up the prize money she was leaving on the table while she recovered. She couldn't blame them for going on with their lives.

And she'd never had time to make friends closer to home. When she was here, she was working. Perfecting her technique. Perfecting Speedo's training.

Being perfect took a lot of time. It didn't leave much room for anything else.

Maybe that wasn't the best way to live your life, but it was the only way Suze knew. She'd never questioned it until now. What if she lost her ability to ride? What would she do then? She had no marketable skills. No education beyond high school. And no desire to do anything but race horses around a cloverleaf pattern at top speed, just as her mother had.

If she couldn't ride, she couldn't live. It was the center of her universe.

Struggling to erase the dire thoughts that crowded her mind, she edged along the counter until she could reach the glasses. Why the heck were they so far from the fridge? It didn't make sense. She was going to fix that as soon as she could.

But who knew when that would be?

Once again pushing all thoughts of her recovery out of her head, she poured herself a glass of milk, drank half of it, then filled it again.

When she reached the foot of the stairs and confronted the task of climbing them one painful step at a time, she felt suddenly dizzy. Stumbling backward, she dropped the glass of milk onto the hardwood floor of the front hall. As the glass shattered, rage and sorrow slammed into hormones and adrenaline, creating a hot tsunami of emotion. Clutching the newel post, she let herself crumple to the floor in a heap and released the painful, wrenching sobs that had been building up for days.

She'd done her best not to cry after the accident. She'd tried to hold in the pain and the fear and the frustration. But now, she couldn't help herself. The sobs were coming from deep, deep inside.

She wondered if she'd ever be able to stop.

Chapter 33

BRADY SHOVED HIS HAND IN HIS POCKET AS HE HEADED for his truck, then groaned. He was always losing his keys.

He retraced his steps in his mind. He wouldn't have left the keys in the barn; he'd had no reason to take anything out of his pockets there. He wouldn't have left them in Suze's room either.

It had to have happened when they were leaning against the counter, eating their sandwiches. His wallet had felt bulky, and he'd taken it out of his pocket and set it on the counter. For some reason—habit, he guessed—he fished out his keys and set them beside it, probably so he wouldn't forget the wallet.

Naturally, he'd forgotten both.

He glanced back at the house. Suze had barely been able to rein in her emotions when he'd left, and she probably wouldn't be happy to see him back. But, heck, he ought to help her up the stairs anyway. The woman was so exhausted, she probably couldn't even get into bed on her own.

Now there was a dangerous situation—him, Suze Carlyle, and a bed. The last time those three things had gotten together, sparks had flown and he'd been burned to a crisp. If he let that same situation happen now, he had a feeling emotions would fly around the room like wild shots from a Smith & Wesson.

But he wasn't going anywhere until he got his keys. Hopefully she'd already gone upstairs.

He glanced around with pride when he passed through the sunroom. That was one thing he'd gotten right. He'd spent hours cleaning the room, and even dragged one of the recliners from the living room out so she could sit in the sunshine and watch her horses.

Make that the horse. Singular. Thanks to him.

It had been hard to resist showing the porch to Suze, but he'd decided not to mention any of the work he did unless he absolutely had to. That way she wouldn't have to acknowledge any kind of debt.

Because there was no debt—not on her side, anyway. On his side? He'd owe her forever for what he'd done.

He eased open the front door and almost stepped in a pool of milk that was spreading across the hardwood floor, away from the crumpled body of Suze, who was lying in a heap at the bottom of the stairs. A broken glass lay beside her.

No. Had she fainted? Fallen down the stairs?

He dropped to his knees. She was breathing, but it was more like gasping. Her shoulders heaved with every breath. Her thick hair had come mostly undone from her braid, but when he tried to brush it aside, it kept flopping back over her face so he couldn't tell if she was pale or flushed.

"Suze? Hey. Sweetheart, hey."

She made a choking sound. Something was terribly, horribly wrong. Was she having a seizure?

"Talk to me, Suze."

She turned away, her shoulders trembling as she struggled to catch her breath. It had to be a seizure.

He tried to remember the first aid classes he'd taken. Like most cowboys, he knew a lot about broken bones and head injuries. But seizures? He couldn't remember what to do.

There was something about the tongue. It was coming back to him.

The patient could swallow it, that's what it was. You had to keep that from happening. And you were supposed to make them bite on a stick. He looked around the room and couldn't see anything remotely sticklike except for Suze's crutches, and they were a little big for biting.

She was still bent over, hiding her face. He didn't see how she could swallow her tongue from that position, but he needed to check. He tried to turn her head, but she fought him, slapping at him with both hands.

It was one powerful seizure. Maybe he'd save her life. Man, she'd *hate* that.

But he had to try. He sat a couple steps up and pressed her head against his thigh. He had to manhandle her a little so he could ease his hand into her mouth. He figured he'd grab her tongue and hang on. It wouldn't be pretty, but what else could he do?

Dang, her tongue was slippery, though. She was trying to say something, but it was all garbled. This was getting scary.

He grabbed for her tongue again and almost had it. Then suddenly he wasn't conscious of anything but pain. Intense, very localized pain. In his finger.

She'd *bitten* him.

Well, it might not be a stick, but she probably couldn't swallow her tongue while she was biting his finger. That was the first thing he'd done right, but how far would he have to take this? The way things were going, she was liable to bite his finger *off*.

Finally, she let go. He tried to grab her tongue real quick, but she got away from him. He grabbed for one of her crutches, figuring there must be something on there she could bite, but since it was leaning up against the wall, he only succeeded in knocking it down. The armrest hit him on the head.

Good thing it was padded.

Suze was still breathing funny, but something had changed in the rhythm of it. Did seizures have phases? He really wished he'd paid more attention to those first aid classes. What did it mean when the patient's breathing was still heavy, still intense, but...

Wait a minute.

"Are you *laughing*?" he asked.

She shoved him away and sat upright, gasping for breath. He was glad to see there was plenty of color in her face, and though her eyes looked glassy and wet, and her lips were swollen, she didn't seem to be having a seizure at all. In fact, she was laughing so hard she could still barely breathe.

Hysterics. What did you do about hysterics?

"Suze." He took both her hands so she wouldn't be able to hurt herself. She hadn't tried, but you never knew. Naturally, she fought him, but he held on.

"Are you all right?" He spoke slowly, so she would understand despite her mental state. "Do you need to go to the hospital?"

"No." She struggled to speak, she was laughing so hard. "I'm fine. Let me *go*." She wrenched her hands away. "What the heck were you *doing*?"

"Trying to save your life," he said. "But you *bit* me."

She was still having trouble containing her laughter. "Save me from *what*?"

"A seizure. I thought you were having some kind of, um, episode."

She only laughed harder. Well, at least she was smiling. He might as well play it for all it was worth.

"I was trying to save your life. Then your stupid crutch clonked me on the head, and all you can do is laugh." He rubbed his head and did his best to look put-upon. Actually, he was mostly relieved. But it was obvious Suze had been crying, so if she wanted to laugh at him, that was fine with him.

She held her stomach, wiping her eyes and gasping. "Maybe you did," she said.

"Maybe I did *what*?"

"Save me," she said. "I was having one heck of a pity party." She sniffed a few times and wiped her eyes again. "It wasn't doing me any good. So you saved me from myself." She chuckled, as if she couldn't help herself. "You made me laugh. It was just what I needed. Oh, Brady, it was so *funny*! Why did you stick your finger in my mouth?"

"I was making sure you didn't swallow your tongue."

"So what were you going to do, hang on to it?"

"Well, what else was I supposed to do? You were breathing funny." He imitated the way she'd been heaving and sobbing and—sobbing.

"Oh." The truth dawned on him. Dang, he was an idiot. "I guess—I guess you were crying."

Chapter 34

SUZE'S LAUGHTER SLOWED, THEN STOPPED. SHE GAVE Brady a wide-eyed look of unfeigned amazement.

"Haven't you ever seen a woman cry before?"

He squirmed. "Probably, once or twice. I—I try to avoid that kind of thing."

"I'm sure you've *made* a few cry. What do you do, run away when the emotions get too hot to handle?"

He looked down at his lap. "Yeah, pretty much."

He expected her to lecture him or make some dismissive comment, but she just shook her head, her smile screwed down tight to hold in more laughter. "You don't even know the effect you have, do you?" She straightened and rested one elbow on his knee.

He wondered if she realized she was touching him. Then he wondered if she realized what that did to him. Then he decided to stop wondering about stuff and just enjoy it.

"It's like you're a big, happy, affectionate puppy, and you jump on people and knock everything over, and then you just go on being happy and affectionate while they try to clean up behind you," she said. "You have no idea the destruction you leave behind."

That didn't sound like a compliment. He bent down and drew her hair back from her face again, noticing her nose was still red and swollen, her eyes damp and bruised-looking. Was that the kind of destruction he left behind when he walked away from a woman? Shoot. Sometimes they yelled at him. Once in a while they even threw stuff at him. But crying? He sure hoped not.

"I've seen women cry before." He stroked her hair absently, as if he hadn't noticed her face. "I've just never seen a woman cry that *hard*. You couldn't even stand up. What happened, Suze?" He bunched her hair up around what was left of her braid so she couldn't hide her face. That made a handy handle so he could turn her head to face him. "I've never seen you break down like that. What's wrong?"

"Well, for starters, I'm not your Howdy Doody puppet." Wrenching her hair out of his hand, she pulled away and shook her head, wreaking more destruction on what was once a tight and tidy braid. "I dropped my glass of milk." She rested her elbows on her thighs, letting her hands hang limp between her knees as she stared straight ahead. "Then I, um..." She lowered her head, as if a sudden pain had struck. "I slipped trying to catch it. That's all."

He had a feeling she wasn't telling the truth. "Did you hurt yourself?"

"No," she said. "*You* hurt me. Remember? Horse? Rope? Dumb move?"

This was the Suze he knew. Things couldn't be too bad if she could still be mad at him.

"I know I hurt you," he said. "But something's going on."

"It got to me, okay? I had to go up the stairs again, and it got to me."

"What got to you? Your ankle? Your wrist? You need to go to the hospital?"

A tear skimmed down her cheek and dropped onto the knee of her sweatpants. "Jeez, Brady, you are so clueless. *Everything* got to me. The whole situation. I'm *worried*, okay? I'm worried I won't be able to ride again, and I'm scared. I get tired of pretending I'm okay, and I *thought* nobody was around. I *thought* I could let loose and cry a little without anybody making a big deal out of it."

"So you didn't slip?"

She shook her head. "Clueless."

Another tear fell, and he couldn't help reaching out and wiping it away with the backs of his fingers. "I'm so sorry, Suze. You can't even imagine how sorry I am."

"Sorry doesn't help much." She looked away again, ignoring the fact that she was staring directly at the side of the newel post, two inches from her face. "I'm hurt, and I'm pretty damned helpless. And unfortunately, people aren't exactly lining up to help, you know?" She sucked in a shuddering breath, and he could tell she was still on the edge of tears. "You're the only person who's offered, and I'm sorry, but you're the last person I want around right now."

"I know," he said. "I understand."

He was lying, of course. He didn't understand a damn thing—not about women in general, and certainly not about Suze in particular. His friends were always calling him a ladies' man, but all he did was love them when they'd let him, and stay away when they threw stuff.

But he couldn't stay away from Suze. He owed her. And if he was honest with himself, she'd been something special to him even before the accident. She was worth ten rodeo queens, twenty buckle bunnies—a million.

He probably ought to tell her that, but he doubted she wanted to hear it now.

Another shudder racked her body and he scooted down a step, so he was sitting right beside her, and put his arm around her shoulders. When she didn't shrug it off, he edged a little nearer. While he'd been trying to figure out what to say, she'd lost the fight to fake it. She was crying again, harder than ever, without shame.

Suze might have every reason to hate him, but Brady knew nobody should ever feel this bad without someone to comfort them. Pulling her head down to his shoulder, he wrapped his other arm around her and drew her close.

To his surprise, she let him hold her. And she wept. That *was* a new experience for Brady. Women cried when they were mad. They sobbed when they thought their hearts had been broken forever. But Suze was weeping, and it was all his fault. Her loss went way beyond anger or heartbreak. She'd lost her sport, her vocation, her career, her everything. She'd lost her*self*, and that's what she was mourning.

He'd done that—him and his ego and that stupid horse, Booger, along with the rope he'd hung on to a second too long.

He whispered into Suze's ear. He didn't know what he was saying or where it came from. It was mostly *there, there*'s and *now, now*'s, along with some nonsense words. It must have made her feel better because her shoulders shook less and less. He swayed gently, rocking her as if she were a child, and she clung to him as if she needed him. He was surprised and ashamed at how good it felt.

All this was his fault. And here he was, using her

misery to get close to her. He was the biggest jerk in the universe. But, dang, it was nice to rub her back, slow and steady, in an easy rhythm he thought might help quiet the tempest of emotions that had demolished her rigid self-control.

He prayed the phone wouldn't ring. He prayed her father wouldn't come home and ruin the moment. He prayed this would last forever, the two of them on the stairs just holding each other, but of course it had to end.

Slowly, Suze regained control. He'd known she would; a great competitor never let things rattle her for long.

She pulled away, but only a little, and scanned his eyes for a long time, as if searching out his deepest thoughts. He never knew what to say to women, and when he tried to express his feelings, he usually said the wrong thing. But he knew how to open up and be honest with his eyes and with his touch. He'd learned that from horses, just as Suze had.

But women liked words, and he liked Suze. So he had to try.

"When other women cry, I feel bad," he said. "When you cry, it's like the whole world's falling apart."

"I'm sorry." She sniffed. "I don't normally cry that hard."

"No, that's not what I mean. I know you don't cry much. That's why it feels like *my* whole world's falling apart. I just want to fix what's wrong so we can get back to normal, and you can ride away mad like you always do."

"Ride away…"

Her expression was so sorrowful he didn't just want

to kick himself; he wanted to pound himself to a pulp in a bar fight. Why did he go and say *ride*?

A tear leaked from the corner of her eye.

"Hey." He wiped it away with one finger and stroked her hair back from her face. And then he kissed her.

Miracle of miracles, she kissed him back.

He went slow, giving her every opportunity to pull away and laugh it off, but she reached up and knotted her fingers in the hair that curled over his collar. She pulled him in and kissed him like she was hungry, like she needed him every bit as much as he wanted—no, *needed*—her.

He ran his hands down her back, moving softly to soothe the bruises and brush burns from the accident. She whimpered—a sweet, kittenish sound he'd never expected to hear from Suze—and wriggled closer to him.

And then she pulled away. He opened his eyes, expecting her to be angry, but she was smiling. They looked in each other's eyes a long while, smiling like a couple of fools, and he felt his world shift, as if everything had changed.

"Brady." She started fooling with the top button on his shirt, and he held his breath, hoping she'd move down and undo the next one, and the next. But she just kept smiling and twisting that same button. "Why do you have to be so darn sweet?"

"What?"

She touched her lips with the tips of her fingers, as if she could still feel the kiss. "I'm mad at you, dang it, and you made me forget."

His disappointment must have shown in his face, because she gave him a pitying look.

"You don't think we're going to carry on some torrid romance while I'm recovering from my Brady-inflicted wounds, do you?"

"No." He raked his hand through his hair. "No, I wasn't thinking that way at all. It's just—I couldn't help it."

"Get a grip, Brady." She huffed out a bitter laugh. "Guys like you don't go for girls like me. Not for the long term, and I don't do the short term." She glanced around the room like a trapped animal, and he knew she was remembering their brief liaison. "Anymore. I don't do the short term *anymore*."

She tossed her hair, then winced as if that hurt too.

He winced with her. "Guys like me? Girls like you? What are you talking about?"

She nodded. "You know." She gazed up at the ceiling as if she needed strength from above to deal with him. "You're a ten, Brady. You can have anybody you want. Someday, when you're ready, you'll find some sweet, pretty, young thing, and you'll build you a little nest, and she'll make it all cozy and nice, and you'll have it made." She sighed. "I might win races, but you win at life."

He ran his hand down his face, struggling for control.

"And what are you going to do, while I'm off nesting with my pretty, young thing?"

She grinned, and suddenly the old Suze was back. "I'm going to win races."

"So if we're so different, how do you explain what happened that night?"

"You mean the night I got drunk and slept with you? Easy. I got drunk."

"You had two beers. Maybe three." He held up three fingers, in case she'd missed his point. "And I'm not talking about sex. I'm talking about everything else. Don't you remember anything about that night?" He sat back down beside her. "Don't you remember how we couldn't stop talking?"

"Until the next morning. You didn't have much to say then."

He tugged at the collar of his T-shirt, as if the room had gotten too warm. "I really did have a meeting, and I was late. I didn't mean to hurt you."

She looked away, seemingly transfixed by the doorknob. "You know, it doesn't really matter to the hurt person whether it was on purpose or not. It still hurts."

"Guess I never thought about that."

"Guess you never did." She started to stand and he stood with her, leaving her nowhere to go. She stared down at her cast. "We're just bad for each other, Brady."

"No," he said. "You're wrong. We're too much alike to be bad for each other. We both lost parents when we were young. We both found solace in horses. We both love taking risks, riding hard. We're alike, Suze." He dodged around, forcing her to look at him. Finally, he took her face between his hands, as if he was about to kiss her. "When you kissed me just now," he said, "you meant it."

She hesitated, then nodded.

"You aren't drunk now." He brushed her lips with his. She let out a little sigh, scented with some sort of mints, and her lips moved, then her tongue, just a little, the tip flicking out to stroke his lower lip.

It was a short kiss but a sweet one.

"So explain *that*." He had her there. He knew it. There was no way she'd be able to explain away that kiss. Not to herself, and certainly not to him.

"Painkillers," she said. "I took a double dose. *Phew*." She wiped her brow with one hand. "Better not do *that* again."

Chapter 35

Suze hadn't taken any painkillers at all, let alone a double dose. Looking at the staircase behind her, she wished she had, but the pills were in her room at the top of the steps. She was going to have to make it up there without pharmaceutical assistance, and her ankle was starting to throb again.

Oddly, it had stopped while Brady was kissing her. But trying to get over her pain by kissing Brady was like swallowing broken glass to help a sore throat. If she loved him and then lost him, the heartache would be a life sentence.

She'd seen it happen to her father, and she wasn't about to let it happen to her. Of course, her mother had died, while Brady would only move on. But imagine if her mother had lived and left her father. Imagine if he'd had to see her happy, in love with someone else. That would be even worse, wouldn't it?

"Can I help you up the stairs?" he asked.

"No. I'll be okay."

He stared down at the floor. She had the impression he was thinking hard, struggling to find a solution to her problems. Well, he could think till smoke poured out his ears. There wasn't a solution.

Finally, he looked up, and to her surprise, he looked pleased with himself, as if he'd thought of a solution.

"You just wait," he said. "People don't even know

what happened yet. Once everybody finds out what happened, you'll have help. You just wait."

She could see where this was going, and she didn't like it.

"Don't you *dare* go telling people how pathetic I am," she said. The last thing she needed was Brady going around, talking folks into helping her like she was some kind of charity case. She wanted friends who would help her out of love—not strangers who would help out of duty.

"You have more friends than you think," he said.

She sighed and set her foot on the first step. "I hate to admit it, but this is one thing I kind of like about you, Brady."

"What?" He put an arm around her, and suddenly she was swept up into his strong arms, cast and all.

She put her arms around his neck instinctively and rested her head against his shoulder. Time seemed to slow down as he turned sideways and carried her slowly, carefully up the stairs, as if she was some precious thing.

She closed her eyes and let herself believe, for a moment, that the warmth glowing in her heart was real, that Brady was carrying her up the stairs to a bed they shared, a double bed in some other house, some other time. Looking up at his face, she saw the delicate tracery of crow's-feet starting at the corner of his eyes, and pictured his brown hair tipped with just a touch of gray. He'd be as handsome in twenty years as he was now.

That sweet, pretty thing was one lucky girl.

He opened her bedroom door, backing and sidling like a horse at a ranch gate, then edged her in feetfirst.

He was breathing hard, and Suze couldn't help laughing. "I'm no delicate flower, Brady."

"It's all that muscle." He grinned and pretended to drop her on the bed, but in reality he set her down gently, and again she felt precious. Oh, she was jealous of whoever ended up with this man! He might be an idiot—an idiot she was mad at, she reminded herself— but he was kind, he was gentle, and he set her heart racing like a jackrabbit over open country every time he came close.

And he was close right now. When he'd put her down, he'd practically fallen on top of her. Now he was just an arm's length away, his hands resting by her shoulders.

"You are not pathetic," he whispered, lifting one hand to tuck a strand of her hair behind her ear. "You are the strongest woman I know."

She shook her head, but she didn't have the energy to argue. It seemed like all her energy was being absorbed by looking into his eyes—his amazing, gold-flecked, brown eyes. She was mesmerized by the shards of brightness, like flakes of gold, that surrounded his pupils.

"You can't do this alone, Suze. I know you're mad at me, but let me help you."

It was a good thing *he* knew she was mad at him, because she'd completely forgotten.

He stroked her hair again and smiled. "No, scratch that. *Make* me help you. Take up all my time. Be demanding and mean and ungrateful and difficult."

She grinned. "I'm already all those things."

"No you're not." He shook his head. "You're faking it. I want you to abuse me for real."

"I'll bet you do." She gave him a sexy sideways smile.

"I'm serious."

"Okay, but I warn you, I'm starting now."

"Okay." He grinned and sat up, folding his hands in his lap like a schoolkid waiting for instructions from the teacher.

She felt a sharp stab of loss, and wondered what would happen if she pulled him back down.

"What are you thinking?" he asked.

She looked away, biting her lip, and he took her chin between his thumb and forefinger, forcing her to face him. "You're thinking the same thing I am."

He didn't stop for confirmation. He just acted, bending low and kissing her again, but this time the kiss was hard and deep and hungry. His hands were fisted in the sheets, and his breaths were short and ragged, as if she'd torn away his ability to breathe.

There went her jackrabbit heart again, leaping and bounding, racing straight toward trouble. She wondered if he could feel it.

She wished he would.

As if he was reading her mind, he moved one hand up her shirt, skimming straight to her breast to squeeze and run his rough thumb over her nipple. She squirmed, letting out a mew of frustration. She couldn't get close enough.

She remembered this part. Brady Caine was a runaway train once you got him going. She'd never been with a man who lost himself so completely in a woman. He was helpless to stop once he'd started. It had made her feel powerful and sexy and strong the first time she'd slept with him, and it was having the same effect now.

Until he stopped.

Apparently, he wasn't so helpless after all.

———

Brady looked down at Suze, sprawled on her bed beneath him, and groaned aloud. He shouldn't do this. He couldn't. Hard as it was—and it was very, very hard—he had to stop.

Would Suze sleep with him if she knew Speedo was missing? While he'd been sitting in the waiting room, chatting up old ladies on their deathbeds and insisting on seeing Suze when she didn't even want him around, someone had gone to the rodeo grounds and stolen her horse.

At this very moment, they might be abusing him, starving him, selling him, or hiding him in a dark stall somewhere. Until Brady either found the horse or confessed his mistake to Suze, he couldn't make love to her. How had he even managed to look her in the eye?

He groaned again.

"Brady, what's wrong?"

Shoot, he was doing it again. Last time he'd walked out on her she'd been angry, but now she looked so wounded that he wanted to take her in her arms and kiss away the pain—but that was exactly what he couldn't do. Kissing would lead to touching, and touching would lead to making love.

"Believe me, I want this," he said fiercely. "I want this more than anything in the world. But you're right, Suze. I hurt you. I'm responsible for this." He gestured toward her cast. "And when you come to your senses, you're going to be glad you didn't sleep with me."

"No," she said. "I'll be sorry if I don't."

He thought of Speedo again. The image of the horse, and of Suze's certain grief if anything happened to him, was the only thing that could pull him away from her.

"Trust me." He gave her the best smile he could under the circumstances. It wasn't much of a smile, because who was he to ask for trust? He was a liar and a fraud, the last person she should depend on. "You'd regret it." He looked up at the ceiling, as if some divine being floated there who would give him inspiration.

The divine being must have been Suze's guardian angel, because a lightbulb went off in Brady's head. There was a way to say no—a way to say no without hurting her.

He made a long face, which wasn't too hard considering how miserable he felt. The thought of Speedo had killed his desire, so he didn't have that kind of misery to deal with, but he knew, no matter how things turned out, Suze was bound to hate him someday soon. Even if he found Speedo, she'd probably find out her horse had been missing. He'd asked too many people for help.

That's why it just about killed him that she was lying there with a come-hither glint in her eyes, believing in him. Believing he was the man he appeared to be.

"It's that double dose of painkillers," he said. "Remember? That's how this all started. I'd be taking advantage of you. Seriously, Suze. It's not the right time."

"Oh, yeah. Tha's right." Suddenly, she was slurring her words. Funny, she wasn't doing that before. Must be a delayed reaction. She actually seemed a little loopy as she lay down and rested her head on her folded hands like a little girl. "C'n I get a rain sheck?"

"Sure," he said. "If you still want to, call it in when you get better. I'll definitely honor a rain check."

He pulled the covers over her. Her eyes were closed as if she was already asleep, but a faint smile and the flutter of an eyelid told him she was faking it.

That was okay with him. He wanted her awake, so she'd feel him settle down beside her, so she'd feel him stroke her hair and feel safe and loved until she fell asleep for real. So he could make her happy, during this brief time before she found out what kind of man he really was.

And so he could touch that golden hair, admire that fine, strong face, and memorize the feeling of being close to her while he still had the chance.

Chapter 36

SUZE SLEPT THE SLEEP OF THE BLESSED THAT NIGHT, but she woke early to the sound of thumping and scraping, bumping and dragging. It had to be Brady. What the hell was he up to now?

She glanced at the clock. Five thirty a.m.

Didn't he have a life of his own? Didn't he have chores to do at Decker Ranch?

The thought made her smile. Both of Brady's brothers were talented horse trainers, and they'd helped her erase some problem behaviors in Bucket and even in Speedo. Whenever she was at the ranch, the brothers had razzed each other about everything from their riding ability to their girlfriends or lack thereof, but the most common theme was Brady's ability to foist off his chores onto Ridge or Shane. Apparently he'd made an art of being a cowboy of leisure.

Which was one of many reasons she was glad he'd put a stop to her foolishness last night. She'd wanted him so much she could still feel the ache, but despite the undeniable attraction between them, they were just too different. The workaholic would be annoyed by the carefree cowboy in no time.

But he was certainly working hard right now. He was also making much more of a racket than he needed to, and it was early. Plus he was apparently tackling something inside the house, which wasn't likely to sit well with her dad, who wanted the place left just as it had been when Ellen was alive.

Suze wished her dad would relax his worship of her mother's memory, just a little. She wondered if Ellen Carlyle had demanded this much attention from her husband when she was alive. Suze remembered her mother as warm and kind, but Suze probably hadn't been a very skilled judge of character at the age of ten. And though she remembered her mother fondly, she also remembered the fights her parents had, fights she didn't understand that left the house simmering with tension.

A loud scrape and a muffled grunt drifted up the stairs. Whatever Brady was doing, she should probably stop him.

Flinging back the covers, she hobbled into the bathroom and gave her hair a few licks with a brush, then rubbed her eyes and rinsed her mouth. That was enough beautifying for now. Brady had already seen her at her worst. She didn't need to put on a face for him—which was kind of nice.

Stop it. He was entirely driven by guilt. She had to keep reminding herself of that fact, because it was easy to believe that he really…*cared*. But what had happened last night was about sex, not caring.

But he made you stop. And he stroked your hair…

She stood at the top of the stairs, which seemed steeper and more perilous every time she faced them. Sighing, she sat down and laid her crutches beside her. The crutches slid quickly to the bottom of the stairs as usual, while she began to bump her way down on her butt.

Whatever Brady was doing must be riveting work if it kept him from hearing her crutches clatter down the stairs. Part of her was glad he wasn't seeing her humiliating descent, but another part wished he'd come up and help her already. Maybe sweep her up in his arms again…

Vivid fantasies swirled through her mind and she hardly noticed the pain as she worked her way downstairs. When she reached the fifth step down, she peeked through the banister to see what was going on in the front hall.

No wonder Brady hadn't come to her rescue; it was her father who was making all the scrapes and thumps. He had her mother's rocker-recliner, the one that matched his own, and he was evidently taking it out onto the sun porch.

Or trying, anyway.

The chair wasn't small, and its spinning base wasn't helping any. He had it stuck in the doorway, half-in and half-out of the porch. But she could see past it, and what she saw was a miracle.

He'd cleaned the porch. Really cleaned it. Somehow, he'd made all the old doors, windows, scrap lumber, and abandoned projects disappear, and then he'd washed the windows and wiped down the walls. The room looked sunny and inviting; a fine place to spend a long afternoon enjoying the long, sage-strewn view of the plains and the pale blue mountains beyond.

For as long as Suze could remember, the porch had been an embarrassment. Every visitor to the house had to wend his way through her father's junk. She'd always hated it, but it was just too big a job to take on by herself, and she'd thought her father would never help her clean it.

But now he'd gone and done it. And he was hauling the sacred chair—Ellen's chair—out there. There could only be one reason he was doing that. He was making a place for Suze.

She felt her eyes tear up. He was making a place for her—a place where she could put her feet up and recover from her injuries, a place where she could sit and watch her horses in the pasture, a place where she could still be a part of the household instead of being banished to her little room upstairs. But most important, by moving that chair, he'd made a place for her in his life, giving up a piece of his obsession with his late wife for her comfort.

She couldn't believe it. No one ever sat in that chair—at least not when her dad was around. A few weeks after her mother's death, it had occurred to Suze that maybe it was forbidden because her mother's ghost sat there. For months, Suze had sat in the chair whenever her dad was away, trying to feel her mother's presence. But all she'd felt was itchy from the chair's ancient upholstery.

But now, the chair was hers. She couldn't hold back any longer.

"Dad!"

She nearly tumbled down the stairs in her eagerness to reach him. It was frustrating to be so hobbled when what she wanted to do was run downstairs and throw her arms around her father.

"Dad, I can't believe it! It's beautiful. I'm just..." She wiped a tear from her eye and shook her head. "I'm just floored. This is the nicest thing anyone's ever done for me. And it's you that did it. That makes it—oh!"

Overcome with emotion, she hobbled toward him, nearly falling in her eagerness. She'd never known how much she'd needed her father's love until this moment, when it was finally won.

But when he turned to face her, he didn't look like a man who had shrugged off the burden of impossible grief and made a place for his daughter in his life. He looked like a man in a rage.

Suze could understand that. Her dad wasn't a patient man at the best of times, and he was apparently frustrated beyond endurance by the chair, which was jammed in the doorway and evidently wouldn't budge.

Suze had wished herself well a million times since the accident, but none of those fervent prayers matched her current desperation. If only she could walk and lift and do all the things she used to do! Together, they could move that chair in no time, and then the two of them could enjoy the newly redecorated sun porch. It needed a little paint, and maybe an area rug, but it was full of light. And love.

She swallowed a sob.

"Why don't you take a break, Dad?" Her father's face was fixed in a scowl so fierce it was almost cartoonish. "Brady'll probably be over soon, and he can help you move the chair."

"Brady," her father spat. "What makes you think your precious Brady's going to fix it? He's the one that made this mess. He's nothing but a meddler." He pointed a finger at Suze—a finger that shook with rage. "You tell that boy he's not a part of this family and never will be." Turning, he tugged futilely at the trapped chair.

Suze felt a little of her elation fade away. She should

have known her father hadn't done this whole project by himself.

It was probably Brady's idea too, not her father's.

The shine was wearing off this new gift awfully fast. But still, her father was letting her have the chair.

"I'm sorry, Dad. He has some awfully big ideas about improving the place, but this was a good one."

Suze listened to herself and wondered when she'd stopped resenting Brady for his interference. At first she'd been steaming mad over the way he'd butted into her life after the accident. Now she was defending him, and it felt absolutely right.

She edged a little closer, braving her father's anger to peer past the chair to the porch.

"This is going to be great, Dad. I'll be able to see the horses from here, and I'll be on the first floor."

She started to say she'd be able to get food easier and wouldn't starve to death up in her bedroom, like she had the day before.

But that would be complaining, and she wasn't going to complain today. Her father might not have cleaned the porch himself, but after the long, dark years of grief, he was finally seeing the light. She wasn't about to harp on past troubles. Not today.

"I'll be closer to the kitchen," she said instead. "Maybe I can make us some nice meals."

When her father didn't respond, she rushed to fill the silence.

"You have to admit, it's nice of Brady to help us," she said. "I mean, I know some of this is his fault, but..."

Her father took a step toward her. "Some of this? Some of it?" He was almost shaking with anger. "It's *all* his fault. He took your mother's chair, and he moved it from where it belongs. He *moved* it, from the spot where *she* sat, and put it out on the *porch*." He shook a finger in her face. "If that meddling bastard shows up, tell him he'd better put it back where he found it. *Right* where he found it."

Suze backed away as he spoke, backing farther and farther until her heel caught on the bottom step of the staircase and she sat down, hard.

Her father hadn't done this for her. He hadn't even helped Brady do it. In fact, he hated Brady for trying to make a comfortable place for Suze to sit.

Her mother's ratty recliner was faded by sunlight and dusty with age. It was upholstered in a fabric that couldn't be described as green or gray or brown, but only as a muddy mess of all three. It was old, it was ugly, and a broken spring caused it to list dangerously to one side. But that chair, ugly, broken, and old, was more important to Earl Carlyle than his own daughter.

Suze doubted her mother had cared a bit about the chair. It didn't seem like the kind of thing dashing Ellen Carlyle would even want. So why was her father so dead set on preserving it?

It was depression, brought on by the grief he couldn't seem to shake. She stood, clinging to the newel post, and smiled as brightly as she could.

"Dad?" she said. "Why don't you go watch your shows? I'll wait here for Brady, and I'll make sure he puts the recliner back."

He gave her a baleful look, and she braced herself for another onslaught of harsh words, but he seemed to have exhausted himself. Slowly lowering the pointing finger, he hunched his shoulders and walked away. But instead of heading for the television, he ducked under the immovable chair and stomped outside.

Just when she thought she was in the clear, he turned. "Tell him to stay out of our kitchen too. I don't need him washing dishes and prettifying everything the way he did. We can do for ourselves."

She stared at him, working the words over in her head to make sure she understood as her father stomped off toward the barn. It was an empty house she spoke to when she finally figured things out.

"So it was Brady, not Dad," she said to no one. "Brady cleaned the downstairs." The stab of disappointment in her father was overwhelmed by the realization of how hard Brady had worked. "Brady did everything."

The clean dishes, the freshly washed curtains, the polished floors—she'd taken them all as signs of her father's love. But it was Brady all along.

She'd been thinking her father was helping, that the two of them could work together as a team until she got better. But her father had never been on her team.

She needed Brady even more than she thought. She'd better clean up her act and start treating him better. He was probably wondering why she hadn't thanked him for all the work he'd done.

She pictured him at the sink, washing dishes; at the window, hanging curtains. She remembered him stroking her hair as she drifted off to sleep. What made a man do that?

Guilt, that was what. She needed to get a grip.

Chapter 37

BRADY STOOD WITH HIS HANDS ON HIS HIPS, LOOKING from the Carlyle house to the Carlyle barn and back again. He wasn't sure quite what to do. He knew Suze had been hurting, but it surprised him that she'd never even mentioned the clean kitchen, the polished table, or the curtains he'd so painstakingly ironed. She obviously didn't care about the housework.

He should probably go look for Speedo. There was nothing more important on the agenda now that he'd fed Bucket and turned him out.

He'd asked dang near everybody he knew to look out for Speedo and call if they saw him. The rodeo cowboy network ran from Texas to Montana, and all the way from California to New Jersey and beyond. His only hope was that someone had hidden the horse somewhere. He'd continue to check abandoned barns today. He still hadn't covered the southern part of the county.

Once that was done, he'd have to fess up and tell Suze so they could get law enforcement involved. He probably should have done that from the start, but the closest town was Wynott, and their constabulary consisted of one man on a bicycle. Officer Jim couldn't find his own butt with a flashlight, so Brady doubted he'd be much help finding Speedo.

He'd given Bucket a quick grooming session before

he turned him out. The poor guy hadn't gotten much attention since the accident, and Brady firmly believed horses needed to be touched every day, if only to remind them of their partnership with their strange two-legged friends.

He wondered if anyone was touching Speedo or if he was hidden in some dark barn, missing the sunshine. Missing Suze.

Bucket had leaned into the brush, enjoying every minute of the massage, but he'd playfully nipped Brady's butt when the cowboy had bent to check his back feet. The whole time, little Dooley had pranced around, seemingly unfazed by the weight and power of the horse's hooves.

Once Bucket was turned out, his stall had to be cleaned. Oddly, Brady had never minded that job. Somebody once told him shoveling horseshit was the closest cowboys ever got to a Zen experience, and he thought that might be true. The repetitive motion felt like a chant, and he let his mind wander. Naturally, it wandered back to the house and up the stairs so it could crawl into bed with Suze.

He pictured her in the early morning, flushed from sleep and satisfied from a night of...

Stop it.

He really needed to find Speedo, so he could make dreams like that a reality.

He stared at the house, hat in hand, and scratched his head. The windows, open to the summer heat, were silent, the curtains motionless. He didn't even hear the television squawk that would tell him Earl was up and watching his shows.

Maybe something was wrong.

He climbed the stairs and jiggled the handle on the screen door.

"Hey," somebody said.

It was Suze's voice, and it seemed to come from above. He backed up, craning his neck and holding on to the crown of his hat. His boot heel hit a rock that jutted from the crispy dry grass of the lawn and he fell flat on his back. He looked up to see Suze, framed in her bedroom window like Rapunzel in her tower, her smile screwed down tight to hold in a laugh.

"If it'll make you laugh, I'll fall down again." He rose and brushed off the seat of his pants.

She shook her head. "Don't go hurting yourself."

That was promising. "Can I come up?"

She nodded, and he stepped inside the sun porch and was immediately stopped by the rocker/recliner he'd hauled out there for Suze. It was half-in, half-out of the door, suspended in the middle of the opening.

Earl. It had to be Earl. Apparently, Brady had moved his cheese.

Well, he wasn't going to help the old guy take Suze's chair away. Ducking under the stuck chair, he headed up the steps.

Suze was in her rolling office chair, which she'd trundled over to the window. Her crutches leaned against the wall, and she had her bad leg propped on a stack of books. With a rigid cast up to the knee, she looked awfully uncomfortable, especially since she had to stick her leg out at an awkward angle from the hip to sit close to the window.

"Let me set you up downstairs." To heck with

Earl. He'd take the chair back out and she could enjoy the sunshine.

"Um, no thanks." She looked away, studying the missing shingles on the barn roof. Darn, he hadn't noticed that. He'd have to get up there and fix it.

"Dad's down there most of the time, watching his shows. Trust me, I'm better off up here. If I have to hear Little Joe whining one more time, I'm going to throw something."

"Where is he now?"

"Out."

She blinked fast, almost as if she was holding back tears. Something must have happened between her and her dad. He hoped it didn't have anything to do with him, but the chair stuck in the doorway said otherwise.

"Thanks for fixing up the porch," she said. "Dad wasn't too happy about it, though."

"Dang it, I didn't mean to make trouble for you. I thought I'd shake Earl up a little, try and make a change." He scratched his head again. "Guess it backfired."

He glanced around the small bedroom. A few tattered novels, obviously read and reread, sat on the shelf under her nightstand. The horse magazines he'd brought her in the hospital occupied a basket by the window. Other than that, the room looked exactly like what it was: a place to sleep in between rodeos. It had all the personality of a cheap hotel room.

She'd go crazy in here.

Suze looked away, suddenly shy.

"It's okay," she said. "I can see Bucket from here when he's out." She bit her lower lip and gave him that sweet sideways look he could never resist, the look women used to make men their slaves from the time they were about six months old. "Do you think you could bring Speedo back?"

Heaven help him, you could see how much she loved that horse just by looking at her face. She was going to kill him when she found out Speedo was missing, and he'd deserve it. Heck, he'd welcome it at this point. He felt so guilty, he could hardly stand to walk around with himself.

Suze might be sweet right now, but he knew she had a wicked temper. If that temper was a shotgun, it would be aimed his way once she found out the truth.

Actually, he suspected Suze's temper was more like a bazooka or a rocket launcher. And once he told her about Speedo, it would go nuclear.

"I really miss him," she said. "I thought maybe Ridge wouldn't mind coming out here to work him. I'd pay him."

Brady cleared his throat, and suddenly found himself choking on nothing. Well, actually, he was choking on words, but they hadn't been spoken yet. They were locked inside, and he couldn't even cough them out.

What words would he use?

Speedo's gone. Somebody stole him.

I left him at the rodeo grounds, and when I went back, he was gone.

He could be anywhere. Somebody might have hurt him or locked him up.

You might never see him—your best friend, your pardner, the other half of your heart—ever again.

He should tell her somehow. But the words stuck in his throat.

He pounded his chest with a fist, wheezing. He couldn't breathe.

"Are you all right?" Suze asked.

"Fine," he said. "Fine." He took a couple deep breaths, preparing himself.

But the words that came out weren't the ones he'd planned to say.

"Did you have breakfast?"

She shook her head.

"Well, you've got to eat. I'll go make you a sandwich. You like peanut butter and jelly, right?"

She sighed. "Sure. Fine."

She looked so vulnerable. Her world was falling apart around her. She couldn't ride, and riding was her life. How could he tell her Speedo was gone?

"What?" she asked.

He realized he'd been standing in the doorway staring at her for way too long.

"Nothing. You look nice, that's all."

"I thought you were going to stop looking at me like that," she said. "Quit going all googly eyed."

He turned away. He couldn't help looking at her like that, but until Speedo was safe in her barn, he should just stay away.

"Sorry," he said. "I'll just make the sandwich and go."

"Wait, Brady," she called as he jogged down the stairs. "I'm sorry. I…"

"It's okay," he called back.

He found the peanut butter in a high cabinet, the jelly in the fridge, but the bread wasn't in its usual spot. As he hunted for it, he noticed a stack of mail piled at the end of the counter. There were a couple things in there that looked like catalogs or magazines. They'd give Suze something to look at.

He flipped through the stack, pausing at a copy of *Western Horseman*. It was the same edition he'd bought for her, so that wouldn't help. He should have known she'd have a subscription.

He pulled a Western clothing catalog out of the middle of the stack and an envelope fell to the floor. It had Suze's name on it, although it was spelled wrong. *Sooze Carlile*. And it hadn't come through the mail, because there wasn't a stamp on it. Even weirder, her name was spelled out in letters cut from magazines that had been taped to the envelope.

What the heck?

Maybe the letter was a joke or something, but it gave Brady a creepy feeling. It looked like an old-fashioned ransom note, the kind you saw in old movies about—

Wait a minute. Ransom. Maybe Speedo hadn't been stolen; maybe he'd been kidnapped for ransom.

It made sense. The horse was worth a fortune, and anybody who knew anything about rodeo knew about the bond between Suze and her horse. Maybe someone saw the big purses she won and figured she had the money to pay.

Glancing around the kitchen, he grabbed a knife from the block by the stove and slit open the envelope. Opening someone else's mail was a federal crime, but this hadn't come through the mail. And if it was about Speedo, he needed to know.

He glanced around again as he unfolded the letter, then cursed as tiny squares of paper cascaded to the floor like confetti.

Evidently the glue hadn't held.

Chapter 38

SMALL CAPS Something behind Brady gave a loud thump. He gave a guilty start and spun around to see Dooley rushing toward him, the doggie door flapping in his wake.

"No, buddy. Down."

Dooley danced and hopped as usual, spreading the slips of paper all over the kitchen.

"Stop!" Brady set the letter on the counter and began frantically sweeping up the confetti with his hands. If this was a ransom note—and he was pretty sure it wasn't a get-well card—he needed to save every letter. It would be a puzzle to solve—something he wasn't particularly good at. Missing letters would only make it worse.

He had almost all the letters brushed into a small pile on the floor, except for one that was stuck to Dooley's paw and a few the dog had eaten despite Brady's pleas.

"Okay." He stood and piled the letters on the counter. "Let's see what's left."

Unfolding the paper, he was relieved to see that the note was mostly intact.

D__r Lezzy B_tch,

> I h_ve your st_pid horse a_d am go_ng to ki_l it if y__ don't put $_00,000 in a b_g and le_ve it at…

After that point, most of the letters were missing.

Great. Brady didn't know how much money the horse-napper wanted or where he was supposed to leave it, or when. For all he knew, the deadline had passed.

He looked down at the pile of letters in front of him and cursed again. It would take him an hour to figure this out.

But Suze could do it. She'd finished every word search and crossword magazine he brought her. She loved word puzzles.

He stared down at the letter, struggling to work up the courage to go upstairs and confess. Just to waste time, he read the letter again, filling in what blanks he could.

Dear Lezzy Bitch,

Where had he heard those words? Someone had called Suze that before.

The smug face of Cooter Banks rose in his memory. He remembered the cowboy's face contorted into a sneer, his hands making some kind of obscene gesture Brady didn't even understand as he'd called Suze a "lezzy," a "stuck-up bitch," and more. Brady remembered how much he'd wanted to punch the guy.

Now he wanted to kill him.

The letter had to be from Cooter. Cooter had been furious when Red had withdrawn his endorsement from Lariat, and Suze had come on board soon after. No doubt Cooter blamed her for his troubles. The man could never accept responsibility for anything, and he was about as bright as your average sex-crazed rooster, strutting and crowing night and day, foolishly unaware that nobody was watching or listening.

But right now, Brady was grateful for Cooter's idiocy. He'd given himself away by calling Suze names. And if Brady wasn't too late, he'd probably find Suze's best friend cooling his hooves in Cooter's barn.

Grabbing his hat from the front hall, he jammed it on his head and ran for the door, almost slamming into the chair. Ducking underneath it, he ran for his truck.

Suze listened to Brady's boots thudding down the stairs and wished she'd swallowed her stupid pride and asked for two sandwiches. Or maybe three. She was so hungry she was ready to gnaw on the furniture.

But Brady was acting weird today. When she'd asked him to quit looking at her the way he did, the warmth in his gaze had turned off like she'd flicked a switch.

Be careful what you wish for.

She heard him cuss once, and then he was hollering at Dooley. Listening to him was definitely more entertaining than the unchanging view outside the window. She rolled the office chair over to the bed, moving as quietly as she could on the uneven plank floors.

It was then she heard the screen door slam, its spring-loaded wooden frame hitting the door frame with a sound like a gunshot.

Moments later, Brady's truck started, and then she heard the unmistakable crunch of wheels on gravel.

He'd left. Just left. Had she been that rude? What had she done?

She was hungry, she was lonely, and she was starting to realize she was a bitch. She hadn't done a thing to thank him for all the work he'd done. And now, here she was ordering him to go get her horse and haul him out here, so he'd have even more to do.

She sighed. It was just as well. Resisting him day after day hurt almost as much as her ankle. If he stuck around, she was likely to end up in bed with him again, and then she'd end up hurting even more.

She should let him go find that sweet thing, a nice girl who would love him and make him happy.

She carefully eased herself from the chair and headed downstairs, using one crutch and the stair railing to support her bad ankle. She didn't know what had set Brady off, but apparently she'd be making her own sandwiches from now on.

—⁓—

Earl Carlyle slouched in his rocker-recliner in the front room, watching *Pale Rider* for probably the twentieth time. The danged cowboy that hung around his daughter wasn't there when he'd gotten home, and Suze herself was taking a nap, so he could relax and watch TV. He normally watched *Bonanza* reruns, but the Ponderosa took a powder from two to four, and wasn't running on any of the stations the satellite pulled in.

He'd seen every episode of that show over and over too, but he felt more comfortable at the Ponderosa than he did in his own home. Lorne Greene had lost his wife—lost three of them, as a matter of fact—but he and his boys just went on about their business. It made Earl wonder if he and Ellen should have had more children.

Once he'd sent Mr. Greene a letter, asked him how he did it. He'd gotten back a signed photograph and an invitation to join the *Bonanza* Fan Club. It figured.

Lorne Greene was just acting, anyway. He probably didn't know anything about grief. Most people didn't.

They'd never lived through the grief and bitterness he endured. He couldn't tell if it was his arthritis and his injuries that crippled him so, or if his unremitting pain was about Ellen.

His heart hadn't ever really broken; it had shriveled up from lack of nourishment, leaving nothing for Suzanne or even himself. He was a hollow man, holding only anger at the unfairness of it all and the deep, aching pain of loss.

It would be easier if he'd had sons, like on *Bonanza*. For one thing, they could do the work around the place, maybe keep up with things better. For another thing, they wouldn't look so much like your dead wife that you felt like you'd been stabbed in the heart every time they walked into the room.

He turned his attention back to the movie. Clint was riding around in that stupid poncho that made him look like a girl. There was a loud hammering noise, and it took him a minute to realize it wasn't part of the movie. Somebody was at the door.

Probably that Brady character, trying to get at Suzanne again. She'd thrown him out a half-dozen times, but he kept on coming back. Those dumb bronc riders were like that, always getting back on the horse even if it tossed 'em off and stomped 'em near to death. Hell, he'd been like that once.

"Just a minute." Earl grabbed the edge of the end table with his right hand and the arm of the chair with his left, levering himself up and onto his feet. Pain shot up from his ankles and his knees ached as he straightened them.

The kid had better have a good reason for interrupting him this time.

He shuffled over to the door, hating the hunched, bent stance the pain forced on him. Once the blood got flowing, it was a little easier to stand, and he straightened as best he could before he had to stoop again to get past that damned chair.

He opened the door to a woman with a round head set on a body that was a perfect square, with stumpy short legs like porch posts. She had no neck to speak of, and her short, straight gray hair swept across her forehead, almost hiding her lively brown eyes. She wore a shabby black peacoat over white overalls so streaked with paint that it was hard to see the original fabric. The effect was strangely festive.

"Hi," she said. "I came to see Suzanne."

Huh. He'd thought he was the only one who called his daughter by her given name. It was always "Suze" this, "Suze" that. He and Ellen had named her Suzanne, dammit.

"You a friend of hers?"

The woman laughed. She might be heavy, but she had a hearty laugh and her eyes flashed and sparkled with good humor. She reminded him of somebody, but damned if he knew who.

"Just her godmother," she said. "I knew you wouldn't recognize me. I'm a friend of *yours*, dummy." She spread her hands as if offering herself for inspection. "Guess it's been too many years and too many pints of ice cream."

He stared a moment. Those eyes...

"Gwen Saunders." Lord have mercy, he felt a smile

spreading across his face. And miracle of miracles, his face didn't crack from the effort. "I knew you looked familiar."

She gave him a good-natured punch in the stomach. Gwen was always like that, joshing everybody, friendly. It was impossible *not* to smile when she was around. He hadn't seen her since Ellen's funeral, but it was like no time had passed at all. He felt his smile softening, his eyes tearing up a bit. He couldn't help it. He'd always liked Gwennie. Liked her a lot.

He'd heard she was living in Wynott. Became kind of a recluse, apparently, living in a junkyard behind a big, high fence. He'd have gone to check on her sometime, because that didn't sound like the Gwennie he knew. But he knew seeing her would remind him, painfully, of Ellen, and all the mistakes he'd made.

He looked at Gwen and waited for that stab of pain, that flash of memory that hurt so bad it made him want to die and join his wife in the grave.

But there was nothing. He was just glad to see her. Imagine that.

She followed him into the house.

"Don't mind that chair," he said. "Got stuck."

She struggled under it, obviously embarrassed by her bulk. But Earl knew he didn't look much better.

"Looks like you lost as much weight as I gained," she said. "You okay, Earl?"

"Fine," he said. "Suzanne's upstairs."

"Really?" Gwen turned and scanned the staircase. "She can get up and down stairs already?"

"No, and she makes me run and fetch everything for her. Drivin' me crazy."

"I heard she has some handsome cowboy running errands for her." Her eyes sparkled, as if she thought it was funny that the damned cowboy was hanging around as if his daughter was a cat in heat.

"She can't stand the sight of him," Earl said.

"Really?" She shook her head, still smiling. "That's not what I heard."

She looked him up and down, and he shifted, uncomfortable. He knew he'd changed. He saw it every time he looked in the mirror. Somewhere along the way, his features had all drawn together into the center of his face and turned small and mean. His brows arrowed down over eyes that seemed to have grown darker with age. His nose was more hooked, his mouth a short, grim line. If Ellen were still alive, she'd never look at him twice. He was just a mean old man.

Then again, if Ellen were still alive, he'd be a different person. When she was alive, he was tall, dark, and handsome. She'd said so herself once.

"You never got over her, did you?" Gwen asked.

He shook his head.

She nodded, then headed up the stairs to see her goddaughter. He supposed he should be grateful that Gwen had turned up, but he felt ashamed of himself, of the way he'd let everything go to hell.

He felt ashamed of the way he treated Suzanne too— but Gwen was the one person in the world who might understand why. She knew the truth about him and Ellen, and the truth about Suzanne.

He hoped she wasn't up there spilling the beans. He hadn't faced the truth when Ellen was alive, and he didn't want to face it now.

Chapter 39

SUZE WAS JUST FINISHING HER SANDWICH WHEN SHE heard the crunch of tires on gravel.

"He's back, Dooley!" The little dog jumped off the bed and barked, whirling in a circle.

"I'm an idiot," she said to the dog. "Why did I assume he was gone for good? Brady wouldn't do that. He wouldn't let me go hungry."

Maybe he hadn't been able to find the peanut butter. Maybe he'd wanted a different kind of jelly, or they needed some more milk. She hobbled to the window, so relieved she wished she could turn a cartwheel.

But it wasn't Brady's Silverado parked in the turnout. It was some old rattletrap truck she'd never seen before.

A heavyset woman eased out of the vehicle. She patted the front fender, as if she was thanking the truck for the ride before she waddled to the front door.

Funny. Suze did that herself sometimes, treating her pickup as if it was a faithful old horse.

Suze heard her father's low voice talking to the visitor and wondered who it could be. Her father sounded almost cordial, and she thought whoever it was must have come to see him, but then footsteps started up the stairs—heavy, lumbering steps, and heavy breathing as well. It sounded like a bear was coming to visit, but the person who appeared in her doorway was a stout little gray-haired woman with laughing brown eyes. She lumbered into the room and sat down on the desk chair without invitation.

The visitor put a fist to her chest, catching her breath, all the while staring at Suze.

"Criminy," she finally said. "It's like seeing a ghost."

Suze glanced around the room. She didn't see any phantomlike apparitions, although judging from her visitor's breathing, the woman might cross to the other side at any moment.

"You, I mean." The woman leaned forward and took a deep breath, then sat up and smiled. "You look so much like your mother, it's scary."

"Thank you," Suze said. "I used to hear that a lot, but not so much anymore."

"People forget." The woman shifted her weight. "New champions come along, and they forget the old ones."

"I always feel bad about that," Suze said. "Sometimes I think it's me that's erasing her memory. When I won my second championship, I beat her record at Thomas & Mack arena. When I found out, I wished I could take it back." She shook her head, hard and fast. "I'm sorry. I don't know why I'm telling you all that. What can I do for you?"

"Nothing. I'm here to see what I can do for you. And the first order of business is to tell you not to worry about your mother's memory. It's your turn now."

"I guess. It just bothers me sometimes."

"Don't let it. She'd be proud." The woman eased off the chair and reached for the photo Suze kept by her bed, pausing before she touched it. "May I?"

Suze nodded and the woman picked it up. Her eyes scanned it almost greedily, her smile widening.

"Did you know her?" Suze asked.

"Know her? I was her best friend."

Suze gasped. "You're Gwennie?"

"Gwen Saunders, in the flesh—and plenty of it." The woman set the photo down and held out her hand. Suze shook it, then clutched it in both of hers.

"Oh, it's so good to see you! I remember you. You used to bring me little horses. Fetishes, you called them." She started to rise, wincing as the pain kicked in. "I still have them. Over there, in the top drawer of the desk."

Gwen opened the drawer and took out a tiny silver pony, then a bronze one, and another carved in stone. They were all tiny, maybe a half-inch long, small enough to fit in a pocket and bring good luck to a girl barrel racer who'd hoped to ride in her mother's hoofprints.

"I still carry one when I ride," Suze said.

"And you still win."

"I know." Suze smiled. "I thought you were a witch."

"Maybe I am." Gwen gave her an impish grin.

"You're a good witch, then. I really thought the horses were magic."

Suze reached over and took the silver pony from Gwen's palm. Turning it over in her fingers, she smiled. "Maybe I need to hold one now."

"Not that one. Not for right now." Gwen snatched away the silver pony and handed Suze the stone one. "Stone, for strength."

Suze clenched it in her palm until the cold stone warmed. "You think it'll help?"

"Sure."

Suze tucked the pony under her pillow. "I'll keep it with me."

Gwen nodded. "I hear you're keeping a cowboy with you lately too. What's going on there? Is it serious?"

"You know about Brady?" Suze could feel her face heating and wished she could control herself better.

"People talk," Gwen said. "Especially in a town the size of Wynott. You and those Decker boys are the pride of the county, so when you get together with one of 'em, it's big news."

"You live in Wynott?"

Suze couldn't believe Gwen lived that close and she hadn't known.

"I own what they call the junk shop." Gwen started to bounce one leg, as though that made her nervous. "Although I don't know why they call it a shop, since I don't sell anything."

"You're the sculptor," Suze said.

She never would have thought, in a million years, that the mysterious recluse who owned the junk shop in Wynott was Gwen. In fact, most people thought it was a man that lived behind the high fence. The place was guarded by spooky figures, men and ogres made of all manner of machine parts, but there was a rumor that the sculptor was a respected artist who sold welded conglomerations of machine parts to big art galleries.

"Why didn't you ever come over?" Suze asked.

"I was ashamed, I guess. A man broke my heart, and I decided to eat my way to happiness. It didn't work. I just loaded on the pounds, and then—well, I didn't want him to see me."

"He lives around here?"

"You might say that." Gwen parked herself on the rolling desk chair.

"I'm sorry." Suze pictured herself years from now, living in some secluded house, mooning over Brady and living on Oreos. She couldn't see it. She wouldn't be able to ride if she got that big.

"Let that be a lesson to you," Gwen said with mock seriousness. "Don't let that cowboy get away."

"You really are a witch," Suze said. "You read my mind. But he already got away, I think, so never mind about that. It's my dad I need help with."

It felt good to talk to Gwennie. She'd been there after her mother's death, a sympathetic ear for a young girl's troubles. But eventually she'd disappeared.

Kind of like a witch.

"What's the matter with your dad?"

"He can't seem to get over my mom's death."

"Maybe it's her life he can't get over. Maybe your mother was the wrong woman for your father."

"No way," Suze said. "He loved her like—well, like she was his life."

"He thought she was." Gwen sighed. "I think your dad needs to face some facts before he can get over your mother. He needs to remember the woman she was, not the woman he wanted her to be."

Suze smiled. "So she wasn't perfect?"

"No. Is that what he told you?"

"Over and over." Suze looked down at her lap and shook her head. "I've been trying to live up to her legacy for years. According to my dad, she was the most beautiful, the smartest, the best at everything. And I don't measure up."

She hated the bitterness she heard in her voice, but it felt good to say it out loud. And Gwen was her godmother. If you couldn't talk to your godmother, who could you talk to?

"Your mother was an amazing woman," Gwen said. "She was strong, she was driven, and nobody could beat her around those barrels. But she liked to shine, and sometimes that meant making the people around her feel dull and drab. Everything came easy for her, and she didn't know what it felt like to lose or to be hurt."

"So she made my father feel dull and drab?"

Gwen nodded. "She made him feel like he never measured up. He spent his whole life trying to please her."

And he's passed all that on to me.

But that meant Suze wasn't a failure. She wasn't a disappointment. She was just as good as Ellen Carlyle. Better, because she would never put down someone else to make herself look good.

"I wish you'd come sooner," she said.

"I know. I'm sorry," Gwen said.

Suze leaned forward, resting her elbows on her knees and her chin on her hands. "Tell me about her," she said. "And don't sugarcoat it. I want to know everything."

———

Gwen didn't know what to think about Suzanne Carlyle.

When she'd walked into the room and seen a clone of her old friend Ellen, she'd expected to find Ellen's spirit too—her crazy, wild spirit. The spirit that knocked flat every obstacle that dared to oppose her. The spirit that was a little selfish, if truth be told, but nobody minded. Ellen's charm had always smoothed the way for her.

Gwen had watched Suzanne ride on TV during the National Finals Rodeo, and smiled to see the girl riding just like her mother had. She'd seen how close to the edge Suze rode, risking everything with every ride.

But while Ellen had raced with a sort of hell-for-leather, dang-everything joy, Suzanne must win through dogged determination. Gwen wondered who she was trying to please—her father or the ghost of her mother.

She wished she'd come sooner. She'd settled in Wynott partly because of its closeness to Suzanne and to Earl—especially to Earl.

But she'd told Suze the truth. As the weight piled on, she hated to go out. People didn't say anything, but she saw how they looked at her. She didn't want Earl looking at her like that.

She shouldn't have worried. Looking at him now, she wondered what she'd ever seen in him. There'd been a time when all she'd wanted was to spend time with Earl, even if it meant tagging along while he mooned over Ellen. Then the mooning led to marriage, and that was that.

Now he was just an old man, and not a very nice one, either. It was kind of a relief.

Her goddaughter needed her help, though, and needed it badly. So like it or not, she was going to have to spend some time with the man Earl Carlyle had become.

She visited with Suzanne a while, telling stories about Ellen. Stories were magic, like the little horses—powerful but only if you believed in them. With stories, she could make Ellen the woman she should have been. The woman her daughter believed she was and needed her to be.

Finally, Gwen said her good-byes and puffed back down the stairs—but not until she'd poked around a little bit. She hadn't heard Earl come up the stairs, so she checked out the bathroom and bedroom to see what kind of house her goddaughter was living in.

Not a very nice one. The downstairs had looked pretty civilized, except for the chair jammed in the doorway. There was probably some explanation for that. But except for Suze's room, the upstairs was a mess—laundry everywhere, and dust, dust, dust. She'd come back as soon as she could and bring a mop.

But she wasn't sure they made a cleaning product that would clean up the mess Earl Carlyle had made of his life.

Chapter 40

IT WASN'T EASY TO FIT ALL THREE OF THE DECKER RANCH cowboys into one pickup, especially Brady's Dodge. He hadn't sprung for the extended cab, so the three of them were jammed onto the one bench seat. He hadn't wanted to pay for an automatic transmission either, so he was feeling up his brother Shane every time he shifted gears.

"You want to watch it with that gearshift?" Shane shifted back in his seat. "That's getting a little too close for comfort."

Ridge glanced back at Brady's empty gun rack. "What kind of posse is this, anyway? We're not even armed. And who brings a horse trailer to a manhunt?"

Brady grinned. His brothers hadn't even asked what they were going to do when he told them he had to get up a posse to take care of some business. That's what being brothers was all about: being there for each other, no matter what.

There'd been a time in his life when he'd only dreamed of having that kind of family, and he treasured his brotherhood with Shane Lockhart and Ridge Cooper—the brotherhood Bill Decker and his wife had pieced together from three lost and broken boys.

"I'd like to use firearms, but it's not an option," Brady said. "This is a persuasive sort of posse. We're going to talk Cooter Banks into letting us take the horse he stole back to the rightful owner."

"Cooter has Speedo?"

Brady nodded. "He sent a ransom note to Suze. It was anonymous, but it was pretty obvious who it was from."

"So Suze knows?" Shane asked.

Brady shook his head. "Um, no."

"Then how did you explain the ransom note?"

"I didn't." Brady squirmed under his oldest brother's dark-eyed stare.

"So you opened her mail?"

"I did." Brady squared his shoulders. He wasn't doing anything terrible. He was just getting the horse back. As long as Speedo was okay, Suze would be happy and Brady would be off the hook.

Shane didn't say anything more, but those eyes stayed on Brady, their expression a mixture of disappointment and surprise.

"I didn't want her to worry," Brady said. "I can tell her after Speedo's safe and sound."

"Sure you can," Shane said. "Sure. She won't notice anything if the horse has been neglected or underfed."

"Yeah," Ridge said. "She'll just blame me."

Brady squirmed. He had no doubt Cooter was guilty on both counts, and he didn't want Ridge's reputation to suffer for his screwup.

Cooter lived in a single-wide trailer that was set against a hillside on a broad stretch of rocky land. A sagging barbed-wire fence marked off a pasture area that was mostly dirt. Two shaggy horses pricked their ears up as Brady drove the pickup up the drive.

After he parked the truck, Shane walked around to the back and opened the horse trailer, dropping the ramp.

"We might be persuasive, but if I lived out here, I'd be armed," Shane said. "We might have to move fast."

"Good point," Brady said.

There were lights on in the trailer, but no one appeared at the window or cracked the door open. Brady was surprised. Living out here, an unexpected guest could mean trouble, and Cooter must have heard them.

"How are we going to do this?" Ridge asked.

"Let's check that shed over there." Brady pointed toward a structure behind the trailer. "Make sure Speedo's here before we start trouble."

"We're not starting anything," Shane said.

Brady bristled. "If he's got that horse—"

"Then *he* started the trouble." Shane shot an elbow into Brady's ribs. "That's all I'm saying."

They strode out to the shed, if you could even call it that. The whole thing leaned to one side, and the windward side had slumped nearly to the ground. Boards and shingles lay all around it. It was hardly an appropriate place to keep a sixty-thousand-dollar barrel horse.

Ridge lifted a rusty latch and the plank door creaked open. The interior of the shed was dark, but not dark enough to hide a white heart that seemed to float at eye level.

"Speedo," Brady breathed. He'd know that heart-shaped blaze anywhere. "Thank God."

"I'll load him up," Ridge said. "We need to keep quiet."

Brady didn't want to be quiet. He'd wanted to punch Cooter ever since that breakfast meeting, and seeing Speedo housed in a dirty old shed made him even madder. His hands clenched and unclenched, his palms literally itching for a fight. But keeping Speedo safe was the priority.

The horse had retreated to the back of the shed. Ridge stepped inside, muttering sweet nothings, but the horse was twitchy, shying away when Ridge reached for his halter.

Brady muttered a few things too, but they were hardly sweet. It was obvious Speedo hadn't been treated well. As Ridge led him out, the fading sunlight revealed his dull, ungroomed coat. He swung his head up and pulled away from Ridge, almost making him lose his grip.

But when he saw the trailer, he calmed.

"It's like he knows he's going home," Brady said.

"He does." Ridge read horses better than anyone Brady knew. His quiet strength was a calming influence, and by the time he'd settled Speedo in the trailer, the horse was comfortably munching hay, as if nothing had ever happened.

"It's your call, Brady," Shane said. "Do we go home, or do we rouse Cooter?"

In response, Brady strode up to the trailer. It was a sorry sight, almost as sorry as the shed where Speedo had been hidden. Siding was peeling off in long strips that flapped in the wind, and there was no skirting to hide the concrete blocks it was mounted on. A swamp cooler on the roof rumbled and coughed.

"Maybe he couldn't hear us over the swamp cooler," Shane said.

"Maybe." Brady finally got to use his fist. It felt good, even if it was just pounding on the door.

"Open up, Cooter," he said. "We know you're in there."

A light flicked on over the door, but that was the only sign of life.

"Let us in, or we'll call the sheriff," Brady said. "He'd be mighty interested in that letter you sent. You know horse stealing's a federal offense?"

He had no idea if that was true, but Wyoming took the crime of horse stealing very seriously. The days of frontier justice were over, but there'd been a time when Cooter would have found himself the guest of honor at a necktie party—more commonly known as a hangin'.

Brady started to pound on the door again, but it opened slightly. A very wide eye peered out at them over the safety chain.

It definitely wasn't Cooter. He didn't have eyelashes that long, and he didn't wear eyeliner, as far as Brady knew.

"Who are you guys?" said a breathy feminine voice.

"We're from Decker Ranch," Brady said. "We've come about the horse."

"Oh!" The door swung shut and they could hear the woman fumbling with the security chain. A moment later, the door opened wide to reveal a skinny, pale girl with long brown hair that was ragged at the ends. She wore cutoff shorts and a bikini top, and she looked about fifteen.

"You guys wanna come in?" she asked. "Cooter's not here. But I could get you some beer." She bit her lip and glanced back at the inside of the trailer, as if Cooter might somehow be watching her.

"We don't want to come in," Brady said.

"Okay," she said. "You wanna buy the horse, though, right?"

"No. We're taking the horse."

"You can't do that!" She stepped outside. She was clearly frightened, biting her lower lip so hard Brady was scared it would bleed, and clutching her arms around her middle as if her stomach hurt. But she looked him in the eye, and he could tell she believed what she was saying. "That horse belongs to Cooter. He spent all his money on it, and he's gonna sell it and make us rich. He says it's a real good horse."

"It is a real good horse," Brady said. "It's also stolen."

"No." She shook her head and backed away as if denying it could make it a lie. "It can't be. He spent all his money on it. That's why we couldn't pay the rent last month."

"I don't know what he spent his money on, but it wasn't that horse," Brady said. "He stole it. I can call the sheriff if you don't believe me."

"No!" Her eyes widened in panic. "Don't call the sheriff!"

Shane stepped forward. "Who are you, anyway?"

She glanced warily from Brady to Shane to Ridge and back to Shane. "I'm Sharlene. Sharlene Banks."

"You Cooter's sister?" Brady asked.

"I'm his wife," she said, lifting her chin as if that was something to be proud of.

Brady didn't think he'd ever felt so sorry for someone in his life. Cooter had somehow talked this little thing into marrying him, and installed her in his barely livable trailer to wait for him while he was mowing through buckle bunnies like a reaper through seed corn.

"How old are you?" Shane asked.

"Old enough." She lifted her chin again. "We are legally married."

"Okay," Brady said. "Well, that horse is legally someone else's, so we're going to be going now."

"You're taking it?"

"You bet," Brady said.

"You can't do that." Fragile yet determined, she confronted the three men. "Cooter'll kill me. I'm supposed to take care of it, but it's mean and I'm scared of it. If he comes home and it's gone, he'll kill me."

Brady looked from Ridge to Shane. "You want to come with us? We'll take you someplace safe."

"No." She skittered toward the door, reminding Brady of a frightened mouse. "He won't really kill me. He just gets real mad."

Shane set a hand on Brady's shoulder. "Let's go."

They piled into the truck, but Brady didn't start it. Instead, he looked over at the trailer. Sharlene had gone back inside, and the place was silent. "We can't leave her here," he said.

"I'll send Sierra out tomorrow," Ridge said. "That kid can't be more than fifteen. Sierra'll know what to do."

Brady nodded. Sometimes it came in handy to have a social worker for a sister-in-law.

"Wish I could be there when Cooter gets home." Brady pictured himself landing a hard roundhouse punch, the kind that shouted "POW!" in comic books.

"Me too," Ridge said calmly. "No horse, no wife, no nothing."

Shane grinned. "Revenge is sweet."

"I'd rather hit him," said Brady.

Brady showed up at Suze's house the next morning with a freshly groomed Speedo riding in the trailer behind him. The horse seemed none the worse for wear now that he'd been fed and exercised.

He'd gotten away with his lies. He should have felt elated, but he felt lower than prairie dog poop.

Speedo nickered as they pulled up, and Suze appeared at her window.

"Speedo!" she said. "You brought him! Oh, *Brady*!"

Brady gave her a crooked smile. He was Suze's hero for the moment, but he felt his sin of omission burning in his gut. She still thought Speedo had been with Ridge all this time, and there was nothing to tell her different. Her horse was here, and he was fine.

Brady didn't have to tell her what had happened. Not today. And being Brady, he wasn't about to reveal the truth until he absolutely had to.

His anger at Cooter had faded as disgust for his own flaws took over. He was a cheat, taking the easy way out, letting Suze think he'd taken care of Speedo when really, he'd almost lost him.

"But why tell her?" the little devil on his shoulder whispered in his ear. Most people had a little angel on the other shoulder to balance things out, but Brady figured his had gotten disgusted and left.

He led Speedo out of the trailer and put him in the corral where Suze could see him.

"You want to come up?" she asked.

He should. He should go up there and carry her downstairs and take her to see her horse. It was the least he could do.

But then he'd have to look her in the eye.

"I've got some work to do in the barn, and then I gotta go," he said. "Sorry."

He heard the window screech shut and knew he'd disappointed her. Hell, he'd disappointed himself.

He was just a disappointing kind of guy.

Chapter 41

BRADY JAMMED HIS HAT DOWN ONTO HIS HEAD AND steadied the ladder he'd leaned against Suze's big red barn. It wasn't ideal roof-repairing weather, but the job needed to be done. He'd discovered mildewed hay bales and rotting wood in a corner of the loft a week earlier, and he couldn't let the damage continue another day.

The damage he'd done to his relationship with Suze was piling up though. He'd continued to take care of the barn and the horses, and he'd done dishes whenever he could sneak in the house without being seen, but he hadn't gone upstairs and she hadn't come down for the past few days.

It was just as well. A relationship built on deception was no relationship at all. It was better to stay away.

The trouble was, she didn't know he'd deceived her. So she didn't know why he'd suddenly deserted her, either. He had a feeling he'd gone and hurt her again.

Hard work wouldn't make up for that, but he had to do something. He planned to get up on the barn roof before the heat of the sun became unbearable, but the wind was whipping up into the kind of tempest that swept up every dead leaf and loose bit of litter and carried them off to Nebraska. Brady knew he'd be okay when he was crouched down nailing shingles, but if he wasn't careful when he stood up, a gust could easily topple him over and send him skidding down the slope to his doom. He wouldn't do Suze much good if he broke his own legs trying to help her.

He watched an enormous tumbleweed bound past and shook off a smaller one that danced across the tips of the grass and clung to his leg. He laughed as Dooley rose from his sentry position on the front porch and took off after the tumbleweed with great leaps, barking as he ran.

With one hand pressing his old straw hat to his head, he started up the ladder. The wind was no friend to broad-brimmed cowboy hats, but in the thin air of the high plains, he'd get one heck of a sunburn if he didn't wear one, and this particular one was a tight enough fit to stick.

Dooley had returned from his hunt, carrying his head high as he pranced home with his prize. Settling at the bottom of the ladder, he began to eat the newly sub-dued tumbleweed.

"I don't think you're supposed to do that, buddy," Brady called down, but the dog ignored him. With all that fur in his ears, it was a wonder he heard anything.

By eight o'clock, Brady had torn off a big patch of old shingles and felt like his skin was dry as an old corn husk from the wind. He sat down on the sloping roof and wiped his brow.

Demolition was the fun part of a job. Now it was time for the real work.

He reached for a box of nails, but his clumsy work gloves made him bobble it, putting on a brief juggling act before it opened up and spilled. Half the nails fell down into the mess of weeds below.

"Dooley, no." Tumbleweeds were one thing. Brady

was sure the dog shouldn't eat roofing nails. "Leave it. Leave it."

Dooley surprised him by dropping the nail he'd caught and lying down with his head between his paws, his back legs sprawled behind him so he looked like a very small, very hairy bearskin rug.

"Good job, Dooley," Brady said. "You're acting almost like a good dog."

Brady reached up and wiped the sweat from his brow with his forearm, accidentally tipping his hat back. The wind whipped up as if it had been waiting for that very moment and flipped the hat into the air.

Cursing, Brady watched his second-best straw hat tumble across the grass and join the tumbleweeds lodged against the fencerow. Well, at least it wasn't going anywhere.

But like the wind, Dooley had been waiting for just this opportunity. Yipping happily, he raced across the grass, seizing the hat in his teeth and giving it a good shake, as if it were a rat that needed killing. Trotting back to the bottom of the ladder, he lay down with the hat between his front feet.

Just then the wind whipped up again and the hat spun out of the dog's grip, sailing toward the fence again. Dooley chased after it.

Brady just watched. Heck, it was an old hat, anyway. It might be wearable at the end of the day, or it might not, but Dooley would be a happy dog.

He fished in his front pocket and took out a bandanna, which he wrapped around his head do-rag style as a stopgap sun block. Then he got to work, sliding the first shingle into place.

He paused with his hammer suspended above the first nail. Suze was probably sleeping, but what was he supposed to do? She probably slept all the time.

He was fixing her barn and entertaining her dog. She couldn't complain too much if he woke her up. Besides, he had a feeling her annoyance would help her heal. Being mad seemed to give her energy.

But he wasn't ready to face her, and he needed a break anyway. Settling down on the roof, he took a can of Coke out of his toolbox and swallowed half of it in one go, then ran the chilled can across his forehead.

Man, that was good. Nothing like a cold drink on a hot, blue-sky day.

Looking out over the Carlyle place from this vantage point, it looked almost idyllic. Speedo and Bucket grazed in the pasture. The area around the house was cleaned up, and he'd mown the lawn too. It looked nice. He'd fixed a lot of problems for Suze.

Did it really matter that he'd had to fix a terrible mistake of his own with that late-night raid on Cooter's place? He'd fixed the Speedo problem just like he'd fixed the lawn problem and like he was fixing the barn problem now.

Maybe he wasn't such a terrible person after all.

He was finishing off the Coke when the corner window on the second floor screeched open and hit the top of the window frame with a resounding *bang*.

"Brady Caine, I always knew you were a pervert!"

It was Suze in all her rumpled glory. A bad case of bed head failed to spoil the effect of a barely there nightie that was worn to sheer transparency and revealed her black lace panties every time she lifted her arms.

Brady almost fell off the roof. How was he supposed to do the right thing when she wore *that*?

"I can't believe you'd go that far," she said.

He started to speak, but she kept right on going.

"I don't care if it's just a joke. It's not funny. People expect privacy in their own homes. And you're not fooling anybody with that toolbox."

As a matter of fact, his tool wasn't fooling anybody either. He wasn't sure how he was going to get down the ladder.

"I can *see* you up there, doing nothing," she said. "Just like *you* can see *me*!"

She lifted her arms to shut the window, revealing that the panties showed plenty of skin in the spaces between their lacy daisies. The sash jammed and she continued to fume while she struggled with it. Brady wished he could take home the work of art framed by the window trim and hang it in his bedroom.

She caught him looking and lowered her arms. "Pervert."

"If I wasn't one before, I am now." Brady winked and pointed the hammer her way. "Nice panties."

She gave the sash a final, useless tug and spun around, covering herself with her hands. Grabbing a blanket from the foot of the bed, she tossed it around her shoulders and reached for the top of the window again. Naturally, the blanket slipped to the floor.

Brady wasn't one for strip clubs, but he'd been to a couple bachelor parties for cowboys who went for that kind of thing, and he'd never seen a strip show that came close to this one.

She scooped up the blanket and clutched it to her

chest. "You could at least have the decency to get down now that I caught you."

"Caught me doing what?"

"Playing Peeping Tom." She gestured wildly toward the barn. "Why else would you be up there, unless you're trying to get a look at me in my skivvies?"

He held up the hammer and the box of nails. "I'm doing roof repairs. Thought I'd get it done before the sun got too hot, but I figured you were sleeping, so I was waiting a bit." He couldn't help grinning. "The skivvies are an unexpected bonus."

"Oh!" She made a sound that was a cross between rage and surprise, and he swallowed a smile as she tugged at the window again.

"I could fix that window too."

"No! I told you. I don't. Want. Any. Help." Each word was punctuated with a tug at the window sash. On the last word, her hand slipped and she toppled sideways. A loud crash and a smothered yelp told Brady she'd taken a serious fall, but she reappeared at the window seconds later, smoothing her hair as if nothing had happened.

"You okay?" he asked.

"Oh, yeah. Fine. Just slipped." She stroked her hair again—a dead giveaway that she was lying. Ditto for the flirtatious fluttering of her lashes. Suze didn't know how to flirt.

She was probably struggling to stay conscious.

Chapter 42

SUZE LEANED AGAINST THE WALL BESIDE THE WINDOW, cussing under her breath. She had been so shocked to see Brady up on the barn roof that she hadn't used her crutches to get to the window. In fact, she'd rocketed out of bed with no regard for her injuries *or* her outfit. She'd probably set back her recovery by two weeks in the process.

Besides that, she'd made an absolute ass of herself. It hadn't even occurred to her that Brady might be repairing the barn roof. Sure, it needed it, but it was the middle of July. Between the high temperatures, the unrelenting sunshine, and the high winds, he'd probably shortened his life just by climbing the ladder. And here she was, worrying about her recovery and her modesty.

She still hadn't managed to pull the window down. She shot the stubborn sash a dirty look and decided to blame it for all her troubles. She leaned over to peek out the window.

Brady's truck was still in the drive, but he wasn't anywhere in sight. He was probably in the barn or out back with the horses.

Good. She'd teach that danged window a lesson. Reaching up, she pulled with all her might, practically hanging on the darn thing. It slammed shut so hard it shocked her and sent her stumbling backward. Fortunately, something stopped her from falling down.

Something warm, that felt suspiciously like a man's muscular chest.

"I knew you were going to do that."

Before she could splutter out the cuss words she had locked and loaded, strong hands began kneading her shoulders right where they hurt. She felt the hair on the nape of her neck flutter. He was close. Too close.

She whirled, nearly falling again, but caught herself quickly enough to hang on to her dignity. Unfortunately, what she caught herself on was the cowboy in question.

"You should have warned me that you were going to be up there."

He looked completely unrepentant. Had Brady ever repented anything in his life?

That morning at your trailer. He regretted over-sleeping. He regretted having to make nice when he just wanted to go...

"If I'd warned you, you would've told me not to do it." He calmly reached over and braced his thumbs on her collarbone so he could dig his fingers into the sore spots on either side of her spine. "I'm not going to warn you about every move I make. That would be exhausting."

"It sure would. You've got more moves than Casanova."

She meant it as an insult, but of course Brady didn't take it that way.

"That good, huh? Thanks." He changed his grip, working muscles she didn't even know she had, and she couldn't help moaning at the mixture of pleasure and pain.

"You've got some moves of your own," he said. "Like climbing out of bed and walking to the window without your crutches. You okay?"

She nodded, but then Brady looked her in the eye and she shook her head.

"Was that a yes or a no?"

"It was an *I don't know*," she said. "It hurts, but it always hurts. I don't think it's any worse than usual."

"What hurts?"

"My ankle."

"It shouldn't hurt that much if you stay off it. It's in a cast."

"I know, but the cast feels too small. It's like it's swollen in there. It aches and throbs. Sometimes it really, really hurts."

Somehow, Brady had managed to steer her over to the bed with his impromptu massage. She sat down gratefully.

"Maybe you're right, and it's too small," he said. "Let's see."

She expected him to look down at her toes, but instead he bent and hoisted her foot into his lap, nearly pushing her over backward. Resting her elbows on the bed behind her, she thanked the boredom gods for the pedicure she'd given herself the day before. Then she thanked the panty gods that her black lace panties were solid where it mattered.

Brady noticed the pedicure. "Pretty toes." He gently touched each one in turn. "They don't look swollen. But it's hard to tell what's going on in there. When did you have it checked last?"

She felt the flush starting at the toes he held in his

hand, rushing up her body to warm her chest, her throat, her face, her ears.

Brady shook his head, still with that gentle smile. Why had she never seen that smile before? It was sweet. Caring.

"You haven't been to the doctor, have you?"

She shook her head.

"Wasn't there an appointment?"

She shrugged.

"Your dad picked you up at the hospital. He'd know when your follow-up visit was scheduled."

"Probably. But he hasn't mentioned it." She shrugged and looked away. "You know how he is."

She knew the appointment was probably a week ago. Now Brady would insist on tossing her in his pickup and driving like a demon, dragging her into the doctor's office, making a scene in the waiting room, embarrassing her in front of all the nurses, who'd fall in love with him and think he was all chivalrous and everything and she was an ungrateful witch.

"Earth to Suze," he said. "You should go to the doctor, you know."

"I will," she said. "I'll ask my dad to take me."

"*Tell* him. Tell him I'll do it if he doesn't. He'll hate that."

"Okay." She couldn't believe she was getting off this easy. She was almost disappointed.

Maybe Brady was learning that she'd listen if he offered advice, but resist him till the cows turned blue if he tried to control her. "Thanks, Brady. And, um, I'm sorry about…" She waved vaguely out the window. "You know, before."

He grinned. "Before what?"

"Before you came up here. When you were on the roof, and I was screaming at you."

"Aw, that was nothing. Besides, it worked out just fine."

Only then did she remember she was still wearing the outfit she'd been so upset about him seeing. And only then did she notice that he'd leaned back on the bed too, resting one arm behind her head.

And only then did she realize he was going to kiss her.

—∿∿—

Brady couldn't help himself. He and Suze were practically in bed together, and she was darn near naked. If she had any problem with that, she didn't act like it. Lies or no lies, he couldn't look at those bruised-cherry lips another second without kissing her.

Besides, it wasn't like his lies had hurt her. Speedo was back, and he didn't seem to have been affected by his brief stay at Cooter's. So Brady might not have told her about Speedo's little adventure, but he'd found him, hadn't he? So it was like it had never happened.

He touched his lips to hers and felt white-hot power shoot from the contact, lighting up every nerve ending in his body. She seemed shocked at first, tensing under his touch, but he put one hand on the bare skin at her waist— the skimpy nightie had gotten hiked up somehow—and did his best to kiss her right.

All thoughts of Speedo, all memory of his deceit, faded away. All he could think of was Suze, warm and sweet and right there. Right there, kissing him back.

He went slow and easy, with moves soft enough to

soothe a spooked filly. First he slid his lips across hers in a chaste, caring sort of caress. When that didn't make her mad, he dared to trace the bottom of that full, bee-stung upper lip with his tongue. Loving Suze was kind of like loving a beautiful but temperamental mare that was eating out of your hand one minute and kicking you in the head the next.

Brady didn't mind. Heck, he rode wild horses for a living. He liked a little excitement in the bedroom—and in the kitchen and the hallway, and every other room of the house, for that matter. He believed life should be lived, not merely survived. And he was sure Suze felt the same way. You could tell by the way she rode.

"I just about went crazy this past week," he said. "Being here. Knowing you were just upstairs."

"You should have come," she whispered in his ear.

The unintentional double entendre stoked the fire raging inside him.

Careful, careful.

He'd nearly lost it with Suze last time he was here. She lit him up like no other woman ever had, and he'd been teetering on the edge of a cliff when he'd pulled back last time.

So this time, he wasn't pulling back.

Problem solved.

Chapter 43

HE STROKED HIS TONGUE ACROSS THE SEAM OF HER LIPS again. When he found the lace border at the top of her panties, he echoed the movement with one finger, running it slowly across and back, across and back. He stroked her lips, stroked her belly, then eased his finger past the elastic on her panties as he slipped his tongue into her mouth.

Judging by the little kitten sounds she was making, the temperamental mare was in a sweet mood today.

He deepened the kiss, bringing his other hand up to cradle the back of her head as she rocked her hips, urging him to take his caresses further. But he wanted to go slow, to show his feelings rather than just slaking his lust.

Not that there wasn't quite a bit of lust to slake. His breath shuddered at the feeling of her breasts pressed against his chest, and he longed to tug down the lace panties and bury himself to the hilt in her warmth. But he needed to take his time. This was for Suze, not for him.

Patiently, gently, he explored her lips and let his tongue dance a slow, sexy tango with hers. It wasn't easy to keep his hands from straying further past the black elastic waistband, but he wanted to make sure she was giving herself willingly. Never again would he take her at a moment of weakness. This had to be something she wanted, and wanted badly.

Not until the kitten noises turned to moans did he lower her head to the pillow and kiss her hot and hard. His lips, his tongue, his hands—they all let her know how he wanted to make love to her, and she answered with an unmistakable yes.

He paused and rested on his elbows, looking down at her. She was lying beneath him, her hurt leg hanging off the bed, the rest of her sprawled in centerfold-worthy abandon on the rumpled sheets. The tiny top she wore, with its worn patches over each breast, was sexy enough on its own; now it had slipped off one shoulder and over one breast, draping just low enough to reveal a pink, tight nipple. Meanwhile, the hem had bunched up around her waist, revealing the full glory of her flat belly and lacy underwear.

"What are you looking at, cowboy?" Her voice was throaty and low—an invitation to sex no matter what words she said. Although the fact that the words sounded like something a loose woman in the Wild West would say didn't hurt. She must have watched enough old movies with her dad to know how the West was really won.

He rested his head on his hand, his elbow on the bed, and considered her question. What was he looking at?

"Not *what* am I looking at," he said. "Who."

He traced the edge of her top, letting his finger ride the wave of one swelling breast before it dipped into the valley in between and rode up the other. She squirmed when he reached her exposed nipple and ran his finger around the areola. He knew his hands were rough and work hardened, so he was gentle as could be.

"With some girls, it's all about the what," he said,

tugging the top up over her breast despite her efforts to writhe out of it again. "What they're wearing, what they're doing. But with you, it's different."

"What, you don't like what I'm wearing?"

"I love what you're wearing."

And he could prove it. The zipper of his Wranglers was strained to the breaking point. Taking it slow was starting to hurt, but he wasn't going to screw this up.

"You could wear anything and I'd feel the same way."

"Anything?"

"Anything. You could wear a baggy old pair of Bubba overalls with a flour sack underneath and I'd still want to take 'em off."

She laughed, rocking back on the bed, her long hair hanging down as she threw her head back. Once in a while he managed to catch a glimpse of this Suze, the real woman behind all the insecurities and issues, and it was then that he knew, without a doubt, that she belonged with him. He could make her laugh; he could make her see how extraordinary she was. He could make her feel loved.

But would that just be another deceit? Was he in love with Suze, or in lust?

All he knew was that this felt different. Making love to Suze rocked his world out of its orbit, while making love to other women left it spinning undisturbed.

He knew this little pocket of time probably wouldn't last. He'd make some wrong move, and she'd be back on the defensive. It really was like taming a wild horse. He had to somehow earn her trust, and there was no way to hurry that process.

But with horses, the ones that were slowest to trust were the ones that loved you the most in the end. Maybe it was that way with women too.

He didn't know. He'd never found one that didn't trust him before.

"What if I wore dirty Wranglers and a do-rag?" Her tone was teasing, but he felt his stomach sink as he reached up and touched his head. Yep, the bandanna was still in place. He tugged it off and tossed it toward the window.

"That's your dog's fault. He took my hat."

"You know Dooley's a shameless reprobate. You shouldn't let him get near anything you care about. Is your hat okay?"

"Dunno. He still has it."

"Oh no!" She jerked as if to leap up from the bed, but he put a finger to her lips and eased her back down.

"No worries," he said. "If that hat is the price of admission to this right here, Dooley can have it. Hell, he can have my 3X black beaver Stetson if he wants it."

She nodded, faking a serious expression. "Okay. I'll tell him that."

Brady laughed, and the two of them stared at each other for a moment before kissing again.

"I really do like you, Brady Caine," Suze said between kisses. "I really do."

I'll take that, he thought. *I'll definitely take that.*

"What is it you like about me?" he asked. "You know I'm as shameless as Dooley. So why do you like me?"

"You're a hopeless optimist," she said. "You believe the best of everybody. Even me."

"You ought to try it sometime. Believe in yourself."

"I do. Every time I race," she said. "I see myself winning, in my head, and it works every time. It's a big part of my strategy."

"Then you already know how. You just need to apply the same kind of thinking to your life, that's all."

"You don't get it." She fell back against the pillows, clearly exhausted. "When I'm racing, I know I can win because it's happened before. But when it comes to everyday life, I just keep on losing. I'm sorry, but it's hard to visualize happiness when you've never really had it."

"Which is why you deserve it more than anyone I ever knew." Brady felt almost fierce. "Just wait. Something will change."

"See?" she said. "You're just a glass-half-full kind of guy."

He traced a slow circle around her areola, and she sucked in a quick breath.

"Right now," he said, "my glass is overflowing."

Suze couldn't believe this. How had Brady ended up in her bed? If anyone had asked her, she would have sworn it was an accident—but nobody would believe that. How did you get a cowboy off a barn roof and into your bedroom in five minutes flat by accident?

Yell at him, apparently.

It didn't matter. What mattered was the moment. She'd been bored out of her mind for days, and while that wasn't a very good excuse for letting Brady back into her bed, she didn't really care. She was tired of worrying about what she was going to do, how she was going to survive, who would help her. Brady would help her, as long as she was nice to him. And if being nice to him meant satisfying her own naughty needs, who was there to worry about it?

Not her father, who was downstairs watching television in blissful and possibly deliberate ignorance of what was going on in his daughter's bedroom. Not her mother, who was long gone and probably would have approved of Brady anyway. Not Dooley, who was too busy eating Brady's hat to care about anything.

That thought made her chuckle.

"What are you laughing at?"

"You," she said, poking him in the chest. That started a tussle that ended with her top hanging from the bedpost and Brady's shirt on the floor. He'd kicked off his boots too, and the two of them smiled at each other.

"You're way overdressed," she said.

He looked ruefully down at his Wranglers. "I'm not sure I can get the zipper down."

"I can help," she said.

"That'll just make it worse."

He stood and liberated himself from the Wranglers, then stared at her in motionless silence, as if he'd been struck by lightning.

"You truly are a goddess," he said.

Suze flushed. "And you've truly lost your mind."

"Yes, I have." He stripped off his boxers too, and returned to lie beside her, his erection nudging her hip. "It's a blissful state. And I'm going to try and help you lose yours."

Her green eyes grew serious as she stroked his hair

Chapter 44

SUZE LOOKED UP AT BRADY, WILLING HIM TO KISS HER again, to touch her, to make love to her. She wanted him so badly. Not just in a sexual way, although her body was begging for him. She wanted something more. She wanted joy.

He bent and brushed her lips with his, and she smiled under the assault as he deepened the kiss and ran his thumb over one nipple. Her heart lightened and lifted, and she surprised him by laughing.

"I'm not laughing at you," she said. "I just feel good. I feel great."

"You *are* great."

And that was the last thing Brady said before they lost themselves in each other, touching and caressing, stroking and exploring. She remembered, in a flash, why the aftermath of her night with Brady had been so painful. He was so totally focused on her, so dedicated to pleasing her. He looked into her eyes so deeply she felt like he saw the real her, like he knew her better than anyone else ever could. He acted like he loved her, and she had to remind herself, firmly, that it wasn't real. Tomorrow would come, and Brady would be Brady again, careless and free. And she'd be hurt.

"What's wrong?" He was stroking her hair again, looking into her eyes.

"You—I—never mind." She ran her hand down his

belly, over the taut ridges of his muscles, and closed
it around his erection. Holding him firmly, she ran her
thumb lightly over the top and felt a bead of moisture in
response. "Playtime's over, cowboy," she said. "Let's
get to the serious stuff."

But it's not serious. He's never serious. She knew
she needed to remind herself of that, but she suddenly
wasn't sure why, and in the next moment she couldn't
think what it was she had told herself to remember. All
she could do was meet Brady's gaze as he held himself
above her, his arm muscles tense with the effort and his
brown eyes staring deeply into her green ones.

This was serious.

That's what his eyes were telling her. This wasn't just
sex; this *meant* something, to him as much as to her. She
could feel it in the faint trembling of his arms, and she
could see it in his eyes.

"Are you sure about this?" he asked. "No regrets in
the morning?"

"No regrets ever."

He slid inside her all at once. It had been so long
since she'd made love that it should have hurt, but her
body was so ready for him there was no shock, no quick
stab of pain. Instead, she felt finally, fully whole, as if a
missing part of her had been restored.

He moved above her slowly. Most men—in her limited experience, anyway—threw their heads back and
closed their eyes about now, and things got purely physical. But Brady kept his eyes open, looking into hers, and
that made the act so intimate she almost shrank away.

Almost.

Because it felt so good, she couldn't stop. She

matched Brady's pace, rocking with him, and he held her eyes with his own even when his thrusts grew fast and deep, and the headboard of the bed banged against the wall as if it was pounding out Morse code.

This was wild, crazy sex, but it was more than that—because he never stopped looking at her. There was a connection that never broke—a connection that was far more intimate than the union of their bodies or even the intimacy of his gaze.

It had always been there, she realized. Always, from the first day they'd met.

But she'd think about that later. Right now, she couldn't think about anything but how *good* he felt, how *right*, how *right*, how *right*..how...

Stars exploded inside her, and wild seas raged. She felt as if she was lifting off the bed, lifting Brady with her on a wave so strong it would carry both of them away forever. She clung to him, praying he wouldn't leave her, because even as the wave subsided and the tide of emotion started to ebb, she felt so good she was almost afraid.

Afraid she wouldn't ever be sane again. Afraid she'd stay in that transcendent state forever, hovering miles above the earth, having risen so high and felt so much that she could never go back to the everyday world again.

She looked into Brady's eyes, which were still fixed on hers, and she really didn't mind one bit. As long as she could take him with her.

—∾—

Brady stroked Suze's hair. He'd decided that was just about his favorite thing to do, besides stroking her body.

But even just touching her hair was somehow satisfying.
It was endless in its loops and curls, like flames spiraling
up from a fire, or waves curling and coiling inward. He
picked up a thick lock of gold and kissed it just as she
opened her eyes.

"I'm sorry," she said.

"Sorry!" The word shocked him. He didn't know
what she was sorry about, but if she was sorry about
anything, then she hadn't understood anything about
what had just happened. They'd made love in a cata-
clysmic, world-shattering, mind-bending way that he'd
never experienced—and she was sorry?

"I closed my eyes," she said. "I broke the connection."

He smiled at her, and she smiled back. He watched
the glow come back to her eyes, and knew he didn't
have to answer her with words. The connection was still
there. It was unbreakable. They could see it whenever
they looked in each other's eyes.

"Oh," she said simply. "Okay. Good."

"Yeah," he said, kissing her hair again. "Good."

She stretched and sighed. Even with the clumsy cast
on one leg and the splint on her wrist, she moved with a
grace he'd never seen in any other woman. She lay in a
slanted ray of late afternoon sunshine and stared out the
window at the barn roof and the blue sky.

"Are you still mad at me?" he asked.

"I don't know." Her gaze slid toward him, and she
narrowed her eyes. "Are you going to leave now?"

He actually did need to leave. He was supposed to
go out to a friend's place on the reservation and teach
some kids to ride. But he wasn't about to walk out on
Suze and let her think he didn't care. Not this time.

Not if the president of the United States was waiting on him.

"I won't leave unless you want me to."

She ran her fingers through her hair, over and over. "I guess you'll have to go eventually."

"Eventually. You tell me when."

She turned her head and graced him with a smile that glowed. "You have something to do, don't you?"

He leaned back against her pillows, resting his head on his crossed arms. "Nothing more important than you."

"Well, I have something to do," she said.

"What's that?"

"Take a nap." She rolled over, resting her head on his shoulder, and stared at the ceiling. "You wore me out."

He looked down at her, thinking he wished he could stay forever, just like this, with her leaning on him, trusting him. "You want me to stay with you?"

"What, and watch me sleep? That would be creepy."

He laughed. "I was thinking I could use a nap too, but I'm supposed to be over at a friend's house, helping his kids learn to ride."

"Oh, that's right," she said. "You have friends."

"They'll be your friends too."

"I hope so." She thought a moment. "I've been living my life the wrong way. So focused on winning I didn't have time to live."

"I think it has something to do with your mother. Maybe she's with you when you ride. When you win."

This time she looked at him a long time, her expression changing from trepidation to wonder.

"Talk about creepy. You know me well."

"It's not hard to figure out. But I think she's with you all the time, win or lose."

She stretched and patted down a yawn. "You'd better go. Don't leave those kids waiting." She smiled. "I bet they're excited, learning to ride from the great Brady Caine."

"I'm not so great."

"You are to me."

She tilted her head and he kissed her, a chaste, gentle kiss. He stood and grabbed his clothes, dressing as quickly as he'd undressed. When he finished, she had her eyes closed. He was pretty sure she was asleep, but he bent over the bed and kissed her good-bye anyway.

She opened one eye and gave him a drowsy look. "Bye, Brady," she said.

She sounded sad. He knew she probably was wondering if he'd meant anything he'd said. The notion that she didn't trust him ate at him, and he wondered how to put her fears to rest.

"Suze?" he said. "You know that connection? The one you thought you broke?"

She nodded, looking up at him, so open and trusting it dang near broke his heart.

"It'll never be broken," he said. "We'll always be connected, you and I. I don't know what it is, but we're two of a kind. Maybe we're both a little lost, I don't know."

"I don't know either." She blinked sleepily. "But for a little while there, I felt found."

Chapter 45

BRADY'S TRUCK SHOOK, RATTLED, AND ROLLED OVER the bone-jarring road to his friend Pete's place. He figured the physical punishment the road dished out was good practice for dealing with Pete's twin boys, who seemed to view Brady as a combination jungle gym, climbing wall, and punching bag.

It was actually Teresa's place now, and Derek and Sam were Teresa's boys. Pete was long gone, which was why Brady and his brothers pitched in and did their best to give the kids some reasonably responsible male role models.

Pete had been a fellow foster kid. He'd aged out of the system about the time Brady and his brothers moved to Decker Ranch, but with no father and no responsible role models in his life, he'd become a bar-brawling, bull-riding biker who lowered his life expectancy every time he set foot in a bar or hoisted himself up on a bull. Shane claimed Pete had had a death wish, and Brady thought he was probably right.

But when Pete met and married Teresa, a slim beauty from the nearby reservation, he changed almost overnight. Teresa was delicate as a summer wildflower, but she somehow took on Pete's demons and won. Marriage and the military settled down the wildness in him, and he scored an assignment as a pilot, flying Apache helicopters.

But the death wish he'd left behind when he'd fallen for Teresa followed him into his new life. Around the time the boys started school, he was deployed to Afghanistan, where he was shot down the third time he flew. No survivors.

Teresa did the best she could to get along on her own, but Brady, Ridge, and Shane checked in on her now and then. Recently, someone had given the boys a couple of ponies. Teresa was worried about the boys' safety, but Brady was more concerned about the animals. They were stout little critters, ill suited for the wild gallops the boys demanded. He spent a little time with them several days a week, teaching them some horse sense and kindness while he held them to a training schedule that would increase the ponies' stamina.

Pete might have passed on, but his memory was everywhere at Teresa's. His old work boots still slumped casually on the doorstep, and his jacket was draped over a chair. And the two little boys' dark eyes glowed with the same mischievous light that had lit their daddy's gaze.

If a man wanted some appreciation, all he needed to do was ruffle the boys' hair, or give them a high five. Derek and Sam were seven now, and they hadn't had a man around the house since they were less than five. They adored their Uncle Brady and tussled madly for his attention. When he looked in their eyes, he saw a totally undeserved hero worship that made him sad. He was just a cowboy. The boys' father was a real hero, and he made sure to remind them of that often.

The kids rode their new ponies with all the fear-lessness of their Arapahoe ancestors. Brady dreamed up games that would channel their energy into competition. He also taught them some rudiments of horse care, so they wouldn't kill the poor animals with their high jinks.

"Thank you," Teresa said on Wednesday, when he brought the boys back into the house. She was still a beauty, with her dark hair and eyes and her slight but strong figure. He was surprised she hadn't taken up with some man by now, but she was careful because of the boys. He had to respect her for that.

"Come in the kitchen. I made you some brownies."

"Thanks. But you don't have to do that." He patted his stomach. "Give 'em to the boys. They need the energy."

She laughed, leaning against the door frame. Her light cotton dress was almost transparent in the sunlight, and her long hair hung loose. Then she gave him a sly, sideways glance with her dark eyes.

"You still seeing that girl? The barrel racer?"

"Uh-huh."

It suddenly occurred to him that being Uncle Brady and helping the boys with their riding might be a sort of audition for the role of husband and stepfather. He averted his gaze from the outline of Teresa's body, so clearly visible under her dress.

"She doesn't appreciate you." Teresa's gaze held his and he realized his hunch was dead-on.

"Suze has a lot going on," he said. "The accident and all. It's kind of hard to appreciate the guy who put you in the hospital and screwed up your career."

"It was an accident." Teresa's dark eyes flashed. "You're only with her because you feel responsible. But it wasn't your fault."

Brady kept his eyes steady on hers, doing his best to make sure she understood that he meant what he said. "That's not true. I'm with her because I love her."

Shoot. He did?

He did.

But, man, he shouldn't have told Teresa before he'd told Suze.

"You should move on." Teresa gave him a sweet sideways smile that told him exactly where she thought he should move to. "You're a good man, Brady." She reached over and ran one finger up his forearm. "In so many ways."

Okay, now he knew for sure what she was trying to do. He needed to put a stop to it before she embarrassed herself.

"I'm not moving on," he said. "I belong to Suze. Okay?"

"Okay." She thrust out her lower lip in a pretty pout that told him it was definitely not okay. If this kept up, he'd have to stop coming for a while. But that wouldn't be fair to the boys.

She suddenly changed from a languorous seductress to a bundle of energy, grabbing a grocery bag from the closet and heading for one of the bedrooms.

"Are you going to Cheyenne anytime soon?" she called out.

"Next week, probably."

She bustled out of the bedroom, the grocery bag now packed full.

"Could you drop off this stuff at Goodwill?" She thrust the bag into his arms.

"Sure," he said. "What is it?"

"Just some old clothes." She stood there, hands laced behind her back, swaying side to side like a little girl.

He cleared his throat.

"Okay," he said. "Well. Ah, see you soon."

Teresa was just another example that showed Brady didn't understand women. He knew she was still in love with Pete—or at least with his memory. But he also knew she struggled, both financially and as a parent. The boys were a handful, and without a man in the house, they ran wild.

He hoped she'd find someone—someone decent, who'd be a good stepdad. It would be a big job, but Teresa, with her dark beauty and pretty ways, would be worth it for somebody. Maybe he'd try and match her up with one of his buddies. She deserved someone to love.

He just didn't think that someone should be Uncle Brady.

Chapter 46

RIDGE COOPER STEERED THE PHOENIX HOUSE VAN PAST the Decker Ranch, heading for the Carlyle outfit. His wife, Sierra, believed deeply that her little brood of foster kids needed to give back to their community in order to grow roots and feel a part of it. She always said the town would save the kids, and the kids would save the town.

She'd sure saved Ridge, so he figured she knew what she was talking about.

She'd saved Sharlene too. He'd taken her out to Cooter's place the day after he and his brothers rescued Speedo. Sharlene was as easy to spook as a wild deer. She wouldn't say how old she was, and she didn't want to go home to her parents any more than she wanted to stay with Cooter, so Sierra had talked the girl into staying at Phoenix House for a little while.

She and Ridge were checking missing persons reports in towns along the rodeo road, hoping somebody was looking for the kid. Meanwhile, Sharlene became a part of Phoenix House, acting as a big sister to Sierra's unruly army of boys.

Now that Sharlene was taken care of, Ridge's wife was determined to save Suze Carlyle, and she'd decided it was Isaiah she'd send to the wrecked rider's rescue, whether he wanted to be a pint-sized knight in shining armor or not.

Ridge was surprised when Sierra chose Isaiah for the job. Suze had a bit of the devil in her, just like Isaiah, and he couldn't see the two of them getting along. But Sierra had pointed out that Isaiah was the only boy at Phoenix House who could stand up to Earl Carlyle, and Ridge knew she was probably right. Carter might have done okay—the boy was so end-lessly cheerful, Earl's hostility would probably slide right off him—but Isaiah was the only kid who had the guts to answer back.

In fact, Ridge would pay money to see Earl and Isaiah go toe to toe. It would be better than an MMA match.

But right now, his job wasn't to speculate on the final outcome of the matchup. His job was to convince Isaiah that the matchup was a great idea.

Unfortunately, Isaiah's life experience had taught him to be deeply suspicious of everything and everyone. He'd come a long way in a year at Phoenix House, but he still questioned authority on every possible occasion.

Glancing at the kid in the rearview mirror, Ridge thought of a neighbor lady who'd declared the boy had devil's eyes in an angel's face. He could sure see the devil today. Isaiah's features were so delicately sculpted that he looked almost elfin, but his dark eyes looked straight through anybody who tried to trick him or lie to him or even shade the truth.

Which was exactly what Ridge and Sierra were doing now. Dealing with Earl, and Suze too, would be a challenge even for Isaiah, but Sierra was determined to think positive.

Isaiah? Not so much.

"So if this Suzy Q is such a nice lady, how come

she needs me to help her?" he asked. "Doesn't she have a boyfriend?"

"Her name is *Suze. Suze Carlyle*, not Suzy Q," said Sierra. "And maybe she doesn't want a boyfriend."

"Yeah, maybe she's a lesbian." Isaiah folded his arms across his skinny chest and nodded, as if the problem was settled to his satisfaction.

"It's none of your business," Sierra said.

"Yup." The boy nodded sharply. "Lesbian. I thought so."

Ridge kept his eyes resolutely on the road. One of these days, Isaiah was going to drive him straight off a cliff. Or crazy. One or the other.

Maybe both at once.

"Isaiah." Sierra's tone was a warning in itself.

"Okay, so she's not."

"Isaiah…" Her tone was even darker this time.

"Well, how am I supposed to help her if I don't know what she needs?" Isaiah bounced in his seat, briefly acting his age before the old soul took over again. "Sounds like she needs a boyfriend. How 'bout if I set her up with one of those Match.com accounts?"

Ridge could almost see Sierra's blood curdling. Isaiah was her biggest challenge, and Ridge tried to help when he could. Right now, that meant changing the subject.

"You met Suze once," he said. "She came to pick up her horse when you kids were at the ranch. Remember? It was the first time you met my brothers."

"Was she the blond with the nice—"

"Watch your mouth," Ridge warned.

"I was going to say she had a nice trailer," Isaiah said, all indignation.

Ridge doubted that had been the boy's intention. Even now, the kid said the word *trailer* in a way that seemed to signify something else. At his age, he probably didn't know what he was saying half the time, but he sure enjoyed saying it. Anything to rile people up.

"Yes, she was the one with the nice trailer." Ridge flushed as he said it. Dammit, now he'd never be able to look at Suze's elaborate horse trailer without thinking of the girl's caboose at the same time.

"Well, she wasn't a nice lady," Isaiah said. "She was mean."

"When was she mean?"

"She was mean to Brady. And he likes her." Isaiah might be a pint-sized package of trouble, but he was fiercely protective of those he loved, and he loved Brady. Of course.

Everybody loved Brady.

"I don't know why Brady likes her," the boy mused. "She treats him like dirt."

"How do you know how she treats him?" Ridge didn't know how he ended up in these crazy conversations with Isaiah. The kid just knew how to push his buttons. As a matter of fact, Isaiah knew how to push everyone's buttons. He'd make a great lawyer when he grew up—if somebody didn't strangle him first.

"You didn't even remember who she was a minute ago," Sierra pointed out.

"Yeah, but now I do." Isaiah pooched out his lower lip, an expression that didn't bode well for anyone. "I like Brady. He's the funnest one of your brothers. He's way more fun than your big brother, Shane."

Ridge grinned. Anything he could rib Shane about was a good thing. "Yeah?"

"Yeah. Shane likes to boss folks around. I wasn't put on this earth to be bossed, you know. Not by him or anybody else."

"I noticed that."

"Yeah. And Brady's a lot funner than you too."

"Why?"

Ridge hated to admit it, but he was a little jealous whenever the boys cottoned to either of his brothers. He was married to Sierra, the group mom for Phoenix House. That practically made him the group dad. *He* ought to be the favorite.

"Why is Brady funner than me?"

"'Cause he talks. You don't hardly ever say a word if you don't have to."

"I'm talking now."

"Yeah, but that's only because I'm goading you into it."

Ridge didn't know if he should laugh or bang his head against the steering wheel in frustration. Fortunately, they'd reached the Carlyle place.

As he turned in the drive, he saw Suze's father, Earl, outside, sitting on the front porch.

"Who's that mean old man?" Isaiah asked.

"That's Suze's dad," Sierra said. "What makes you think he's mean? You haven't met him yet."

"He just looks mean," Isaiah said. "Look how his eyes and nose and mouth are all squizzened up into a little knot in the middle of his face. And how his chin sticks out like he wants to fight." Isaiah nodded. "He's mean, all right. I got my work cut out for me at this place."

As the van rocked up the pitted drive, Suze's father stood and peered at the vehicle, using one hand for a sunshade. Ridge wondered if the old man really was spoiling for a fight. If he was, he just might find himself on the losing end of things.

Because Sierra was right; if anyone could take on Earl Carlyle, it was Isaiah.

Suze had always liked Sierra Cooper. She'd blown into town as the temporary group mom for Phoenix House, and stayed to marry Brady's brother Ridge. The sunny social worker and the gruff, laconic cowboy were an odd match, but they seemed to make it work.

So the sight of the Phoenix House van pulling into the driveway wasn't unwelcome. Rising from her seat in the shadows of the broad front porch, she tucked her crutches under her arms and limped down the steps and past her father to make sure Sierra and her cargo got a happier greeting than her dad would provide. Earl had been sulking on the porch steps all morning. Sure enough, as she exited the shade of the porch, her father stomped into the house.

The big side door to the van opened and a boy stepped out and stood in the drive with his hands on his hips, gazing around the Carlyle ranch like a pint-sized real estate mogul. He was a skinny kid with skin the color of a triple-shot latte and bright eyes that seemed to take in every dilapidated detail as they flashed from the barn to the house to the front door, which was still blocked by Ellen's old chair.

When the kid turned to Suze, his dark brows

arrowed down over his eyes to make him look almost comically angry.

"What is this, some kind of crazy house?" He pointed at the recliner. "You got a chair stuck in the door, there. How're people supposed to get inside?"

"Isaiah, *hush*," Sierra said. "That's rude."

But as she approached the house, Sierra looked from Suze to the chair and back again. Suze didn't know what to say. How could she explain the series of events that led to the chair jammed in the doorway?

"It's kind of a Brady thing," she finally said.

"Oh." For Sierra, that seemed to be enough of an explanation. She ducked under the chair and motioned for the boy to follow. "Isaiah, it would be much nicer if you offered to help with the chair, now, wouldn't it?"

"I can't help with that chair," the boy said. "That thing's dang near as big as I am."

Suze couldn't help smiling. The kid was all city smarts until he cussed like a born cowboy. He'd evidently spent some time hanging around Decker Ranch.

"Why don't you and Ridge go visit Suze's horses?" Sierra asked.

"Because I'd rather find out what's going on with that chair." Isaiah's bright eyes flashed. "Our teacher said there's stories everywhere, and I bet there's one in that chair."

Sierra gave the kid a hard look. "That wasn't a suggestion." Her tone was mild but evidently effective. Isaiah headed straight for the barn and Ridge hastened to follow.

"How are you, Suze?" Sierra asked as Isaiah's chatter

faded into the distance. "I heard about the accident and thought maybe I could help."

Great. She *knew* Brady wouldn't listen to her. He'd gone around behind her back and told folks how pathetic she was. "Brady sent you, didn't he?"

"Not really. He told Ridge and me what happened, of course. He feels awful about it, but I'm sure you know that."

Sierra headed over to the long bench that sat in the hallway beneath a row of hooks that held jackets, hats, and various implements ranging from an ancient fly-swatter to an assortment of dog leashes. Relieved to get off her feet, Suze joined her.

"I'm afraid my motives aren't entirely pure," Sierra continued. "I've been looking for ways the boys can give back to the community, and I couldn't help thinking this was a great opportunity."

"An opportunity?"

"A chance for them to help someone."

"Someone less fortunate." Suze picked at her cast, trying not to let the implication of what Sierra was saying bother her. She'd suddenly become less fortunate than a bunch of motherless, fatherless foster kids. When had that happened?

"It's not like that." Sierra touched Suze's arm, and the look of compassion in her green eyes made Suze feel a little ashamed of herself.

Which was an improvement over feeling sorry for herself. Maybe she was evolving. They always said adversity made you a better person. This was the first hopeful sign she'd seen.

"Everybody sees these kids as charity cases, and they

know it." Sierra kept her voice low, even though Isaiah had gone off with Ridge.

Suze knew she couldn't let Isaiah volunteer here, no matter how bright and amusing he was. She didn't want the poor kid running afoul of her dad. Isaiah would be scarred for life.

"So it's important for them to help others," Sierra was saying. "It gives them a feeling of self-worth, and makes them feel like a part of the community."

Just then, Suze heard Ridge's voice hollering, "*Isaiah! Get back here!*"

A youthful voice piped up in the living room. "Whatcha watching?"

Suze realized Ridge was too late. Isaiah had found the back door. She braced herself for her father's answer, but there was no response.

Isaiah didn't give up, though. "Hey, your chair matches the one in the doorway. You oughta bring that one in here and then you'd have a matched set. You could maybe even invite a guest to sit down, so he doesn't wear himself out watching TV standing up. Right?"

Chapter 47

SUZE HAD TO RESIST THE IMPULSE TO SLAP HER HAND over her mouth. She and her father had avoided the topic of the chair since the day he'd discovered it. Brady refused to move it, and so it hung there, jammed in the doorway, a constant reminder of their problems.

Now this poor, innocent kid had brought it up. She waited tensely for her father's answer.

"I was *trying* to bring it in here," her dad finally said. "That's how it got stuck."

"Maybe Ridge and me could help you unstick it."

"That's 'Ridge and *I*.' And 'unstick' isn't a word."

"Well, it oughta be." Isaiah seemed completely unfazed by her father's hostility. Suze was starting to like this kid.

"Can we keep him?" she asked with a grin as Ridge ducked under the recliner.

"I heard that." Isaiah came rushing in from the living room. "I'm not some puppy in the pet store you can just pick out, you know." He punctuated his words with a jabbing finger. "I'm a full-grown human being." He looked down at his slim frame. "Well, almost." He looked up, frustrated. "You know what I mean."

"I know you're not a puppy," Suze said. "First of all, a puppy would have tucked its tail and run when my dad used that tone of voice." She deliberately spoke loudly, so her father would hear.

"That's right." Isaiah puffed out his skinny chest as best he could. "I'm no sissy puppy. I'm one of the big dogs!" He made a snarling sound and lunged at Ridge, who looked pained and backed away. Suze smothered a laugh.

"Isaiah, sit down and behave." Sierra moved over, making room on the bench.

"Do I have to? I'd rather go watch *Bonanza* with that old guy," the boy said.

"All right. Then go. And his name is Mr. Carlyle." Sierra glanced at Suze, who nodded her approval.

Isaiah went.

"What do you think?" Sierra asked. "If you channel that energy, he could be a big help."

"Doing what?" Suze asked.

"I was thinking he could come over for a couple hours after school and take care of whatever you needed," Sierra said. "He could put dishes in the dishwasher, do some light housework, and just generally help out. And he makes a mean peanut butter and jelly sandwich."

"Brady *did* send you," Suze muttered, but the idea didn't make her mad anymore.

Sierra lowered her voice. "We talked a little, sure. And from what he said, it sounds like you'd be a good mentor for Isaiah. He's a little bit of a handful, but that's mostly a defense so people won't see he's vulnerable. He's bright and funny and kind—and determined nobody will find out he can be hurt."

"I'm not sure how much help I'd be," Suze said, almost laughing. "I think a lot of people would say the same thing about me—the handful part, anyway."

"Exactly." Sierra smiled. She had such a kind face

that Suze felt somehow blessed, and knew she'd been right: she and Sierra really could be friends. "I've heard you fit the other part too."

"Well, don't tell anybody."

Sierra laughed, but then she shifted into a more serious mode.

"Isaiah loves to cook, although he'll need some guidance as far as following recipes and making up menus. Be careful, because he'll put you on a constant diet of chocolate cake for breakfast, lunch, and dinner if you let him."

"Does he make good chocolate cake?"

"It's pretty darn good," Sierra admitted.

"That might not be so bad, then."

"True." Sierra smiled. "All the boys have learned basic horse care and safety from Ridge, but they have different levels of interest. This one is capable, but he's not horse crazy. I understand your horses are valuable and highly trained, so I didn't think you'd want a kid who wants to ride them."

"Not unless he's highly trained too," Suze said. "But this sounds like a lot of work for a kid."

"Isaiah has a lot of energy. And I'm also going to ask for something in return."

There was always a catch.

"Okay," Suze said.

"Make him feel needed, like part of the family. He especially needs a fatherly or even grandfatherly force in his life. I'd like him to spend some time with your dad. And it seems like that's already working out."

"For now," Suze said. "But my dad'll never agree to it. He's—he's not an easy man."

The truth was, he wasn't even fatherly to his own daughter.

."So don't ask him. Just let Isaiah spend some time with him. I don't care if they just sit and watch TV."

"I thought Ridge was their father figure."

"They have to share him. Isaiah needs somebody all his own."

"I hate to tell you this, but Isaiah's getting a pretty tough grandpa."

"That's what he needs." She clasped her hands, pleading. "Give it a try, please? He's a great kid."

Suze felt a smile twitching at the corner of her lips—a mischievous, knowing smile. "He's driving you nuts, isn't he?"

Sierra nodded. "School can't come fast enough."

"Okay," Suze said. "Let's do it."

Sierra let out a little whoop, her smile lighting the room. Suze couldn't help envying her, with her pretty face, her handsome horse-trainer husband, and a job that truly made a difference to the world.

"I don't really care if he does any work or not," she whispered to Sierra. "I just want him around to annoy my dad. And he's funny."

"He is, but it'll be hard at first. He'll need some watching."

"I'd better check on him," Suze said. "They're awfully quiet in there."

Suze started to rise, giving Sierra an appreciative nod when the woman grabbed her elbow and gave her a boost. Slipping her crutches under her arms, she stumped over to the other side of the hallway as quietly as she could so she could see into the living room.

There sat her father, in his usual chair. And there sat Isaiah, cross-legged on the floor in front of him. The boy looked totally enraptured by the big doings on the Ponderosa, and as she watched, he leaned back against the front of her dad's chair.

"What's that guy's name?" Isaiah asked, pointing to the screen.

Suze waited for the fireworks, or at least a bad-tempered admonishment, but her dad simply said, "Hoss."

"Sure fits him," Isaiah said. "We got a guy like that at Phoenix House. My friend Carter. I think I'm gonna start calling him 'Hoss.'"

Earl grunted. But it was a nice grunt.

"Dang," Suze said. "We'll take him."

Chapter 48

BRADY STOPPED AT SUZE'S HOUSE EVERY MORNING and every evening. He knew Sierra was bringing Isaiah out, and the kid was capable of feeding the horses and turning them out, but what if one of the horses was sick? What if one of them got injured? Someone with experience ought to be around to keep an eye on a horse like Speedo.

Besides, there were kisses to be stolen and glances to share. Everything seemed to have changed between him and Suze. She'd apparently changed her mind about him. He didn't know why, but he didn't really care. He just liked the result.

The only problem was Isaiah. The kid was probably his favorite out of all the Phoenix House boys, but he was always there, watching with those dark eyes. And he didn't miss a thing.

"You two getting married?" Isaiah asked him once, as he was leaving.

Brady knew Suze could hear them, and it took a couple beats too long for him to think of an answer. "I guess that would be up to her," he said.

Actually, Isaiah wasn't the only problem. There was also Earl Carlyle, lurking in the living room like some malevolent presence in a horror movie. Ridge and Isaiah had moved the recliner back into the living room, so Brady had lost that fight, but he'd found a beautiful old rocking chair in the attic at the ranch, with tapestry upholstery that was only a little torn, in places where you'd barely notice it. Suze spent most every day ensconced in its old-fashioned comfort, watching her horses and knitting.

But Earl wouldn't be a problem today. His truck wasn't in the drive. No, the only problem Brady would face today was the Big Lie.

It might be a sin of omission, but keeping Suze in the dark about Speedo's kidnapping at the hands of Cooter Banks just felt wrong. Besides, he was bound to be found out. His brothers knew about Speedo's kidnapping. So did Cooter, and anyone Cooter had told. Plus he'd asked about the missing horse all over the county. Suze would find out about it sooner or later. And if she didn't hear it from him, there'd be hell to pay.

There might be anyway.

On the day he decided to come clean, he arrived at the Carlyle ranch late in the afternoon. Taking the stairs two at a time, he swung into Suze's bedroom to find a rumpled bed, a half-filled water glass, and a paperback novel splayed on the pillow. Gently, he touched the sheets with the back of his hand to see if they were warm. They weren't. He adjusted the pillow, inhaling her familiar feminine scent as he punched it into plumpness.

He glanced back at the bedside table. He was used to seeing the photo of her mother there. But never before had there been another photo stuck in the edge of the frame, nearly obscuring her mother's face. He leaned closer.

Dang. It was the photograph he'd seen in her underwear drawer. The one of the two of them, him and Suze, sitting on a fence on a summer day.

Their faces were open, laughing, young, and alive. They weren't thinking about the future; they were thinking about that moment, that single, golden, magical moment. And each other. They'd definitely been thinking about each other.

Apparently, they still were.

Both of them.

She loves me back. Holy crap, she actually loves me.

It had to be true. No way would she allow that photo to obscure her mother's face unless it really meant something to her.

His hand shook a little as he stuck the picture back in its place and intensified his search. She wasn't in the bathroom upstairs, or the living room or the powder room downstairs. She didn't seem to be anywhere.

She loves me. That wasn't going to make it any easier for him to tell her what he had to say. But maybe it would make it easier for her.

He checked the downstairs.

No Suze.

Could she have gone town with her father? He doubted it. She was doing better, but a full day in the truck would be torture for her.

She loves me. She loves me. The words repeated with every beat of his heart. He knew it for a fact now. There was no other reason for that picture to be there, where she could see it as she drifted off to dreamland.

But she wasn't here.

Head hanging low, he walked back to his truck. As he

opened the door, a thought occurred to him. Slowly, he closed the truck door and headed toward the barn.

Dooley raced to greet him. Last time he'd been with Suze, she'd accused him of alienating the little mutt's affections, and maybe she was right. The dog jumped in place like a jackrabbit with no place to go, pink tongue panting, hind end wiggling in ecstasy every time he hit the ground.

"Poor buddy. Were you lonesome? Huh? Were you lonesome?" He gave the dog a wild belly rub while the dog rolled happily in the grass. Suze would kill him if she saw him getting her dog so dirty, but hey, Suze wasn't here.

"Are you all by yourself? Huh, Doolers? Did they go away and leave you, Dooley-pants?"

He played a brief game with the dog, jumping from side to side as the dog tried to rush past him. They'd played for quite a while before a voice behind him made him jump higher than Dooley.

"*Dooley-pants*?"

Brady squinted into the shadowy depths of the barn. "Where are you?"

"Right here." Suze stepped out into the sunshine.

What he noticed first, before anything else, was her smile.

What he noticed next was that she'd left her hair down, and it spilled in twisting spirals over her shoulders.

Then he noticed her legs—both of them—and the cane.

"You—aw, honey, you got it off! And no crutches!" This was cause for celebration.

He couldn't tell her about Speedo now. It would

spoil her good day, and God knew she didn't get enough of those.

He reached her in three long strides and scooped her into his arms, spinning her around and around. When he put her down, he pulled her against his body and they kissed like a couple of teenagers, right out there in the middle of God's outdoors.

"Where's your dad?" Brady asked when they came up for air.

"He went to town," Suze said. "He'll be gone all afternoon."

Brady stroked her hair back from her face and kissed her again.

This was definitely a good day.

Chapter 49

EARL SAT IN THE FRONT SEAT OF HIS PICKUP, CHECKING the list he made every week of the items he needed in town. He'd gone clear to Cheyenne to do the grocery shopping, and then circled back to Wynott to pick up a few miscellaneous items at Boone's Hardware. He did this every week, just one time. If Suze forgot to add something to the list, she had to wait for the next trip. It was over an hour's drive.

He'd left early this morning, before she was up. She'd probably have a fit about something she hadn't gotten to add to the list. Well, let her fuss. In his experience, women enjoyed it.

He started the truck and eased out of his parking space. There was no traffic in Wynott, even on a Saturday. If it wasn't for Boone's and that new home for kids, the place would be a ghost town.

Of course, there was Gwen's sculpture studio, but if you didn't know what it was, you'd think it was just another crazy small-town junk shop. You'd never know the owner was a sculptor who'd sold her work as far afield as Chicago and New York. So Gwennie had said, anyway, when she came to visit Suzanne.

Suzanne. Not him. For some reason, that rankled.

He didn't begrudge his daughter the company. But there'd been a time when Gwen Saunders didn't have eyes for anybody *but* him, and he hadn't realized, until she'd stopped by, how much he'd missed her sunny disposition and her joking demeanor. She had a way of lightening things up, Gwen did.

Gwen was the only woman he knew who didn't like to fuss. When things went wrong, she'd always reacted with a smile and a wave of her hand, as if she were erasing the problem. Funny thing was, it usually went away for her, just like that.

Maybe he should have asked her to do that the other day when she'd come to visit. He could use that smile and that wave of her hand that erased the past. If only she could erase his grief, erase Suze's accident, erase their money troubles.

When she was just a little thing, Suze had always insisted Gwennie was a witch—a *good* witch, she'd said. Sometimes it seemed like she was right. Gwennie would show up and rough roads would turn smooth, old arguments would be forgotten, and the sun would come out from behind the clouds. He'd seen it happen. Maybe that was why she and Ellen had been so inseparable.

On impulse, he pulled over next to the junk shop.

Studio. He meant studio. That's what she'd called it.

Maybe he'd go on in and see what it was she did in there. From what he'd heard, she rarely left the place, and she didn't talk much to anyone in town. She was a bit of a mystery.

That didn't sound like the Gwennie he'd known. She hadn't looked like the Gwennie he'd known either. Lord knew she'd gained a whole 'nother Gwennie while they were apart. But she was still the same bright-eyed girl at heart.

He pulled over onto the shoulder of the road and

parked by the gate that offered the only visible access to the six-foot fence surrounding Gwennie's peculiar fortress. He knocked on the gate and waited, but nobody came. Glancing right and left, he lifted the latch—a complicated contraption made out of the head of a hammer welded to a hinge—and let himself in.

It sure looked like a junk shop. Matter of fact, it looked like a junk*yard*, with defunct cars all over the place and a rusted Caterpillar earthmover lording it over them all, its toothy bucket filled with soil that had sprouted a healthy crop of weeds.

He made his way through the mess, which wasn't easy. There were tangles of barbed wire, stacks of what appeared to be roofing shingles, and old wheels lying all around the place.

He could hear the hum of an air compressor, and the weird zippery sound of a welder. As he came around the back of the building, he caught sight of Gwen—or at least, he thought it was Gwen. It might have been Neil Armstrong, for all he knew. She was dressed in what was probably a fire-retardant suit and welding helmet, but she looked like an earthbound astronaut. She was welding a bunch of gears and flywheels together. The device she was working on wasn't much bigger than a box of Kleenex, but a few much larger creations stood around the shop. They didn't make a lick of sense, but they were so complicated, they were fun to look at. Kind of like those old Rube Goldberg cartoons, where a big, complicated machine did something simple like pet a cat.

"Do they *do* anything?" he asked.

He had to repeat the question twice before she heard

him. Flicking off the welder, she flipped up the see-through mask, revealing her round, smiling face.

"They all do something." She pointed to a shining contraption made mostly of stainless steel medical equipment, from scalpels to stethoscopes. "That one's called *Time*. It heals all wounds." She pointed to another contraption, one that looked a little like a catapult. "That one throws caution to the winds."

"And it's called…"

"*Youth*."

"That fits," he said. "And this one?"

Her eyes sparkled and she grinned. "This one repairs broken hearts."

"Hah," he said. "What do you call it, then?"

"*Love*," she said.

"Well, that doesn't make any sense."

"No?" She didn't seem bothered by his scoffing tone, but then, it had always taken a lot to bother Gwennie. She wouldn't stand for cruelty or meanness. But that was about all that would ruffle the smooth waters she sailed in life.

"No. Love *causes* broken hearts." He spoke with the certainty of the afflicted.

"What do *you* think the cure is, then?" she asked, her head tilted, her smile playful.

"There is no cure." He sat down heavily on the running board of an ancient pickup truck that had rusted to a uniform shade of brown. "And I'm speaking from experience."

"Oh, Earl." Gwen sat down beside him and the truck groaned, shifting slightly from her weight. "I know Ellen broke your heart."

Earl nodded. "When she died."

Gwennie stood and the truck rose about six inches, almost pushing Earl to his feet. "I thought she did it way before that."

"Like when?"

Gwennie dropped the shield back over her face. "Like a little bit at a time, every day, from the moment you met her."

Flicking a switch, she brought the air compressor back to noisy life, making further conversation impossible.

Chapter 50

EARL SAT THERE AWHILE, HIS ELBOWS ON HIS THIGHS, his hands dangling uselessly between his knees. Ellen had been the love of his life. She'd made his world a better place just by being by his side.

Hadn't she?

Gwennie finished welding one more piece onto her sculpture, then took off the helmet and shook out her mop of gray hair. "Remember that necklace Ellen wanted?"

Earl remembered, all right. It was made with some fancy blue stone that matched her eyes, and it cost more than two weeks' pay.

"She pestered you and pestered you until you bought it, remember? And then she lost it the first time she wore it."

"I know. I thought she'd be upset, but she shrugged it off like it was nothing." Earl had done his best to admire Ellen for that. At least she hadn't raised a ruckus or cried or anything.

But it had hurt at the time. He'd scrimped and saved for that necklace, and she'd barely bothered to look for it.

"Once she had it, she didn't care about it anymore." Gwen gave Earl a long, considering look. "Maybe you're not ready to hear this, but that's how she was with you."

"What do you mean?"

Gwennie shed the fire-retardant suit and sat down on a crude wooden bench that stood beside the studio's big back door. "I had a crush on you back then, you know that?"

"I knew." He eked out a smile. He hadn't used those muscles in a long time.

"She took you away from me," Gwennie said. "And then she didn't care anymore. She'd proven she could do it."

Earl sat in silence for a while. What Gwennie was saying hurt like a blow to the chest, and he was having trouble catching his breath.

It was true. And the truth hurt. For all these years, the years of his marriage and the years after Ellen's death—he'd been hurt by that truth.

Everyone had recognized it but him. He'd refused to believe he couldn't make Ellen love him, so he'd followed his wife around like a servant, bowing to her every whim—trying to make her love him.

It was embarrassing, that's what it was.

"We had some good years," he said. "When she was sick, she was a different person."

"Because she was scared. And she needed you."

He scowled. "I thought you two were friends."

"We were. That's why I understand. It was the same way for me."

"You weren't there when she was sick." He knew his tone was accusing. He didn't care. He'd never understood why Gwen had abandoned her best friend when she needed her most.

"I would have been there for you more than her,"

Gwen said. "I was afraid she'd think I was waiting for her to die. It seemed best to stay away."

He hadn't thought of it that way. Ellen might have believed that, even of Gwen—because she'd been that way herself.

They sat in silence for a while. Earl was used to silence—the long, uncomfortable silences that hung in the air between him and his daughter, a silence made of secrets. But this silence was different. Comfortable. Comforting, even.

"You need to tell Suzanne the truth," Gwen finally said. "About everything. Even about Slim."

He shook his head. "Slim Harris took enough away from me. I'm not giving him anything else. She's the closest thing I've got to family."

"Suzanne loves you."

"I've never given her a reason to." Earl looked at Gwen a long time, making up his mind whether he'd trust her.

He decided he would.

"I can't stand to see her," he said. "She looks so much like Ellen. She's a reminder of my failure." He struggled to speak through the hard, aching lump in his throat. "I never made Ellen happy. I try to honor her memory because I failed her in life."

"You didn't fail," Gwennie said. "She just made you feel that way. You did the best you could. Sometimes that's as close as we can get to success."

They sat together a long while, watching the sun drop in the sky. Earl thought he finally understood why Gwen lived here. He felt safe behind her high fence—safe from cruelty and secrets and lies. Safe from life.

He looked at a sculpture labeled *Absence* and felt a stirring in his heart, as if it was coming to life after a long hibernation.

"You want to stay for supper?" Gwen asked.

"I do," he said. "I surely do."

Suze sat on her rocking chair on the sun porch, watching the driveway for her father's truck. He'd left for town early that morning. It was nearly eight, and he wasn't home. Her dad might drive her crazy, but he was all she had, and she was worried.

Crickets chirped in the tall grass as the sky turned a luminescent blue that faded until there was only a faint glow on the horizon.

Brady stepped out onto the porch carrying two glasses of iced tea. The two of them had celebrated her freedom from crutches all afternoon in her upstairs bedroom. He'd fallen asleep and she'd let him rest, tiptoeing down the stairs to wait for her father. But as the day drew to a close, the warmth in her heart was fading as fast as the light.

Brady took one look at her and knew something was wrong. "What's the matter?"

"Dad should be home by now," she said. "He left before I got up, and he's still gone."

"You know where he might be?"

"Maybe Gwen's place." She explained who Gwen was and described the sculpture studio in Wynott.

"I know that place," Brady said. "Kind of weird. You want to drive by? See if his truck's there?"

"Yes. Please."

What a relief. She could probably manage to drive with the cast on her foot, but she wasn't supposed to.

Brady opened the truck door for her, but the passenger side was littered with fast food wrappers and empty Coke cans.

"Looks like you had a party in here."

"No party. Just kids."

He made a quick effort to clean up the mess, stuffing trash in a McDonald's bag and throwing the empty cans behind his seat. He shoved a bag that sat on the bench seat onto the floor, which was fine because the truck had enough leg room for a long-legged cowboy, and Suze only needed about half that much space.

"Kids? Is that what you've been up to?" She kept her tone light, as if she didn't care where he went when he wasn't with her. As if she wasn't one bit worried about what he might be doing.

"I've been over to the reservation," he said. "Doing horse stuff with some kids."

"Teaching them to ride?"

"Sort of."

He seemed oddly evasive. Maybe he was embarrassed to be caught doing even more good deeds. How could she ever have thought he was anything but a good guy?

Searching for a change of subject, she nudged the bag with her feet. "What's that?"

"Some old clothes. I need to take 'em to Goodwill next time I go to Cheyenne."

"Oh."

They drove in silence. The road to Wynott was a blacktop highway, one lane each way. Brady took it slow, looking out for deer and praying they wouldn't come upon her father's truck anywhere but Gwen's. Suze's dad was getting old, and Brady wasn't sure how good his eyesight was. Brady prayed he hadn't been in a wreck.

That must have been what Suze was thinking, because she kept twisting her fingers in her lap as she stared out the side window. Brady reached over and took her hands in his.

"We'll find him. It'll be okay."

Suze swallowed and nodded, but she went back to twisting her fingers as soon as he let go, and kept it up until they hit the tiny town of Wynott. The town occupied a Y where two state highways met. There was a bar, a hardware store, and a string of Victorian houses that had seen better days. The most impressive building in town was Phoenix House, with its freshly painted gingerbread and welcoming front porch.

The studio was across the street from Phoenix House, and sure enough, Earl's truck was parked outside.

Brady pulled in behind it. "You want to go in and check on him?"

Suze shook her head. "No. Long as he's here, he's fine."

Brady gave her a sideways look that would have been a leer on a less handsome man. "You think he'll spend the night?"

"Maybe." Suze didn't really want to think about what her father might be doing with Gwen. Going over old times, probably. Reminiscing about her mother.

Or something else. *Ew*.

"I hope he does," Brady said. "It would give us some time alone."

As they pulled into Suze's driveway, Dooley raced across the yard to greet them. He made a flying leap the instant Suze opened her door, greeting her with an ecstatic *yip* and a liberal supply of sloppy kisses. She finally had to fight him off. He was small, but not *that* small, and he was liable to hurt her when he was this excited.

She rested in the truck while Brady headed out to check the horses. He could do it quicker than her, and they wanted to make the most of the time her father was gone. She sat sideways on the bucket seat, dangling her legs over the side and resting her head on the cool leather of the seat. She was tired, and it would be nice to lean on Brady on the short walk to the house. She wasn't used to leaning on anyone. It was a good feeling, to know you had someone who would catch you if you fell.

He must have gotten tied up with the horses, though, because he took forever in the barn. Dooley, crouching at her feet, got bored and started attacking the clothes in the grocery bag on the floor.

"Hey, leave that alone," she said as he shook a T-shirt like it was a rat. "Drop it."

For once, Dooley obeyed. She picked up the shirt and started to put it back in the bag, then paused. It was a T-shirt, all right. But not a man's T-shirt. This was clearly something a woman would wear. As a matter of fact, it was pink, and the rhinestone script across the front read "Foxy." She definitely couldn't see Brady wearing it, even if Lariat Western Wear ordered him to.

He'd said, "Old clothes." He hadn't said they were his. But still…

She pulled out the next item. A pair of jeans. Size four, ultra-low rise.

Hm.

She started pawing through the bag a little faster. Next came a silk nightie that was practically see-through. Then a bra.

A *bra*.

What kind of friend gave a man a bra to get rid of? It wasn't even an old bra. It was in good shape, a lacy one from Victoria's Secret. Expensive.

When she pulled out the panties, she knew she'd been had. This wasn't a bag for Goodwill. It was an overnight bag, a whole change of clothes for some other woman. Some *size four* woman. And it was right in the front seat of his truck.

Chapter 51

SUZE FELT LIKE SHE'D BEEN WHACKED OVER THE HEAD with a hammer—a hammer that felt strangely familiar. Did she need to be thumped any more or any harder before she'd see the truth? Brady hadn't changed a bit. He was still a player. And he was playing her.

She flung herself back in the seat, nearly reopening her wound by conking her head on the gun rack.

What the heck was wrong with her? Why did she fall for his charm, over and over? Through the dust on the windshield, she could see the grass Brady had mowed, the fences he'd mended, and the barn where he was caring for her horses. How could she not fall for him? He was a good guy with a good heart. He really was.

He just couldn't be trusted where women were concerned. Brady loved women—a little too much. And that was a deal breaker for her—as it should be.

She sat there, the bra dangling from her fingers, and tried to make the merry-go-round in her mind turn and spin the other way. She needed the crazy carousel music to run backward and unwind the past two weeks. Brady wasn't her lover. Brady was her friend. Her friend. Her friend.

Hammering that thought into her thick skull was tiring work, and it hurt. She felt a little bit stunned, a whole lot tired, and hurt beyond healing.

The sun was warm, the truck cab warmer. She sat

there, staring, her thoughts going round and round until she wanted to scream. And she did just that when Dooley jumped out of the truck and snatched the bra from her fingers. Before she could even shout his name, he'd run off into the barn.

Oh, well. She didn't care. Let him greet Brady with that dangling from his jaws. That would wake the man up and spare her the trouble of explaining her change of heart.

But Brady didn't say anything when he got back.

"Did you see Dooley?" she asked as he helped her out of the truck.

"No, why?"

"He took off with something out of your bag," she said.

"My bag?"

Oh, so innocent.

"Yeah, you know. Your *old clothes*."

Don't cry, don't cry, don't cry.

He still looked puzzled, and she gave him a wry smile that was a true work of art, considering how she really felt. "The bag you meant to get rid of, remember?"

"Oh." He waved his hand. "That's okay. Doesn't matter."

"It probably matters to somebody. You know. Somebody who wears size four jeans. And a bright yellow, 34C bra."

―⁘―

Brady couldn't believe what he was hearing. He'd completely forgotten about Teresa's bag of old clothes, and Suze was on a roll, cataloging the contents.

"And *panties*, Brady. *Panties*. Someone left a complete change of clothes in your truck. A handy little overnight bag." She leaned back against the pickup, arms folded over her chest. "If you can explain that, go for it."

"They belong to a friend," he said. "And, yeah, she's probably about a size four."

"And she just happened to leave an entire change of clothes in your car, including her sexy lingerie?"

In a heartbeat he saw what Teresa had done. He'd been too dumb to realize she'd really set her sights on him. And now she'd set him up.

Maybe she'd given him the clothes so Suze would find them, or maybe she'd just hoped Brady would notice the sexy underwear and get the message. Either way, he was screwed unless he could get Suze to believe him.

Surely, over the past weeks, she'd learned to trust him.

She shouldn't trust you. You almost lost Speedo, and you didn't tell her.

"Teresa is my friend Pete's widow," he said. "She's the mom of the boys I'm working with on the rez. Sam and Derek. They're twins."

Suze nodded and swallowed hard. It looked like she was trying to believe him.

"I used to help her out, because of loyalty to Pete. I swear, I've never felt anything for her but what a brother would feel. I realized last time I was there that she was, um, flirting with me, so I'm not going back."

"What about her clothes?" Suze asked. "You'll need to bring those back."

He reached over and touched her chin, turning her to face him.

"I don't feel anything for Teresa. You're the only woman I love. I mean that. I swear."

She nodded, but she looked so sad it made his heart ache. "I just—I need some time, okay? I just need to go lie down."

"Okay," he said. "Let me help you upstairs, at least."

She shook her head and started toward the house. He watched her go, wondering what she was thinking. She held herself so straight and tall, even after all she'd been through. There was no way to read her. No way to tell if their relationship was merely broken or shattered beyond repair.

Finally, he couldn't stand it any longer. He strode up behind her and touched her shoulder with a gentle hand.

"Hey."

She turned and looked up at him with sea-green eyes that held so much hurt it made him want to carry her inside and feed her, fix her, make everything right.

"Let me—"

"No, Brady." She wouldn't even let him finish the sentence.

He wasn't at fault. There was nothing going on between him and Teresa. But he had a history with women, and he was paying for it now.

"Okay." He looked into her eyes and tried to make her believe in him. "But have sweet dreams, okay? I love you. I really do."

He took her in his arms and kissed her. And she let him. Actually, she did a lot more than just let him kiss her. She kissed him back, long and hard.

But he had the feeling she was kissing him good-bye.

—◆—

Suze was leaning against the corral fence, weaving her fingers through Speedo's blond forelock, when Gwen's ancient pickup came up the drive, rattling like a rolling barrel of bolts. It was a hot, sunny day, the kind of day that made Suze wish she could climb on Speedo's bare back and take a slow, aimless ride to nowhere. That was what she'd always done when she had a problem to think through—like the problem with Brady.

She knew she should trust him. She loved him.

But deep down where it really mattered, a nasty little demon of doubt had taken up residence in her chest overnight. He squatted there, leering at her, hinting at all the things Brady might be doing with this Teresa woman. The little demon wouldn't shut up, and he wouldn't go away.

And she couldn't deal with Brady until she got rid of him.

So she was happy to see Gwennie, who eased herself around until she sat at the edge of the driver's seat. She let her short legs dangle over the dusty driveway until she slid from the seat and landed with a thump.

"Whatcha doing, girlie?"

She ambled toward Suze, her face alight with good humor. Despite the demon and his ugly stories, Suze felt her spirits rise.

"Just standing around."

"Probably feels good after all that sitting."

"It does."

"Let's go talk to your dad, though," Gwen said. "He's got some things he needs to say."

Suze stilled, her hand holding Speedo's mane so tightly he jerked his head away and gave her a gentle nip.

"My father never talks to me."

"He will now. It's important."

Suze followed Gwen into the house, wondering what was going on. Her godmother seemed serious, almost grim. Maybe her dad was sick.

Suze felt a flutter of panic knocking around in her chest, like a bird trying to escape a dark room. She couldn't lose her father. He was all the family she had. Gruff as he was, she loved him. And without him tying her to this place, she'd be alone and adrift—an orphan, for heaven's sake.

When they entered the house, her dad was already at the table. It was a trestle table, jammed into a corner of the small kitchen so one bench was up against the wall. Her dad was back in the corner, Suze's usual seat. She sat there because she always liked to have her back against the wall. It felt safer that way. Nothing could happen that she didn't see coming.

She wished she could sit there now, but maybe it was too late to find a safe place.

She sat across from her dad, and Gwen lowered herself onto the bench beside her, sliding her bulk behind the table with care.

"Gwen has convinced me that it's time to tell you the truth about some things." Her father's voice sounded choked, as if his subconscious didn't want to let the words out.

"Past time," said Gwen.

To Suze's surprise, her father nodded. She'd never

seen him take criticism so gracefully. Bewildered, she looked from her father to Gwen. "What's going on?"

"It's not what's going on. It's what went on, before you were even born," Gwen said.

Suze wanted to get this conversation rolling. It didn't sound like they were bringing her good news, so whatever they had to say, she wanted it all at once. She believed in ripping off Band-Aids as fast as possible.

"Out with it, then," she said. "You two are making me nervous. Whatever it is, just tell me."

"Okay." Her father breathed in a deep breath, then exhaled as if he was letting all the poison out of his body. Only then did he start his story.

"Years ago, your mother and Gwen and I were friends. The three of us were inseparable." He smiled at Gwen, and for a minute he looked almost handsome.

Something was going on here, Suze thought.

"I admired your mother a great deal."

Gwen snorted. "He followed her around like a puppy dog with his tongue hanging out."

Her dad cleared his throat. "Yes, you might say that."

"One night, you mother, er, made herself available. Very available."

"You mean she slept with you."

Her dad nodded, then took a deep breath. "A few months later, she informed me she was pregnant. I was young, with no experience with women. Marrying her seemed like the right thing to do."

"Wow." Suze stared down at the tabletop. She could feel the mythology of her childhood slipping away, the perfect mother, the princess in every family fairy tale, tarnishing a bit.

"When you were born," he continued, "I realized she'd probably lied." He cleared his throat. "About your parentage. About who the father was."

Chapter 52

THE FATHER.

The words hit Suze like a jolt of electricity—quick, hard, and painful. She parsed Earl's words in her head, once, twice, three times. There was only one way to interpret it.

"You're not my father."

"I don't believe so."

She'd always wondered why beautiful, talented Ellen Carlyle had married an insurance salesman. Now, it turned out she'd trapped him into marriage—trapped him with a lie.

Suze suddenly couldn't sit another second, despite her ankle. She shoved her side of the bench back hard enough to shift Gwen, who clutched the edge of the table. Gwen probably wasn't used to being pushed around.

Suze crossed the kitchen and leaned against the counter by the sink, folding her arms over her chest. She might not be sitting in the corner, but that was how she felt: cornered, by Gwen and Earl and this revelation.

How many times in her life had she wished for a different father, a different life? But now that the dream was real, it looked a whole lot less attractive. She wished she could turn back the clock, pretend she'd never been told.

Bracing her hands on the counter, she glanced around

the familiar kitchen. It felt far too small to hold her emotions, but it was all she had.

All she had.

She used to think her father was all she had. He was her only family—or so she'd believed. But he wasn't even related to her. She had nothing. Nobody.

An orphan.

Her mind kept stuttering and stalling, gears grinding, wheels spinning. She looked at her father—at Earl; she should probably call him Earl now—hoping for some reassurance that she mattered to him anyway. He was still staring at the tabletop, avoiding her gaze.

She had never felt so alone in her life.

And then she had a thought. A hopeful thought. One that could change everything.

"So who's my father?"

Maybe he was someone *normal*. Maybe he'd moved on after her mother married Earl. Maybe he'd had another family, a whole pack of kids who would be her half brothers and half sisters. Maybe she wasn't alone at all.

She stared at her used-to-be father. He looked about as defeated and ashamed as a man could look. He'd lied to her all her life. Kept her with him, even though she didn't really belong to him. Kept her from that other life. Surely it would have been better. Surely her real father would have loved her, at least a little.

"Who was he?" she insisted.

Her father got out an ancient and yellowed envelope. "Private" was scrawled on the front in black marker, and the flap was taped down. Suze had seen it before, at the bottom of her father's file cabinet, and been tempted to peek. But she never had.

Her dad dumped out a pile of photos and clippings. He turned away, as if he couldn't bear to look.

"Your father," he said.

Suze pushed off the counter and sat down to look. They were old photos, most of them candid snapshots. Every one featured a tall, good-looking cowboy with a James Dean slouch. He stared insolently at the camera in every picture. He always had a toothpick or a cigarette stuck in his mouth, and in many of the photos he was shirtless.

The clippings were mostly from old rodeo magazines, although a few were from South Dakota newspapers. They showed him riding bucking horses, heels down, free hand high, the toothpick still miraculously dangling from his lips.

He was handsome, he was young, and despite the faded color of the photos, Suze could see that his eyes were green. Her green eyes were the one thing that set her apart from her mother and from Earl.

He and her mother would have made a stunning couple. Why didn't she marry him?

"He was a rodeo cowboy named Slim Harris," Gwen said.

Past tense.

But of course. He wasn't *still* a rodeo cowboy. He was probably a rancher or a stock contractor. A lot of cowboys moved on to jobs like that.

Suze sorted through the pictures. She could see her own face in the shadows of Slim Harris's, like a ghostly imprint. Her full mouth, her strong nose—all the features that didn't match her mother's matched his.

She'd always thought her parents were an odd

couple. They simply didn't go together, like dolls from two separate toy companies. As a child, her mom had tried to pass off some Barbie knockoffs as the real thing, but the fake Barbies just didn't look right next to the real ones.

That was how she'd thought of her father and mother: a pair that didn't quite match. As her memories of her mother faded, she had more and more trouble picturing them together.

But she could see her mother with Slim Harris.

"Why didn't she marry him?" Suze asked.

Her father winced as if the words hurt, and Suze wished she'd asked some other way. She hadn't meant to hurt him.

"She figured I was a better bet," he said. "I had a job, and I didn't have anything to do with rodeo."

"And Slim?"

"He was a wild one." Gwen smiled as if she'd liked Suze's father. "He rode like a demon and drank like a fish. Your mother knew he'd make a terrible father, if he'd even marry her."

So much for that ray of sunlight. She doubted there'd be any joyful reunion with her real father.

"Was she right?"

Gwen nodded. "He found out she was marrying your dad and went on a toot that lasted for months. Rodeo to rodeo, bar to bar. They finally took his PRCA card away because he showed up drunk so many times. Then all he could do was small-town stuff." Gwen's brown eyes sought Suze's, and the sympathy in them made her feel even worse. "He rode a bronc at a ranch rodeo he'd saddled himself while he was drunk. The cinch was loose, and when the saddle slipped—well, he didn't make it." Gwen shook her head sadly. "You weren't even a year old."

"So she tricked my dad into marrying her. And broke my real father's heart so he self-destructed." She put a fist to her mouth as emotions threatened to overwhelm her. Did you cry for a father you'd never known? Or for a mother you suddenly did?

"She didn't mean to hurt people," Gwen said. "She had no idea the destruction she left behind when she went on to her next win, her next triumph."

Suze's mind was a whirl of spinning thoughts, truth and lies blending together until she couldn't tell one from the other. A question for her father finally flew out of the mix.

"Why were you mourning her, then? She lied to you. She cheated. Why did you stop living when she died?"

"She was a different person when she got sick. She was good to me then." He shook his head, chuckling softly as if he couldn't quite believe what had happened. "We fell in love. We really did. And then she died."

It took Suze a while to grasp what he was saying. Finally, she said, "You were mourning what could have been."

"What should have been," Earl said. "Her illness made her realize how precious even the most ordinary life is. Even the most ordinary love."

Gwen had slid over on the bench so she sat across from Earl. As Suze struggled to sort out her feelings, Gwen reached over and clasped her father's—Earl's—hand. The gesture was simple, but there was so much affection in it that Suze suddenly wished, with all her heart, that her father would have the sense to see the bright-eyed girl inside Gwen's body. It was obvious she cared for him.

Suddenly, two pieces of information came together for her, like pieces of a puzzle. "The man who broke your heart," she said to Gwen. "He was…" She suddenly realized she might be outing a secret. "Never mind."

"No, you're right. He was me." Earl turned his hand over to clasp Gwen's. "I was a fool."

He looked like a fool, the way he was looking at Gwen now. She'd never seen her father's face soften like that. All the hard lines and creases relaxed, and he looked like a different person.

Good for Earl. Good for Gwen. But it was hard to celebrate their long-delayed love affair when she'd just discovered everything about her life, from her birth to her mother to her father himself, was a lie. There were hidden reasons behind every hurt, and nothing was as it seemed.

"No wonder you never loved me." The words came out flat and emotionless. She felt numb, stupefied by the sudden onslaught of truth. "I wasn't even your child."

"I did my best," he said.

"You made me feel so bad. Comparing me to her. Making me feel like I was never good enough. Why did you make her out to be so perfect when you knew she wasn't?"

"I didn't realize how you'd take it. I was trying to make sure you knew she was special, that's all. She wanted you to be a champion, like her, and I thought I should push you."

"Men don't get it," Gwen said. "They don't understand emotions unless you run them over with a tractor.

Then they understand what pain is." Her brown eyes met Suze's. "He didn't realize you thought you weren't good enough. He just wanted to give you an example to live up to, that's all. And he wanted you to love your mother."

Earl ran a shaky hand over the thin strands of his comb-over and cleared his throat. "I wanted you to have one parent you could look up to."

A new truth flooded into Suze's heart. If Earl wasn't her father, then he owed her nothing. Once her mother died, he could have walked away. With her father long dead, she would have been an orphan for real.

She thought of the kids at Phoenix House, fatherless and motherless because no one cared enough to take them in. Maybe Earl had made her feel bad about herself, but how bad would she have felt if he'd dropped her off at some adoption agency and left?

She needed to think, and she couldn't do that with Gwen and Earl staring at her. Opening the refrigerator, she faked interest in the scant supplies on the lighted shelves. The thought of eating made her gag, but once she regained her self-control she knew what to say. Everything had changed, nothing was as it seemed, but there was one truth at the heart of this mess: Earl had taken care of her when he could have walked away. He wasn't made to be a father. It didn't come easy for him. But he'd tried.

She closed the fridge and turned around.

"If I'd known the truth, I would have looked up to you, Dad." She felt tears building up, hot behind her eyes. "You didn't have to take care of Mom when she got sick. You didn't have to raise me. You could have walked away from both of us as soon as you found out about my father."

"I couldn't."

"I know." Suze set a hand lightly on his shoulder. They rarely touched, and now she understood why. Raising a teenaged girl who wasn't your kin was a delicate operation. "You might be a grumpy old cuss, but you took care of me." She put her other hand on his other shoulder and squeezed.

It was as close as she dared come to a hug.

Chapter 53

SUZE WOKE THE NEXT MORNING WITH HER HAIR LOOKing like a bird's nest gone terribly wrong. She had a habit of playing with it when she was emotionally distraught, and evidently she'd been distraught even in her sleep.

As she tugged a brush through the tangles, she winced at the pain and thought about the revelations of the night before. Oddly, she wasn't that surprised by the truth about her mother. Something had always seemed off about her father's grief.

She picked up the photo of her mom that sat by her bedside. She could see nuances in that face now, where once she'd seen only perfection—a shadow, maybe, deep in her eyes. Had she loved Suze's father? Had she mourned his death?

She tugged at a knot in her hair and looked at herself in the mirror. Who was that person? She wasn't Earl's daughter or the child of a brilliant, saintly barrel racer. She was herself, a woman alone. Her strength, her will to win, and her smarts were all she had.

Except...

She looked down at her little dog and sighed. "I miss him, Dooley."

Dooley sat at her feet, gazing up at her with unaccustomed gravity.

"But how can I trust him? He had another woman's

underwear in his truck. I'd be a fool to call him. Wouldn't I?"

The little demon in her heart nodded yes. Dooley whimpered. Picking him up, she held him close. He needed a good brushing too. But first, she needed to solve the Brady problem.

"I can't help it. I just can't believe he'd lie to me. I mean, he's Brady. You wouldn't think he'd be *able* to lie."

She kissed the dog and set him down. "I need facts. Hard, cold facts. Maybe I could go to the reservation and find this Teresa person." She looked down at the dog, who was panting with excitement. "Is that what I should do, Dooley? Should I go out there? Should I find out?"

Dooley punctuated her questions with a tremendous leap that landed him on top of the vanity. Well, that explained the recent disappearance of her toothbrush — and the minty-fresh scent as Dooley panted in her face.

"You think I should, don't you? You think I should find out."

Jumping off the vanity, Dooley squatted at her feet and peed on the floor.

"Oh," she said. "You think *you* should *go* out."

Grabbing a paper towel from under the sink, she cleaned up the mess. She didn't scold the dog. It wasn't his fault he'd had an accident. She'd been so involved with herself and her troubles she hadn't even realized the dog had been shut in her room all night with no access to his doggie door.

Just another example of what a crappy person she was. She couldn't even take care of a dog.

But she could walk now, and she didn't see why she

couldn't drive. To hell with what the doctor said. She was heading out to the rez, and she was going to find out the truth about that bag of size-four, sexy clothes.

―⁂―

By late afternoon, Suze was losing her enthusiasm for her fact-finding mission. She didn't know where Teresa lived. She didn't know the woman's last name either, so she couldn't look her up or ask for directions. And she'd forgotten how big the reservation was—how many roads there were, how many little houses. Teresa could be anywhere.

She wasn't sure she wanted the truth anyway.

She was heading home when a cloud of dust in the road ahead cleared to reveal two small riders on fat spotted ponies tearing down the road like Butch and Sundance running from the law. She slowed as she passed them in case a horse spooked. The little outlaws looked as if they barely had the animals under control.

She'd left them behind before she remembered what Brady had said about Teresa of the sexy lingerie. *Two little boys...hard for her to handle...new ponies...*

She jerked the truck to a screeching, dust-raising halt and rolled her window down, watching in her rearview mirror as the riders approached. They slowed, then stopped, staring curiously at the strange truck.

They probably knew better than to talk to strangers.

Just as she was about to drive off, one of the boys nudged his pony into motion and strolled up alongside her driver's side window with all the dignity of a state trooper making a traffic stop.

"Ma'am." He tipped an incredibly dirty cowboy hat.

Suze rested her elbow on the car door. "Howdy."

It was hard for her to keep a straight face. The kid was covered with dust from the top of his hat to the scuffed toes of his boots. He looked like a seasoned cowhand who'd been riding drag on a miniature cattle drive.

The other boy eased closer, hanging behind his brother. At least, she assumed they were brothers. They looked enough alike to be twins.

"You fellas know Brady Caine?" she asked.

The boy's serious face creased into a huge smile, showing two missing teeth that made her realize he was even younger than she'd thought. He must be seven, maybe eight at the most.

"Sure do," he said. "He's teaching us to ride Apocalypse and Doom."

"Apocalypse and Doom?"

"These horses, here." He patted his mount's shoulder like a born cowboy. "This here's Apocalypse. My brother's horse is Doom."

Apocalypse nodded his head as if acknowledging the introduction, then blew a massive raspberry, decorating Suze's elbow with horse snot.

"Brady's teaching you guys to ride?"

"Not really."

Ah. Here came the truth.

"We already know how to ride." The little cowboy's chest swelled with pride. "He's teaching us to ride like *champions*."

There. That line had Brady written all over it. He'd told the truth; he was just teaching the woman's kids to ride. This Teresa might have put the clothes in Brady's car to spark his interest or to stake a claim. But Brady himself, like so many men, might be too dense to see what she was up to.

Why had she doubted him? Brady was right; love couldn't survive without trust and respect. He wasn't the one who was lacking in this relationship; she was.

Her mind backpedaled through their relationship, as off-balance as an amateur unicyclist on a downhill slope. She'd behaved so badly she couldn't help wondering about her own feelings. Did she love him? She didn't trust him, and that meant she didn't respect him. Without trust or respect, what was left? Sex. Sex and ownership. She wanted to *own* Brady, and that wasn't what love was about.

"Excuse me. Ma'am? Are you all right?"

She jerked out of her reverie to see the little cowboy staring at her. "Sure," she said.

"Can we help you with something?"

"No," she said. "No. I just—I bet Brady's a good teacher, huh?"

"He sure is." The other boy edged forward with eagerness, his pony jockeying the other one aside. "And he's gonna marry our mom and be our new daddy."

Oh.

Suze felt like the kid had whipped out a gun and shot her in the chest.

Looking from one boy to the other, she prayed for some sign of wishful thinking or outright lying, but all she got was great, gap-toothed grins of absolute certainty and a whole lot of nodding.

"You're sure about this?"

"Yup," said the first boy. "He's gonna make an honest woman of her."

Suze felt the jolt of this new knowledge like a knife in the heart. *An honest woman.* Then they'd already done the deed.

Only then did she realize that she hadn't really been on a fact-finding mission. She'd been hoping to discover Brady was telling the truth. But the real truth about Brady was something she didn't want to hear.

She waved good-bye to the little renegades, who took off at a gallop on their ponies. Putting the car in gear, she thought about where she should go from here.

Home. She'd go home — back to the barn, back to her horses and the only world she could trust. Her thoughts came back into balance, as if that unicycle rider was pedaling, smooth and steady, in a straight line. Brady might have taken away her hopes for love and a family, and he might have done a number on her confidence, but soon she'd be able to ride again.

She'd take a good horse over a man anyway. You could always trust a horse.

Chapter 54

IT WAS DOOLEY WHO TOLD SUZE BRADY WAS BACK.

The little dog was prone to excitement about everything and everybody, but Brady inspired a special sort of idiocy in the hairy little creature. He raced from the window to the bed, alternating between barking ecstatically and leaping on Suze, licking her face and hands.

"What is it, buddy?"

She couldn't let herself believe it. Brady was busy with his buddy's widow, making an honest woman of her, being a father to her adorable little boys. So why would he be coming to visit *her*?

She steeled herself against his charm and swore to herself she wouldn't believe his lies. But when she saw that familiar truck pull up, her heart kicked in her chest, leaping with the same unfettered joy Dooley displayed and rolling in the knowledge that Brady was here.

She and Dooley were two of a kind. She was loyal as a dog. It was pathetic, really. The only thing in her life that gave her real joy was the man she'd promised herself she'd forget.

A big part of her wished she still believed Brady was hers, and hers alone. That he loved her the way a man should. She'd been through so much the last couple days. Brady would listen to her. He'd help her sort out the truth about her mother. He'd help her figure out how to deal with her father.

Earl. Just Earl. He wasn't her father anymore. He never had been.

Brady would know just what to say, just what to do. He'd make the whole thing seem simple.

But no. She deserved to be loved the way her father had loved her mother. To be loved so much she was forgiven for her flaws and admired for her strengths. Brady wasn't capable of that kind of love.

She headed downstairs to tell him to go away.

When she opened the door, he was standing there with his thumbs in the belt loops of his worn jeans. His shirttail was half-in, half-out, and his old straw Stetson was tilted rakishly over one eyes. She could see the part Dooley had eaten at the back.

"Hey." His eyes were soft with concern. "I talked to Gwen. She told me you might need to talk. What's going on?"

Darn it. Gwen needed to stop trying to play matchmaker.

"I—it's nothing." She shrugged one shoulder. "She and Earl sat me down and explained that he's not my real father. Turns out my mom cheated on him and lied about it." She tilted her chin up. "Gwen probably figured you could tell me something about that."

"I, um, I don't know." He looked genuinely confused. "Wow. You must be really upset. Can I come in?"

"No."

"Oh." He looked down at his boot tips, then turned and looked over his shoulder, squinting into the far distance as if he expected to be rescued at any moment by Clint Eastwood, riding across the pasture.

He turned his gaze back to her, and she wondered

why he had to have such impossibly long eyelashes. Why he had to have brown eyes soft as Bambi's in a face tanned by hours on horseback. Why he had to be so kind and look so damn good.

"So you thought I knew something about your mother? I swear, Suze, I never—"

"Not about my mother," she said. "About lying and cheating."

He shook his head. "We're not back to that again, are we?"

"Yeah," she said. "We are. I went out to the reservation and got the truth. I found out about Teresa. About how you're going to marry her and make an honest woman of her."

He actually laughed. It was convincing too, the laugh of a man who'd just heard the most ridiculous idea ever. "I'm not going to marry Teresa. Who the hell did you talk to?"

"Never mind." Belatedly, she realized she didn't want to get the kids in trouble. Brady seemed to be really good with kids, and she doubted he'd take it out on them, but who knew?

"Well, whoever it was is shining you on," he said. "I help Teresa when I can. Her husband was like a brother to me. Like Ridge and Shane. It would be like me putting the moves on Sierra."

"I wouldn't be surprised," Suze said.

She wanted to take the words back as soon as they left her mouth. Brady might have many flaws, but when it came to his brothers, he was loyal as the day was long.

He stepped back as if he'd been slapped. Those brown

eyes didn't have a thing in common with Bambi's any-more; they were hard as granite.

Brady had never looked at her like that before—as if she were a stranger. A stranger he didn't even like. She felt her knees buckle, and again wished that she'd never found out the truth.

But this had to be done. She'd do it fast—like pulling off a Band-Aid. She'd gotten through that conversation with Gwen and Earl, so she could get through this.

"Your debt is paid, Brady," she said. "You don't need to come around here anymore."

He looked at her a long time with those hard, cold eyes.

"I'm—I'm sorry," she said.

"Are you?"

She nodded. "It's just—I can't be with a man who lies to me. Who hides the truth. It turns out I've been lied to all my life, and I'm through with that kind of thing. You can't build a relationship on deception. You just can't."

He nodded. "You're right, I guess. I did my best, Suze. People make mistakes. People lie. Your dad did what he thought was best. Are you going to be able to forgive him?"

She shook her head, staring down at the floor. "I don't know." She looked up at him. "Did you lie to me, Brady?"

He looked deep into her eyes, and she willed him to say no. Instead, he slowly nodded his head.

"I did. But it's not what you think. I never lied about love."

He sucked in a deep breath, and his brown eyes met hers. "After the accident, Ridge went over to the rodeo grounds to make sure Speedo was safe. He put him in a stall, because he didn't have a trailer with him."

She nodded, wondering where this was going. Something cold clutched at her heart. This felt like another truth she didn't want to know.

"I was over at the hospital, trying to get in to see you. I needed to know you were okay." He turned away from her, leaning his long, lean body against the house, gazing off across the fields. "I should have gone and gotten Speedo. I should have made sure he was safe. You didn't even want to see me, remember?"

She nodded, even though he wasn't looking at her.

"Somebody took him. I looked for him for days. Finally, you got a ransom note."

She frowned. Was he making this up? Was it some kind of parable?

"I didn't get any note," she said.

"I know. I found it in your mail, and I took it. I figured out from the note it was Cooter Banks who sent it. He's not exactly a criminal mastermind."

She stepped out onto the porch, her fists on her hips. "Cooter Banks had Speedo?"

He nodded, his eyes full of sorrow.

"And you didn't tell me?"

"You couldn't have done anything about it. I found him, and he was okay."

"But you told me he was with Ridge. You told me he was doing fine."

"I know," he said. "I lied."

Her eyes filled with tears. "My father isn't my father.

My horse wasn't where I thought he was. You've got another woman's underwear in your truck."

"I lied to you about Speedo. I'm coming clean on that. But I didn't cheat on you. Teresa set me up."

"Do I have a big 'Lie to Me' sign on my forehead or something? Or does everybody just think I'm stupid?"

He sighed. "Maybe everybody's trying to save you from pain."

"Which pain do you think I need to be saved from? Maybe you think you need to save me from the pain of knowing you cheated on me. How would I know?"

He kicked at a pebble on the step, and it flew off into the yard. "I guess you wouldn't." His eyes narrowed. "I guess you'd have to trust me."

"I can't," she said. "You just proved to me that I can't."

He shrugged. "Then I guess we're done here." He started toward his truck, then turned as he opened the door. "You know, Suze, nobody's perfect. People make mistakes. Sometimes you have to trust the people you love to do the right thing."

"But they never do," she said. "So how can I trust anyone?"

Brady didn't answer. Instead he climbed into the truck, slammed the door, and drove away in a puff of dust.

Chapter 55

TWO DAYS LATER, SUZE WAS RELIEVED TO SEE SIERRA pull into the turnaround in the Phoenix House van. A visit from Isaiah was just what she and her dad needed. They'd talked more in the last couple days than they had all year.

Her nights were even more stressful than those long days spent talking about the past. She wasn't in pain anymore. At least, her leg didn't hurt. But her heart did, and she knew most of the wound that made it ache so was self-inflicted. Her regret for the way she'd talked to Brady was so strong she woke from a dream to find herself actually reaching out her arm, trying to claw back the words.

She and Brady were done. That, she could accept. But she wished it had ended differently, and she wished they could still be friends.

Fortunately, she and Earl had decided to continue on as they were. The fact that he wasn't her real father put a new spin on their relationship so far. He'd taken care of her all her life, and she realized she was only just beginning to pay him back. He wasn't the kindest man in the world, or the most softhearted. He'd made a lot of mistakes, but he'd done his best. So Suze would stay, and she'd do her best as well. Maybe, in dealing with Earl, she'd learn to be more loving. More forgiving.

Sierra hopped down from the van's driver's seat, and

Isaiah extricated himself from the passenger side. He'd just turned twelve and was reveling in the distinction of being legally allowed to sit in the front seat of the van. He was the oldest boy at Phoenix House, and Suze suspected he'd laid claim to that seat. If another boy turned twelve, he'd have a tough fight taking over.

Isaiah opened the sliding door and two more kids leaped out of the back of the van. They hit the ground running and were halfway to the barn before Suze realized who they were.

It was the little riders from the reservation. Teresa's kids.

"What are *they* doing here?" she asked Sierra. She really needed to learn to think before speaking. She sounded so *mean*. It had only been two days since she'd cut Brady loose and already she sounded like a bitter old woman.

"You know Derek and Sam?" Sierra grinned and Suze couldn't help smiling back. "They're great kids, aren't they? A little high-spirited, but so *happy*."

Suze nodded. "I only met them once. I just happened to run into them on the reservation. But you know, Brady's dating their mother."

"He *is*? Oh, Suze, I'm sorry. I thought you and Brady were…" Her words faded away. "Oh no." She pulled Suze into a hug.

Suze wasn't a hugger, and she usually shied away from touch. But she *needed* this hug, dammit, and Sierra's sympathy felt good. She blinked back her tears—she wouldn't go so far as to cry on Sierra's shoulder—but it felt good to lose herself in a little human warmth.

"Are you guys *done*?" said an annoyed voice.

"Isaiah," Sierra said. "Why don't you go in and see Earl?"

"I think I'd better stay outside and watch these little Indians," Isaiah said.

Sierra shot him a stern look.

"Well, they *are* Indians. And they are pretty little."

"Just be nice," Sierra said. "Be a big brother to them, okay?"

"Okay." Isaiah assented as if he were agreeing to a life sentence in Sing Sing. Sierra and Suze smothered their laughter as he literally dragged his feet on the way to the barn.

"How did you end up with them?" Suze asked Sierra. "They're not foster kids."

"No, but they need a little guidance," Sierra said. "I thought it would be good for Isaiah to learn to manage them a little. He has such strong leadership skills. I try to find ways to channel that."

Suze thought Isaiah was just bossy, but Sierra saw the best in everyone.

She and Sierra sat out on the sun porch for a while, Suze in her rocking chair and Sierra in a side chair she'd carried out from the kitchen. Suze made a pitcher of iced tea with some of the mint that grew like weeds around the foundation of the house, and they talked about everything from riding to relationships.

Suze had trouble opening up, even to Sierra, but she did manage to tell her about Earl. Brady, however, was a subject she wanted to avoid.

When the pitcher ran dry, Sierra rose and gathered their glasses.

"I can do that," said Suze. Her leg hurt, but she wasn't about to force her guest to clean up the dishes.

"No, I'm good." Sierra headed for the kitchen. "Tell you what, if you'd check on the hooligans out there, I'd be grateful."

Suze wondered if Sierra was trying to make her feel useful. She was big on that kind of thing.

"See if you can sneak up on them a little," Sierra said. "I'd love to hear how Isaiah's treating the boys."

Suze doubted she'd be delivering good news on her return, but she never minded a trip to the barn.

She stopped at the bench outside the barn door. Earl had built it years ago for Ellen, so she could sit outside the barn and watch the sun rise. Suze had sat there so many times, believing she could feel the spirit of her mother as she watched that same scene play out. Leaning her back against the dark red wall of the barn, she let the last remnants of the day's summer heat warm her back and listened to the boys chattering. She could watch them too. The setting sun glowed through the back door of the barn and cast their shadows, elongated into alien forms, on the grass in front of the barn.

The boys were sitting in a row on the hay bales Brady had thrown down a few days ago. Earl hadn't gotten around to stacking them against the wall, so they made a nice conversation pit for the kids.

"They're named Apocalypse and Doom," one boy was saying. "They're quarter horses, mostly."

That was a pretty generous description of the ponies she'd seen the boys riding. There might be some quarter horse in them, but they were mostly Shetland pony.

She straightened and leaned toward the barn door when she heard one of the boys mention Brady.

"He's, like, the best rodeo cowboy in the world," the boy boasted.

Suze couldn't help smiling. Good thing Brady wasn't around to hear this. He'd be unbearable for a week.

"He's teaching us to ride Apocalypse and Doom," the other boy added. It was hard to tell the two apart until they spoke. Derek had a slightly higher-pitched voice.

"And then he's going to marry our mom and be our dad," Sam said.

"No way," Isaiah said.

"Way," said Derek.

"Yeah *way*." Sam wasn't about to be left out of this argument. But Suze had heard enough. She rose to leave, but then Isaiah jumped back in the fray and she paused to hear what he'd say.

"That's just a load of crap, 'cause Brady Caine is crazy in love with my lady in there." His lanky shadow gestured toward the house. "I know, 'cause I take care of her and her dad." She could picture him defending her, his brows arrowed down fiercely, his lower lip jutting out in a pout. "You better find yourself some other dad, 'cause you're not getting *him*. He's *ours*."

There was a long silence as the twins digested this new information. Suze was sure they'd have a comeback, and she was right. It just wasn't the one she was expecting.

"Well, then, Chuck Norris is gonna marry our mom and be our dad," Sam said.

"Yeah!" The smaller boy wriggled with pleasure.

"Chuck Norris. He's gonna make an honest woman out of her."

"Don't say that about your mom," Isaiah said. "You should never talk about your mom that way. It's disrespectful. I'd never say that about my lady, even though she does the nasty with Brady Caine pretty much every chance she gets."

"What's the nasty?" Derek asked.

Any other time, Suze would have stuck around to hear Isaiah's answer, but first she needed to digest what Sam had said.

Chuck Norris is gonna be our dad. He's gonna make an honest woman of her.

They were the same words he'd applied to Brady the other day, spoken with the same certainty. But they were a total fantasy.

Brady had been telling the truth.

He'd loved her, truly and deeply. She'd seen it in his eyes. But she just couldn't accept love at face value. She had to dissect it, take it apart, examine it. If it were a sweater, she'd tug at all the threads until it unraveled.

It wasn't that she couldn't believe in Brady, she realized.

It was that she couldn't believe in love.

Chapter 56

Suze wasn't supposed to be walking much. She wasn't supposed to be driving, either. So Sierra's offer to take her along when she and Ridge drove some of the kids to the Rooftop Rodeo in Sheridan over the weekend offered just the opportunity she'd been looking for.

She'd get out of the house and even out of Wynott. She'd get to be outside all day, in the stands. And she'd get to see Brady ride. Maybe she'd even get to see him and apologize. She doubted it would do much good, but she'd feel a little better if he only knew how bad she felt.

The Phoenix House van was almost full when Ridge pulled it into the turnout.

"Hey, lady, you can have the front seat if you want," Isaiah said. He was sitting beside Ridge, but as Suze approached, he slid to the ground and waved her into the minivan with a courtly gesture.

Suze slid into the seat. "Thanks. Hi, Ridge."

He just looked at her, his expression stony. Ridge was always quiet, but she was pretty sure she was feeling some heavy-duty waves of hostility emanating from his gray eyes.

Normally, Ridge seemed to like her. She wondered what Brady had said to him.

Sierra, who was sitting in back with the boys, moved over to make room for Isaiah.

"That was nice, Isaiah, but you shouldn't call her 'Hey, lady,'" Sierra said gently. "You know her name."

"It's okay," Suze said. Ever since she'd heard Isaiah defend her claim on Brady as "my lady," she'd accepted the name. "It's something we got worked out."

If Isaiah hadn't offered the front seat, she'd have had to ask. Her ankle still gave her trouble, and the knee on the same leg got sore if she sat for a long time. Soon Isaiah would be calling her, "Hey, old lady." And she'd have to answer.

Actually, she'd answer to anything the kid wanted to call her. Isaiah had been a godsend. Having him around was like having a mischievous sprite in the house. Unfortunately, mischievous sprites were known to eavesdrop occasionally, and he'd overheard Suze and Earl talking about their newly defined relationship. But his frank appraisal of their new situation made them both laugh.

"So he's not the guy that knocked up your mom," he'd said. "That doesn't matter. He's still your dad, 'cause he does all the dad stuff."

Suze and Earl had laughed, and the tension in the house had ebbed a little bit, as it did every time Isaiah was there.

Sierra introduced Suze to all the kids. Teresa's little munchkins were there, along with Sierra and Ridge's boy, Jeff. Then there was a beautiful brown-eyed, olive-skinned boy named Frankie who was wearing the most disreputable-looking Panama hat Suze had ever seen; a chunky, cheerful kid named Carter; and a new boy, Adam, who seemed a little overwhelmed by the energy level in the van.

As Ridge jockeyed the van over the potholes and cor-rugated concrete of Wyoming's country roads, Suze felt free for the first time since the accident. She watched a center-pivot irrigation system creep slowly across a farmer's field like a huge robotic centipede, and saw two horses running in a pasture, nipping at each other as they galloped over the prairie. She saw livestock trucks hauling cattle, and hay trucks bearing huge round bales that sagged over the sides of their flatbeds.

The only thing that spoiled her pleasure was Ridge's unfriendly presence. He only grunted in response to her efforts to make conversation, and she caught him staring at her with a grim expression once when they stopped for a light.

As they neared the rodeo grounds, she saw more and more pickup trucks, all of them driven by men in cowboy hats. Sure, there was the occasional pickup with a "Stupid Boy, Trucks Are for Girls" bumper sticker, but rodeo was still a man's game.

Unless you were a barrel racer.

"Is it going to be hard for you to just watch?" Sierra asked.

"No. It's such a treat to get out of the house today, I won't mind at all," Suze said. "I'm going to drink beer and gorge on fair food, and have myself a good time."

Sierra grinned. "Sounds like a plan. I'll join you."

"You can't drink beer," Isaiah said indignantly. "That would set a bad example for all these little kids."

Despite the fact that he was only a year or two older than the rest of the kids, Isaiah had always referred to them with a hint of scorn as "little kids." He evidently considered himself a miniature grown-up, and at times his odd blend of wisdom and gravity made him seem precisely right.

But he certainly had the energy of a kid. No sooner had Ridge pulled into a parking space than he was out of the van, opening Suze's door and practically dragging her out of the front seat he'd offered so kindly a few hours earlier.

"Come on, lady. Let's go. I want nachos and some of that beer."

Suze was beginning to regret her mention of alcohol. "I don't really drink beer, Isaiah," she said.

It was true. She'd only drunk beer once, and that had led to her first night with Brady. She shivered at the thought.

"You okay?" the boy asked.

"I'm fine."

"You gonna come with us to see Brady?" he asked.

"I don't think so."

His dark brows lowered over his eyes, and he scowled. "Well, are you gonna cheer for him?"

"I sure am." Suze smiled. "Louder than you, I bet."

"No way." Isaiah puffed out his chest. "Nobody cheers louder than me!"

"No, I'm the loudest," Carter said.

"No, me." Frankie joined the fight, and they argued about it until Sierra let out a piercing whistle.

The boys fell immediately silent and stood waiting for whatever she had to say.

"Nobody is going to be loud," she said. "We are going to be polite and kind to each other and the people around us." She swept the little crowd of kids with her eyes, then ducked down to their level. "You know why?"

"'Cause we're secret agent men from the planet Zorg and revealing our true identities could cause discovery and *death*!" the boys shouted in unison.

"Okay, let's go." Sierra led the way, with the boys doing some sort of awkward Igor walk behind her. Evidently, that was how secret agent men from the planet Zorg got around.

Once the kids were absorbed in the menu at the concession stand, Sierra moved over to stand by Suze.

"You sure you don't want to see Brady?"

"I'm sure," Suze said. She and Sierra had become friends, just as Suze had hoped, and she'd confided in Sierra about everything from her harsh words to Brady to her discussion with Earl and Gwen. "Just seeing him ride'll be nice."

"He's loved you for a long time," Sierra said. "One fight can't have made that much difference."

"I hurt him one too many times," Suze said. "I think he's over me."

Sierra's smile was serene, as if she knew better. "I doubt it."

But Sierra hadn't seen Brady's face that last day, when Suze had accused him of everything from courting Sierra herself to lying about his involvement with Teresa. He actually hadn't looked hurt. He'd looked cold, as if he'd shut down his emotions for good.

That was one reason she'd wanted to come to the rodeo. She wanted to see him ride with his usual abandon, and watch his fancy dismount. Incredibly, she wanted to hear that joyful whoop of his again, in some context other than her own accident. Surprisingly, she felt like it would be healing to see the old carefree

Brady, without their troubled relationship shackling his good humor.

She loved him. That would never change. It was trust that was the problem—trust, truth, and forgiveness.

What a mess her life had become.

Once the boys had spent their grubby, creased dollar bills on a selection of gloriously unhealthy rodeo food, Sierra sent them up to their seats with Ridge.

"You take them, okay?" was all she had to say. The man was a saint.

"You really got lucky with Ridge," Suze said as they sat down at a picnic table to eat their hot dogs.

"Brady's his brother," Sierra said with a knowing smile. "You could get lucky too."

"Brady's nothing like Ridge, though," Suze said. "Ridge is so quiet and responsible. Brady's the anti-Ridge."

Sierra sighed. "You have a point. *Quiet* isn't a word I'd use to describe Brady," she said. "Although he did take responsibility for what he did to you."

Suze nodded.

"And you know, Brady was raised by Bill Decker, just like Ridge and Shane," Sierra said. "He lives by the Code of the West, just like they do."

"I'm not sure what part of the code applies to our relationship," Suze said wryly.

"It applies to life, though. Think about it. Brady's honest. He's tough but fair. He rides for the brand. And he's loyal as the day is long."

Suze nodded. All those things were true.

Except, wait. The first one wasn't. He wasn't honest.

"He lied to me, though," she said.

"People do." Sierra sighed in a put-upon big-sister sort of way. "Don't take this wrong, but you haven't had a whole lot of experience with love."

"I know." Suze flushed. "I've only slept with three guys."

"I don't mean sex." Sierra laughed. "I mean *love*. With your mother gone and your father the way he is, you never had it growing up. It's no wonder you don't know it when you see it now. And it's no wonder you have trouble trusting people."

"I don't know," Suze said. "I spent a lot of time with animals. That'll teach you about love."

"Unconditional love," Sierra said, nodding. "Kids are good for that too."

They ate for a while in silence, watching the people flow around them.

"I'm not sure I'm right for Brady," Suze said. "I do care about him. So much. But I think maybe it's best if I let him go, and I care enough to do that." She finished off her hot dog and crumpled her napkin. "I'm not here to talk him into taking me back or anything. I just want to see that he's okay. And then, somehow, I'll move on."

She wasn't sure how she'd do that, but that wasn't Sierra's problem. It was hers. All hers.

Chapter 57

As soon as Suze and Sierra got back to the stands, Sierra started checking on the kids, handing out napkins, and gathering up trash. Meanwhile, Ridge sat stonily at the end of the row, staring down at the day sheet that listed the cowboys and indicated what horses they'd ride.

Sierra took one look at him, and asked, "Ridge, what's wrong?"

He handed her the day sheet. "Brady drew Tornado."

"You're kidding."

"Isn't that the horse that rolled over on you and messed up your hand?" Isaiah asked. The kid was always direct, Suze thought.

Ridge just nodded. Suze knew he'd had to give up rodeo when a bucking horse threw him and rolled over on him, damaging two vertebrae in his neck and causing nerve damage in his riding hand. He couldn't hang on to a basketball, let alone a bucking rope.

"Maybe Brady'll get revenge for you," Isaiah said. "Maybe he'll whip out a gun and shoot that sucker dead!"

"Yeah!" chorused Teresa's kids. Suze was starting to see some hero worship in their eyes when they looked at Isaiah. Next they'd be trying to get the kid to marry their mother and make an honest woman of her.

Sierra gave Isaiah a look that would freeze a fire. "That would be totally inappropriate, Isaiah. As was your comment."

When they'd come back from the concession stand, Sierra had sat down on the far end of the line of kids, so that she and Ridge would act as bookends. But now, with a quick glance at Suze, she moved down the line and sat beside him, taking his hand. The two of them stayed silent, almost motionless, but Suze could see Ridge relaxing simply from his wife's presence.

That was the kind of relationship Suze wanted—quiet, unspoken, and deep.

Again, words that didn't describe Brady.

And yet, he was the man she wanted. The man she loved—quietly, unspoken, and deep inside her heart.

—◆—

Suze couldn't help watching for Brady. As the cowboys lowered themselves carefully onto big bucking horses twitching with nerves, she listened for his name. Her ankle was throbbing with every beat of her heart. She'd foolishly worn a normal boot on her bad foot as well as her good one, and if she didn't take it off soon she'd have to cut it off.

A tussle in the chutes drew her eye. Six or eight cowboys were trying to help a rider mount a horse who clearly wasn't planning on being ridden today. The animal lunged and reared, then stood just long enough for the cowboy to lower himself onto its back before it slung itself sideways, slamming the cowboy's leg into the rough boards of the chute.

The horse leaned against the chute, pressing the cowboy's leg against the unforgiving wood.

"He's going to get hurt before he even gets out of the chute," Suze heard Ridge grumble.

"That's Brady?" She leaned over so she could talk to Ridge. "That can't be Brady. This is the bareback riding. He doesn't do that."

"He does now," Ridge said. "Tornado's a bareback horse. Guess my little brother's got a death wish. Wonder why." His gray eyes fixed on Suze, expressionless. A taut muscle pulsed in his jaw and Suze realized why the kids behaved so well around him. You didn't mess with Ridge Cooper. Or his family.

"All right, everybody, you might want to watch gate five," the announcer said. "That's Brady Caine, getting ready to ride Tornado. That horse has never been ridden yet, and you can see he's not planning to take Caine for a pony ride today!"

Suze wished the announcer would shut up. He yammered on, announcing the next cowboy, but she barely saw the bronc burst out of the chute and toss his rider almost immediately. Somersaulting off the horse, the rider landed on his very attractive cowboy butt, then hopped to his feet and waved to the crowd.

Suze glanced down at Ridge, who was hunched forward, resting his elbows on his knees and his chin on his hand. His pale gray eyes were fixed on chute five, where Brady had managed to get himself into position and was hammering his hand into the rigging.

"Aaaaand now for Brady Caine on Tornado!" hollered the announcer. "Ladies and gentlemen, this is the horse that dang near killed another Decker Ranch cowboy last year. Ridge Cooper hung up his spurs after Tornado rolled over on him in a wreck. Now Caine's here to take his revenge. Those boys are like brothers, ladies and gentlemen. So, *do you think he can ride him?*"

The announcer's voice rose to a frantic pitch on the last words, and the crowd roared. Half of them wanted Brady to give them a good wreck, but the shouts of "No!" were practically drowned out by the Phoenix House kids, stamping on the bleachers and hollering for Brady.

Suze was shouting encouragement too, until Brady glanced over his shoulder and tipped his hat for the kids. Then she shrank back down in her seat, hoping he hadn't seen her.

"Eleven rodeos and twenty-two tries, this horse has never been ridden," the announcer continued. "And now—*whoa, there he goes!*"

The gate swung open and the horse reared up for a heart-stopping second, nearly tumbling over backward before plunging into the arena. The shaggy paint horse hit the dirt with his front hooves in what had to be a tooth-jarring landing for Brady.

And then the dance was on. The big horse plunged and kicked, leaped and sunfished, twisting his body so hard his belly turned toward the sky. He spun into Brady's riding hand and then reversed, almost throwing Brady off balance.

Almost. The cowboy wrenched himself upright through pure strength of will, his legs never losing the rhythm of the ride as he lifted his free hand high.

Suze knew eight seconds could seem like a long time when you were in the saddle getting your insides pureed, but she'd never realized how long it could take when you were in the stands, praying for it to end safely for someone you loved. She found herself leaning forward with her hands clenched in her lap, chanting "please,

please, please," over and over as Brady's body whipped forward and back, forward and back, like a willow branch in a wild windstorm. He was strong, she knew he was strong, but Tornado's power was legendary.

"That's an even-Steven matchup of cowboy and bronc if I ever saw one," the announcer said. "Brady Caine's been on a winning streak these past few weeks, and it looks like he's going to…"

The announcer's words were drowned out by the roar of the crowd as the horn sounded.

He'd done it. Brady had ridden Tornado.

Suze waited for the fancy dismount, but apparently Tornado had taken everything Brady had, because he tumbled from the horse in a graceless nod to gravity. From where Suze was sitting, it looked like he'd landed on his head. She stood, along with half the crowd, waiting for the cowboy to move.

Please move. Just move. Please. Please.

She found herself mumbling the words aloud again as a sort of prayer as she watched Brady lie in the dirt of the arena, still as—well, a lot stiller than she wanted him to be.

Chapter 58

It was probably only five seconds before Brady twitched, stood, tipped his hat, and started toward the chutes, but it felt like five hours to Suze.

It had never occurred to her that anything could happen to Brady. He was a force of nature, invincible. Always there, like a river flowing. Like the Wyoming wind.

When the score lit up the screen, the crowd roared.

"That's a ninety-one, ladies and gentlemen, an arena record," the announcer said. "I'd say this man avenged his brother for what that horse did to him, don't you think, folks? Let's hear a big hand for Brady Caine, riding the unrideable *Torrrr-nado!*"

It had been an epic ride. Suze waited for the wild, winning whoop, the tip of the hat. But Brady didn't even turn to look at the scoreboard. When he reached the fence, he climbed up to the top rail and hung there a moment, scanning the crowd. As he turned his head, Suze caught a glimpse of the back of his hat. A piece of the brim had been chewed out by a certain hairy little dog.

The realization he was wearing the hat Dooley ruined gave her hope for some reason. She knew she was a fool, but she couldn't help leaning forward and waving, and letting out a little whoop of her own.

She caught him in the middle of waving to the boys.

His eyes lit on her and for a brief second, his smile straightened to a grim line and his eyes grew as cold as they'd been the last time she'd seen him.

And now she had her answer. He'd never forgive her. Never.

Ridge left his seat and made his way down to the contestant area, nodding as some of the cowboys greeted him. When he reached Brady, there was some backslapping and an awkward sort of sideways hug, and then the two disappeared under the stands to the cowboy ready area, where contestants put on their gear and readied themselves for their rides, relaxing out of reach of the fans.

Suze couldn't sit in those stands another minute. She felt like she'd jump out of her skin if she didn't move, walk, think. She was hurt by the look Brady'd given her, but no more hurt than he'd been by her cruel words.

But when had she ever taken no for an answer? She'd been kicked, stomped, thrown, and bitten by horses. She'd knocked over barrels, even skipped one once by accident. And still she won races.

And her life was a lot like her career. She'd been unwanted, unloved, alone, and unhappy. And still she survived.

Brady Caine might be able to subdue Tornado, but he wasn't going to beat her. Not without a fight.

She jostled a few people on her way down the bleacher steps and out the alleyway. She walked out from under the bleachers and turned left, entering the area across from the Cowboy Ready area, where the livestock was kept in corrals made of iron piping. She passed the big Brahma bulls, who calmly chewed their cud, waiting for the moment when they'd be driven into the chutes and have their own moment in the hot Wyoming sun. She passed the big, hammer-headed bucking horses, pausing to pet a couple who lifted their noses over the top of their corral.

She stopped where the roping horses were kept. Next to barrel horses, roping horses were the smartest animals on the circuit—even smarter, the ropers would argue. She clicked her tongue and was deep in silent conversation with a pretty chestnut when she recognized the man standing beside her stroking the nose of a blue roan.

"Ridge?"

He didn't look happy to see her. But then, Ridge rarely looked happy, and he'd just watched his brother ride the horse that almost killed him.

"I thought you were talking to Brady."

"Brady's not talking," he said.

"Brady? Not talking?" She shook her head. "He used to brag on every ride till even the buckle bunnies got bored."

When he didn't answer, she glanced at his face—hard and unreadable, as usual.

"You okay?" she asked.

"Fine."

"Good."

She wanted to ask him if he minded that Brady had ridden Tornado. She wanted to ask if it felt like revenge or if he was sad to see the legendary horse defeated, like she was. She wondered if he was angry with his brother or proud. But none of that came out. What came out was the question she most wanted to ask.

"What's wrong with him?" she asked. "Where's the whoop? The trick dismount? He didn't even tip his hat."

Ridge shrugged without so much as looking at her. "Guess you took the Brady out of Brady." He patted the horse's neck. "He's been quieter than me these last couple of weeks."

She looked down at her boot tips, feeling small. "You must hate me."

"I don't hate you," he said gruffly. "Not yet. But you'd damn well better fix him."

"How do I do that?"

Ridge finally looked at her. "You reach down deep, grab your heart, rip it out of your chest, and hand it over. No bargains, no strings, no safety net." He wiped his brow as if even remembering the experience was traumatic. "Dang near killed me, getting together with Sierra. You hand your life over too, you know." His gray eyes softened. "It goes with your heart. You have to trust. It's hard."

They stood side by side, patting the horses as Suze digested what Ridge had said. "Sometimes I think I'm all wrong for him," she finally said. "I'm grouchy, and I'm difficult, and I'm not good with people."

"I know."

She almost laughed. You could always count on a cowboy to tell you the truth.

"But for some reason he wants you," Ridge continued. "Kind of like Sierra wanted me." He shoved his hands in his pockets. "I'm grouchy, and I'm difficult. I'm better with people than I used to be, though. I'm a better man because of Sierra. And she knows we're stronger together."

Suze mulled over what he'd said. Ridge had a point. He rarely spoke, and when he did, it was usually to make some harsh but honest observation that rubbed people the wrong way. Sierra was the Brady of their couple— friendly and compassionate, with people skills and charisma that made her universally loved. They were oil and water, but the marriage worked.

And when danger stalked the kids, Ridge was there for her—strong, silent, and driven by love.

Suze pictured herself handing her heart to Brady. Then she pictured him looking at her with that grim stare, throwing her heart to the ground, and grinding it under his boot.

"Take the chance," Ridge said. "Let him decide."

He turned and walked away, the crowd parting as he strode back under the stands to see his brother.

Chapter 59

SUZE GLANCED OVER AT THE COWBOY READY AREA. She could see Brady behind the fence, sitting on a bench with his hands dangling between his knees, staring at the floor. Once in a while another cowboy walked up and slapped him on the back, congratulating him on his ride.

He thanked them, gave them the briefest of smiles, and went back to staring at the floor.

Suze could probably go in there. She was a competitor, after all, and the cowboy watching the door knew her. But did she really want to declare her love in front of a roomful of cowboys?

No. She wanted to declare her love in front of the whole world. She'd spent enough time alone, obsessing over Brady. One way or another, she was going to solve this problem.

Bidding a quick good-bye to the horse she'd been petting, she strode out of the rodeo grounds and into the parking lot.

Brady drove a Dodge Ram, like dozens of other cowboys. It was red, which hardly set it apart. But since he didn't often tow a trailer, he'd been able to customize it with a lift kit and giant tires that made it literally rise above the rest.

Suze leaned against it and waited.

—᠁—

Brady knew the other cowboys meant well, with their backslapping and congratulatory comments. They thought his ride on Tornado was the kind of thing you celebrate over beer and everybody wanted to buy him a Bud.

But it wasn't like that. Riding Tornado hadn't been revenge, exactly. It was just taking care of business. The horse had hurt his brother. Tornado had hurt a lot of cowboys, but Ridge had lost the use of his riding hand and with it his rodeo career.

Brady and Ridge had never talked about the incident, but it rankled every time they'd heard Tornado described as "unrideable." Somebody had needed to tame that sucker, and it needed to be a Decker Ranch cowboy.

Brady knew his brother didn't want him to do it. It had been years since Brady had competed in bareback, which was far more punishing physically than the more refined saddle bronc riding. Bareback riders needed to be strong, quick, flexible, and agile—just like the horses they rode.

Ridge hadn't called Brady "chicken" in a long time. Lately, he hadn't even called him "little brother." But Brady knew what his brother thought of him. What everyone thought of him. The last time he'd tried to prove himself had been at the photo shoot, when he'd ridden that danged Jim Dandy and hurt Suze so bad she might never ride again.

Hurting Suze, then falling for her and losing her, had taken the joy out of life. He'd needed to do something big. Something exciting. And riding Tornado sure fit the bill.

He'd thought making the buzzer would make him

feel good again. But for some reason, it just didn't matter. Nothing did.

He headed out to his truck, glad to escape the congratulations of the other cowboys. He needed to go home. Maybe he'd saddle up one of the old lesson horses that still lived at Decker Ranch and go for a long, slow ride. Or maybe he'd just take a nap.

He'd seen Suze in the crowd and wondered what she'd thought of the ride. She probably knew he was trying to prove himself to his big brother, and she probably knew what a fool he was to think it made any difference.

Good thing it didn't matter what Suze thought anymore. His servitude was over, and he wouldn't have to have his heart smashed under her boots anymore. Not today, not ever.

Lately, his heart felt about as dry and torched as the crispy brown grass that made up the lawn. But he could move on now. Find another girl. Suze thought he'd find somebody to love, somebody sweet and pretty.

Maybe she was right.

So why did he feel so miserable?

—⁂—

Suze watched Brady approach the truck. His head was bowed, and his fringed chaps flapped around his legs with every stride. He looked like a cowboy who'd been beat, not one who'd ridden a horse no man had ever ridden before.

Taking a step toward him, she wanted to hug him. She wanted to cry all over his wrinkled denim shirt. She wanted to beg for forgiveness. But when he saw her, he stopped midstride, as if he might turn and walk away.

She pretended not to notice.

"Nice ride."

He shrugged. "I'm not as much of a loser as you think. I win once in a while."

"I know that. You think I'd hang out with a loser?"

"Apparently." He walked past her and set one foot on the running board of his souped-up pickup. "A man would be a loser if he cheated on you. He'd be a loser if he lied to you about something you needed to know, or if he almost lost your horse. And he'd sure as hell be a loser if he hurt you."

"You didn't do those things," she said.

"Yeah, I did. All but the first one."

"But I hurt you too." She gave him a crooked smile. "We're even."

"Okay." His tone was brutal. "So why are you here?"

She tried to reply, but the words wouldn't form. Her throat was dry and parched. "Brady, I'm sorry," she said. "I never meant to hurt you."

"Hurt me?" He climbed into the truck and a whoosh of hot air blew out of the sunbaked interior. "You damn near killed me. You think that accident ruined you? Well, you ruined me. We're even now."

"I'm sorry, Brady." She was crying now, shamelessly, letting the tears run down her cheeks. "I'm so sorry. I tried to trust you, Brady. But I—I just couldn't. Everything in my life was upside down. I'd just found out my own father had been lying to me. He isn't even my father, and everything I believed about my mother and about myself was a lie."

"That's too bad." He shoved the keys in the ignition and rolled down the windows. "I'm sorry for what happened to you, Suze. But when you love somebody, you have to be able to trust them. You take them at their word. And you can't do that." As the engine roared to life, he tipped his hat and nodded, his expression blank as he backed out of the parking space.

"Brady, wait." Suze grabbed on to the window frame on the passenger's side and hiked herself up onto the little step outside the door. "Don't go."

He revved the engine.

"You can drive off if you want," she said. "But I'm hanging on. You won't be able to shake me. Not ever again, no matter how hard you try. I promise, Brady. And I keep my promises."

Grimly, she hung on, her good leg balanced on the step, the bad one dangling. She'd worn a sundress and cowboy boots, and the dress whipped in the wind, twisting around her legs. Her wrist was starting to hurt, but she held on tight.

"You're going to look pretty funny, tearing down the highway with a woman hanging out the window," she said.

"I've made a fool of myself before."

He turned onto the road and headed toward the exit. The gate attendants were two older cowboys who sat in lawn chairs, drinking beer.

"Hey, Caine," one of them said. "You picked up a hitcher." The two of them laughed, har-de-har-har.

"Can't shake her," Brady said. Without another word, he drove through the gate. When he reached the main road, Suze braced herself for the turn. But instead of pulling onto the road, he steered the truck into a grassy field that was used for overflow parking during night shows.

He stopped the truck and Suze started to pull herself through the window, but he popped the locks and nodded toward the door handle.

"I'm not taking a chance. I'll step away and you'll drive off." She hiked herself up on the windowsill, then pitched forward into the truck. The men at the gate got a nice view of her panties as she kicked her way into the passenger seat, but she didn't care.

"Those guys are watching," Brady said. "One of 'em's got a pair of binoculars."

"I don't care." She settled into the seat, fluffing the skirt of her dress so it covered her legs. "I've made a fool of myself before too. And I'm hoping to do it again."

Brady shut off the engine and they sat there, side by side, like they were watching a drive-in movie. But the only thing they could see through the windshield was the darkening sky, and the sounds of the Wyoming dusk rose around them—the chirping of crickets in the grass, the cautious hooting of a mourning dove on a telephone wire.

"Listen," she said.

He tilted his head. "What?"

"Don't you love this time of day? The daytime birds are singing themselves to sleep, and the nighttime birds are just getting up. And the sky's so pretty." She peered out the open window. "The stars are coming out. Remember that shooting star we saw?"

He nodded.

She twisted her hands in the skirt of her dress. "I wished for us to be together," she confessed. "What did you wish for?"

He shrugged and looked away, resting his elbow on the window frame. "Same thing."

She tried to smile, but it trembled at the edges. "How did we get so mixed up, when we both wanted the same thing at the beginning?"

"I'm not sure," he said. "It's been a long story, hasn't it?"

"It has." She reached for his hand. "Talk to me, Brady. Even if the story's over, it could have a better ending."

Squeezing his hand, she squeezed her eyes shut too, praying for courage, praying for strength, praying for the right words to come from her heart.

"Come on," she said. "Let's go for a walk."

Chapter 60

SUZE KNEW EXACTLY WHERE TO GO. SHE'D SEEN IT ON the way here, a corral fence just like the one in that old photograph she'd kept of her and Brady at a high school rodeo.

She sat on the top rail of the fence, just like she had all those years ago. She knew exactly where he'd stood, and she wondered if he'd take the same spot. For some reason, it seemed like that would mean something.

She held her breath as he approached, then let it out when he leaned against the fence. If he wanted to, he could grab her leg and pull her off the fence. She almost wished he would.

She looked down at him and that day came back to her in a rush—the heat. The dust from the contestants, who'd ridden steers and broncs, who'd roped calves and run the barrels. The blue of the sky, the gold of the grass—it was all the same, except for the dust.

"I'm not very good at this," she said.

"At what?"

She looked down at him and almost lost herself in those brown eyes. She had to grab the fence post before she fell over backward. Lying on her back in the dirt would *not* help her get this done.

"At love." She looked toward the horizon, where a single bright star glittered and glowed. "My father didn't love me. He did his best, but I was a reminder, every day, of the mistakes he'd made, of my mother's lies. I always felt like he'd get rid of me if he could, and I never understood why. I thought he was my real father, and I couldn't figure out why he didn't love me."

Brady didn't move or nod or acknowledge what she'd said.

"My mother was the one person in the world who loved me, and she left me. I know she couldn't help it. I know it wasn't her fault. But it hurt anyway."

She paused. Staring up at the sky for inspiration.

"I never had anyone I could trust before. I didn't know how, Brady. But you taught me." She took a deep breath. "I know you love me. I know I can trust you. And you can trust me now. You've taught me how. You've helped me change."

He gave her a long look, and she tried to do what Ridge had said. In her mind, she reached down deep and took hold of her beating heart, tore it out, and handed it over.

"My heart belongs to you," she said. "You can throw it away, or you can take it. But I don't want it back."

Ridge hadn't warned her about this part, where you waited to see if the other person was going to accept your gift or stomp it to smithereens. This was the hard part, and Brady let her wait, looking down at his hands as if he really was holding her heart.

"Trust me, Brady. Trust me to trust you. I love you, and I know you're a good man. You keep your promises. You care about your family. You care about me, and I don't make it easy." She kicked at the fence rail below her. "I *know* you now. And the more I know you, the more I admire you. I think you're bigger on the inside than you are on the outside. I think you have a heart that's stronger and finer than anybody knows."

He squinted over at the rodeo grounds, clearly a little embarrassed by the praise.

"I think you get hurt easily, and you don't want anyone to know. When you were a kid, it was safest to just laugh everything off, wasn't it? You must have been in some rough places."

"Sure was," he said.

"I have a picture of us, back in high school," she said. "We're sitting together at a rodeo. I'm on the fence, and you're down there, just like that."

"I know." He finally smiled. "I found it in your underwear drawer when you were in the hospital."

"Shoot. That was my big secret."

"It didn't have to be."

"No. But the fact that I held on to that picture all that time ought to tell you something," she said.

"What should it tell me?"

He looked her in the eye and she knew, in that moment that she'd done it. She'd won the biggest challenge of her life.

She'd won back Brady Caine.

"It should tell you that I've loved you most of my life."

Reaching up, he grabbed her leg and pulled her down into the grass, cushioning her fall with one strong arm. She shrieked in mock terror and they rolled over a couple times, laughing like kids, and when they stopped, he was looking down on her, his eyes soft and serious.

When their lips met, he brushed his gently over hers.

Then she grabbed the back of his head and kissed him for real, putting all the frustrated, foolish, foiled love she'd saved up the past few weeks into one single, desperate kiss.

They rolled again, over and over, in the soft overgrown grass beside the arena, kissing. She had grass stains on her knees, on her elbows, on the heels of her hands. But she had Brady, so it didn't matter.

When they pulled apart, Brady lay in the grass and let out his rebel yell, that wild whoop of joy she'd missed so much at the rodeo.

The two men at the gate applauded and Suze groaned. Brady rolled over and hiked himself up on his elbows so he could gaze into her eyes. His own were soft and grave with worry.

"I didn't hurt you, did I? If I hurt you again, I'm retiring that stupid whoop for good."

"I'm fine," Suze said. "Only thing you hurt was my reputation, and I don't care about that." She grinned. "You can whoop all you want. In fact, you'd better keep it up or your big brother will kill me."

"What?"

"Ridge said I took the Brady out of Brady, and I'd better put it back."

She looked up into his eyes. He was smiling down at her, his face framed by the brim of his hat and the blue Wyoming sky. In that moment, she had everything she'd ever wanted. Love made the world around her shine with a new light, and she was never going to let it dim.

That's why she kissed him again.

―◆◆◆―

The drive home was long and quiet. Suze let her hand dangle outside the window, savoring the cool touch of the air rushing by.

When they reached the house, Brady helped Suze out of the high truck and took her by the hand.

"Where are we going?" she asked as he led her past the house and barn.

Around the corner, at the back of the barn, was a patch of sunflowers. Suze had always loved the cheerful, unruly tangle of blossoms, but she hadn't been behind the barn since spring.

It was twilight, and the only light came from the motion-sensor light at the corner of the barn, but she could see they were blooming again, surrounding a rustic bench that sat just in front of them. A few flowers had grown through the slats, lifting their cheery heads as if to welcome her.

"When did you do this?" she asked, stroking the bench's smooth finish.

"Shane's been teaching me woodworking. I finished it a few weeks ago. Set it up one day when you were in town, seeing the doctor."

Tears sprang to her eyes. She imagined what it would have been like finding the bench if she and Brady hadn't made up. She'd probably have grown old alone without him.

A sudden image of a much-older self crossed her mind—a much-older self, white-haired and bitter, sitting on this bench and remembering her brief happiness with the man she loved. Remembering how she'd lost him to her selfish pride and her foolish fears.

But now it would be different. Now the future was

in her hands. If she loved Brady enough, if she trusted him and won his heart, her life would always be complicated. It would always be a tangle of happy accidents, like this patch of sunflowers. It wouldn't be organized. She wouldn't be able to control it. You couldn't watch videos and improve your technique when it came to love. There were no do-overs.

Although she seemed to be getting one now.

Oblivious to her thoughts, Brady sat on the bench and pulled her down beside him.

"I figured this way you can sit in sunshine even on cloudy days," he said.

There was no sunshine now. Brady picked a sunflower and began to pluck the petals off, one by one. When he finished, he passed the naked stem to Suze with a smile.

"What did it say?"

"It said I love you. But I already knew that."

"So you destroyed this poor innocent flower for nothing?"

"Hey, I dang near destroyed you," he said. "The flower's nothing."

"You didn't even come close to destroying me."

"That's true," he said. "You're one tough cookie. But I was bound to you until I made it right."

"That's not true. You're bound to someone if they *save* your life. Not if you ruin theirs."

"You *did* save my life." He tossed the flower on the grass. "Everybody thought I was happy, but my life was shit, Suze. It felt wrong, ever since I got out of school. Maybe even before that. I didn't know what was wrong until Shane pointed out that the only reason I did rodeo was for buckles and babes. And I knew the only reason I was alive, the only purpose to my life, was to do rodeo."

"So your whole life was about buckles and babes."

"Exactly. And you changed that. You opened up my life and made it worth something."

"Really? Because of me, you ended up with no buckles and only one babe. I'm not thinking I did you any favors."

"It's the right babe, and that makes all the difference." He settled back and stared up at the sky. "That cowboy whoop, that rebel yell? The first time I let it out was when I saw you thundering around your dad's arena on that old horse you had."

"Sherman."

"Yup. You were the prettiest thing I'd ever seen, and you still are. I fell for you right then, and I've never gotten over it. The rest of my life has just been waiting for a chance to prove to you I'm worthy."

"You're worthy," she said. "More than worthy."

He reached for her hand and their fingers twined together as a shooting star arced across the southern sky. "What are we going to wish for now?" Brady's voice was hushed, as if he was in church.

"I'm going to ask to always be this happy," she said. "To always have you beside me."

"Good." He cleared his throat. "I need to talk to you about that."

"About what?"

"About forever."

He slipped off the bench and dropped to one knee so fast she half expected him to tip his hat and whoop. It was a dismount worthy of the rodeo.

"Suze Carlyle," he said, "I loved you the first time I saw you and I've grown to love you more every day since then. You're strong, you're stubborn, and you're the only woman I know who can make me behave without making me miserable."

She laughed. "Well, that was original."

"Just concentrate on the first sentence. I practiced that one. Wrote it out and everything."

"When?"

"A long time ago." He smiled, a faraway look in his eyes. "You know that picture of the two of us? The one you kept?"

She nodded.

"It was about then."

"I never knew," she said. "I never thought you'd pick someone like me."

"I never thought I deserved you."

She looked over at the old barn where Speedo bunked with his friend Bucket. Her gaze shifted to her bedroom window—the window where she'd watched that first day when Brady came to make things right. Where later she'd shown up in that terrible worn-out old nightie and yelled at him for peeping when all he was doing was fixing the barn roof. She looked at the sunroom, where she spent every morning drinking coffee and watching the dawn sky, and at the neat, well-groomed lawn and the baby lilac bushes he'd planted beside the front steps.

He'd changed her life, one chore at a time.

"So what's your answer?" he asked. He was still on one knee, still watching her face.

"You didn't ask a question."

"Oh." He took a deep breath. "Will you marry me, Suzanne Carlyle?"

"Yes," she said. "Yes. My life is yours. My heart is yours. You'll always have the power to break it, but I trust you to keep it safe. I'd marry you a hundred times, Brady Caine, and a hundred times more after that."

Brady picked her up, bounced her once to make her squeal, and spun her around until the world was a blur. Lifting his face to the sky, he let out a whoop so full of love and wildness and pure cowboy joy that she lay back in his arms, stretched her arms wide enough to hold the whole of the sky above them, and spun in the starlight, trusting the man she loved to hold her tight and keep her safe.

Epilogue

SUZE HADN'T WANTED DIAMONDS FROM BRADY ON their wedding day. She couldn't imagine what she'd do on a beach vacation. What she wanted, what she *needed*, was a new barrel horse so Speedo could retire. And that's what Brady had given her.

Her new mount, Hilo, was calm when she mounted him, despite her unconventional riding attire. It might be crazy to run barrels in a wedding dress, but Suze couldn't wait. Besides, wrestling with her dress made her forget her ankle, her knee, and everything else. After fighting with the yards of fabric for nearly a minute, she finally hiked the dress up to her waist and pushed the mountains of fabric behind her like an old-fashioned Victorian bustle.

And then she was in the saddle at last.

"You sure you don't want some help?" Brady asked.

He stood at the gate, which had been decorated with white netting and rosebuds for the wedding. She could only imagine how tense he was. He probably hadn't expected her to try out her gift right away, without even changing her clothes.

But being with Brady had changed her. He'd taught her to enjoy life, to be impulsive and happy and free. When she felt like saying something, she said it. When she felt like doing something, she did it. And if she wanted to ride a horse in her wedding gown, nothing was going to stop her.

Sitting there in the saddle, her heart filled with joy. She was right where she was supposed to be: high on a horse and ready to ride.

"I'm fine," she said. "Just fine."

The tickly fabric that was draped around Hilo's haunches didn't seem to bother him a bit. One ear flicked back to check on her as the other focused forward.

The arena beyond the gateposts gleamed like a white sand beach—a beach with three battered, rusty barrels set in the sand. Wedding guests stood in small clusters around the fence, but in her mind, Suze could hear the roar of a rodeo crowd, the chatter of excited children, and the shouts of the cowboys.

One of Sierra's kids let out a whoop and set Hilo dancing for one high-stress second before he caught himself and calmed. She could feel him through the saddle, through the reins, feel his focus and his ambition and his determination. He was in charge of this ride. He was taking care of her, scoping out the situation and readying himself to make the best run he could.

Speedo had taken care of her like that. Some riders would have hung on and let the horse rule the ride, but Suze knew it was up to her to make it the best it could be. Hilo would lean into the turns and she would nudge him a little closer to the edge, push him one degree beyond where he wanted to be. That way, he'd run a little harder to keep the two of them in balance. The horse might make a perfect ride on his own, but she'd push it beyond perfection. He was the runner and she was the urge to run. He was the racer and she was the will to win.

She thought about moving forward, just thought

about it, and Hilo walked to the gate before she even had time to cue him. She looked at the mark Brady had drawn with a boot heel and he stopped, front hooves dancing with impatience.

Suze looked at the first barrel and visualized the run in her head. In response, Hilo flicked his right ear back and she felt something she could hardly believe. She'd had a rare experience with Speedo. She'd truly felt that he could read her mind, and she'd never expected to find another horse so in tune with her thoughts.

But Hilo was with her on that imagined ride. They were hurtling around the same ethereal cloverleaf, taking the turns together, riding the perfect ride. He was in her head, and she figured she was probably in his.

Whatever Brady had paid for this horse was nowhere near enough. She'd found a once-in-a-lifetime horse— for the second time in her life.

It wasn't that long ago that she'd felt cursed. She'd truly believed her personal patch of sky was darkened by clouds beyond her control. She'd never expected to find true love. To find real happiness. To find peace.

But now, in the saddle, she felt charmed.

She willed Hilo to settle, and for a moment she and the horse hung suspended out of time, hovering in the hot summer air like a hummingbird the second before it darts for a flower. Then he gathered beneath her, the muscles bunching and tightening.

She thought, *GO!*

Hilo shot forward like a rocket from a launchpad and exploded into the arena, a fury of dust and flickering hooves and high spirits. It didn't matter that there was no timekeeper, no competition. Suze was still aware of time passing a second at a time, ticking toward success or failure, counted out by the horse's hooves and the beating of her heart.

They took the first turn in balletic unison. The horse was a genius. He was made for this; he'd found his groove the same as she had, and he lived for racing just like she did. As they ran the second barrel and the third, she felt joy coursing through the horse's bloodstream, the joy of a born barrel horse pounding for home after cutting three perfect loops in the sand.

Brady knew he was watching his new wife fall in love all over again—and nothing could make him happier. He could see her and the horse joining up, becoming one. Hilo's tail waved behind him like a flag, and Suze's long hair, long escaped from her wedding updo, formed the same wave, a visual echo.

He'd been riding in opposition to his mounts so long that the sight of their unity made him ache. She and the horse flowed like a current of air, blowing around the barrels like wind through the trees. He'd known the first time he saw her ride that she could fly, and now he knew she'd launch herself into the record books riding the horse he'd bought for her.

Watching the two of them together for the first time was a moment he'd never forget. He hoped Stan, who'd offered to photograph the wedding as a gift, had captured some images of his wild bride, riding a perfect race in her wedding finery.

She pulled Hilo to a stop at the gate, then trotted him right up to Brady. Now that the race was over, reality washed over him and he looked up at her anxiously, watching for signs of pain in her eyes.

"How's your ankle?" he asked. "How's your knee? You looked really good out there. Are you okay? How do you feel?"

She slid off the horse and into his arms. Unfortunately, the hem of her dress caught on the saddle horn, offering the guests a private view of her lace panties.

"Hold it," Brady said. He freed the dress, tucked his arm under her bottom, and hoisted her into his arms.

"How do you feel?" he asked again.

She looked up at him with a smile that glowed.

"I feel lucky," she said.

Her hair was a mess, and she'd gotten her expensive gown dirty. She'd looked like an angel when she'd met Brady at the altar, and she still did—but her halo had tipped a little to the left.

"I feel lucky too," he said.

He set her down and they turned and walked back to the Carlyle house, back to their guests. The house was theirs now; Earl had moved into Gwen's high-fenced sanctuary, and proudly claimed he hadn't watched an episode of *Bonanza* since. He'd given Suze away, and the groomsmen had been Ridge, Shane, and Isaiah. Sierra had been a perfect maid of honor, settling Suze's jitters even as she kept her boys in line.

The reception had barely begun. There were dances to dance and cake to cut, but the best part of the wedding was behind them.

Brady knew for certain, though, that the best part of the marriage had only just begun.

How to Wrangle a Cowboy

COMING SOON FROM
JOANNE KENNEDY AND
SOURCEBOOKS CASABLANCA

SHANE LOCKHART'S EX CLIMBED BACK INTO THE CAR and started the smooth, purring engine. Releasing the brake, she slung the Beemer into reverse, peering over her shoulder as she backed up, then shifting into drive and gliding out into the darkness. Gravel crunched under the tires, and then the sound disappeared along with the red glow of the taillights.

So this was how it happened, Shane thought. It didn't take long to leave a child behind, to create an emptiness that would last a lifetime.

His son would be all right. He'd *make* him all right. He was good at that—bending people to his will. Bending *life* to his will. He'd make this work, and he'd tell Cody that his mother loved him. He'd tell him she'd had to leave and had wanted to stay.

He'd tell lies to his son and save him the pain he'd endured himself.

Shane looked down at the sleeping child in his arms,

at the way his lashes lay against his cheeks. His dark hair, dark as Shane's own, clung to his forehead, a little damp with sweat. Shane felt his heart swell.

Mine. My boy.

Shane felt joy pouring into him, filling the empty spaces Tara had left behind when she'd stolen his son. He was a father. He had his boy back.

Cody's lashes fluttered, and he stirred in Shane's arms. Shane held his breath as the boy's eyes opened and met his.

The boy's eyes were dark as Shane's own. His nose was more delicate, but he was a six-year-old kid, right? Kids were delicate.

The truth was, Shane could see himself in every feature of the boy's face. And he thought he could see his own fears and insecurities in the shadows of those sleepy eyes. He'd find a way to give the boy courage. Courage and strength. Both would flow from love unending, love that would last as long as he lived.

"Are you my dad?" the boy asked sleepily.

Shane's voice came out hoarse from a throat tightened by emotion.

"Yes," he said. "I'm your dad."

Cody looked puzzled for a moment, and Shane held his breath. What if he asked where his mother was? What if he wanted to go with her?

The boy blinked twice, then nestled against Shane's chest.

"I thought you'd be bigger," he said and went back to sleep.

―◆◆◆―

"Let's get this sucker in the ground." Alice Ward turned away from the gleaming casket poised above the gaping grave and tugged at her escort's arm. "He was a good-lookin' sumnabitch and it's a shame he's dead, but, Lord, that preacher about talked us all into our graves already, and here he's getting ready to start jawing again."

A gasp rose from the compact crowd of mourners surrounding the gravesite. Alice might look delicate, but her voice was as vibrant and clear as it had been in her brief Hollywood heyday.

"My husband won't take kindly to me being gone so long at some stranger's funeral," she continued.

Bending his black-hatted head over her slight figure, Shane reminded her, as gently as possible, that the good-looking sumnabitch in the velvet-lined casket *was* her husband.

As foreman of the Y4 Ranch, the duty of "seeing to" Alice had fallen to Shane with the death of her husband. He stood beside her, staring down into the latest hole in the small, sad family graveyard. The cemetery held Alice's daughter, who'd died young in a car crash, and two small graves she never spoke of. Now it would hold her husband, and Alice would be alone in the world, except for a granddaughter she hadn't seen in years.

Knowing Alice might take a turn toward tragedy and hurl herself into her husband's grave at any moment, Shane gripped her arm firmly. Drama was never more than a heartbeat away when Alice Ward was around, but her histrionics were usually harmless. As for Shane, he loved her like family. She'd been kind to him, and lately she'd been a substitute grandma to his son.

The trouble was, you never knew what to expect from her. She'd been inconsolable over Bud Ward's death, which had occurred at the intersection of a cowardly cow horse and a petulant porcupine. A day later, she'd chatted with an invisible Bud over her morning eggs and ham as if he was alive and irascible as ever.

Shane actually welcomed the brief appearances of Bud's ghost. His phantom presence kept Alice calm, and she was less liable to wander off if she believed he was out fixing fences or tending cattle.

But right now, she seemed certain he was waiting back at the house.

"Come on, cowboy." She tugged at Shane's arm again. "All this sad stuff is giving me a headache."

Again the mourners stopped their sniffling and foot-shuffling, and all heads turned toward Alice. The only sound was the trill of a meadowlark, shattering the sorrowful atmosphere with unseemly joy.

Shane wished he'd given in to Alice's urging a little sooner. The entire town of Wynott—all three blocks of it—would be buzzing with the news that Alice Ward had lost her mind. Worse yet, she'd insulted the redoubtable Reverend Bannister from First Methodist. Being from Hollywood, she and Bud had always been fodder for gossip, and Shane had a feeling that wasn't going to change with Bud's death.

Not that he could blame folks for their interest in the Wards. Bud had been a rough-riding stuntman and Alice a Hollywood ingenue when the two had met, and they'd made three movies together during the heyday of the Western. Bud mostly fell off horses while Alice played various meek and frightened pioneer lasses. In reality, she could ride nearly as well as her husband, and swear just as lustily. When Bud was injured in a stagecoach accident, he married Alice and carried her off to the Y4 Ranch.

Alice's ingenue days were far behind her, but she was still bright and birdlike in a voluminous scarlet scarf that wafted around her slight figure and caught every hint of a breeze. She'd refused to wear black to the funeral.

"We were black-and-white in the movies," she'd said when Shane protested. "Bud always said he liked me in color. And, besides, I don't want my only granddaughter to think I'm some old crone."

Shane nodded, doing his best not to reveal his feelings about Alice and Bud's granddaughter. Lindsey Ward hadn't visited in at least five years. Alice claimed she'd been busy setting up a successful veterinary practice in Charleston, South Carolina, but Shane knew something had happened between Bud and his prodigal granddaughter, something Bud had never forgiven.

Shane didn't really care what the problem was. Abandoning folks as good-hearted as Bud and Alice must mean the granddaughter had no heart at all.

Supposedly, she was flying in from Charleston, but she'd missed the funeral. Shane doubted she'd show up at all, unless it was for the reading of the will. If love for the two fine people she was fortunate enough to call family hadn't drawn her to Wyoming, maybe inheriting some portion of Bud's millions would do it. Shrewd investments and a fine head for cattle breeding had made Bud a wealthy man.

As the minister droned on, Shane noticed a slight figure climbing the dirt trail that led to the Ward family cemetery, which was set high on a hill behind the ranch house. The latecomer, a slender, dark-haired woman perched on impossibly high heels, paused briefly to stand on one leg like a heron. She removed a shoe, then rubbed her foot and replaced the shoe without wavering, but she nearly fell when she skidded on a patch of gravel at the graveyard gate.

"Lindsey!" Alice lurched away from Shane and enveloped the new arrival in a generous hug. Despite her small frame, Alice was enormous in her affections and expressed her feelings with verve.

While Alice greeted her long-lost granddaughter, Shane couldn't help staring. Not because Lindsey was young, slim, and lovely—though she was—but because the sight of her made something in his heart clench and twist, and not in a good way. Dark hair flowing down her back; large, heavy-lidded blue eyes; an angular, well-formed face; and a fine jaw with a determined chin made her just Shane's type.

The type he needed to avoid.

"I'm so sorry, Grandma," the woman said. Her sky-high heels made her tower over Alice, but she shared her grandma's petite build. "I had an emergency with a cockapoo."

A cocka-what? Judging from Alice's effusive greeting—which had earned a stern glare from the reverend—all was forgiven where Lindsey was concerned. And yet a cockapee—which sounded like some sort of exotic bird—was more important to her than her own grandfather's funeral.

Hopefully, Lindsey Ward wouldn't stay long. After all, she had that successful veterinary practice. With any luck, she'd spend a few days at the ranch, admire how smoothly and profitably it ran under Shane's guidance, and go back to her cockapees.

Shane felt his son clutch at his pant leg and glanced down to smooth the boy's hair. He expected Cody's eyes to be fixed on the casket as it was lowered into the grave, but instead the boy was gazing wide-eyed at the new arrival.

Of course he was. She was a woman. She had dark hair. And she was pretty, if you went for that type.

Which Shane didn't. No way. Not anymore.

But his son looked like he'd just seen a fairy godmother, Glinda the Good Witch, and his runaway mother, all rolled into one.

Chapter 2

LINDSEY STEPPED INTO THE FRONT HALL AND WAS instantly enveloped by the sweet scent of home. Even after all these years, the masculine, outdoorsy scents of sage, saddle leather, and dust, combined with the more civilized odors of home-baked cookies, Lemon Pledge, and her grandmother's perfume, overwhelmed her with a rush of nostalgia.

The front room was filled with mourners standing awkwardly about, balancing plates of cheese pinwheels, shrimp with cocktail sauce, and ambrosia salad, all brought by neighbors.

Edging past the door and into the dim hallway that led to the back of the house, she dabbed at her eyes. Her sorrow over the loss of her grandfather was almost overwhelming, but she didn't want to break down in front of this crowd. She'd never really understood funerals. Grief, for her, needed to be nursed in private. She'd experienced enough loss to know.

There was only a faint bar of light showing from under her grandfather's study door. Later, the will would be read there. That laconic foreman, Shane Lockhart, and some hired hands had set up rows of folding chairs rented from the community hall, so everyone could sit and hear Bud's last will and testament.

Beyond the study, the hall turned toward the more private parts of the house, including the bedrooms.

Lindsey could swear she heard a rustling sound coming from the darkness, and then a board creaked.

Holding one hand over her rapidly beating heart, she felt a prickle of awareness, as if a cold shadow had fallen over the spot where she stood. Slipping off her borrowed shoes, she padded down the hall and peered around the corner.

An old oak china closet stood against the wall, filled with rodeo trophies and mementos of Bud's and Alice's film careers. Lindsey had always loved to explore the contents, begging her grandfather to tell the stories connected with each object—a gold buckle, a pair of spurs, a diamond necklace, an ancient rodeo program.

Apparently, she wasn't the only one interested in the contents of the hutch. A tall stranger stood before it with the door wide open. He held a buckle in his hand and was tracing the raised image of a bucking horse with one finger.

The Pendleton buckle. Lindsey held her breath. It would be easy for the man to slip it into his pocket. What would she do if he turned out to be a thief?

Get Shane.

She gave her head a quick shake, annoyed that the foreman had come so quickly to mind. She didn't need Shane Lockhart to help her. The man wasn't going to attack her—especially not if she announced her presence before he'd taken anything.

She cleared her throat, and the man gave a guilty start. Replacing the buckle, he shoved his hands in his pockets.

"He was quite a guy, wasn't he?" His tone held a heartiness that struck her as utterly false. "Quite a guy."

"Yes, he was. And who are you?"

"Oh, I'm nobody," the man said, his smile tentative and unsteady. "Nobody at all. Not compared to Bud, you know."

Lindsey remembered a poem she'd read in school.

I'm nobody. Who are you? I'm nobody too.

"No, really. Who…?"

The man shoved past her and headed back toward the front of the house.

She really should put aside her foolish pride and find Shane Lockhart. He might be rude, but in this case, that could be a good thing. If he didn't know him, maybe he'd eject the man from the premises. That would be something to see. Lindsey smiled to herself, picturing the foreman's dark brows, his square jaw. He was cute when he was angry.

She set out to find him. He wasn't in the room with the food, where a group of men were drinking and reminiscing. He wasn't with Alice, who was chatting with a group of ladies in the kitchen.

Pausing at the back door, she glanced out at the hillside where her grandfather lay. And there he was, a lone figure silhouetted against the sky. The black hat was off, pressed against his chest as he stared down at her grandfather's grave. But there was no mistaking Shane's erect figure, even with his head bowed.

Slipping back into the torturous shoes, her ankles aching from the unaccustomed exercise, Lindsey started the long walk up to the family plot.

Acknowledgments

This is my eighth book, the second in the Cowboys of Decker Ranch series. I believe I've thanked most everybody by now, so for once I'll spare the typesetter and keep my gratitude short and sweet. Mind you, that's not easy. I've had a couple of difficult years, and everyone who's touched my life deserves a big dose of gratitude. So please know that I appreciate all of you, even if you're not mentioned by name. You know who you are, and so do I.

I'd like to thank Deb Werksman, Danielle Dresser, Susie Benton, Skye Agnew, Eliza Smith, Dominique Raccah, and the whole Sourcebooks family for sharing my successes and sticking with me through the tough times. I'm also grateful to my agent, Elaine English, who has nurtured my career from the start and has never let me down.

I'd like to thank Brian Davis for making it through pilot training, for selling us his sweet Jeep, and for making the world safe for democracy. I'd like to thank Alycia Fleury for sharing her awesome kids (that's *you*, Ashton and Kaelan and Myla!), and Scott McCauley and Aminda O'Hare for huckleberry bear claws and the most amazing wedding ever.

I'd like to thank the Southern contingent of the McCauley family for being my friends as well as my relatives.

Most of all, I want to thank Scrape McCauley for loving me always, and for realizing that great risks bring great rewards. Thank you for believing in the Stillwater Nation, and for believing in me.

How to Handle a Cowboy

Cowboys of Decker Ranch Series
by Joanne Kennedy

His rodeo days may be over...

Sidelined by a career-ending injury, rodeo cowboy Ridge Cooper is desperate to find an outlet for the passion he used to put into competing. So he takes on the challenge of teaching roping skills to troubled ten-year-olds in a last-chance home for foster kids, and finds it's their feisty supervisor who takes the most energy to wrangle.

But he'll still wrangle her heart

When social worker Sierra Dunn seeks an activity for the rebellious kids at Phoenix House, she soon learns she's not in Denver anymore. Sierra is eager to get back to her inner-city work, and the plan doesn't include forming an attachment in Wyoming—especially not to a ruggedly handsome and surprisingly gentle local rodeo hero.

"Realistic and romantic... Kennedy's forte is in making relationships genuine and heartfelt as she exposes vulnerabilities with tenderness and good humor."—*Booklist* Starred Review

"The sex scenes are juicy...and the plot moves seamlessly."—*RT Book Reviews*, 4 Stars

For more Joanne Kennedy, visit:

www.sourcebooks.com

Slow Hand

Hot Cowboy Nights Series
by Victoria Vane

In rural Montana...

Wade Knowlton is a hardworking lawyer who's torn between his small-town Montana law practice and a struggling family ranch. He's on the brink of exhaustion from trying to save everybody and everything, when gorgeous Nicole Powell walks into his office. She's a damsel in distress and the breath of fresh air he needs.

Even the lawyers wear boots...

Nicole Powell is a sassy Southern girl who has officially sworn off cowboys after a spate of bad seeds—until her father's death sends her to Montana and into the arms of a man who seems too good to be true. Her instincts tell her to hightail it out of Montana, but she can't resist a cowboy with a slow hand.

For more Victoria Vane, visit:

www.sourcebooks.com

Rough Rider

Hot Cowboy Nights Series

by Victoria Vane

―~~―

Old flames burn the hottest…

Janice Combes has adored Dirk Knowlton from the rodeo sidelines for years. She knows she'll never be able to compete with the dazzling all-American rodeo queen who's set her sights on Dirk. Playful banter is all Janice and Dirk will ever have…

Until the stormy night when he shows up at her door, injured and alone. Dirk's dripping wet, needs a place to stay, and Janice remembers why she could never settle for any other cowboy…

―~~―

Praise for Victoria Vane:

"Erotic and sexy…absolutely marvelous." — *Library Journal* on the Devil DeVere series

"The Mistress of Sensuality does it again!" —*Swept Away by Romance*

For more Victoria Vane, visit:

www.sourcebooks.com

The Trouble with Texas Cowboys

by Carolyn Brown

New York Times and *USA Today* Bestselling Author

—⁓—

Can a girl ever have too many cowboys?

No sooner does pint-sized spitfire Jill Cleary set foot on Fiddle Creek Ranch than she finds herself in the middle of a hundred-year-old feud. Quaid Brennan and Tyrell Gallagher are both tall, handsome, and rich, and both are courting Jill to within an inch of her life. She's doing her best to give these feuding ranchers equal time—too bad it's dark-eyed Sawyer O'Donnell who makes her blood boil and her hormones hum…

—⁓—

"Brown's modern storytelling is humorous, heartwarming, and full of sass and spunk. The banter between Jill and Sawyer is infectious, and the chemistry between them sizzles. Add a solid, well-crafted plot filled with distinctive characters, and readers will be left with one entertaining read." —*RT Book Reviews*, 4 Stars

For more Carolyn Brown, visit:

www.sourcebooks.com

How to Marry a Cowboy

by Carolyn Brown

New York Times and *USA Today* Bestselling Author

She's running from her past

Mason Harper's daughters want a new mama in the worst way, and when a beautiful woman in a tattered wedding gown appears on their doorstep, the two little girls adopt her—no ifs, ands, or buts about it. Mason isn't sure about taking in a complete stranger, but Lord knows he needs a nanny, and Annie Rose Boudreau stirs his heart in long-forgotten ways...

And he's the perfect escape

Annie Rose is desperate, and when a tall, sexy cowboy offers her a place to stay, she can't refuse. After all, it's just for a little while. As she settles in deeper, her heart tells her both Mason and her role as makeshift mama suit her just fine. But will Mason feel the same way once her nightmare past catches up with her?

For more Carolyn Brown, visit:

www.sourcebooks.com

The Cowboy's Mail Order Bride

by Carolyn Brown

New York Times and *USA Today* Bestselling Author

She's got sass...

Emily Cooper promised her dying grandfather that she'd deliver a long-lost letter to a woman he once planned to wed. Little does adventurous Emily know that this simple task will propel her to places she never could have imagined...

He's got mail...

When sexy rancher Greg Adams discovers his grandmother Clarice has hired Emily, he decides to humor the two ladies. He figures Emily will move on soon enough. In the meantime, he'll keep a close eye on her—he doesn't quite buy her story of his grandmother as a mail-order bride.

A lost letter meant a lost love for Clarice, but two generations later, maybe it's not too late for that letter to work its magic.

"While the romance is hot, there is an old-world feel to it that will bring out the romantic in every reader, leaving them swooning and wishing they had their very own cowboy."—*RT Book Reviews*, 4 Stars

"Carolyn Brown's characters become my friends and I find myself laughing with them, crying with them, and loving with them."—*Bitten by Love Reviews*

For more Carolyn Brown, visit:

www.sourcebooks.com

Cowboy Heaven

by Cheryl Brooks

———

When you find yourself in cowboy heaven...

When lonely widow Angela McClure hires a gorgeous hitchhiking cowboy with an affair in mind, she knows they'll have to be discreet: her old-fashioned father and the stern ranch foreman adamantly discourage any interaction between her and the ranch hands.

Things can get hot as hell...

Despite their attempts at secrecy, the heat between them is undeniable. To divert suspicion, Angela forms a new plan: she'll flirt with all of the ranch hands. Suddenly Angela has a whole stable full of sexy-as-sin cowboys to play with, but only one can win her heart.

———

Praise for Cheryl Brooks:

"Cheryl Brooks knows how to keep the heat on and the reader turning pages!" —Sydney Croft

"Ms. Brooks delivers plenty of sexual tension, suspense, and pleasure in simply being alive." —*Romance Junkies*

For more Cheryl Brooks, visit:

www.sourcebooks.com

To Love and to Cherish

A Cactus Creek Cowboys Novel

by Leigh Greenwood

USA Today bestselling author

—⁓—

Torn between a desire to be free...

When Laurie Spencer said "I do," she just traded one pair of shackles for another—until her husband's death leaves her with an opportunity to escape her controlling family. Determined to be independent, Laurie approaches sexy rancher Jared Smith with an offer she hopes he can't refuse...

Jared's determined to make it in Texas, but with the local banker turned against him, his dream may be slipping through his fingers. When Laurie offers a partnership, it looks like his luck may be changing...but when she throws herself in the deal, Jared's not sure he'll be able to respect the terms of their agreement and keep his hands to himself.

There's something about Laurie that awakens every protective instinct Jared has...and when all hell breaks loose, there's nothing and no one who'll be able to keep this cowboy from her side.

—⁓—

"Greenwood is a master at Westerns!" —*RT Book Reviews*

For more Leigh Greenwood, visit:

www.sourcebooks.com

About the Author

Joanne Kennedy's lifelong fascination with Wyoming's unique blend of past and present inspires her to write contemporary Western romances with traditional ranch settings. She is the author of *Cowboy Trouble, One Fine Cowboy* (nominated for a RITA award for best single title contemporary), *Cowboy Fever, Tall, Dark and Cowboy, Cowboy Crazy, Cowboy Tough*, and, first in the Cowboys of Decker Ranch series, *How to Handle a Cowboy*. Her fascination with literature led to careers in bookselling and writing, but at various times, Joanne has dabbled in horse training, chicken farming, and bridezilla wrangling at a department store wedding registry. She lives with two dogs and a retired fighter pilot in Cheyenne, Wyoming. The dogs are relatively well behaved.

Joanne loves to hear from readers and can be reached through her website, www.joannekennedybooks.com.

Praise for
How to Handle a Cowboy

"Realistic and romantic... Kennedy's forte is in making relationships genuine and heartfelt as she exposes vulnerabilities with tenderness and good humor."

—*Booklist* Starred Review

"The sex scenes are juicy... Each character is essential to the story line and the plot moves seamlessly."

—*RT Book Reviews*, 4 Stars

"Emotionally driven, extremely heartfelt, and beautifully executed."

—*HEAs Are Us*

"If you love a good cowboy romance, this one is a cut above the rest."

—*Debbie's Book Bag*

"Kennedy did an excellent job at drawing me in and making me care about all the characters... Everyone should read this book if they like stories with HEAs and ones with a few twists along the way."

—*Romancing the Book*

"For anyone who is a fan of cowboys, then this one is a must, and I only hope Ms. Kennedy will have stories to tell for Ridge's brothers, Shane and Brady. Having met them in this story and learning a little about them, I'm rather captivated by these other cowboys and want to learn more about them."

—*The Reading Cafe*

Also by Joanne Kennedy